PRAISE FOR WILLIAM BERNHARDT

"Bernhardt is the un ... drama."

— ...RY JOURNAL

"Political infighting and backstabbing. Kincaid faces it all."

— NEW YORK DAILY NEWS

"William Bernhardt is a born stylist, and his writing through the years has aged like a fine wine and is now sharper, deeper, and better than ever."

— STEVE BERRY, NEW YORK TIMES BESTSELLING AUTHOR OF THE CHARLEMAGNE PURSUIT

"Plot twists, sly wit and political intrigue make this book exciting reading."

— TUCSON CITIZEN

"Captivating...A welcome addition to the fictional bar."

— NEW YORK LAW JOURNAL

"Bernhardt skillfully combines a cast of richly drawn characters, multiple plots...and a climax that will take most readers by surprise."

— CHICAGO TRIBUNE

JUSTICE RETURNS

WILLIAM BERNHARDT

BABYLON
BOOKS

JUSTICE RETURNS

by William Bernhardt

For sweet Laurisa

"We shall never end wars, Mrs. Barham, by blaming it on the ministers and generals, or warmongering imperialists, or all the other banal bogeys. It's the rest of us who build statues to those generals and name boulevards after those ministers."

Paddy Chayefsky, *The Americanization of Emily*

PROLOGUE

His arms were chained to the wall. They had been that way so long he could not move them or feel them. He was naked and dirty, unable to move or scratch or pee. They woke him constantly, deprived him of sleep for days at a time. They blasted heavy metal music into his cell, endlessly, painfully. Time was an erratic stream connecting when they tortured him and when they did not torture him. He did not know what day it was, or if it was morning or night. His windowless room provided no clues.

He thought he'd been here for three weeks.

He told them everything he knew the first day.

They didn't believe him. Or said they didn't believe him. Or wanted something more. He didn't know.

He knew he couldn't endure this much longer.

Waiting. Dangling. Crushing boredom and crushing pain. And it was so hot. The first week it had been unbearably cold, and they gave him nothing to wear. Now it was searing, as if he were back in the desert, no oasis in sight, melting by inches, the air so thick he couldn't breathe.

Being crucified on the wall did not help with the breathing.

He heard the creaking of a distant door, followed by the muffled echo of combat boots.

They were coming back.

The cell door opened. Nazir, the worst of the trio, stepped inside, followed by two assistants. He didn't know their names. The fat one and the young one—the one who seemed to enjoy it.

Nazir did not make eye contact. "Unchain him."

The two lackeys fulfilled his command. He couldn't feel the difference, even as his arms slammed to his side.

Nazir pointed to the wooden chair.

They pushed and dragged him to it, the only furniture in the cell, near the stinking toilet bucket that had not been emptied in a week. Someone jabbed the back of his knees. He collapsed into the chair.

Nazir peered down at him. "Does it work?"

Speaking did not come easily. He had done little but scream for so long. His throat was dry and his lips were chapped. "I don't know what you're talking about."

Nazir did not blink. "Does it work?"

"I told you before, I don't know anything. I wasn't in long and I didn't do much. I just want to go. Please let me out of here. Please."

Nazir's jaw tightened. "Does it work?"

"Don't keep saying that. Listen to me. I beg you."

"You beg me." Nazir curled his lips. "And you call yourself an American."

"Why are you doing this?" He tried not to whimper. "I don't know anything that can help you."

"I don't believe you."

Tears sprung from his eyes. "How can I make you believe me?"

"You can't. Because you lie."

A single, bright overhead light illuminated the small cell. He watched as Nazir pulled it down and pointed it at his face.

"You do not look well. I think it is time you gave up your foolish resistance and talked."

"About what?"

Nazir spat in his face. "I could kill you now and no one would know. No one could do anything about it if they did know."

"Please don't kill me. Please don't kill me."

"Then tell me what I want to hear."

"I don't know what you want to hear. I don't."

"Does it work?"

"What? Does what work?"

Nazir grabbed him by the throat. *"Does. It. Work?"*

"Yes! Yes, it does. It works magnificently well."

Nazir's eyes narrowed. "What does it do?"

He hesitated. "Whatever you want it to do?"

Nazir slapped him hard. "Do you think you will outlast me? Do you think if you are strong enough I will release you?" Nazir shoved him backward, rocking the chair. "I will never let you go. You are my personal fuck toy, now and always, to do with as I choose."

Nazir kicked the chair leg, making it fall over, sending him crashing downward. His head hit the stone floor, forcing more tears from his eyes.

"I could take you by force," Nazir said. "I could humiliate and disgrace you. I could humble you before our Creator and every man on this earth."

"Please don't. Please don't. God no. Please."

"Do you think I will be kind? You are a traitor."

"I'm not."

"Did you imagine yourself Snowden? Assange? You stupid, petty cockroach." Nazir shoved his head down on the stone floor and kept pressing.

One of the lackeys spoke. "Let's give him the water treatment. We haven't done that for a while."

"Not again." His body shook violently. "Please don't hurt me again."

"Who are you working for?"

"I'm not working for anyone."

Nazir crouched down. "You will tell me everything you know. You realize that, don't you? All this suffering is so futile."

"I already told you everything."

"They all break eventually. Everyone does, and you will, too."

"I would help you," he gasped. "I would. If I could. I don't know what you want. Maybe I could find out. Maybe if you let me go, I could find out what you want to know."

"Worthless American. Worthless, filthy, traitorous American."

"I'd do anything you want."

"Then tell me. Tell me *now*."

"I don't know anything!"

"Then you will be with me forever."

Nazir walked to the back of the cell. "This is your last chance to avoid a lifetime in hell. Talk to me."

"I don't know anything!"

He motioned to his assistants. "Chain him back up."

He closed his eyes, unable to bear the thought of being strapped to that wall again, maybe all day, maybe for the rest of his life.

"There is no escape for you," Nazir said, teeth clenched. "I can hold you forever. I have the authority. I can do whatever I want with you. Because you are a person of interest. And I am the Central Intelligence Agency."

PART I
SUSPICION OF EVIL

CHAPTER 1

I watch as the foreman grips the document that will determine the future, life or death, for at least three people in this room: my client, the woman sitting in the gallery, and me.

His fingers twitch, rustling the pages together. I wonder whether this man fully comprehends his power. Perhaps he does. Perhaps that's why he grips the paper so tightly, and perspiration soaks through the parchment. But how could he fully understand when he knows so little of the truth? Ninety percent of what lawyers do at trial is designed to limit what the jurors know, not to inform them. Could he read between the lines? Could he understand what no one was permitted to say? In his normal quotidian life, he's the assistant supervisor on a loading dock. But today he's Solomon and Torquemada and Jack Ketch. Today he has the power to decide who lives and who dies.

This trial—an appropriate term—has dragged on for weeks. The relevant information could probably have been conveyed in an afternoon. But these exercises in amateur theatrics are not about efficiency, nor are they about justice. Today they are about politics and the societal need for retribution—a code word for vengeance, the pettiest of motives. This is bread and circuses, a performance designed to amuse and placate the masses.

The reporters, commenters, and bloggers who have covered this case nonstop are scavengers circling for carrion. My client is the prey, while I and the others wearing blue and gray suits exist somewhere in between. There was a time when I considered us officers of justice. But now I see that we are little better than mechanics oiling the wheels of the machinery. Churning through cases. Through people's lives. And their deaths.

The only opinions that matter now are the twelve opinions sitting in that box, those twelve random souls chosen not for their wisdom, not for their powers of perspicacity, but because they hold a driver's license. On those opinions now rest futures, families, perhaps even the fate of nations. The sword of Damocles hangs over our heads, suspended not by a thread, but by a faith in an abstract notion: jury of one's peers.

I've sat in this room and listened to that judge speak the same words on many previous occasions. These words are litany, like the incantations of a religious sect. Presumed innocent. Beyond a reasonable doubt. We brandish these catchphrases as if they actually mean something. But that is not how jurors decide cases. Some will try to do what they think is right. Some will acquiesce to the majority. And some will do whatever gets them out of here the quickest. Words are empty air when confronted with realities of this magnitude.

And sadly, words are the only tools lawyers possess.

My client glances at me nervously, running his finger through his hair, hoping for a sign. He thinks I can read the foreman's expression and tell him what lies ahead.

And he's right. I can. But early knowledge will not benefit him in the slightest. Better to let the service reach its own benediction.

The woman in the gallery also stares at me. I know what she's thinking. That I've failed her. Again.

I brace myself. The judge opens the document and nods. The bailiff returns the document to the foreman. The twelve look like pallbearers standing over a grave.

The foreman speaks.

The world erupts in a searing flash of desperation and fury.

Nothing will ever be the same again.

CHAPTER 2
SEVEN MONTHS EARLIER

This is the most important case I've ever handled, so I'm keeping a detailed record. I want to remember every second of it in the days to come. Some people think my actions were inexplicable. I get that. All that matters to me is that I remember why I did what I did. I'll never forget how it ended. I don't want to lose the details that got us there.

I've been a trial lawyer for many years, maybe too many. Ben Kincaid, attorney-at-law. Almost twenty years now. And in all those years, I've managed to learn only two things. First: being a lawyer is way more complicated than most people realize.

And second: every trial has a critical turning point.

Just like a good novel, a trial always reaches a place where the story line veers suddenly in an unexpected or decisive direction. Sometimes it is a moment of clarity. Sometimes it is a moment of despair. It may not be immediately apparent to others. But when you've done this as long as I have, you can feel it in your veins.

I had just reached such a turning point in the Overnight Express trial, the one I handled immediately before Oz came back into my life. It was a dull affair about mismanaged phone orders for package deliveries. Judge Perkins knew this was tedious. I could see the weary haze in her eyes. She's a heavyset woman, never married, never so far as I know even close to it, and that worried me initially. I represented the plaintiff, Powers Leone, who had a reputation for being a would-be playboy—exactly the type of man a serious single woman of indefinite sexuality might dislike. My ace in the hole was supposed to be the current witness, Leone's mistress, who for the purposes of this trial we were calling his fiancée. She was supposed to verify Leone's testimony and clinch the case.

She did an admirable job. Three days of witness prep reaped benefits. I asked the right questions, and she responded appropriately, never going on too long, never speaking so evasively that jurors had any reason to doubt her veracity. I've always rehearsed my witnesses extensively. We review everything: how to dress, how to sit, whether to cross your legs, whether to look at the jurors, whether to hide emotion or show it, whether to speak loudly or softly or somewhere in between.

Kyra Kubrick had little to do with the order-fulfillment business. She was present during a conversation during which the defendant allegedly admitted that his company mishandled calls, resulting in a large loss of income over the Christmas holidays. Kyra was a tall woman, slender, pale and brittle as bone china, just attractive enough to potentially arouse resentment from female jurors. I cautioned her to go easy on the makeup and to let her hair fall naturally. She'd had an accident in the bath the day before and wore a bandage on the right side of her face—which I considered a blessing. I didn't want her to look glamorous. I wanted her to look like an honest woman caught in a feud between well-heeled power brokers.

"Any further questions, Mr. Kincaid?" the judge asked.

"Just a few." I addressed Kyra. "Was this the first time you met the defendant, Brian Wagner?"

She cleared her throat. "Yes."

"Probably heard your fiancé mention his name before, though?"

"Oh yes."

"Why were you at the Roundhouse?" As the jurors would know, the Roundhouse was one of the nicest restaurants in Oklahoma City.

"We were celebrating. It was our anniversary." She looked down and smiled. "We'd been together two years."

By modern standards, a millennium. Very good. "So this was a special occasion?"

"Powers is a very special man. No one ever treated me the way he does."

Wonderful. If a client starts talking about how terrific he is, jurors are likely to think he's a blowhard. But if it comes from someone else, particularly an adoring woman, that's different. If she likes him, they subconsciously surmise that he must be a likeable person.

"Were you expecting Mr. Wagner?"

"No. He just appeared suddenly."

"What was his demeanor?"

"At first he seemed angry. He said he knew Powers had been talking to attorneys. He said Powers should think carefully before he—" Her voice dropped a notch. "Do I have to use the same word he did?"

Adorable. Couldn't play better here in the reddest of the red states, Bible Belt Oklahoma. "I'm afraid you do, Kyra."

She swallowed. "He said . . . that Powers should think carefully before he tried to screw with him."

Such language. I hope his mother washed his mouth out with soap. "What happened next?"

"They argued. For two or three minutes. I was afraid the manager would throw us out of the restaurant. And then, all at once, Wagner started crying."

Several eyebrows rose in the jury box. They were paying attention. "Did you understand why he was crying?"

"Not at first. It seemed like . . . a strange mood swing."

"What did you do?"

"I offered him a napkin. He was crying all over himself."

"What did Mr. Wagner say?"

She hesitated, only for a second, but in that second, everything changed. I mentioned that every trial had a turning point? This was it. This testimony, coming from a likeable witness, could save the day for my client.

"He said four things," she replied, and just after she did, she glanced at my client. Then her hand brushed against the side of her face, the bandaged side.

And that's when I understood everything.

Something about the way she replied, the way she gave me a topic sentence instead of an answer seemed wrong. As if she had memorized a list. And that hadn't happened during our practice sessions. This was something I hadn't heard before. Something new.

Something that wasn't true.

Why perjure herself? Of course, she loved Leone and wanted to please him, but most people would draw the line at lying in court. Unless... .

I saw the look Leone gave her. A tiny furrow between the brows. A coldness in the eyes. Stern. Uncompromising.

A warning.

And then she touched the bandage.

Damn. How could I be so stupid?

The saddest part was, I think she really did love him. And for that and probably a host of other psychological reasons, she stayed with him, even though she knew she should go.

As an attorney bound by the Rules of Professional Conduct, I had a tricky decision to make, and about three seconds to make it. This woman was about to perjure herself. I knew that as well as I knew my wife's middle name. I could probably pretend I didn't, but I did.

On the other hand, her testimony was crucial. Wagner supposedly confessed that the phone orders were mishandled, and we had the burden of proof to demonstrate the mishandling by a preponderance of the evidence. Our best evidence was the weepy confession at the restaurant.

But it was a lie. A lie Leone bullied her into telling.

I can't honestly say I've never done anything the Disciplinary Committee of the Bar Association might condemn. I have. But always for a good reason. And today, I didn't have one. This was just a squabble between two businessmen over a big pile of money.

And what if she got caught? Sure, she probably wouldn't, but what if she did? Leone was no fool—he got someone else to take the risks. Should I allow her to put her neck in the noose?

If I asked what were the four things Wagner said, she would undoubtedly tell me. So I didn't ask.

"After Mr. Wagner left, what happened?"

Kyra blinked several times rapidly. "Nothing. We finished our dinner."

"Thank you. No more questions." I returned to the plaintiff's table.

Leone controlled his emotions well, but I could read the message in his eyes, and the language was considerably harsher than "screw you." For that matter, the opposing attorney seemed fairly dumbfounded.

At the break, I concocted some excuse, some alleged strategic reason for not eliciting the perjury. And I found another way to make the same point with someone else. My cross-examination of Wagner also showed how badly the phone orders were bungled. So I didn't hurt my client. But I also didn't allow an innocent young woman to sell her soul and endanger her future.

And no one in the world would ever know what I did.

Like I said, being an attorney is way more complicated than most people realize.

CHAPTER 3

During the lunch break, I called my wife on my cell.

"Hey, Chris. You at home or the office?"

"Office. The twins are in All Souls' Mom's Day Out till five." I knew there was more to that thought, but she kept the rest to herself. "Need something?"

"Do you still volunteer at Harmonium?" A local battered women's shelter.

"Of course. Why?"

"I'd like you to contact someone I know. Kyra Kubrick. Tell her about Harmonium and the help they can offer. I think she's been abused for some time."

"I'll call. But you know, people rarely respond to phone calls about something like this. They go into denial mode. Usually we can't do anything until they're ready to seek help themselves."

"I know. But she just dodged a major bullet, so she might be receptive."

"I'll give it a try. How's the trial going?"

I'd save the details for later. "Not bad, given that the brains of our partnership aren't in the courtroom."

I could feel the smile on the other end of the phone. "I think you can handle this one yourself." Which was her loving way of saying civil cases bored her to tears. They did me, too, but bills must be paid. "Home by seven?"

"Likely. Want me to pick up sandwiches at Napoleon's?"

"No. The mighty trial warrior deserves a home-cooked meal. Just let me know if you're going to be late."

"Will do. Anything else on your mind?"

"No." A few moments of reflection and hesitation. Funny how sometimes you can feel so much pain packed into a single syllable. "No."

So we weren't going to talk about it yet. Fine. I guess. "You know you're what keeps me going, right?"

"In the sense that you'd probably forget to eat if I weren't around to remind you?"

"No." The problem with having an elephant in the room is that the damn thing makes it so hard to see the door. "In the sense that, no matter what has happened or will happen, I keep moving forward because I know you've got my back." That was about as close to talking about it as I could get without actually talking about it.

"No dark moments of the soul?" A Fitzgerald reference. I knew what she meant.

"When I say 'no matter what,' I do mean 'no matter what.'"

Only a slight pause. "See you for dinner."

"See you then."

I slid the phone back into my pocket. At times, I feel as if my entire life has been a long series of mistakes and accidents. But there's one brilliant exception, one that made up for all the goofs, a thousand times over. Lots of men said stuff like this, but I knew it was true. Marrying Christina was the smartest thing I ever did.

Not everyone understood my devotion to my spectacular wife. When I first met her, she was running around in colored tights and crazy *Alice in Wonderland* hair. She's matured—not that I didn't adore her then. She's smart, useful, hardworking, and everyone likes her. I, on the other hand, am slow, neurotic, antisocial, and I fully expected to be alone till the end of my days, the pathetic geezer you see at the cafeteria complaining that his Salisbury steak isn't cooked enough.

Christina gave me a life, gave me a family. I'd do anything for that woman.

The sandwiches in the snack bar on the first floor of the Oklahoma County Courthouse were old and sadly deteriorated, not unlike the building itself, but I grabbed a ham and cheese and some chocolate milk and started back to the courtroom. I wanted to review my notes and some of the deposition transcripts before the trial resumed.

"Ben?"

I pivoted in front of the world's slowest elevators. Michael Hickman, associate prosecutor in the US Attorney General's office, offered his hand. We'd had a few cases opposite one another since I moved to Oklahoma City. He struck me as a fairly typical government lawyer—ambitious, political, and, too often, completely self-oriented. For me, being a lawyer was always about the clients. But lawyers in the AG's office represented the government—in other words, they didn't really have a client. They had a cause. To me, that changed everything.

Hickman had mop-top curls that wreathed his head like a halo. His soft Irish smile was hard to resist, even for someone like myself who'd spent most of his life resisting.

"Hey, Michael. What brings you to the wrong side of the tracks?" The attorney general's office was a few miles away, and its cases generally lande in the federal courthouse.

"This is a closely guarded secret, but the coffee is much better here." Which seemed extremely unlikely. "Days like these I need all the help I can get. Every day is a Monday, right?"

Generally speaking, I like lawyers, but I weary of the bromides we exchange as a substitute for real conversation. "True dat."

"What are you up to, Ben?"

"Toiling in the civil courts today. Breach of contract. Tortious interference with business."

"Any chance on the tort claim?"

"Not really. But torts raise the possibility of punitive damages, which sometimes puts goose bumps on corporate flesh. It's worth pleading, if only for settlement purposes."

He gave me a baffled expression that I immediately distrusted.

"Too complicated for me. I'll stick to criminal work. Right and wrong. Black and white. That's hard enough for a Muskogee boy."

Right. He was about as rural as I was. "If you'll excuse me, I need to prep for—"

"Hear you've got a new client."

I slowed. "I do?"

"C'mon, Ben. Privilege doesn't extend to the fact of representation."

So this wasn't a chance encounter. This was a fishing expedition. "Sorry. Haven't had a new case or client in several weeks."

"If you don't want to tell me, fine. But don't lie to me."

There are many things in this profession I will grudgingly tolerate. But being called a liar is not one of them. "You're mistaken. Unless you know something I don't."

"Well, I know who's sitting in your office right now."

My first thought was, How? But I knew asking that question would be pointless. "You're monitoring my office?"

He glanced down at his coffee. "We can't do that. But we can monitor persons of interest."

My eyes narrowed to tiny slits. "Michael, I'm tired of tap dancing. What are you talking about?"

Hickman looked both ways down the corridor, then pulled me to one side, as if somehow that would convey more privacy. "Look, I'm only doing this because I bumped into you and we're friends."

Three fibs in one sentence. Must be a record of some sort. "Doing what?"

"Cautioning you. Against getting involved in a whole mess of trouble you don't need or want."

"I still don't know what you're talking about."

"I'm talking about that sweet family of yours. They don't need you wrapped up in something you might never get out of. Your record's dodgy enough as it is. Your license wouldn't survive jail time."

"Are you threatening me?"

He held up his hands, palms outward. "Of course not. Calm down. I'm just trying to help. I don't want to get caught up in the cogs."

"If you want to help me, the best thing you could do is stop babbling in riddles and explain what you're talking about."

He laid his hand on my shoulder and pulled me about as near as it was possible to be without kissing. His voice dropped to a whisper. "Give him the boot, Ben. Let the court-appointed drone handle it. Better for everyone. Especially you."

He gave me a little squeeze and walked away, dropping his coffee into the nearest trash can.

CHAPTER 4

I didn't know what to make of that. This was not the first time I'd been on the wrong side of government officials. But usually I at least understood why. This time I was completely clueless.

On a hunch, I pulled my cell phone out of my pocket. Sure enough, I found a message from Tanya. I silenced the ringer while I was in court, so I missed the usual panpipe that told me I had a message.

POSS CLIENT N OFFICE. TOLD HIM U WERE N COURT. WONT LEAVE TILL HE TALKS TO U.

Normally, leaving the courthouse during a trial, even during lunch, would be unthinkable. The trial at hand always takes precedence. But on this occasion, I thought I'd best make an exception. I was unlikely to be able to concentrate on anything else till I figured out what was up.

AFTER A BRISK JOG TO MY OFFICE, I WALKED THROUGH THE FRONT doors. No one sat behind the reception desk. Or so it initially appeared. Upon closer inspection, I found someone behind the reception desk who was not immediately visible. Because her head was under the desk. And her nineteen-year-old rear was thrust up toward the heavens.

I am completely and unalterably devoted to my wife. But did I notice that Tanya was wearing thong underwear? I'm devoted, not blind. Cute little butterfly tattoo, also.

"Drop something?" I asked.

"It's the net server. We've lost our connection again. I can't do a thing without it." She withdrew her head. "When did we all become so dependent on computers?"

Coming from a woman about the same age as my car, this was more than a trifle risible. "The world runs on the Internet."

"I wish people would forget email exists. I spend half my day answering it."

"Twenty years ago, you would've spent half the day playing telephone tag. This is better."

"If you say so." I heard a click that told me she'd replaced a connection. "Let's see if the reboot works." She stood up a little too fast, dislodging the contents of her low-neck blouse and giving me an unnecessarily generous view of her two strategically placed crescent moon tattoos. "You need to get to the conference room, Ben. He's been waiting a long time."

"What's his name?"

She glanced down at her desk. "Omar al-Jabbar."

Now I understood Hickman's use of the phrase "person of interest." "What's he been charged with?"

"Don't really know. Wants you to file a lawsuit."

Curiouser and curiouser. "Tanya, have you noticed anything . . . unusual around the office?"

"Like weirdo guys who won't leave, won't make an appointment, and stare at my tats?"

"You have tattoos?"

"Duh. If you weren't so head over heels with your wife, you would've noticed."

"Love is blind. But I was thinking more in terms of . . . being watched."

"Guys are always watching me."

"But . . . anything unusual? Like maybe someone watching this prospective client?"

"Not that I noticed. What is he, ISIS?"

I didn't comment. Because I didn't know and also because despite her bravura attitude, I thought Tanya seemed a trifle skittish about this man, perhaps even scared. She'd worked for me about six months. It was an adjustment. I was accustomed to having a seasoned professional and semimature adult at this station. But Jones didn't want to move to OKC, so Christina took over the office-management duties, and Tanya filled in at the front desk.

I met Tanya when she turned state's evidence on one of my clients. She was from a small town in Western Oklahoma, Dill City, who thought she'd won the lottery when she was asked out by the high school quarterback. This was an Oklahoma town that completely revolved around high school football—well, actually, they all do. Consequently, she didn't say anything even when it became clear he used performance-enhancing drugs, not only on the field but in the classroom. Her deal with the DA kept her out of jail but left her a pariah in the only town she knew. I gave her a job to help her get back on her feet. She took night classes at UCO, hoping to be a teacher one day. Her secretarial skills were rudimentary at best, but her attitude was excellent, which I found a pleasing change.

"I don't know what he is. Guess I better find out. Hold my calls. I have to be back in the courtroom by one."

Tanya nodded, and I headed down the corridor. I braced myself for what was bound to be an unpleasant conversation. Probably because of my reputation for handling civil rights cases, not to mention hopeless cases, I'd been approached before by men of Middle Eastern descent protesting their treatment by the federal government. For good or ill, the Patriot Act gave law enforcement enormous powers, and no judge yet had the courage to declare the law unconstitutional.

I had another problem, though one I never discussed or admitted to anyone, not even my wife. I had a hard time understanding foreign accents, particularly those of the Persian variety. It may relate to a hearing loss I suffered at an early age from an ear infection. I once dated a lovely woman with a French accent, but I had to end it because constantly asking her to repeat herself was making us both batty. Having a client you couldn't readily understand was almost equally impossible.

So I braced myself for a conversation that would be somewhat tortured and, for him, unavailing.

"Ben! How the hell are you?"

I froze in the doorway. Most people have probably had the awkward experience of being recognized by someone you couldn't recognize back—but it happened to me all the time. Part of that is because my legal exploits, plus the two books I wrote, have given me a higher-than-average profile. Part of it, I suspect, is because you have only so many memory slots in your head, and so many of mine are consumed by litigation details and piano chords and obscure Scrabble words, some faces have been pushed out.

"I'm . . . fine."

"Good Lord, Ben. How long has it been?"

And the other problem is that I was expecting to see someone with a darker skin tone. But the man standing before me was just as Caucasian as I am. More so, actually, since he had more hair in a lighter color. His ramrod posture and close-cut hair suggested military.

"How's Julia? I haven't seen or heard anything in years."

The reference to my sister was the memory jog I needed. They used to date. But the name wasn't right. Something didn't match up.

And then the light dawned. Did Tanya get the name wrong? "Oz?"

He smiled again and stopped shaking my hand. "I'm sorry. I should've left both names with your receptionist. Who, by the way, is quite the hottie." He jabbed me in the side. "Does your wife know about her?"

I didn't know what to say, so I maintained my stunned and silent demeanor.

"I'd have gone to law school if I'd known there were perks like that. After your sister, I didn't date again for three years."

It *was* him. Oz Kirby. Oz, short for Oscar, and who could blame him for abbreviating that? "Oscar" must've been a terrible burden for a teenager.

I was embarrassed for not recognizing him sooner. We had a lot of history. Most of which I would prefer to forget. "Oz . . . do you know if anyone followed you here?"

"I'm certain someone did. They've been following me for months."

"Why?"

He was completely straight-faced when he said, "They think I'm a terrorist."

The pieces were coming together. "Do they have any evidence?"

The corner of his lips turned up. "Do they need any evidence?"

CHAPTER 5

Even though I recognized him, there was still a jigsaw piece missing. How did Oscar Kirby—a rich kid growing up in Nichols Hills, one of the most affluent neighborhoods in Oklahoma City, a track star and, if I recalled correctly, Eagle Scout—become Omar al-Jabbar?

"I can't believe I'm seeing you again, Ben, after all these years. Good grief, we haven't talked since—"

"I remember."

"Did you ever do anything about—"

"No."

"Your sister—"

"No."

"I hear she married. Several times."

"What brings you to my office today?" I asked, hoping he would take the hint and change the subject.

He did. "Like I said, the government thinks I'm a terrorist."

"I can't help you with that. The Patriot Act gives the intelligence community the power to investigate pretty much anyone they want, at home or abroad. And I only have a little time before I need to be back in court." I paused. "How did Oscar become Omar? And what should I call you?"

"Call me Oz, like you always did. It's a long story. And not all that interesting, at least not to others. Believe me, I've tried it out in singles bars, and I've seen the eyelids droop. I don't know if you followed this, but after Julia and I split, I left Oklahoma. I was having some issues."

He was kind enough not to mention that they were probably all my fault.

"Had a hard time adjusting, you know, going from high school sports star to, basically, nobody. Tried a semester of college, but it wasn't for me. Tried some low-level management positions, but turned out I wasn't good at working for the man. Ended up in the military."

"Really." The kid I knew in high school was the last person on earth I would've expected to end up in camo.

"Tell you the truth, Ben, I got myself into a bit of trouble. More than a bit. Of the available options, joining the army looked best. After basic I got posted overseas. Ended up in Iraq."

"But you came back okay."

"More than okay. Multiple decorations. Even got the Silver Star. I was wounded once, during my second tour of duty. More shell-shocked than anything. I got over it. Did a year of PTSD therapy. Not all that many doors opened for returning vets, especially ones with a history of mental issues. Yeah, I got to board planes first, got ten percent off at the movies. But did anyone offer me a job? No. With no degree and the economy in the dumper, I had serious problems."

"All too common, unfortunately."

"And then, somewhere along the way, I discovered Allah."

"You converted to Islam?"

"I'm not sure that's the right word, since I'd never been much of a Christian. But I adopted the Muslim faith, and that led to changing my name."

Over the years, I've learned to watch people carefully. As a trial lawyer, that's essential. If you want to know how a trial is going, you don't ask someone in the gallery, and you don't ask the judge. You watch the jurors. Unlike the litigants, they aren't told to maintain a poker face, and they usually don't. Someone shifting their weight, or raising their hand to their chin, can speak volumes.

I tried to read Oz, but it wasn't easy. I got the distinct impression he held it all inside. Masking, to use a litigator term of art. And why would he do that?

"I eventually bumped into someone I'd been in service with. At a VA meeting. Abdullah Ali. He's Muslim, too, except he was born to it. Still an American, mind you. Born and raised in Iowa. But he had troubles after 9/11. The feds suspected him of complicity with terrorist cells. Completely baseless, but they monitored him to such an extent that he couldn't work. Eventually he started a nonprofit organization to protest the Patriot Act. He calls it PACT—Patriot Act Challenge Tribunal. They educate people on the facts and pursue legal and political avenues to overturning the Patriot Act."

"Part of it has expired."

"The parts pertaining to NSA bulk collection of US phone records. Not the parts pertaining to rendition, detention, or interrogation. The USA Freedom Act left almost all of that intact. And the NSA is still collecting millions of US citizens' phone metadata without warrants.".

I'd heard of PACT. So far as I knew, they were a legitimate lobbying group. I worked in Washington for a time and played a role in preventing the passage of a significant expansion of the Patriot Act.

"I believed in the cause, and I needed work," Oz continued. "Abdullah provided it. And if that weren't perk enough, I started dating his sister, Mina. Till the CIA grabbed me."

"What happened?"

"I was detained and interrogated. On American soil. Arrested me at the airport, put a bag over my head, dragged me to an undisclosed location. Despite the fact that I'm an American. Despite the fact that I'm a vet."

"They do have that power. It may seem unconstitutional, but Congress thought the need for domestic security justified it."

"Ben, they held me three weeks."

"Three weeks?"

"I was strip-searched. Three times a day. Cavity searches. Even assuming they could justify it the first time, what did they expect to find afterward? They took my clothes and left me naked in a dirty cell. I demanded to be released. They ignored me. In fact, they laughed at me."

"Did they . . . hurt you?"

"Define *hurt*." His lips tightened.

"Did they torture you?"

"Damn straight." I couldn't help but notice that his hands shook. "They didn't *wound* me, if that's what you mean. They didn't penetrate my skin. But they tied me to a chair, or handcuffed me, and left me like that for hours, grilling me, accusing me, telling me they knew I was a terrorist and I was going to get the needle for it. They waterboarded me. Do you know what that means?"

"I think I—"

"It's not like what you see in the movies. They came up with a cute name to minimize what it was. Waterboarding. Sounds like a sport, doesn't it? Like surfboarding. Loads of fun. What they're talking about is drowning someone. Not just threatening to drown you, but actually drowning you. Not so much that you die. But they completely block off your airflow so long everything goes black and your brain goes dead and all you can feel is panic, the gasping, helpless panic that comes when your lungs can't get anything and your whole body starts to self-destruct—"

He turned his head away. Probably because his eyes were watering, and he didn't want me to see. "They did it over and over again. Chained me to the wall. Bombarded me with painfully loud music. Disgusting food. Filth and squalor. People think all that ended after bin Laden was executed, but they're wrong. My primary interrogator was a man named Nazir. I'd known him a little back in Iraq, before he conveniently switched sides and joined the CIA. He's got a serious bad-on against me. It's personal, and this gave him the perfect opportunity to act on it. That bastard would lean into my face with a sick grin, and he'd say, 'We're never letting you out of here. We're going to play with you and hurt you over and over again for the rest of your life. And there's nothing you can do about it.'"

He covered his face with his hand. "And I believed him, Ben. I believed every word. I would've done anything to get out of there. And I did."

CHAPTER 6
WITNESS AFFIDAVIT
CASE NO. CJ-49-1886

I had been watching al-Jabbar for hours, even before he entered the lawyer's office.

The surveillance had been uneventful. Nonetheless, my handler assured me it was important and my vigilance was critical to our mission, so I stayed at full alert, ready to strike, retaliate, or defend myself. Some might question these actions, especially given all that occurred afterward. I did not. Not then and not now.

Once they left the central lobby, with its large street-side window, I was unable to maintain visual contact. Using my infrared and heat sensors, I could establish that there were three persons in Kincaid's office, and two were gathered in a smaller room in what appeared to be a posture of conversation.

Since I could not hear what they said, I was unable to determine whether critical secrets were revealed. At this time, all I could tell was that two people—in all likelihood Kincaid and al-Jabbar—were engaged in a protracted discussion. At various times, the smaller of the two figures, most likely Kincaid, reached out to the other in a gesture of comfort or support. Beyond that, I could not assess what was said or its threat potential.

My handler broke radio silence, a quaint antiquated term, given that our means of communication had nothing to do with radio waves.

"Target acquired?"

"Yes."

"In sights?"

"Yes."

"Within range?"

"Not within visual or strike range."

"Threat assessment?"

"Impossible. I cannot discern what is being said. I cannot hear them, and the lack of visuals makes lipreading impossible. Recommend planting listening devices in the office at the earliest possible opportunity. Perhaps tonight."

"Recommendation accepted."

"Don't you need—"

"No. Recommendation accepted."

"It shall be done."

The chain of command is complex and often convoluted. The smart soldier obeys orders and avoids power struggles. Commanders come and go. Soldiers are forever.

I descended from the roof into an alley, crossed the street, then moved to the rear of the building. I found a fire escape, which, coupled with some gymnastics and a grip honed by years of strength training, allowed me to gain access to the roof without taking any actions that would leave overt traces of surveillance. Once on the roof, I measured my distances carefully, then withdrew the nylon cord from my backpack. I tied one end to a stationary pipe jutting from the center of the roof, then tied the other end around my waist. I checked for tautness and to ensure that my measurements were accurate.

That done, I stepped off the edge of the roof.

The rope held me tightly enough that I could defy gravity. I took six steps down the side of the building, checking the cord at each step. It held, and more importantly, it held me. When the cord was at its full length, I hovered just above the window I calculated to be Kincaid's interior conference room.

Slowly, carefully, I lowered myself to my knees. The Oklahoma wind fought me for control. Strength training comes of value in the most unexpected circumstances. When I was certain I was secure, I laid down flat against the building, my head poised just below the top of the window. I knew I could not maintain this position forever. Eventually the blood rushing to my head would impair cognitive functioning.

From this position, I was able to employ the MKX-Audio 9, essentially a high-tech stethoscope. I placed the reception disc against the window and listened.

"Did they . . . hurt you?"

"Define hurt."

"Did they torture you?"

"Damn straight."

I knew I would not be able to listen to the conversation as long as it was likely to proceed, so after a few minutes, I contacted my handler for further instructions.

"I have obtained limited access to the conversation. Al-Jabbar is providing details of his incarceration and questioning."

"And beyond that?"

"So far, he has not progressed beyond that."

"Any discussion of his affiliation with other organizations?"

"Only PACT."

"Any discussions of concern to our operations?"

"Not at this time."

"Monitor the situation as long as you can safely."

"I will."

"You must not be detected."

"Then I will not be."

There was a pause in the flow of my instructions. "You understand . . . if the threat assessment should turn negative, you will be required to take action."

"Of course."

"We cannot allow anything to threaten or compromise our long-range plans."

"Absolutely not."

"A situation could well arise in which you would be required to take extreme sanctions against the target."

"But which target?"

"Either of the targets. Or quite possibly both."

CHAPTER 7

I didn't feel I knew Oz well enough to comfort him. I hated encouraging him to continue talking when he was in pain, but I couldn't help him if I didn't know the whole story.

And I had only about ten minutes before I had to rush back to the courthouse. Typically, clients weren't appreciative when you made them bare their souls on a deadline.

"You were released. Eventually."

"Yes." His eyes remained cold. "Eventually."

"Why?"

"I don't know. I told them everything I knew the first day. Sorry if that sounds weak. See how long you can hold out, being drowned, shivering naked in your filthy cell, no support, nothing for comfort. I didn't feel I'd done anything wrong. Why shouldn't I talk? Problem was I knew very little. Almost nothing they wanted."

"What did they think you knew?"

"Nazir repeatedly asked, 'Does it work?' I have no idea what that meant."

"They must have been looking for information about something."

"I think they were after Abdullah, because his political activities were causing them problems."

"They can't use the Patriot Act or the Freedom Act to go after lobbyists."

"They can do anything they want with a person of interest."

I tried a different approach. "Do you think Abdullah was a legitimate person of interest?"

"No. They never brought charges against Abdullah. I don't think they ever planned to. They may have been trying to scare him, because his nonprofit got in their way. But he's no terrorist, and they damn well know it."

"Why go after you? If they wanted to scare Abdullah, surely the best course would be to detain Abdullah."

"Not necessarily. He might be willing to sacrifice himself, but less willing to sacrifice a friend."

"They could detain you to secure your testimony, or to prevent you from fleeing, but they couldn't hold you on suspicion of being a terrorist unless they had at least a glimmer of evidence."

"Exactly."

"So you believe you were held in violation of the law."

"And I want to sue the bastards. For what they did to me."

"A civil suit for wrongful imprisonment. If what you say checks out, you've got a prima facie case. At least enough to get past the sniff test."

"Meaning we win?"

"Meaning we go to trial. Assuming the judge agrees with my assessment."

"Then you'll take my case?"

I held up my hands, startled. I'd been considering the facts and issues from a purely intellectual and legal standpoint, something I tend to do (too much) in the early stages of a case. For the clients, of course, it's never an intellectual exercise. They want justice. Or perhaps revenge. "I don't know, Oz. I'll have to give this more thought."

"What's to think about? You're a civil rights attorney, aren't you?"

"Sometimes."

"Then why the hesitation?"

Truth was, filing a civil suit sounded like Oz was asking for trouble with little chance of material gain. And it was always possible he was exaggerating. Melodramatizing.

Then again, Hickman wasn't trying to scare me off just because he was afraid of a civil suit or bad publicity. Something more was going on here. Much more. "Life has taught me to think carefully before committing to anything."

"Are civil rights cases your most important work?"

I thought a moment before answering. "Every case is important to the client."

"And civil rights cases are important to everyone. And this is a civil rights case. A huge violation of personal liberty."

"Potentially."

"And we go way back, right?"

Was he trying to guilt me? "I need to do more investigation. A case like this will be long and frankly expensive."

"I think I can get Abdullah to foot the bill."

"Bad idea. You need to completely distance yourself from him, especially financially. Don't give them any ammunition."

"Then I'll find the money somewhere else."

"Let me check this out first. Talk to people. Talk to my wife."

"She makes your decisions for you?"

Ah. So now he was going to play the "pussy-whipped" card. Fortunately, the older I got, the less I felt I had to prove my manhood and the less I cared what other people thought. "I need to give this some serious deliberation. I don't want to waste your time or mine." I glanced at my cell phone. "And right now, I just don't have time to think it through."

"Are you scared?"

That surprised me, but I supposed it shouldn't have. "If you think I run from controversial cases, then you don't know anything about me."

"Truth is, Ben, I know almost everything about you. I did my research before I came here. I picked you for a reason. Your record screams courage. I know taking on the government is dangerous. There's no limit to how much they can screw with you, or how much they can take away from you. They could seize your assets, freeze your bank accounts. They could circulate false information. They could arrest and waterboard you on some pretense, just like they did me. If it's too much for you to handle, I get it."

"I never said that."

"Then what are you saying? Ben, this should not have happened to me. I'm not some flaming liberal. I'm a veteran and a Republican. I come from a good family. I'm a card-carrying NRA member. I supported the Patriot Act when it passed. But what they did to me—and what they're doing to others like me—is wrong. And I don't think it has anything to do with national security. I think the government is abusing its power for a completely different reason. Why won't you help me do what's right? Why won't you stand up for freedom?"

Somehow, he'd managed to get me on the defensive. "I said I need time to think. And I don't have time right now. Leave your contact information with Tanya. I'll call you tomorrow."

"All right." He pushed himself out of his chair. He didn't say anything, but his disappointment—along with the accompanying approbation—was apparent. "I'll wait for your call. Just remember Ben —if they can do this to me, they can do this to anyone. We accuse other nations of civil rights violations, but who watches the watcher?" He paused. "And I don't know what it means to be a civil rights lawyer if you don't have the balls to tackle the greatest civil rights violation in the history of the nation."

CHAPTER 8

I didn't get home till almost eight thirty. I had a lot to do, and a lot on my mind, and I was more than a little shaken by my lunchtime conversation. I got through the afternoon in court, but I knew I wasn't functioning at top capacity. This is another reason why when I'm in trial, I typically don't go to lunch, don't watch television at night, and basically become a miserable person to be around. Because the only way to do the job right is to give the trial everything. The second the judge snaps that gavel, you're in a submarine that doesn't come up until the foreman reads the verdict. That's why most trial attorneys have multiple marriages and burn out early.

I managed to get some decent admissions out of Wagner. Not as good as having an adoring girlfriend testify about what he said, but keenly damaging, just the same. I felt certain the jury could put two and two together.

During the drive to Nichols Hills, I hands-free dialed Mark Ames. We're both small-office lawyers, and we cover for each other when possible. He was going to be at the courthouse anyway and agreed to appear for me in court whenever the jury returned its verdict. He'd already entered an appearance, so it wouldn't offend client or court. I hadn't made any decisions about Oz's case, but one way or the other, I had a hunch I'd be busy tomorrow and didn't need to be jerked out of it just to hear the verdict read live. I could never predict how long it would take a jury to finish. Even in the simplest cases, there were too many variables. Do they have a strong foreman? Do they have any rebels? Is there anything good on television?

The Nichols Hills neighborhood still seemed like a foreign country to me. It shouldn't have. I grew up here, and I'd been living here almost a year since I moved back. Long rows of huge front lawns professionally trimmed, each blade of grass mowed to precision-measured height. Clothes closets bigger than most people's homes. Foreign cars in every driveway, just below the porte cochere. Big change from the place Christina and I had in Tulsa.

As I eased off Sixty-Third, Francis Bolton waved from the botanical garden he called his front yard. He trimmed his hedges like other people trimmed their soul patches. He had a lot of time on his hands. Back in the day, he'd been a highly successful orthodontist, with offices in three different metro suburbs. He'd wrangled some sort of government contract, providing braces to the underprivileged, which turned out to be a great way to amass a fortune. He owned half the office space in Bricktown.

I slowed and rolled down my window. "Hey, Fran. If you run out of hedges to trim, feel free to start on mine."

"That's not gonna happen, Ben. Not that they don't need it."

I didn't take that as a slam. I knew most of the men in this neighborhood were much more interested in yard work than I was. Of course, most had bought their own houses, so they understandably took more pride in them. Most had gardeners, too, but they still made a point of appearing every now and again in those one-piece jumpsuits with a pair of clippers.

"I'm not really trimming, anyway," Francis added.

"Just taking in the air?"

"Watching for speeders. People come off Sixty-Third driving at the speed of light. They don't realize they've passed from the highway to a residential neighborhood. Where children play."

Other than myself, I didn't think anyone here raised small children, but whatever. "So you glare at them as they race by?"

"I take down their plate numbers and call the cops. Bastards need to be taught a lesson."

"Do the cops do anything?"

"I don't call the city cops. They're worthless. I call NH Security. They know who's paying their salary."

"But they don't have jurisdiction over anyone who's left the neighborhood."

"Then they'll get them the next time. Hey, you know people at the police station, don't you?"

"More than I'd care to admit."

"Maybe you could pull a few strings."

I pondered. I did want my neighbors to like me. "Sure. Maybe if you see a particularly egregious driver, I could talk to my friends."

"Thanks, Ben. You're a stand-up guy. That's what I was telling them down at the neighborhood association meeting. Some of them weren't crazy about it when you moved into your mom's house."

"It's only temporary."

"Yeah, you said that six months ago. Hey, I get it. If you've got a house here, you're crazy not to use it. But some of the others think you didn't earn it. You know what people say. Kids today don't know how to work for a living. They want to do as little as possible and have as much as possible. The world doesn't work that way."

"Not usually."

"And doctors don't love lawyers. That's a universal truth. Oilmen aren't too crazy about them, either. Course I adored your mom. Everyone did. Never saw a woman who aged more gracefully. She was something else."

"That she was."

"So I stood up for you, pal." He punched my shoulder. "I told 'em you were Nichols Hills born and bred, and a man never shakes his roots, right?"

I declined to comment.

"So don't be surprised if you get recruited to be an officer. We always need fresh meat."

They need someone desperate enough to be accepted that he'll do the grunt work. It wouldn't be me. "Well, thanks. I better get home."

"Say hi to that cute little wife of yours for me."

"Will do." I rolled up the window and drove the rest of the way home.

I pulled into the ridiculously large driveway leading to the four-car garage. I would never get used to living in a forty-six-thousand-square-foot home. Our little place in Tulsa was just fine for me. But my mother's health diminished when she hit her mideighties. My wild-child sister, Julia, could not be located, and my father died years before, so that left the eldercare to me. After months of traveling up and down the turnpike with wife and twins in tow, I realized it would be simpler to live here. Fortunately, this house was more than large enough to accommodate us all. I leased our house in Tulsa. When my mother finally passed, turned out she'd left the place to me and my sister in her will. So we just stayed here.

The irony was not lost on me. As soon as I was old enough to leave this place, I bolted, never once looking back. My cardiologist-scientist father and I never got along, for good and valid reasons I won't rehash. He completely disowned me, left me nothing in his will.

And now I had everything. And lived in that same house I'd turned my back on all those years ago.

Turns out Wolfe was wrong. You can go home again. It's just not home anymore.

🕉

I WALKED THROUGH THE GARAGE INTO THE HOUSE. I COULD HEAR Christina goo-gooing with the girls in the playroom, and I could smell something delicious emanating from the kitchen. She'd been busy. Even more impressive, since I knew she'd been in the office till late afternoon.

"The wheels on the bus go round and round, round and round, round and round . . ." I felt as if I were being sung around the corner. There she was, sitting on the floor, one tiny girl in each arm, Elizabeth on the left, Emily on the right.

We were neither of us as young as we'd been when we met, all those years ago, working our butts off at Raven, Tucker & Tubb. But the years had been kinder to her. To me, time only brought crow's-feet and a receding hairline. To her it brought wisdom and elegance, or so it seemed to me. The red hair mellowed into a dustier pink, the freckles were less prominent, and she was all the lovelier for it. I could see worlds inside her pellucid green eyes. This one man still loved the pilgrim soul in her, and always would.

"Look, Daddy's home!" Christina swung around and passed a beautiful eighteen-month bundle to me. I knelt down to receive.

"Hello, Lizzie!" I said with a bug-eyed expression that passed for animated engagement. Chris made fun of the way I played with the girls. Truth was I had no experience with babies at all, save for a brief period when I had custody of my nephew, when he was about the same age the girls are now. I knew next to nothing about children. But I managed to get by. Instead of nursery rhymes, I recited poetry. Instead of lullabies, they got show tunes.

"Nothing's gonna harm you," I crooned, *"not while I'm around . . ."* Elizabeth made a gurgling noise, which I recognized as the universal indicator that she loved me. I pressed my face, goo-goo eyes bulging, into hers. "Who loves the little girl? Who loves the little girl?"

She giggled and squirmed. The tickling no doubt helped. "Dad-dy," she cooed, with admirable precision and diction.

I have never felt such unrestrained love in my entire life.

"Don't forget her little sister by forty seconds." Christina passed Emily into my unoccupied arm.

"Who loves this pretty girl?" I said, redirecting my bug-eyed facade. "Who loves the pretty, happy girl?"

No reaction, except perhaps a slightly quizzical expression. Probably gas.

"Emily . . . I just met a girl named . . . Emily." I tried something else. *"Emily had a little lamb, little lamb, little lamb* .

Nothing.

I pulled her close and hugged her tight. "What's going on in there?" I whispered. "Why won't you talk to me?"

I stared into those beautiful eyes. The lids were open, but it was as if nothing looked back. Not that the head behind the eyes was vacant. More like the eyes were pointed inward rather than out.

"Talk to me, Emily," I whispered. When I caught Christina's expression, my heart felt as if it had dropped to the pit of my stomach. "Just one word. Tell me you're in there."

But no words came.

Not from Emily. Elizabeth flung herself at me with such force it almost cracked my clavicle. "Fambly hug!" she chirped, as she nestled in beneath my chin.

Christina wrapped both girls and me in her embrace. We hugged as tightly as seemed safe. Her face was pressed to mine, and our tears commingled.

By nine we had both girls asleep and in bed. Emily always took longer. She might not talk, but she definitely knew how to cry. And I was still too much of a softie to leave a crying child alone. She had to fall asleep in my arms. My college friend Mike knew more poetry than anyone on earth, but even using his cheat sheets, I found that putting Emily to bed usually drained my resources.

"She's not Joey, you know," Christina said, when I came to our bedroom. "Some children develop at different speeds than others."

"Twins?" I tossed off my bathrobe and climbed under the covers. "One talks, the other doesn't. One follows directions, the other acts oblivious. That's not normal."

"What is normal, anyway?"

"There are standards."

"From everything you've told me about your father, he had miserable social skills. Didn't get humor. Didn't say goodbye at the end of phone calls. Was awkward around other people. He probably could've been diagnosed as autistic. And yet he became a doctor and a scientist and made a ton of cash."

"I want our girl to be normal."

She placed her book, something by Tess Gerritsen, on the nightstand. "And why would you expect your children to be normal? They share your DNA, after all."

"That's not funny."

"Neither is you assuming your daughter is autistic just because your nephew is."

"I spent a lot of time with Joey—"

"As I recall, I spent a lot of time with Joey while you tried your big murder case."

"We both spent time with him. And we both know how difficult he was."

"I adored Joey."

"I'm not saying—" My entire body felt cold. Perhaps I needed to check the thermostat. "I loved Joey, too. But we both know that his future options are limited."

"Everyone's future options are limited by one thing or another. Mine were limited by money. Yours were limited by neurosis and deep-seated dodo-headedness. And yet, we both ended up with law degrees, making a living, more or less."

"Joey is not going to be a lawyer."

"Perhaps, but he could be a fine engineer. Or computer programmer. My friend Sally works in Silicon Valley, and she says half the guys out there are autistic. But they're making big bucks, which means they can attract mates, which means their genes reproduce, which means their genes may be the dominant strain in a few generations. Maybe this isn't an abnormality. Maybe this is the evolution of the species."

"Thank you, Carl Sagan. I don't care about the species or neurodiversity. I care about my little girl. You're being brave, but I know you're concerned. I can see it in your face. I can hear it in your voice."

"No, what you're seeing and hearing is my concern about you, you thundering dunderhead."

"Why would you be concerned about me?"

"Because I know how you obsess and fret purposelessly given the slightest cause."

"You can't pretend you haven't worried that Emily might be autistic."

"I think it's too soon to worry. You, on the other hand, never think it's too soon to worry. You were worrying about the girls before they were born."

"The ultrasound looked weird."

She laid her hand on my shoulder. "Honey, let's wait till we have a good reason, okay?"

I took her hand and pressed them between mine. "You're claiming you're not worried about her? I saw your eyes watering up when mine did."

"Because you looked so sad."

This conversation was not remotely satisfying, but I could see that my worry was worrying her more. Worry is like yawning—highly contagious.

"Tanya told me you have a new client," she said, changing the subject.

"Maybe." I told her about my encounter with Oz. "What do you think?"

"I think he's hiding something."

"Every client is hiding something."

"Yeah, but this one doesn't make sense. I don't think the feds would interrogate him for three weeks, or follow him around now, just because he worked with this Abdullah guy. There must be more."

"We only had a few minutes to talk."

"He probably wouldn't have told you anything useful if you'd had all day. You need to talk to someone else. Someone who might give you the straight skinny."

"Oz wants to file a civil suit. You know the feds will counter with take-no-prisoners tactics. They can't afford bad publicity. And they don't want the Freedom Act subjected to a constitutional challenge."

"Maybe that will inspire them to settle."

"Not if the press gets wind of the story. And it will."

"Gag order? Transcript under seal?"

"Wouldn't help. Even if we got it. Which I think unlikely."

"Will you be able to handle the negative publicity? I mean, you personally."

I felt my brow crease. "Why do you assume the publicity will be negative?"

"Put on your big boy pants, Ben. You know as well as I do that the feds will portray themselves as the thin red-white-and-blue line between the terrorists and the American way. They'll portray you as the shyster attorney trying to set the terrorists free so they can bomb again."

"Not everyone is so easily led."

"True. But some will be. And you are the most sensitive person on the face of the earth. The hating will go viral, and you'll have clueless nerds pontificating on Internet bulletin boards about you and your case and making ugly assertions about your motivations. I don't know that you can take it."

"I've outgrown my insecurities. I don't need everyone to love me."

"You so do. Your feelings get bruised if someone frowns at you in traffic."

I pondered a moment. "This case might be more trouble than it's worth."

"Clearly."

"On the other hand, I have known Oz a long time."

"Loyalty to boys from the decadently wealthy hood?"

"If even half of what he says is true, he has been wronged." I loved talking cases with Christina. Just the process of thinking out loud with her as devil's advocate helped crystalize the issues in my mind. "His civil rights were compromised in a frightening way that could happen to anyone, innocent or guilty."

"True enough. And you say he has money?"

"Can get it."

"Well, that's different. I don't want to be the venal Lady Macbeth, but we have a property tax payment on this house coming up that's roughly equivalent to our combined annual income .

I frowned. Why couldn't life be easier? At least occasionally. "Okay. I'll pursue the possibility of taking his case."

"And you'll stop worrying so much. You're too young for ulcers. Or Xanax."

"Not as young as I used to be."

"No one is." She scooted over and laid her head on my chest. "Wanna know a secret?"

"Desperately."

"Your daughter loves you. Both of them."

I felt the fountain gushing up toward my eyes again. I couldn't speak.

"And you wanna know something else?" she continued. "So do I."

CHAPTER 9

I scored an appointment with the chief prosecutor in the US
Attorney General's office with surprising ease. The fact that I
knew Hickman, and I was already on their radar, probably
helped. The attorney general himself was typically too busy with political and administrative obligations to keep a close eye on the legal
issues that came before his office. The staff attorneys handled the
criminal and civil appeals with federal jurisdiction, as well as requests
for advisory opinions. The chief prosecutor ran the shop, which made
him one of the busiest men in the office.

So why was he so willing to carve space out of his day to chat with
me? Clearly, he knew who I was and probably knew what I wanted.
Given that they knew Oz was in my office before I did, I had to
assume they were still one step ahead of me. And far more knowl-
edgeable.

The receptionist waved me right into his office. The chief prosecutor, Roger Thrillkill, sat at his desk studying a stack of papers. He was
a tall, big man with a ramrod straight back. His shirtsleeves were rolled
up with precision, each to exactly the same height.

Michael Hickman, the associate who'd chastised me in the courthouse yesterday, stood beside him.

Thrillkill met me as I was halfway into the office, his outstretched hand blocking my progress. "Ben Kincaid. At last we meet."

I took his hand. He favored what I thought of as the Vulcan Death Grip, like most politicians in this state. "Sir."

"Call me Rog. Everyone does. Ever since I was a short piece of scrub back in Wewoka."

There was nothing scrubby about him now. He was something like six foot three, which made him about a head taller than me. He was a bear of a man, round in the middle, but vigorous and strong. He had an eyes-lock gaze and a one-dimple grin that made disliking him challenging. "Pleased to meet you, sir. Thank you for finding time for me."

"Least I can do for such a distinguished officer of the court. Who did time in Washington. Handled big cases all over the country. Make the rest of us look like pikers."

"I hardly think so. You'll probably be in Washington yourself in a few."

"Me?" Thrillkill pressed a hand against his chest as if I'd just suggested he ran a cockfighting club. "I'm just a small-town boy."

"Running the USAG's office."

"And already in over my head." He slapped me on the shoulder and showed me to a chair. I noticed he did not sit. He preferred to tower over me. "You know more about big-city politicking than I ever will. You're a Nichols Hills boy, right?"

He'd done his research. I wasn't surprised. "Only in a technical way."

"And you've moved back there. Joined the country club yet?"

"I'm afraid my golf game isn't worth much."

"Oh, golf, who has time for that? It's about networking, Ben. That's what you pay those membership fees for. Say, if you like, I could talk to Frank Hamish about sponsoring you at Gaillardia."

"Thanks, but I'll pass."

"He runs the History Center, too, and I know they're looking for board members."

I decided to end the tap dance before it got out of control and I actually accepted one of his inducements. "Do you mind if I ask you a few questions?"

He spread his arms wide. "That's what I'm here for. Why did you want to see me?"

"Well, my first call was to the OSBI, but my contact there said the CIA had more contact with your office."

"CIA? The national boys? Sounds like something big. What is it?"

As if he didn't already know. I nodded toward Hickman. "I think your associate there already knows. It's about an old acquaintance of mine. Nowadays he goes by the name Omar al-Jabbar."

"Is he your client?"

"For the moment, he's a guy who used to date my sister."

"Mmm." Thrillkill leaned against the edge of his desk. "I thought this might be about him. That's why I asked Michael to join us." He gestured vaguely toward the man beside him. "You two know each other, right?"

"We do. Had the pleasure of getting trounced by him in court once or twice."

Hickman smiled a little. "That's not the way I remember it." But I sensed he relaxed a trifle just the same. Never hurts to compliment a man in front of his boss. "You held your own just fine."

"Michael's the head of the Criminal Department. These days he spends most of his time liaising with the big boys."

The Justice Department? The intelligence community? Anytime there was an ongoing federal investigation involving a state citizen, this office was supposed to be notified. "Can you tell me why Omar was arrested?"

"I don't know that he was."

"Okay, detained."

Hickman glanced at the boss. A curt nod gave him the okay to proceed. "The investigation was initiated by the Central Intelligence Agency. They believed your man was engaged in terrorist activities."

"My client thinks he was held because he engaged in lobbying activities. That you wanted information about Abdullah Ali. The leader of PACT."

Another boss check. Did the man need permission to go to the bathroom, too? "We don't know anything about that."

"And no charges were ever brought against Abdullah."

"That's correct. Although they believe he engaged in dangerous and hostile terrorist activities. But they didn't obtain enough evidence to proceed."

"Even after they held Omar for twenty-one days?"

Hickman drew in his breath. "Yes, that was unfortunate."

"But true?"

"They got wind of some new terrorist weapon in development and thought your boy knew something about it."

Thrillkill gave me an aw-shucks expression. Sort of like Andy Griffith by the fishing hole. "You know how that goes, Ben. Not every lead pans out. But we don't want the boys in Washington to stop trying. You don't want another 9/11 on your conscience, right? I know I don't."

"No one does, but that's not really the point. Holding Omar in retaliation for legal political lobbying would be improper even under the Patriot Act."

"Of course you can't believe everything these camel jocks say."

My jaw dropped. Hickman squirmed, then said quietly to his boss, "Actually, Omar al-Jabbar is Caucasian. He changed his name when he converted to Islam."

"Oh. Well. I didn't realize."

"What's more," I said, "Omar believes he was singled out in what amounts to a vendetta by an interrogator named Nazir. I don't have to tell you that if that were true, it would be a major civil rights infraction."

Thrillkill didn't say anything right away. Which meant I was getting somewhere.

"Do you know Nazir?" Thrillkill asked, eventually.

"Can't say as I've had the pleasure."

"I have. Hard working as any man you'll ever meet, even if he doesn't believe in our Savior. I don't believe he would allow himself to indulge in any vendetta. Frankly, I don't think he has enough of a personal life to have a vendetta."

"Who said the vendetta was based on something personal?" I replied. And thank you for the helpful clue. "It might be political."

"I just don't believe it."

"Neither do I," Hickman said, jumping back into the conversation. "But I believe it's possible someone else might have a vendetta."

That caught my attention. "Like who?"

"I don't have any names. But anyone who lives the way your boy lives is bound to have some enemies."

"I don't know what you mean."

Hickman took a step back. "Perhaps I've said too much."

"Don't be a tease. Explain your comment."

Hickman and Thrillkill exchanged a long sideways glance. Ending with a shrug of the boss man's shoulders.

"First, your man's working for someone we know has terrorist connections, whether we can prove it or not. Abdullah's involved in an ongoing plot to develop a weapon that will take terrorism to an unprecedented level. We're talking about the next 9/11 and then some. Something that will make 9/11 look like a minor unpleasantry."

"And your proof of this?"

He ignored me. "Second, your man is messing with the wrong woman."

"Are you talking about Abdullah's sister?"

"Is that what he called her?" His smile broadened. "Boy, you really don't know anything about this guy, do you?"

"Perhaps not as much as I should."

"And third, your man works with ISIS."

"What? That's preposterous."

"That's a fact."

"You can't prove it."

"Has your man denied it? I don't think we have to prove openly acknowledged facts."

I felt my heart thumping in my chest. ISIS? That would certainly explain the interrogation. "Tell me why you think he's with ISIS."

"Never mind. Just forget it."

"It'll come out in discovery."

"Are you threatening us with a lawsuit?"

"You and I both know that's a possibility. That's why we're having this meeting. And I also know you've been surveilling Omar in what is increasingly sounding like illegal data gathering, even given the enormous powers granted by the Patriot or Freedom Acts."

Hickman jumped in. "I never said anything about watching your man."

"You knew he was in my office yesterday."

Hickman did not confirm or deny.

I continued. "You know a great deal about his activities. And way too much about his personal life."

"I had twenty-one days of interrogation transcripts to review. Look, Ben, I tried to warn you off as a personal favor."

"Or as an attempt to interfere with Omar's constitutional right to counsel."

He inhaled deeply. "You know, Ben . . . you are starting to make me wish I hadn't tried to help you."

"And I'm starting to think this is exactly the kind of arrogance that leads people to think they can hold someone against their will for twenty-one days and get away with it."

"Gentlemen, gentlemen." Thrillkill held up his hands. "Let's calm down. There's no need for anyone to do anything rash."

"Like file a civil rights lawsuit?" I said. "To draw attention to a gross miscarriage of justice? Just before election year?"

His smile thinned. For a moment, I almost thought I might see a crack in his jovial armor. But he reined it in. "Did I mention that this current term is not my first time to work in this office?"

I resented his attempt to derail the conversation. But I went along with it. "No, I don't believe you did."

"I worked here almost twenty years ago as an intern, while I was in law school. Same time you were interning at the DA's office, I believe."

More background research. Scary background research.

"And before that, I worked under Mike Turpin while he was the state AG. I loved that man. Bigger than life, full of energy, always a good word for anyone he met. He was a huge role model for me. But why was I working there? Not to brag, but I was Order of the Coif, top five percent. I could've gone anywhere. I could've worked at a big law firm, like you did."

"For about ten minutes."

"But I didn't. I worked for the AG because I cared about justice. Just like you. I bet we both went to law school for the same reason. Because we felt justice had disappeared from this country, and we wanted to see justice return. We took low-paying jobs that allowed us to see the justice system up close so we could figure out how to make it work better. Isn't that why you did what you did?"

"That," I replied, "plus I really wanted to piss off my dad."

"Sure, we followed different roads later on. You've taken all those bleeding-heart cases, standing up for the little guy. I admire that. I went into government work, another keenly low-paying venue, because I was committed to public service. You're still taking those cases because you see the cracks in the system. But I see something bigger than a crack. I see something that threatens to destroy the entire country."

I wasn't buying it. "If you had any evidence that Omar or Abdullah were planning a terrorist attack, you'd have brought charges. The fact that you haven't suggests that you're just trying to scare me off. And you wouldn't bother doing that unless you thought I had a potentially damaging case."

"Ben, you're not hearing me. If we allow terrorists to destroy the country, niceties like civil rights won't be anything but a nostalgic glimmer in a downtrodden eye. You think those boys in the Islamic nations care about civil rights? Most of them are worrying about where their next meal is coming from and whether they can get it without being beheaded by the latest fascist of the week."

"That's not—"

"I don't want to live in a nation like that. I see the world the same way Dick Cheney did. You're either with us or you're helping the terrorists." He leveled a squinty-eyed glare. "And right now, it doesn't look like you're with us."

CHAPTER 10

I tried to get Oz on the phone, but he didn't pick up, so I moved to the next interview on my list. Preliminary research can be tedious, but it's the only way to get the information you need to make smart decisions. I've tried farming this kind of work out to associates in the past, but I usually regretted it. With the exception of Christina, no one ever got the information I needed to answer the questions that mattered. So I had to tough my way through the grunt work. If we went to trial, life would be plenty exciting in a hurry.

Getting in to see Nazir was a good deal more difficult than seeing the prosecuting Tweedledum and Tweedledee. But necessary. I never like filing a suit naming someone I haven't met, but that was especially true here, when different people were spinning different stories and some of them didn't make sense. Maybe Nazir would provide the key piece of information that made sense of the puzzle.

Probably not. But I wanted to give him the chance.

I managed to get in just before the end of the day. The location was an unmarked hard-to-find former strip mall in one of the less pleasant parts of OKC. The signage suggested that this was a HUD office, but I suspected that was a cover for the CIA. No one would tell me Nazir's status or job title. At first, they wouldn't even acknowledge that he existed, till I identified myself as an attorney and made noise about a possible wrongful imprisonment suit. Once someone contacted Nazir, I got an appointment.

There was only one possible explanation. He wanted to see me just as much as I wanted to see him.

"Mr. Kincaid. How can I help you?" Unlike Oz, Khalid Nazir was Middle Eastern, as his dark complexion and hair made apparent. He spoke with an accent, slight but discernible. He was about my age, trim, obviously athletic. I did not believe for a minute that this man worked at a desk most of the time, even if he was currently poised behind one.

He moved straight to the point, so I did him the courtesy of doing the same. It wasn't as if he didn't know why I was here. "I understand that you were an interrogator during the interrogation of Omar al-Jabbar."

His gaze dropped a notch. His lips pursed. "Yes. That is correct. That was an unfortunate business."

So he denied nothing but, at the same time, suggested regret. "He believes he was held improperly. Unconstitutionally."

Nazir shrugged. "Perhaps he is right."

This response I did not expect. "Is that an admission?"

"That is an acknowledgement that I am not a lawyer and know nothing about such legal niceties."

"Omar says he was mistreated. Not because you thought he was a terrorist but because you thought he had information about his boss, Abdullah."

"I cannot comment on that. Except to say that as an interrogator I do not choose my targets nor determine the goals. My job is simply to determine how best to achieve those goals."

"Did you have evidence that Omar was involved with terrorism?"

"The term is 'suspicion of evil.'"

"Okay. Did you have 'suspicion of evil?' Is that why he was detained?"

"You're asking the wrong man. I did not make that decision. I was asked to interrogate, and so I did."

"Did you ask Omar about Abdullah or about himself?"

"Anytime someone works with a known terrorist, there is cause to inquire. That does not mean it was the primary reason he was detained."

"He says he was tortured."

"Our government does not define waterboarding as torture."

"Then our government is kidding itself. I thought President Obama banned waterboarding."

"And President Trump has said he believes it is necessary." Nazir smiled. "If you had seen what I have seen, particularly in my home country, you would see waterboarding as little more than—what is it they call the standard interrogation technique here? Good cop, bad cop? The waterboard is the bad cop."

"And the strip searches?"

"A security necessity."

"Repeatedly?"

"Sometimes weapons are smuggled into holding facilities. You know this."

"Taking his clothes. Leaving him naked."

"Weapons are easily concealed in clothing."

"The loud music? Filthy living conditions."

"All standard interrogation practices. Not forbidden by the Geneva convention, even were it applicable."

"You have no end of excuses, Mr. Nazir. But it all adds up to improper treatment. In violation of the US Constitution."

"A piece of paper." He looked down at the desk. "And completely meaningless, if there is no nation to be governed by it."

"So the end justifies the means? I have to tell you—that's not the view of the law. Or the Supreme Court."

"Is it not? I understood that constitutional infringements are permitted when there is . . . what is the term? Substantial state interest."

I was expecting a brute, not a man so articulate and obviously intelligent. It threw me more than I cared to admit. "Maybe for small matters. Time, place, and manner restrictions on the right to speech. But here we're talking about holding a man who was not charged with a crime but held prisoner for twenty-one days. And tortured."

Nazir walked up to me and, before I even knew what was happening, placed his hand on my shoulder, digging his thumb firmly in the space behind my clavicle. His gaze was penetrating, plainly intimidating. He wasn't interrogating me, at least not officially, but he still made my heart beat faster and my tongue get thicker. If I were naked and tied to a waterboard, he would be terrifying. "Terrorism is serious business, Mr. Kincaid. Do you understand that?"

"Of course." I willed my voice not to tremble.

"Good. We do not have to be enemies. I sense we are not so far apart in our thinking as you imagine."

The thumb hurt, but damned if I was going to tell him that. "I have yet to be convinced."

"Then please allow me to try." He removed his hand. "Perhaps some fresh air. It is a lovely day. Will you walk with me?"

Ten minutes later, after we passed through some security checkpoints, we were outside. I wondered if he meant to be ironic when he said it was a lovely day. This time of year, the weather in OKC was rarely lovely, mostly hot and humid, and this part of downtown wasn't even close. OKC had made great strides in recent years. Bricktown had been converted to a genuinely attractive pedestrian center for shopping and dining. But other parts of the city remained an eyesore.

And then there was the matter of the wind. Chicago was known as the Windy City, but statistically speaking, OKC was windier. The downtown area had a system of underground tunnels so workers could avoid going outside indefinitely. If the wind wasn't bad enough, the sun was. Summer in OKC typically varied from too hot to miserably too hot, till you got to August, when it was simply best to be somewhere else.

"You have not asked about my background, Mr. Kincaid. Are you curious? Or has your crack research team already told you everything you need to know?"

More satire? "I don't know anything about you, actually. There's nothing online."

"That is one of the great perks of working in intelligence. I cannot say the same for you, Mr. Kincaid. You are all over the Net. And some of it I am sorry to report is rather unkind."

"All my sins remembered."

"Yes, this information age has too often put the least accurate or flattering data in the hands of those least equipped to use it wisely. I would not like every insecure hatemonger with a web browser to be able to review every mistake I have ever made."

"Mistakes made here? Or in Iraq?"

"Both, I am sorry to say." He walked at a brisk and steady pace. I had to work to keep up with him.

"What did you do in Iraq?"

"I was a member of the Republican Guard. Do you know what that means?"

"It means you were in the Iraqi army."

"Correct. I was in intelligence. An interrogator, there as here."

"Omar mentioned that he had some contact with you in Iraq."

An eyebrow rose. "Indeed? I do not recall that. But I was very busy, and I saw many Americans. I was very good at my job. Which is what brought me to the attention of the CIA."

I remembered what Oz told me. "You switched sides."

"There were no longer sides. The Hussein reign of terror was over, and the Guard was disbanded. The government was in chaos. I had to eat. The US government was aware of my . . . activities. And how effective my work had been."

"You tortured US soldiers?"

"I interrogated them. On a few occasions. Most of my work pertained to Iraqi citizens, before the operation you know as Desert Storm."

"So the US recruited you."

"They needed help. Intelligence gathering was at an all-time low. It is now commonly accepted that the decision to invade Iraq was based on poor intelligence. And you may believe that if you wish. If their intelligence gathering were to improve, they needed men who knew how to persuade prisoners to talk. I was not the only man recruited from the Guard. After the US withdrew from Iraq, I was transferred stateside so I could use my talents on domestic prisoners."

"Like Omar. Did you learn anything of value from him?"

He hesitated.

"If I file a lawsuit," I said, "you will be required to testify and to produce all records."

"Not if there is a national security issue."

"Then the records will be produced in camera—for the judge's eyes only. But they will still be produced."

Still no response.

"My client suggested you had some kind of grudge against him. Not relating to terrorism. Something personal."

Nazir didn't blink. "I never allow personal matters to affect my work."

"Roger Thrillkill told me the interrogation was part of an investigation into some alleged terrorist plot," I said. "Something about a new weapon."

"It is much more than alleged. The threat is real. It is imminent."

"So I'm supposed to believe that terrorists are swarming around Oklahoma City?"

"It has happened before, has it not?"

His words hit me like a sledgehammer. All at once, I realized why he'd brought me out here. We'd ascended the crest of a hill, and only a few blocks away I could see the Oklahoma City National Memorial, built on the site of the former Murrah building. The place where a terrorist bomb killed 168 people. The Memorial made sure no one ever forgot. The Gates of Time marked the moment just before and just after the devastation. The Reflecting Pool allowed people to peer in and see someone forever changed by what happened. The bronze chairs reminded everyone what was lost. One chair for each death. Nineteen tiny chairs for the children.

"You are probably aware that terrorists love anniversaries," Nazir said. "The Oklahoma City bombing was on the anniversary of Ruby Ridge. 9/11 was on the anniversary of the British mandate allowing immigration into Palestine. It would be extremely difficult for terrorists to strike again at the newly rebuilt World Trade Center. Oklahoma City is far more vulnerable."

My mouth went dry. I searched my brain for some rebuttal, but I couldn't come up with one.

"How many people do you know who work in this area, Mr. Kincaid? How many friends? How many loved ones?"

I did not answer.

"I believe you and your wife share an office downtown, correct?"

"That doesn't mean—"

"If you had been in court the day of the Murrah bombing, you would feel differently. I have seen my homeland ravaged by terrorists. And war. By evil allowed to flourish undeterred."

He turned toward me, once again placing that firm hand on my shoulder. "You are a smart and caring man, Mr. Kincaid. Compassionate. I am sure you feel strongly about your country. And your friends and loved ones. Instead of being enemies, let us work together to stop this looming threat in our midst."

I cleared my throat. I had a difficult time forming words. "No one wants to see another bombing."

"Agreed. And if I can do anything to stop it, I will. Anything."

CHAPTER 11

Thursday night is date night for Christina and me, so we already had a sitter lined up to watch the girls. As usual, we spent the night playing Scrabble.

If other people enjoy date night at a Bricktown dance club, or catching the latest Marvel movie, more power to them. I don't. I'd much rather spend a quiet evening at home with my wife. We had dinner at the Roundhouse, then came home after baby bedtime.

Other people play card games for relaxation. Some people find that chess helps them concentrate. We like Scrabble. What can I say; we're word people. And I've been playing this game so long my brain anagrams letters on autopilot. Even when I'm driving, my brain compulsively rearranges the letters on billboards or bumper stickers. I don't know if everyone realizes that "Pontiac" is an anagram of "caption," but I do. I never looked at the back of one without doing the mental rearrangement.

Christina says this is a sign of deep-seated psychosis. I prefer to think of it as quirky.

"So cutting to the chase," she said, as she laid a *Z* on a triple-letter square, "you're going to take this impossible case, aren't you?"

"I haven't made up my mind." I was distracted by her play. Her *Z* adjoined not one but two perpendicular *A*s, thus making the word "za" twice, scoring over sixty points. "And that is just not right. I don't accept 'za' as a real word."

"Take is up with the editors of the *Scrabble Players Dictionary*."

"No thanks. I think they jumped the shark with the fourth edition."

"Like you've never played *za*."

"That's beside the point."

"Then I must've missed the point." She totaled her score and recorded it. "I don't know the real reason the CIA interrogated Oz so long, but I suspect they thought they were acting in the best interests of the nation."

I extended her "za" into "zaftig," making a modest twenty points. "But the end does not always justify the means. Some means are acceptable under the law and some are not."

"Yes, I went to law school, too. But don't you think there are times when national security becomes more important than abstract rights?"

"I think any time we face serious trouble, there will be someone who thinks it's permissible to rewrite the Constitution."

"Lincoln did it. FDR, too. And they were not bad guys." She referred to Lincoln's suspension of habeas corpus and Roosevelt's restrictions on freedom of speech, both done during wartime by executive order—meaning they didn't go through Congress.

"True. But one of the primary injustices the founding fathers hoped to eliminate was the crown seizing people without informing them of the charge. And I can't believe anyone thinks torture is acceptable, even if it works. Most of the studies conducted by Amnesty International indicate that the information obtained by torture is rarely reliable. Subtler approaches produce more beneficial results."

She drew more tiles out of the bag. "But bottom line—is this a case you want to be associated with?"

"I'm planning to keep a low profile."

"The press will be all over this the instant you file. The feds will have to make some public comment. And then the twenty-four-hour news crowd will weigh in. You may have the heart of Clarence Darrow, but they'll make you out to be Satan incarnate. Particularly here in the heartland, where televised debates mean two speakers compete to see who can be the most right-wing."

"You're exaggerating. I can handle a little negative publicity. It's not like it's never happened before."

"Yeah. But when you're all sulky and moody because you think everyone hates you, I'm the one who has to live with it."

"I am never sulky."

"Ri-i-ight." She laid down "goofy," using the *G* in my "zaftig." I hoped she was just playing the game, not making commentary.

"Or moody."

"You were moody last night."

"That was different. That was—" I stopped. This was date night. I wouldn't drag my concerns about Emily into it. "I can't shy away from tough cases. That would defeat the whole point of getting into this business."

She sighed. "Would you at least make sure this Oz character can pay his legal bills? And that he isn't a paranoid freak?"

"I think he genuinely believes he's been wronged, and he wants me to believe it, too."

"You said before he's got a girlfriend."

"Abdullah's sister." Maybe. I remembered what Thrillkill said.

"So those two are into each other in an even bigger way. And you know what that means."

"Not yet. You gonna tell me?"

"If Abdullah is involved with terrorists, like all those feds say, then his sister must know about it. Odds are she's involved, too. Terrorism tends to run along family lines."

"Let's not make any stereotypical assumptions. That's not necessarily true."

"It's not necessarily true that drug addicts are unproductive or that OU football fans are obsessive or that poets are insane. But when have you ever known one who wasn't?"

"We have to take a strong line against stereotyping, especially when it runs along racial lines. Maybe Abdullah has been subjected to so much scrutiny because he's Middle Eastern and rich. I've wondered if the feds didn't originally go after Omar because his name made them think he was Middle Eastern. Must've been a shock when he turned out to be whiter than me."

"No one is whiter than you, Ben."

"What does that mean?"

"Are you going to play?"

I laid my tiles down. I played "yacht" extending from the *Y* in her "goofy." Which put me exactly two points ahead. Now was the time to make my full-court press. I could win this game yet. After all, I was the king of anagrams. And I had the *J* on my rack. "Take that."

"Oh my. I'm trembling."

"I think I've made up my mind. I hope you won't be upset."

"I knew you were going to take this case a long time ago, husband."

"He says Abdullah will pay his legal fees."

"And I predict that will fall through."

"How can you possibly know?"

"Call it a hunch. Based on experience. And you'll continue representing him anyway."

"What are you, the oracle of Delphi?"

"Those who do not study history are doomed to repeat it."

"I'm not as predictable as you think."

"You are to me."

"Am not."

"You played "yacht" because your rack was consonant heavy. You played into the bottom line, thinking next time you're going to build horizontally into the triple-word square. You're saving your best tile, the *J*, so you can triple it and win the game."

The worst part was now I couldn't play "junket" without proving her right, and I was really looking forward to that. "I'm pleading the fifth."

"Thought so."

"But I am taking the case."

"I know. But ask yourself one question. How much of your decision is based on the cause being just—and how much is based on guilt?"

"Guilt? Guilt about what?"

"I don't know. You haven't told me yet. But I know that look in my boy's eyes."

"I don't know what—"

The doorbell rang. Christina looked just as puzzled as I was. We didn't socialize that much, and unexpected visitors were a rarity at any time, much less this late at night.

"I'll go," I said throwing on a robe.

Christina held me back. "Ben . . . maybe you shouldn't."

"What do you mean?"

"Word is already out that you've been talking to a . . . person of interest. Maybe even that you're planning to represent him. Given your history of taking on lost causes, it wouldn't be a big leap."

"You think they've already put out a fatwa on me?"

"I think I love my husband, and I don't want to lose him."

"You're being silly."

"Ben—"

"I promise to look through the peephole before I open the door."

And I did. But nothing on earth could've prepared me for what I saw. A terrorist with a rocket launcher would have been less surprising.

CHAPTER 12

"Julia!"

My little sister didn't say a word. She just walked into my arms and stayed there. I hadn't seen her in years. I hadn't had a hug from her in that much longer.

Once upon a time, growing up in Oklahoma City, we were the best of friends. We're only two years apart. Many siblings squabble and compete. We never did. I tell people this, and they say, "Sure you did. You just don't remember." But they're wrong. We were not only siblings but best friends. Until all that ended .

I suppose it's inevitable that relationships change. But perhaps not as dramatically as they did for us. Part of it was high school. She acquired a new set of friends and engaged in activities I didn't like. Including dating Omar—not that it was any of my business. But my disapproval of her spoiled-rich-kid-jock boyfriend was a big part of why the relationship didn't last. By college we were in completely different orbits. She disappeared, lost a lot of weight, gained a lot of weight, married my college pal Mike, divorced Mike, married a much wealthier doctor, had a son, left the doctor . . . etc. Real life stuff.

The nadir was probably when, in desperation, she dumped her infant son, Joey, on me. I did my best, but parenting did not come naturally or easily, and with a trial practice exploding all around me, I just didn't have time. That era was full of surprises. One was the shocking discovery that Joey was autistic. The other was the perhaps even more shocking discovery that Joey was actually Mike's son—something even Mike didn't know.

Julia finally got her life in order (temporarily) and returned for Joey, abruptly, unexpectedly, just as the kid and I were learning how to live with one another. I haven't seen her since. Have tried to track her down repeatedly. Without success.

"You came home," she said, her long blonde hair cascading off her shoulders. I was relatively certain the color wasn't natural, but what adult blonde's hair color is? She appeared trim—the best shape I'd seen her in since we were kids. "I never would've believed it."

"It doesn't seem like home. I mean, you know. Like it used to be."

"Thank God for that." She took a few steps into the cavernous living room. "I like what you've done with the place. Which would appear to be . . . absolutely nothing."

"Mother already had it furnished far better than I could have done."

"What about your wife?"

"She has better things to do than blow money at Mathis Brothers."

"Speak for yourself." Christina emerged, wrapping a robe around herself. "I don't recall you inviting me to blow money at Mathis Brothers."

An ear-to-ear grin spread across Julia's face. "You must be Christina."

The two women sized each other up. "And you must be Julia. I've heard a lot about you."

"Likewise."

"About me? From whom?"

"Well, I still talk to Mike from time to time."

"You do?" I was surprised. I stayed in touch with Mike, too, and he'd never mentioned it.

"Plus, there's a lot of stuff about you two on the Internet."

Christina blinked. "Good or bad?"

"Oh, both. Like for any other celebrity. Some will praise, some will be insanely jealous because you've accomplished something with your life and they haven't."

I stepped in. "Wait. Let's go back to the word *celebrity*."

She gave me a playful jab in the arm. "Don't be so modest. Some of your cases have gotten a lot of coverage. You're a big shot, Ben."

"I am so not."

"You are."

"I haven't done anything except plod through courtrooms and try to keep my head above water."

Christina laid a hand on my arm. "That's Ben for you. He never thinks anything he's done is of any importance."

"Yeah," Julia said. "Well, I know where that comes from."

The two women exchanged a look.

"I confess I've wanted to meet you," Christina said. "But I'm surprised to see you tonight, out of the blue, without warning."

"Did I come at a bad time?"

"Oh, no, no," Christina said, simultaneous with my "Well, we were playing Scrabble ."

"I've been wanting to see you two for a long time," Julia explained. "Especially since I heard you'd married. How did you ever get this waffley wishy-washy worrywart to commit?"

"You can't believe how hard it was. Or how long it took."

"I can imagine."

"But you're dodging the question. What brings you here tonight? I mean, I'm glad to see you, and you're welcome to stay as long as you like. It's your house, too."

I cut in. "After Mother passed, we tried to find you—"

"No worries, Ben. I don't want the house. I couldn't live here. Gives me shivers. Frankly, I don't know how you stand it. But if you don't mind, I might stay a few days. Are you using my old bedroom?"

"Actually," I said, "we've got that closed off."

"Oh." She looked at me. "Of course."

Christina's eyes narrowed. "Ben told me it was to save on air conditioning."

Julia sat on the oversize sofa. We followed her lead, sitting on either side of her. "Ben, I know you've seen Oz."

"How can you possibly know that?"

"I've stayed in touch with him, too."

"How do you manage to stay on good terms with your exes?" Christina asked. "Every time I broke up with someone, they started acting like I was demon spawn."

"Don't get me started. His father currently has custody of Joey, in case you're wondering. He convinced a judge he could provide a more stable home."

"Didn't you fight it?"

"I tried. But he hired one of those—" She stopped herself. "Never mind."

"You can say it," Christina said. "Divorce lawyers. Here we call them the second-floor Mafia."

"I get it. Put the money in the bag or you'll never see your kid again. He hired some big old windbag bully, who filed motions and subpoenas and discovery requests I didn't understand. I ran out of money to pay my attorney after the first month. They told the judge I was a horrible person. I didn't know how to defend myself."

"So he got Joey?"

"It would be more accurate to say he bought Joey." Her face twisted up in a way I found difficult to describe. The bitterness was plain.

I brought the subject back home. "Julia, I know you liked Oz in high school. But he's a different person today. In fact, he might be . . . dangerous."

"And yet you talked to him."

"Like an attorney to his potential client. I don't want you in the line of fire."

"But you're putting yourself there, aren't you?"

"How do you know that?"

"Because I know you. You haven't changed that much from the scrawny kid who tried to save the robin with the broken wing. Anyone could see it was hopeless. But you didn't stop trying."

"It fell out of its nest."

"Yes, well, didn't we all. I hope you'll represent Oz. He's been through some seriously rough stuff. I mean, he's been tortured, for God's sake. He needs a friend."

Christina leaned in. "It doesn't have to be Ben."

"Isn't that what Ben does?" I loved the way these two women talked as if I were in another room. "Defending the defenseless? Taking cases no one else will take?"

"It's different now. He's married. He has a family."

Julia's face brightened. "Which reminds me! I want to see the girls!"

"In the morning," Christina said levelly. "They're asleep. I know we just met, Julia, but you need to understand something. Ben has two girls who depend upon him. He can't risk our security, not to mention our income stream, on some political hot potato."

"So you're okay with the government holding citizens for an indefinite period of time? Torturing them? Even when they've never been charged with a crime?"

"I haven't opposed him taking the case, but—" Christina drummed her fingers on the coffee table. "We should get some sleep. Can we continue this discussion in the morning?"

"Of course." We said a few more words, and I showed Julia to the guest room.

"That was quite a surprise," I said, returning to our bedroom.

"Not as surprising as what I'm about to do."

I raised an eyebrow.

"I'm about to play *quixotic*," Christina explained.

"Oh." I scrutinized the board. "Once you play that bingo, the game will be over."

"Yup. You're toast."

"What kind of person looks at a rack of letters and sees *quixotic*?"

She just smiled. "The kind who's married to you."

CHAPTER 13

Monday morning I was in the federal courthouse the moment it opened. I had a case to file and a few docket calls on other cases. An hour later I was back in my office. Where sixty-seven phone messages awaited me.

"I guess the word is out," I murmured.

Tanya pursed her lips. "If by that you mean people know you filed Oz's suit against the CIA and the Justice Department, then the answer is yes."

"I assume most of these people called to offer their support."

"Then you are more naive than you look. Some want to interview you. Some want to educate you. A few want to kill you."

"Lovely."

"You need to start returning those calls," Tanya said, as I slid the pink slips off the spindle. "Our phone lines can't handle many more. Neither can I."

"Getting receptionist's ear? A strange malady that only affects law office personnel."

"The worst was Nancy Grace."

"You talked to Nancy Grace?"

"Yes, and she sounds just like she did on television."

"So you got to chat with a big deal. Guess you didn't know how many perks there would be when you took this job."

She pushed some more paper my way. "If Brad Pitt calls, I'll be impressed. Speaking of celebrities, FOX News called. They want an interview. If I were you, I wouldn't do it."

"I never do interviews about pending cases, but just out of curiosity, why not?"

"Because I listened to them during my break, and they're already talking about how this case demonstrates the dangers posed by terrorist sympathizers. They're hinting that your client is linked to an international terrorist ring. Allegedly."

"Based on what evidence?"

"An unnamed source. And an interview with a so-called expert who said he didn't think the government would've held Omar without a good reason."

"That's fair and balanced."

"I know the receptionist doesn't normally get a vote, but I think you should drop this case."

"You're right."

"I am?"

"Yes. The receptionist doesn't get a vote."

"Ben, some of these people are complete cranks, and they sound kinda nuts. They say we've got to blow up terrorists and their accomplices. Before they blow us up."

"Do any of these people realize Oz is an American? Not to mention white?"

"I don't even think FOX News has twigged onto that yet. But I'm not sure they'll care."

"Whatever. We'll be okay."

"Easy for you to say. You're not on the front lines. Some whack job goes postal and comes through the office door, I'll be the first one he sees."

"And when he realizes how lovely you are, not to mention how white you are, his anger will fade, and he'll perceive the error of his ways. Probably ask you to marry him."

"Sometimes I think you are completely twisted."

The outer door slammed. Oz raced through. He looked breathless. Sweat ran down the sides of his face. "Ben, you need to lock that door."

"I'm fairly sure that would be bad for business."

"I'm not joking. Do you know how many reporters are swarming on the street outside?"

"I didn't see anyone when—" I stopped. "But I came from the parking garage."

"On the street you've got maybe forty people desperate for a sound bite. All the local stations. Some national."

"Already?"

"Yes. Someone recognized me, and they went into attack mode." We both heard the crystal chime of the elevator. "They're he-e-e-e-e-e-e-ere."

A throng appeared on the other side of the acrylic outer office doors. A few carried minicams.

"Ben," Tanya said. "Tell me I can lock the doors."

I hesitated. "We don't want to appear to be hiding anything. Or from anything."

"Ben," she repeated, a decided edge in her voice. "Tell me I can lock the doors."

Safety first, my mother always said. "Do it."

Tanya sprung up, key chain jingling. Oz and I followed her movements, though I wasn't sure if Oz was following the keys or the thong peeking out over her slacks.

The crowd hit the door seconds after Tanya locked it. A few shouted questions.

I had to do something. But I wasn't sure what.

Christina emerged from her office and gave me a wry look. "Would this be an example of you keeping the case on the down low?"

"Saying 'I told you so' is so petty."

"It's all over the Internet," Christina informed me. "You went viral about ten minutes after you filed. For possibly the first time in your life, you're trending. Blogs, Facebook, Twitter, Instagram. People are videoing their ill-informed opinions and posting them on YouTube. Personally, I prefer the Jenga-playing kitty."

The crowd outside the door got louder. And angrier. I've always felt lawsuits should be tried in the courtroom, not in the media, especially given telejournalists' proven difficulty grappling with issues requiring more than thirty seconds of discussion. But I also recognized that this story was going to make the news, and I didn't want the first image my potential jurors received to be Oz and his lawyer cowering behind locked doors while some newswoman intoned gravely that they "declined to comment."

I told Oz to wait for me in my office. I walked to the front doors. The noise level dropped, but to their disappointment, I did not unlock the doors.

"I'm sorry," I said, loud enough for them to hear, "but I'm conducting a private and confidential consultation. I can't allow anyone in the office at this time."

"Will you be giving a press conference?" the brunette in front shouted.

"No. We're raising serious constitutional issues best addressed by the courts, not infotainment—"

"Roger Thrillkill has announced a press conference at noon at the state capitol."

That seemed rather sudden. But not completely surprising. Thrillkill probably started marshaling his forces the instant I left his office.

"I'm sure he doesn't want this case tried in the media any more than—"

"He says he will release evidence demonstrating that your client was questioned properly and that he is involved with terrorists."

In other words, he *was* going to try the case in the media. He didn't have enough evidence to press charges in court, but he had enough to convict someone on television. "That's not how I roll, and I won't be baited into—"

"Can we take that as an acknowledgement that your client is guilty?"

Of what? He's never been charged. "No, you may—"

"Why are you siding with the terrorists?" a tall man in the rear shouted.

"I'm not. I'm siding with the Constitution."

"If the prosecutor can prove your client is a terrorist, will you drop the case?"

"If they had credible evidence, they would have charged him already."

"So you're siding with the terrorists."

"No one has even been charged—"

I felt a tug at my sleeve. Christina. "Ben, you're needed urgently."

I turned, more than a little annoyed, mostly at myself. "What is it?"

"That private and confidential meeting you mentioned. We've started. We need your expertise." She smiled at the reporters. "We'll let you know when we're ready to make a statement."

She tugged me away from the doors.

"What are you doing?" I asked, as soon as we were out of sight.

"Saving your bacon."

"Meaning?"

"Meaning, the point of not talking to the press is to not talk to the press."

"I wasn't talking to them."

"You gave them three separate sound bites, which they will edit to make you look evasive and disreputable."

"I can deal with the press."

"That explains why you were handling it so masterfully. Now go to your office and stay there till the vultures have left the desert."

"Thank you, but I do not need a handler."

"Even Don Quixote needed Sancho Panza. You have people in your office waiting for you."

"People?" That caught my attention. I knew Oz was here. Did he bring friends? I gave her a kiss on the cheek—a reminder that I loved her even when I felt crabby—and headed down the corridor.

Oz waited in my office with two others—a petite woman with dark hair that flowed past her shoulders, and a young man. Unlike Oz, she was undeniably of Middle Eastern descent, and also undeniably beautiful. Her eyes had a darkness that seemed both haunting and haunted. The kid looked like he didn't want to be here.

I stood awkwardly in the doorway. "May I ask . .

Oz grinned a bit. "They snuck in through the parking garage. I mentioned Mina before, remember? My girlfriend. And this is her little brother, Kir."

Ah. "Nice to meet you both, but this is a confidential meeting. You don't need to be present."

Mina shook her head, letting the hair dance freely about her face. "No, you want to talk to me."

"I'm sure I would love that, but right now we have to—"

"Seriously. You want to talk to me. Right now. I'm the one those fools outside are looking for." The olive-skinned beauty smiled. "I'm the terrorist."

CHAPTER 14

There are moments in the practice of law when your head spins with so many potentially conflicting interests, all of which you are supposed to mentally balance lest you incur the wrath of the Bar, that even the most ethical person can be confused and the mightiest brain can be addled.

This was one of these moments. "Ma'am, I will have to caution you against making any self-incriminatory remarks. Since we don't have an attorney-client relationship, I could be compelled to testify in—"

Her expression was uncomfortably close to a sneer. "Relax, Counselor. I have not confessed to anything." Her English was excellent, vernacular and easy to understand, only a trace of an accent. "But I am trying to give you insight into what this case is truly about. Why they held Omar for so long. And why they will come after you with everything they've got."

Needless to say, that stimulated my interest. "Oz, do I have your permission to talk to this woman?"

"That's why I brought her."

"Your personal relationship will not protect her in court, and the attorney-client privilege will not extend to her."

"Got it, Ben. Do your lawyer thing."

"This is serious, Oz. You saw that vampiric throng outside? There's already an enormous amount of interest in this case. We've had phone calls from national markets. That's likely to increase. It's going to affect both of you. And possibly create some unsavory temptations."

"I'm not quite sure I follow—"

Mina cut in. "He's afraid I'll sell what I know to the *National Enquirer* for a million bucks."

"Oh." He shrugged. "I don't think that's going to happen. Maybe you should just hear her out, Ben."

"If you wish, Miss .

"My name is Mina Ali. I am from what was once one of the most prominent Iraqi families, under Saddam Hussein. After your government murdered him, my family suffered for the association."

"Wasn't he executed?"

"Call it what you will. You invaded our country and replaced our leaders. After a show trial, he was killed."

I opted not to get distracted by politics. "How did you come to the United States?"

"My family had money, some of which has survived the invasion. And my brother lives here. His name is Abdullah Ali. I believe Oz has mentioned him."

"Oz's boss. The one the feds think is a terrorist."

"Precisely. I had both of the essential qualities for emigration—money and connections. This has allowed me to come to the United States. But I also . . . attracted unfortunate attention. Both in Iraq and here."

"Did you know Nazir?"

"At first—only by reputation. And later, in a much more . . . personal way."

"I don't understand."

"Unlike Nazir, I never made a profitable realignment. And that cost me dearly."

"How so?"

"I was arrested, after the Hussein regime fell out of power. They accused me of spying against them."

"Was it true?"

"Of course it was true. I was attempting to survive. The Americans invaded us. The country was in chaos. As you will recall, the formal fighting was of short duration. Sadly, unofficial acts of warfare continued. Bombings and suicide missions and the pointless loss of life."

"Terrorism."

"If you wish to call it that."

"Isn't that what it was?"

"If another nation occupied the US, and local resistance operatives struck against the occupiers, would you call them terrorists? Or freedom fighters?"

"I grasp your point, ma'am. But rehashing past acts won't help anything. My focus is on winning Oz's lawsuit."

"Yes, of course. There is money to be made. And Americans prioritize profit above all else."

I've never been anyone's puppet patriot, but the woman was beginning to annoy me. "I assume you're telling me this because you eventually had some contact with Nazir."

"Indeed." A shadow crossed her face. The dark eyes burned with a smoldering intensity. "I was arrested. Questioned for days without food, without sleep, without rest. They wanted information about the local resistance efforts. So I was tortured."

"Waterboarded?"

"Raped." A hush fell across the office. I felt as if someone had vacuumed the air out of my lungs. "Over and over again. For weeks."

My voice cracked. "I . . . am so sorry."

Her eyes seemed hollow. "It was a long time ago."

"Who—"

"Officially, it was done by Iraqi operatives. But who do you think pulled their strings? Was Nazir working for Iraq when he did this to me, or for the US? Soon after, Nazir's new alliance was made public."

"Americans would never condone—"

"Which is exactly why they got Iraqi pawns to do it for them."

"I don't believe—"

"At the time, your president insisted Americans do not torture. Until there was overwhelming evidence that they did."

I bit down on my lower lip.

"It is no matter what you believe," she continued. "What was done was done. One day, they stripped me naked, put me up on a table, let old men circle around and bid on the right to rape me. The others held me down while the highest bidder took his pleasure. If I tried to resist, they beat me." She paused, pushing her hair back with her hand. "But it made little difference who won. Once the highest bidder had his fill, the others took their turns."

I was without words. "That's . . . horrifying."

"Sadly, that is commonplace. To this day, ISIS systematically rapes women and girls of the Yazidi religious minority. It is part of their theology—as is slavery. Because these people are conquered and not in the proper sect, it's considered halal. They say raping Yazidi women is a prayer to God." Her lips tightened. "Nazir and his brutes were much the same."

"And you talked?"

"Not then. They could invade my body, but not my conscience. Not yet. Not till the hot irons."

I knew I didn't want her to continue. But I had no way to stop her.

She turned around and lifted her blouse. Her younger brother averted his eyes. "See the scars? They laid me flat on the floor—still naked—and threw hot irons on my back. The metal seared into me. I smelled my own flesh. I felt it peeling away from my body."

"Why . . . would anyone do this?"

"Their goal was to break me. And I am sorry to say they succeeded."

"You told them what they wanted to know?"

"I told them almost nothing because I had almost nothing to tell. I knew of a few small-time resisters, no more. But I babbled like a child. I would have told them anything. I wept and cried and begged for mercy like the weakest of cowards."

"I think it's understandable—"

"There is no excuse for weakness." Her chin rose and her back straightened. "Never before in my life did I display such frailty. And never will I do so again."

"Was Nazir in charge of your interrogation?"

"Yes. It was always done in the dark, with a hood over my head and a knife pressed to my throat. I never knew the names of my rapists. But so far as I am concerned, they were all Nazir. He was the cruel bastard who orchestrated the attacks. And he was rewarded for his cruelty with a trip to the land of opportunity and a comfortable government position. While I spent months in an institution in a virtually catatonic state, babbling and drooling on myself like a broken toy. This is how justice was administrated in Iraq—after the US military accomplished their mission and brought us freedom."

CHAPTER 15

I wished Christina were here. She was always better at nurturing than I was. Not that my heart didn't go out to this broken woman. But I wasn't sure how to show it, or even whether that would be appropriate.

Throughout her horrific narrative, I kept an eye on her young brother, Kir. He appeared to be a teenager, or maybe early twenties. He remained silent, but I could see anger burning in his eyes. I could hardly blame him for being protective of his sister. I had a sister, too.

And I knew how painful it felt when you couldn't help her.

"You seem much better now," I said.

"Yes. But it has taken years to recover myself. To find some semblance of the woman I once was."

"Are you working?"

"With Abdullah. My work is political. And that is why, once again, they seek to stop me."

"You also work for PACT?"

"I work for a division of PACT that uses a different name. JUSTICE IRAQ."

I started to get an uneasy feeling. "I don't know what that is."

"The division that Omar works for focuses on lobbying for Arab-

American rights, challenging the Freedom Act and anti-Muslim initiatives. But these legal niceties are of little importance to me. I know that this government will do what they wish regardless of their laws. If they can accomplish what they did to me, they can do anything."

"What's the focus of your organization?"

"To see that justice returns to my country. To address the sins of the invasion and force Congress to make reparations."

"I don't see that happening anytime soon."

"Did not your nation demand reparations after World War II?"

"That's very different."

"Indeed. You were not invaded. Your country was not razed, your men were not slaughtered, and your women were not raped. Your economy was strengthened, not decimated. And yet still you demanded reparations. So shall we."

I was getting an ugly premonition not only about this woman but about this case. I was also beginning to understand why the feds were pulling no punches. "Would it be fair to call JUSTICE IRAQ . . . radical?"

"Radical is in the eye of the beholder."

True enough. "Would you call it a terrorist organization?"

"Of course not. That would be foolish."

"But would it be true."

She hesitated much too long before answering. "We are a political lobbying group. We seek retribution through legal avenues. I have seen the impact of violence. I have no desire to see it repeated."

Oz cleared his throat. "JUSTICE IRAQ has appeared on the CIA's list of known or suspected terrorist organizations."

I felt my eyelids close. "And you're just now telling me this?"

"It's got nothing to do with me. I don't work for that organization."

"Your girlfriend does. The sister of your boss does." My voice rose of its own bidding. "This completely changes the case." And I hadn't even had a chance to ask the question that really burned in my brain.

"I'm your client, Ben. I'm not a terrorist."

"But you're sleeping with one!" I wished I hadn't said it the second the words were out of my mouth. Especially since her brother sat right beside her. But there was no taking it back.

"I have the right to be with whomever I choose. My personal relationships are of no relevance."

"The government will claim that they are. I guarantee it. What's more, they'll say that this lawsuit is part of *her* vendetta. That both of you want revenge against Nazir."

"Are you telling me to break up with her?"

I wasn't going to say it. He could see reality for himself and decide whether he wanted to win this suit. "It might be helpful if Abdullah would come forward. Explain that your work was nonviolent and completely legal."

"That will not happen," Mina explained. "Due to the government penchant for detention and torture, my brother has gone dark."

"Meaning?"

"You can't contact him. And neither can anyone else."

"Is that what this is about? The government wants to find an undercover terrorist, so they go after his friend and his sister?"

"We are not terrorists," Mina said. "We only seek to make the world aware of the crimes that have been committed."

"But you hate Nazir. I'd hate him, if he'd done to me what he did to you. Or if he'd done it to my wife."

"But Omar's lawsuit is not about personal hatred. It's about the difference between right and wrong."

I continued to press. "Admit it, Oz. You hate Nazir. He tortured both of you."

I sensed Oz's discomfort. "I don't know why you're—"

"Because it matters. You hate him."

"I am not going to—"

"Stop wasting my time and admit it. You hate him."

"All right then. *I hate him!*" His voice was so loud it shook the beams in the walls. I wondered if the reporters outside could hear. "He let them rape Mina. Repeatedly. And he tortured me. For twenty-one days. Of course I hate him. If it had been you, you'd hate him, too. He's a sick, evil bastard, and he deserves to die. *Painfully!*"

For all that his voice had rattled the rafters, the silence that followed was even more shattering.

I WASN'T MESSING WITH OZ AND MINA JUST TO AMUSE MYSELF. I was trying to demonstrate what would happen as soon as the prosecutor got him or her up on the witness stand and started pressing hard. They couldn't deny their enmity toward Nazir and the CIA, and even if they tried, no one would believe them.

For the first time, Kir spoke. Despite all the turmoil surrounding him, he remained amazingly calm.

"If I may speak, sir."

"Of course."

"I have known my sister all my life, of course. She has a strength such as I have never seen anywhere else. I would do anything for her. I have sometimes suggested revenge against our oppressors, and she has always insisted that I resist such impulses. That I follow a more peaceful course. The woman who taught me this, the woman with such moral courage, would never act for any reason but her belief that it was the most just course of action."

Mina beamed at him. For the first time, I saw the faintest trace of what might be called a happy expression. "He is a smart boy, is he not? The top of his class at school. His science teacher calls him a . . . what is it? A whiz kid. And so calm, so measured. Not like me at all."

Kir's eyes lowered. "I have only taken advantage of the opportunities you have made possible."

Mina wouldn't have it. "We make our own opportunities in this life."

I thought it was time to move in a different direction. "Oz, the feds think you're aligned with ISIS. Is that true?"

"Of course not." Pause. "Not anymore."

My head felt light. "You mean you *were?*"

"It was a brief flirtation. I was never really a member."

"What the hell does that mean?"

Mina cut between us. "I am an Iraqi patriot. Do you think I would be associated with a member of ISIS?"

"What I think is—"

"Excuse me." Christina appeared in the doorway. "Are you aware that some of those reporters have extremely powerful microphones? Maybe you should stop shouting your conversation."

"You think they could hear?"

"I think Helen Keller could hear." She glanced at her watch. "We should head downtown. We don't want to miss Thrillkill's press conference."

"I don't want to be there."

"Yes you do."

"If I'm there, the reporters will want me to give them a rebuttal."

Christina looked at me, arms akimbo. "And you'll give them one. You don't want Thrillkill to be the only voice on the evening news."

"Cases should be tried—"

"Then that's your rebuttal. But you will give one."

I noticed she used the imperative *will* rather than the suggestive *should*. And I'm no fool. "All right then."

Oz pushed himself out of his chair. "I'll accompany you."

I raised a finger. "Absolutely not."

His face flushed red. "No one knows more about this situation than I do."

"All the more reason not to be there. That goes for all three of you. I don't want you anywhere near that place. We've filed suit. We're seeking justice in an appropriate manner. Go home. I'll contact you if I need anything."

"*But—*"

"Look, you hired me to advise you, so take my advice. *Go home.* I'll be in touch."

Oz frowned but returned to his seat.

Tanya appeared in the doorway. "I just heard a news flash. They're preempting local programming on most networks to cover the press conference. The feds say they have new evidence of 'plots against the United States.'"

Christina and I didn't even have to exchange a glance. We were out the door.

CHAPTER 16

By the time we arrived at the state capitol building, a significant throng had assembled on the south plaza. Usually, when they hold this sort of event, the speakers assemble their own staffs on the steps so the press can shoot over their heads and make it look like a much bigger deal than it is. When I'd interned at the DA's office, press conferences were frequently scheduled at lunchtime so everyone in the office could attend. We hoped curious passersby might inflate the flock.

This time the crowd needed no artificial enhancement. I estimated more than four hundred people were in attendance, completely filling the plaza, and they didn't all come from the USAG's office or the CIA. I recognized some of the attendees as reporters who had been outside my office earlier. Others were lawyers and personnel from the various cogs of the criminal justice system. And some appeared to be concerned citizens. Judging from the placards, many had already determined that this lawsuit was a threat from foreign powers and had come to show their support for good ol' 'Merica.

As I approached, I heard chanting and shouting, some of it angry. In the past, the Oklahoma capitol building had been famous for three reasons: because it had working oil rigs on the premises, because it was one of only two capitol buildings in the country without a dome, and because it had a Ten Commandments monument. Someone finally drummed up the funds for a dome, and court cases and vandals eliminated the Commandments, but the rigs were still there. They didn't pump as much as they once did, but the capitalist symbol remained, even now, when scientists told us fracking and wastewater reinjection had turned Oklahoma into the most earthquake-ridden state in the Union.

Thrillkill read his prepared statement, interrupted every time he said something that fanned the flames of the reactionary lookie-loos. This was obviously stage-managed to influence popular opinion about the lawsuit, but I tried not to let it bother me. I love this state, and it was no news flash to me that it leans red. Around here, people use the term "Oklahoma Democrat," which translates to "what the rest of the world calls a Republican." I also know 9/11 had genuinely unnerved many. Any time a public official talks about terrorist threats, people get scared. Scared people make poor decisions.

But they're great when you're trying to stir up support.

Thrillkill spoke in short bursts, as if the speech had been written not in sentences but in sound bites. No point in giving a press conference if the news crews can't use it on the evening broadcasts. "I have been asked to make a few comments regarding the recently filed lawsuit challenging the authority and actions of the United States of America."

Well, that was one way to put it. I wondered who, if anyone, "asked" him to make comments. I suspected this conference was scheduled on his own initiative—*sua sponte*, as we say in the law—by an intelligent lawyer well aware that an election year approached.

"We categorically disagree with the charges made in this pleading. I speak on behalf of the US Attorney General's office, the Central Intelligence Agency, the Justice Department, and all branches of the US government. In fact, 'disagree' is not a strong enough word. We find these allegations vile, self-serving, and frankly motivated by the desire to undermine American intelligence efforts."

A cry of approval erupted from the crowd. Possibly a plant, but I had to admit it sounded spontaneous.

"The suggestion that either the Justice Department or the Central Intelligence Agency would resort to extralegal measures is both factually incorrect and completely offensive. We did not do this, and we have no need to do this. The Freedom Act is generous in the power it gives law enforcement to prevent threats to this nation. We will contain ISIS just as we've contained terrorist threats in the past."

Low-level rumblings of support. Thrillkill knew how to play this crowd, and he was handling it well.

"The Petition alleges false imprisonment and illegal detention, and yet the Freedom Act allows us to hold and question suspected participants in terrorist enterprises. And that includes"—he glanced down at his notes, as if he didn't already know the names—"Omar al-Jabbar, who has significant links to ISIS and other terrorist forces."

He paused a moment, allowing the pure Persianness of the name to sink in. Unsurprisingly, he did not mention that Omar was completely Caucasian.

"We will of course defend this nation against all those who would derail our national defense through civil unrest, lawsuits, or any other unscrupulous chicanery. Let me make two matters absolutely clear. First, there is no merit to this lawsuit whatsoever. Second, we will defend against all threats to the integrity and security of this nation."

That would be the strategy not only during the pretrial stage but most likely during the trial. Justify the incarceration and torture as necessary to national security. Remind people of 9/11 whenever possible. And completely avoid the constitutional issues raised by the Patriot and Freedom Acts.

Christina tugged on my sleeve. "I think this is going to be a tough one."

"Aren't they all?"

"Thrillkill may think this will scare you off. But I know better."

"They do seem to be playing the trump cards, right from the start."

"But that's good. They're not holding anything back. So you know exactly what you need to do and how to do it."

As always, I appreciated her confidence in me, however misplaced it might be. At this point, I had no idea what to do, much less how to do it.

"Excuse me. Aren't you Benjamin Kincaid?" The words came from a short woman with long hair and heavy makeup. I recognized her from television, though I couldn't place her name. Judging from the camera operator behind her, I assumed she was a newsreader. She must sit on an apple box when she's on television. "Are you going to speak next?"

"Definitely not," I said quietly. I didn't want to attract any attention.

"We'd like to get your response to the prosecutor's comments."

"No thank you."

"So we can quote you as agreeing with what he's saying."

Christina and I exchanged a glance. "Since I haven't given you a statement, it would be a gross violation of journalistic ethics to claim that I did, wouldn't it?"

"I'll put you down as 'refused to comment.' But didn't you file this lawsuit?"

"It's inappropriate to comment on pending litigation."

"Hasn't stopped Thrillkill."

I tilted my head to one side. "True."

"Even if you can't comment on the legalities, could you say something about the political situation?"

"My only interest is my client, not politics."

"Didn't you used to be in politics?"

"That was—" I felt another tug at my sleeve. Christina.

"Mr. Kincaid, you're needed elsewhere." She looked down at the newswoman. "Sorry. Previous engagement."

She dragged me away, and I offered no resistance. Obviously, she thought I was handling the press here about as well as I did at the office. Meaning not at all. And she was undoubtedly correct.

By the time we repositioned, Thrillkill concluded his remarks. "But you don't have to take my word for it. I wasn't there. I've invited someone who was there during the questioning to give you some insight into what really lurks behind this lawsuit. Ladies and gentlemen, let me introduce a patriot, an intelligence fighter for this great country—Abdul Nazir."

Now that was a surprise. I expected face-saving sound bites. I did not expect Thrillkill to call witnesses. And not in a million years did I think he would put Nazir in front of the microphones. I suppose it made sense in a way. Nazir knew more about his situation than anyone, and he was clearly of Middle Eastern descent. Perhaps Thrillkill wanted to make the point that this was about security, not racism. I suspected there was more to it, but at the moment, I had no idea what that might be.

Nazir fidgeted with his microphone, cleared his throat several times, then coughed. His first words were too soft, then he moved so close to the mike that it caused a sonic squeal. If his goal was to show that he was unaccustomed to public speaking, he was doing an excellent job.

"Pardon me. As Mr. Thrillkill was kind enough to point out, I work in intelligence. Not public speaking."

"Louder!" someone behind me shouted.

He pulled the microphone closer. "As you have no doubt noticed, I am not originally from this place. I was raised in Iraq, but I had the great fortune to be recruited by the American army, fulfilling a lifelong dream of working for the forces of freedom. Your government used me first in Iraq, and later here in the states, to obtain information about possible terrorist threats by appropriate means."

Given what I'd heard from Oz and Mina, I couldn't help but wonder if "appropriate means" included rape and torture.

"I did in fact know the plaintiff in this lawsuit, Omar al-Jabbar, and I did interrogate him regarding his ISIS connections, as well as his work for the terror—" He jumped forward abruptly, as if jabbed from behind. He and Thrillkill exchanged glances. "Regarding his connections to the *alleged* terrorist Abdullah Ali."

Skillfully done. They maintained the legally necessary "alleged" but made it clear they had no doubt Abdullah was a terrorist.

"During the interrogation," Nazir continued, "the plaintiff confessed that he worked for Abdullah." That of course was never in doubt, but the way he phrased it suggested Oz confessed to working on terrorist schemes. "I continued questioning him for the purpose of learning the extent of that work." I had to admire how flat Nazir kept the tone of his voice, never giving in to emotion or giving anyone any reason to suspect he had a personal interest. "This interrogation lasted several days, but that of course is not unusual. Few witnesses reveal everything they know in the first ten seconds."

"Death to terrorists!" a high-pitched voice screamed from the rear, followed by some scuffling sounds. "Muslims go home!" Out the corner of my eye, I saw security forces converging. I wasn't sure if that remark was in support of Nazir or in opposition. Either way, I knew the person who said it would miss the rest of the press conference.

"I do not doubt that this was an unpleasant experience for the plaintiff, though I endeavored to make it no worse than it needed to be. I did not determine the parameters of his incarceration. I only questioned him in a lawful and what I hoped would be a productive manner. And although the investigation against Abdullah was discontinued, we did in fact obtain several pieces of information that proved useful in various contexts."

"Send the sand niggers back to the desert!"

This time, almost everyone on the steps, hundreds of people, whirled around, trying to spot the speaker. The commotion level rose as spectators spoke among themselves, craning their necks to see what was happening. The shuffling was such that I began to lose my balance. I felt Christina clutch the back of my suit jacket, hanging on for dear life.

Nazir glanced up from the podium. For the first time, I had the impression that he departed from his script. "Please, my friends. There is no need for this animosity."

He held up his hands, trying to quiet the crowd, without success. The noise level grew rather than subside. I could see some sort of struggle behind me, but I couldn't tell what it was.

Nazir raised his voice. "We do not need to erect more barriers. Yes, we must maintain security for our families. But blind unreasoning hatred—this is what fuels terrorism. We want to defeat them, not become them. We can be better than this. We can—"

Only a few times in my life have I been so unfortunate as to be near a weapon in action, but I have learned to recognize the sound. And that was why, at that moment, I knew I was not hearing a car backfire or a cell phone sound effect or a talented voice mimic.

Someone fired a gun.

The shot blasted somewhere behind me. I threw my arms around Christina's.

"Terrorists!" someone screamed, and in less than a second the capitol steps descended into chaos.

More panicked voices followed. The shuffling became blind panic. Everyone wanted to get to safety, but no one knew where safety was. The crowd shifted every which way at once, pressing and shoving, getting nowhere. I felt my heart thumping in my chest. No one knew what was happening. Everyone was scared.

"Not again!" a high-pitched voice squealed. "Not here. *Not again!"*

Some oaf in a trench coat rammed into Christina. She fell against me and we both tumbled to the concrete. I bashed my face against the corner of a step. Pain seared through my head. I stifled the cry, glad I cushioned the fall for her.

"Are you okay?" I asked. She nodded faintly. I could tell she was shaken but strong as ever. I pulled in our hands and elbows, trying to avoid being trampled.

"Hold on to me," I said, helping her to her feet. "We're getting out of here." I pressed a hand to my head, wondering how bad the damage was. Sticky blood trickled down the side of my face. I didn't have time to worry about that. I needed to get my wife out of there.

The pandemonium continued. More people raced back and forth on all sides of us, screaming and sobbing and moving without thought to what lay before or behind. I kept an arm wrapped around Christina's waist, determined no one would separate us.

I spotted an open patch of lawn not far from where we'd parked. I thought that was the safest direction to travel. Most everyone seemed to be moving in the opposite direction, either back toward the capitol building or the public parking lot.

Not until I had Christina in relative safety did I stop to take my bearings. I had not heard another shot since the first, but that didn't mean it wasn't possible.

I scanned in all directions. I saw a lot of people running, but no guns, no gunshots, and no shooters.

Only then did I think to look back at the podium.

Emergency medical personnel surrounded the fallen figure of Abdul Nazir. The pool of blood surrounding his head was so great I could see it from where I stood.

He did not move. I did not think he was ever likely to move again.

And I spotted one other item of interest, about fifty feet away, down the steps and off to the far right. Three security officers held someone in custody. They'd cuffed him and pinned his arms behind his back. They shoved him roughly into the back of a patrol car.

The suspect was silent, a resolute expression on his face.

The suspect was my client. Omar al-Jabbar.

Oz.

PART II
NECESSARY LIES

CHAPTER 17

I had to fight my way through a mob just to get inside the holding jail. I'd never seen so many reporters and rubberneckers and protesters and thugs of unspecified allegiance. I got the impression they were hanging around just hoping a fight would break out so they could hurt someone.

"Mr. Kincaid!"

Damn. Recognized again.

"Still stand behind your client? Still worried about his rights?"

I tucked in my chin. The smart thing, as Christina had told me a million times, would be to keep my mouth shut. But when had I ever done the smart thing? Not recently. "I stand behind the right of all American citizens to be protected against wrongful imprisonment and torture. One hundred percent."

"And for a murderer?"

I felt my temper rising. "Don't you mean an alleged murderer? Since my client hasn't even been charged, much less convicted."

"Let's say it turns out he's guilty." The reporter kind of winked. "Still think the government was wrong to detain him?"

"Anytime the government does anything that violates the Constitution, I'm not going to like it." That was general enough to be unobjectionable, I hoped, even on the evening news. I left it at that and pushed through the crowd.

Maybe I imagined this, but the crowd seemed to thicken rather than thin the closer I got to the front desk. I all but collided, chest to chest, with a woman in a blue blazer. Only after I recovered and apologized did I realize that I knew her.

"Mina." I was more than surprised to see her here. Surprised and concerned. I hesitated to even speak aloud, but this crowd was so loud and frenzied there was little chance anyone could eavesdrop. "Should you be here?"

"I must see Omar," she said, barely audibly.

"I'm sure you're concerned. But they won't let you see him unless you've got a law degree. Frankly, I don't think you're safe here."

"What do you mean?"

I glanced over my shoulder. "I don't think all the sheriffs on earth could protect you from this crowd if they learned of your . . . sympathetic relationship to the accused. Or his boss."

"Or my hatred of the victim?"

"What happened anyway? I told you two to stay home."

"And you thought he would? Then you do not know him well."

That was becoming abundantly clear. "I wish you'd listened. I wish you were listening now. You shouldn't be here." I saw Kir just behind her. "Especially not with your brother."

"People should be able to hold opposing beliefs without resorting to violence."

"I don't know if you've noticed, but this crowd isn't composed of the high school debate team. Go home. I'll call you as soon as I know something."

Kir leaned in. "Can we get a message to Omar?"

I didn't want to make any promises until I knew what the message was. Anything cryptic and I would say no. I didn't need anyone later suggesting I'd helped subversives conduct their business. "Depends on the message."

Kir's lips tightened. "Can you not see that my sister cares for him?

She will not rest until they have spoken." I started to reply, but he continued. "Can you not see that this is part of the government's plan?"

"All I can see is that I need to speak to my client as soon as possible."

"Tell him that I love him," Mina said quietly. "And tell him that the scars I bear and the scars he bears will only make us stronger."

"I can do that." Though I might paraphrase it a bit.

"Will you be able to get him released?"

"I don't even know the charge yet." I paused. "But I think that unlikely. I'll call you as soon as I know anything about his situation."

Her head tilted slightly to one side. "This is a promise?"

"It is. And whatever failings I may have, I keep my promises."

After a few moments' contemplation, she acquiesced. "I will await your call."

One potential disaster eliminated, a fistful more to tackle. I recognized the burly man standing just before the admissions desk. Not personally, but I'd seen him around. He led some conservative group, Occupy This or Tea Party That or whatever it was this week. The vocal minority posing as the silent majority. Normally I wouldn't even notice, but the room was too crowded to get around him, and since he was roughly three times my size, I couldn't push him out of the way. I considered crawling over him, but it seemed undignified.

"I pay your salary," the man shouted at an elderly officer behind the desk. "You work for me."

Well, he was half-right. The man behind the desk had the sense to keep his mouth closed.

"The government of the people should serve the people. We need to take back the government that belongs to us." And a few other catchphrases. He was trying to get some kind of chant going, but praise heaven it wasn't catching on.

"Ben!"

This voice I would recognize anywhere, and unlike the voice of the reporter, it was one that demanded my immediate attention.

"Christina. I thought you were going to stay in the car."

"I thought you were going to come home. This isn't safe."

"I need to speak to my client."

She frowned. Actually, "frown" wasn't the word for it. More like "expression of long-suffering toleration." "How you gonna do that from way over here?"

"Well, I'm trying—"

"Frank!"

Especially coming from such a tiny woman, her voice had impressive heft. The buzz in the room dropped several decibels, for at least a second or two.

We both knew the man on duty, Frank Gorman. He'd been working this desk for about 105 years, far longer than I'd been around.

"Any chance my dopey but endearing husband can see his client?"

Frank cracked a grin. "Ben reps the shooter? I should've known." He checked his clipboard. "I don't think we're allowed to say no to counsel of record. Even when we suspect it might be for your own good."

I stepped forward. "Get me in as soon as you can, Frank, okay?"

"I'll see what I can do. They're still running through the preliminaries."

That would mean the printing and the mug shot and the phone call and the stripping and changing into bright orange coveralls. Which they would draw out as long and painfully as possible. Jail wasn't supposed to be fun. And the people in charge generally made sure it wasn't. I worried about what could happen here to someone with a Persian last name. Especially someone suspected of murdering a CIA agent.

"As soon as you can, Frank."

"I'm on it."

THREE AND A HALF HOURS LATER, FRANK ESCORTED ME INTO A small room separated by a Plexiglas screen from another equally small room. Once he left, I launched right in.

"What the hell did you think you were doing?"

Oz looked like he'd been through the wringer, which I suppose he had. "Ben, you have to believe me—"

"Let me caution you before you say a word. You do not have to tell me anything. Anything you tell me is privileged, but if you confess to anything, the Rules of Professional Conduct do not permit me to aid you in perpetrating a lie, which might impair my ability to represent you to the best of my ability." I'd rattled this off so many times I could do it by heart. The lawyer's equivalent of a Miranda warning.

"I did not shoot that man."

That was good to hear. Even if it was a total lie, it would make my job much easier. "The feds think you did."

"They've been after me forever. They finally got their chance."

"Because you gave it to them."

"They were watching me from the moment I showed up at the press conference. Just looking for an excuse to tie me up and torture me some more."

"I told you not to go."

"I had to go."

"You chose to go. And it was a bad choice." I pulled out my phone and punched up a report. I'd had a lot of time to Google while I waited to see my client. "According to an unverified report in the Huffington Post, you were arrested with a gun in your possession. Which might provide an even more convincing explanation of why you were arrested."

He didn't say anything. That worried me more than a little.

"You are not required to speak to me." This was where it got sticky. "At the same time, if you send me into the courtroom without critical knowledge, especially critical knowledge that the prosecutor might possess, you send me into a gunfight armed with a slingshot."

Oz's chest rose, then slowly fell. "I don't know what happened. I must have tripped. Stumbled. Hit my head. I was dazed. That crowd was crazy."

"What's the first thing you remember?"

"Lying flat on the ground, a police officer shaking me." He hesitated. "And there was a gun in my hand."

I closed my eyes. "It just magically appeared there?"

He didn't answer right away. "There was so much going on. So much happening all at once. I was . . . confused."

No doubt. But the prosecutor wouldn't buy it. And sell this story to a jury? I didn't look forward to it. "If someone planted the gun on you, the police would've likely seen it."

"Unless the police were the ones who planted it."

Okay. That was the first good point he'd made. I'd known cops who thought they were justified in planting evidence when they wanted a conviction.

"For that matter," Oz continued, "given how many people were around, it should have been impossible to fire a gun without being seen. But someone accomplished it."

Okay, two good points for the defendant. "Did you say anything at the press conference? Anything that might suggest you were on a killing spree?"

"Just the usual words of protest."

"Such as?"

"I voiced my opposition to torture. Isn't that my First Amendment right? To speak my mind?"

"Yes, but like most rights, it comes with a price tag. Did you do anything else to give the feds a reason to suspect you?"

"Not to my knowledge."

"They're filing charges as we speak."

"To bring pressure on their political opponents. Me. Abdullah."

"A crime was committed."

"For all I know, it was a CIA assassination."

"Nazir worked for the CIA."

"And you think this would be the first time they killed one of their own? I can assure you that it is not."

I swept a hand through my rapidly thinning hair. "Can you prove any of this?"

"When I see footprints in the sand, I know someone made them. Even if the person is no longer there."

Wisdom or paranoia? I had no idea. "Oz, this is a murder case now. In all likelihood you'll face the death penalty."

"They can bring all the pressure they have to bear. I will not give them what they want. I will not tell lies. I will not inform on Abdullah."

"You'd rather die."

He looked me squarely in the face. "I would rather die." Several seconds passed before his face cracked slightly. "But I would prefer to do neither."

"That would be my preference, too."

"Talk to the prosecutors. See what they want."

"Wait a second. I haven't accepted this case yet."

"But you're my lawyer."

"In the civil case, sure. That doesn't mean I have to take on this potentially life-threatening can of worms."

"You've handled controversial criminal cases before. I know you have."

"This is beyond controversial. This will be all consuming. For months, at the very least. Probably longer."

"If you don't represent me, at this point—who will?"

And I knew he was right. No one would, that's who. The court would appoint someone, and they'd probably do the best they could, but . . . it wouldn't be the same as having someone in your corner who actually cared. Someone you had some history with.

Christina had already suggested I was motivated by guilt. How far could that take me? "I'll see what they've filed, Oz. I can explore the possibility of a plea, though I think it's unlikely at this stage."

"Then you will take the case."

I sighed heavily. It would be smarter to text my wife first . . . "Yes. I'll take the case."

"Thank you, Ben. If I could embrace you, I would."

"Just as well. In the meantime, talk to no one. I mean *no one*. You may think that cellmate or convict is your friend, but they're not. They'll do or say anything to get out, so don't give them the opportunity. Feds use jailhouse snitches all the time."

"I'll keep my mouth closed. Can you get word to Mina?"

"Yes." I repeated her message to him.

"And Julia. Keep her informed as well."

I paused. "Okay .

His eyes darted upward, then away. "Thank you. From the depths of my heart. I am in your debt for all eternity."

A lovely thought. But I might not have an eternity, I suspected, because my wife might not let me live through the night.

CHAPTER 18

It was almost dark by the time I headed home, but it felt as if it were about three in the morning. The whole day had played out in a bizarre slow motion. I was ready to get back to normal speed. I could hardly keep my eyes open.

I waved at Bolton as I passed his house. He saw me, but he didn't wave back, much less come out to the car and chat. The next neighbor down the street was worse. He stood in his driveway with his arms folded like Mr. Clean and glared at me as I cruised by.

So word was out. If Bolton knew I was representing Oz, everyone knew. This neighborhood was about to get a lot chillier.

To my disappointment, the twins were already asleep. I could have used some sweet, high-pitched chirping in my ear. Christina gave me permission to hover over their beds, although she threatened me with a death sentence if I woke them.

Lizzie was deep asleep. She was always the easy one. Sing her a song, recite a little Shakespeare, and she was gone.

Emily flipped and flopped restlessly. I knew it was dangerous to make any sound at all because that might give her an excuse to wake and demand more attention. I left the lights out but bent down low beside her and whispered. "Let us not to the marriage of true minds /

Admit impediments. Love is not love / Which alters when it alteration finds, / Or bends with the remover to remove. / O no! it is an ever-fixed mark . . ."

Guess my pal Mike made more of an impression on me than I realized. I have no idea why I remember that stuff.

Emily fidgeted and made a gurgling noise. All at once her eyes shot open, as if a cannon had fired in her ear.

Even in the dim lighting, I could see her beautiful eyes.

The vacancy in those eyes terrified me.

I don't even know how to describe it. She was there, but she wasn't there. She saw me, but she didn't see me. Like she was peering through the looking glass, seeing a dim reflection of what lay on the other side without actually comprehending it.

She was in her world. And I was in mine.

"You're imagining it," Christina told me later, over hot chocolate and coffee cake. "Babies are weird. No one knows what's going on in their heads."

"She never talks."

"Or maybe she has a language of her own, and we don't know it."

I almost laughed. "I used to love Sheldon Mayer's Sugar and Spike comics. Those two tykes had their own language—which of course sounded like gibberish to the grown-ups."

"See? If it happened in a comic book, it must be true."

"But at least Sugar talked to Spike, and vice versa. Emily doesn't talk to anyone."

She laid her hand atop mine. "She will, Ben. Be patient."

I heard padded footsteps on the kitchen tiles. Julia was in her bathrobe, rounding the island. My mother built the biggest kitchen I'd ever seen with more marble than most quarries. "Is this a private party, or may I join you?"

"Please sit down," Christina said. "You've done a yeoman's work today."

"Watching the girls? Are you kidding? Those two are precious. I could do that all day long."

Christina arched an eyebrow. I knew what thoughts traveled through her brain. The original plan, once we knew Christina was pregnant, was for her sister to come watch the girls so Christina could maintain some semblance of a career. That hadn't worked out, so she was limited to a few hours here or there when she could find an acceptable Mom's Day Out program.

"Those girls are smart," Julia continued. "I suppose that shouldn't be a surprise, given who their parents are."

Okay, now I was suspicious. We'd never been a family of flatterers.

"Heard you had some excitement today, Ben." The air of casualness didn't work. Julia was no actress. "Did you get in to see Oz?"

"I did. Thanks to Christina."

"You two make a good team. She's got the chutzpah and the street smarts, and you've got .

"Yes?"

"I don't know. A big briefcase. Anyway, how's Oz?"

"As well as could be expected." I took a long drag from my hot chocolate. It's not as good when it doesn't scald a little. "They've put him through the wringer. He's behind bars without a friend. If the other inmates learn who he is, they'll probably try to rip his throat out with their teeth."

Julia's hands flew to her mouth.

"Just an expression," I added. "In his mind, he's a political prisoner, held unjustly, not for the first time, because the authorities believe he's associated with this Abdullah guy, or because he had the obviously anti-American idea of exercising his freedom of religion and converting to Islam."

"Do you think the government is behind this?"

"I would be lying if I pretended I had any idea what's going on here. What I am concerned about is this murder. Someone assassinated Nazir. In a crowded area with decent security. And still managed to escape detection. That suggests a high degree of sophistication. I don't think Oz operates on that level."

"But you don't know that," Christina said, her voice low. "He could be playing you."

"Every attorney has to deal with the possibility that his client might be lying. But we proceed on the assumption that they're telling the truth."

"Is there anything we can do for him?" Julia asked. "Maybe get him a private room?"

"This is jail, not the Hyatt Regency."

"Surely they have some obligation to safeguard him from danger."

"Some. Not much."

"What about bail?"

"We'll have a hearing in a few days. Don't hold your breath. He's going to be charged with a capital offense in a high-profile case. The easiest course for the judge is to leave him locked up."

Julia reached across the table, pushing aside my plate. She grabbed my wrist. "Ben, you have to help him. Surely you can do something. Pull a rabbit out of your hat."

I gave her a hard look, trying to see what was going on behind those eyes. "Mind if I ask why you're so concerned?"

"Why wouldn't I be? I've known Oz forever. We were high school sweethearts. Don't you have a sweet spot for your high school sweetheart?" She paused. "Oh. You didn't actually have one, did you?"

"We're making up for lost time," Christina said.

"Thank goodness. In high school, my friends thought he was gay. No way, I told them. He's just shy." Her voice dropped a notch. "But I was never really sure."

"Could we stop talking about me like I'm not here? Julia, it's obvious that this is more than just a casual interest in a guy you knew decades ago. And it's also probably not a coincidence that you showed up here at the same time that he boomeranged onto my doorstep. What's going on?"

"Nothing. I just want to make sure Oz is okay. And the only reason I came back here is . . ." Her eyes darted away. "Because I don't have anywhere else to go."

I felt like a complete heel.

"My ex-husband doesn't want me back. He's got custody of my son. I've tried working crap jobs, but I'm not good at it. I'm not trained for anything."

"You're a nurse."

"Not anymore. He filed some trumped-up complaints to get me out of the hospital. They're in the system. I seriously doubt anyone would hire me. I've been drifting around with no place to go for . . . a very long time."

Christina reached out to her. "You should've come here sooner."

"I didn't want to impose."

"It's your house."

"It isn't. Really."

Christina pushed away from the table and cut a slice of cheesecake for Julia. "Eat this. You'll feel better."

Julia reluctantly took the fork and nibbled a bit at the corner. "Thank you."

"Look," Christina said. "I don't know what's going to happen with this case. But I know it's going to get a lot worse before it gets any better. The politicians and protesters and reporters have been storming the castle all day. I predicted this case would be trouble, and now it is. The kind of trouble that ends careers."

I couldn't argue. I couldn't blame her if she tried to talk me out of it.

But she didn't. "Here's my point, Julia. Ben is going to need my help."

"I believe that."

"If our family and our livelihood is on the line, I'm gonna be right there making sure no one takes advantage of my boy. And if he needs my help, I need your help."

"You mean with the girls?"

"And the house. And the shopping. And a thousand other problems that will likely arise. We've run a relatively low-visibility practice since we moved to OKC, but that's about to change. We're understaffed and overwhelmed. They'll bury us if we let them." She paused. "So what do you say? Will you pitch in?"

"I guess . . . I could try. If you're sure you need me."

"I'm sure. You can start with watching the girls. Who knows? Before this is over, we may have you cross-examining witnesses. One thing at a time."

"I don't want to be a bother. But . . . it would feel good to be wanted." Pause. "Needed."

"And we're going to pay you, so don't even argue about it."

"That's not necessary. I—"

"Did you hear the part about no arguing?"

Julia buttoned her lip.

Christina turned to me. "You have a problem with this, oh mighty trial warrior?"

As if I would've said anything, even if I did. If this meant I'd have Christina at my side as we plunged into this big hot mess, terrific.

I needed all the help I could get.

CHAPTER 19
WITNESS AFFIDAVIT
CASE NO. CJ-49-1886

I could see Kincaid and the other two in the kitchen as clearly as I could see my own shadow. Satellite triangulation allowed me to find the house. The numerous neighbors prowling about, plus the propensity for neighborhood police to investigate parked cars, complicated securing a safe berth. But I managed. I did not have audio access yet. But I would remedy that in time. If they took out their cell phones, I would be able to watch or listen, even if they never made a call.

Earlier that day, Kincaid texted his wife:

Story credibility issues. Failing memory. Jury won't buy bonk on the head.

And the woman replied:

Maybe true assailant was bonker.

Three minutes later, Kincaid texted back:

Need better SODDIT than "Bonker."

I am no lawyer. But I could interpret the communications. He had contacted al-Jabbar, who had provided a provisional alibi. Kincaid either didn't believe it or didn't believe he could convince a jury.

Two other electronic actions seemed noteworthy. First, one from Kincaid to the shameless whore who works in his office:

Batten down the hatches. Firestorm coming.

Translation: He will represent al-Jabbar on the criminal charges.

Also noteworthy: His wife added a contact to her cell phone. Julia Kincaid Morelli McKeown.

And perhaps of even greater interest: Kincaid called a contact from his smartphone. Charles Corwin. A simple data search revealed that the person in question was a private detective.

Mobile electronic devices have made my work much simpler. People grouse about privacy and perform childish maneuvers with passwords and VPNs, but they reveal their entire lives on their laptops and cell phones and Facebook and Instagram, oblivious to how easy it is to access that information. They surveil themselves. Their lives play out in bits and bytes, read by the ever-increasing number of people conversant in that digital language.

The temptation for al-Jabbar to open his mouth, to say what must be said to liberate himself, must be great. He could resist torture, as a man must do. But the thought of life imprisonment, or death with ignominy, is different. The Koran speaks of rewards for those who perform holy work. They will spend eternity with bountiful riches, food, wine, and a large number of virgins (though I have always been troubled by the Book's failure to specify where these virgins come from, or to specify their gender). But what rewards can be expected when one perishes with a cloud over one's head? Perhaps Allah can sort out the truth. But what of the seven billion people residing on the planet?

My handler instructed me to ensure that al-Jabbar does not speak of the unspeakable. Not to anyone. Not even an attorney.

And I was further instructed to make sure that if he did speak, the information did not travel far. And there is only one way to ensure that a secret is not spread. Eliminate all those who know the secret.

I delight in the irony of these so-called high-security residential areas. Neighborhood watch parties. Private cops. And my favorite, the illusion of gated security. The gates certainly did not complicate my entrance or egress. All they did was slow down whatever emergency vehicle might be tempted to venture this direction.

None of which mattered. I had no intention of being detected. I have operated in the shadows for years. Tonight would be no exception.

Even though it was not critical that I be able to audit this particular conversation, I decided to move closer. There would be later times, I suspected, when I would need to know what was being said inside that house. Better that I work out the parameters while there was no urgency about it.

I crossed into the target's backyard. The six-foot stockyard fence was so little inconvenience as to induce laughter. Who exactly did these capitalists think they excluded with a fence a child could mount without effort? I found a hideaway in some shrubbery not far from the house.

Windows. Large windows. Perfect for letting in light. And anything else that wanted in.

I could not help but note that this position, with visual access to almost every room in the house, would make a perfect sniper's loft. Extraction would be equally simple.

My lipreading skills are excellent. Using binoculars, I could follow the general trail of the conversation, with only occasional lapses when the wife spoke, as she sat with her back to me. First the parties present discussed al-Jabbar's situation. I sensed that more was not being said *than* said. Then the conversation turned to the sister and her situation. Even less was said there.

My tiny MacIV Listening Scope was only slightly more sensitive than the listening devices one could obtain at Toys R Us. But it was more than sufficient at such close range. The reception through my earpiece was almost static-free and immediately transmitted to the recording mechanism. I had an automatic backup file, in case my memory lapsed. Not that my memory ever lapsed.

"Mind if I ask why you're so concerned?"

"Why wouldn't I be? We've known each other forever. We were high school sweethearts. Don't you have a sweet spot for your high school sweetheart? Oh. You didn't actually have one, did you?"

"We're making up for lost time."

I ensured transmissions and recordings would continue even when I was not present. I crept to the back of the house and wedged the subsonic transmitter through a tiny aperture on the side of the door using a shish kebab stick. The magnetized adhesive took hold.

A remote possibility of detection existed, but I thought it unlikely. Given the minute size of the device, even if someone noticed, it was far more likely they would mistake it for a splotch of dirt or a dead insect. I did not believe anyone in this household bore the level of intelligence sophistication necessary to recognize this for what it was.

The conversation ended, and the parties retired. Once the house was still, I climbed over the fence and departed, careful not to be seen. The risks were too great to take chances. The fate of nations lay in the balance. With stakes of this magnitude, the lives of individuals were less than meaningless.

CHAPTER 20

As I rode the elevator to my office the next morning, my mind was filled with questions but no answers. Who killed Nazir? What did Oz want? Why did he go to that press conference? Why was my sister so interested? What game was Mina playing? Who and where was this mysterious Abdullah?

All of which could probably be summarized in one overarching question: What the hell was going on?

I was so wrapped up in my own thoughts I was halfway through the lobby before I noticed the devastation.

My office had been trashed.

I'm not talking about a few upended chairs. I'm talking about an office that looked as if one of Oklahoma's infamous twisters came through and tap-danced for a few minutes. Paper covered the floor like carpet. Case files were dumped and scattered. Two of the windows were cracked. The seat cushions in the sofa had been ripped open. The end table was splintered right down the middle. Tanya's workstation was a mess. It was like—

I put my simile on hold.

Tanya's workstation .

Where was Tanya?

A chill gripped my chest.

Stay calm, I told myself. Don't panic. Don't assume the worst—even though that is always my natural instinct.

I willed my limbs back into action. I took one step, then another, then another. I rounded the curved desk that separated Tanya's station from the rest of the lobby.

Tanya huddled in a fetal position, hands wrapped around her knees, head pressed against the wall, her entire body quaking. She cried so intensely she could barely catch her breath. Tears and snot streamed across her face. Her shirt was hiked so high it revealed not just a butterfly but a kaleidoscope of them.

I crossed, crouched beside her, and gently laid my hand on her back. "Tanya, it's all right. No one's here but you and me."

She looked up at me, her eyes wide and frightened, then looked away. She didn't speak. I wasn't sure she could speak.

"What happened?"

Eons passed before she answered. "Don't . . . know. Found it . . . this way .

"Did you see anyone?"

Her head bobbed. "Wore ski masks. Rushed out when I came in."

"How many?"

"S—saw three. Might be more."

"Did they hurt you?"

"One . . . knocked me down. Didn't have to. Wanted to. Knocked me down with a single swat."

I saw a welt on her face that would soon be a nasty bruise. I felt guilty about pressing her to talk about something she obviously didn't want to remember. But I had to know what happened. I comforted myself with the idea that it might be good for her to get this out of her system. "Did they say anything?"

It took her longer to reply. "The one who hit me. Said . . ." Her voice trailed off, degenerating into gasps and sobs.

"What, Tanya? What did he say?"

"He said, 'Tell your boss he doesn't know who he's fucking with.'"

She turned suddenly and wrapped her arms around me. I'm not

sure I've ever felt anyone squeeze so tightly. Like she thought body heat might chase the demons away.

I'll admit I felt a strong chill myself.

"I'm scared, Ben. Really . . . really scared."

"Nothing's going to happen to you, Tanya."

"I'm scared for *you*." I felt tears drop onto my neck.

I knew we had a lot of work to do. And I knew it would take much time to reassemble this office. But for the moment, surely, the best thing in the world I could do was hold her and let her cry it out.

⊛

"WELL, NOW. GOOD THING I'M NOT THE SUSPICIOUS TYPE."

I was still on the floor holding Tanya when I looked up and saw Christina hovering above us. "I can explain."

"Don't bother," she said, gazing around the room. "I think the state of the office is explanation enough." She crouched down and wrapped an arm around us both. "You two okay?"

Tanya wouldn't look up. "I don't know."

"She ran into the intruders," I explained. "One of them hit her on his way out."

Christina nodded. "Take some time and get over this, Tanya."

"I . . . don't want to be a crybaby."

"You're not. Look, I've been manhandled once or twice in my life. I didn't like it. Makes you feel vulnerable. Like, if that can happen, anything can happen. You take all the time you need."

Tanya looked up, her face streaked with tears and blotches. "This—this has happened to you?"

"'Fraid so."

"You're the toughest woman I know."

Christina turned her head. "Oh, pshaw."

Tanya wiped her nose. "If you can work through it, so can I."

"You should probably go home and—"

She pushed herself to her feet. "Nah. Someone's got to clean up this mess."

Once she was out of earshot, I gave my wife a hug. "Remind me to tell you how special you are someday."

"I didn't do anything."

"You did what I didn't come close to doing. Because you understand people."

"You're getting better."

"I'm not even in your league."

"True." She sifted through the debris. "You think the haters did this? Racists? Lynch mob?"

"I wish I did. But I don't."

"Nazir's family?"

"No."

"You think it was the government."

"I wish I didn't. But I do."

"Which particular branch of the government?"

"I don't know. I probably never will. The possibilities are endless."

Christina walked down the main corridor, cataloguing the damage. "There may be more to this than scare tactics. They might've been looking for something."

"What? I don't know who killed Nazir. Or even who would have a motive. And I don't know how to find Abdullah."

"But your client might. And someone might be worried about him talking."

We sat down in my inner office. "If that's true, it would be useful to know who it was and what exactly they were worried about."

"Yes, and we're not going to learn that from chatting. Ben, call in Loving."

"I can't do that."

"Ben, it's been years."

"I don't care. Not doing it." Aloysius Loving had been my private investigator. We met when he held me at gunpoint. I represented his ex-wife in their divorce, and he wasn't happy about it. We worked past that and became close friends. He helped me on innumerable cases. But on the last one, he was seriously injured and almost killed. He decided to take some time off, which I thought a good idea. And much as I could use some help, I wasn't about to risk his life.

"Ben," Christina said, "Loving would do anything for you."

"That's the problem. He never says no—even when he probably should."

"He wouldn't mind."

"He should. And you should, too. You should be home with our girls. This is looking dangerous."

"That's why I'm here."

"So you can be the next target?"

"To keep my girls from losing their good-hearted but occasionally thickheaded father."

I knew from experience there was no point in arguing with her. But I wouldn't draw Loving into the fire. "I already called Corwin about the case. He's good."

"He's no Loving."

"He'll have to do."

Christina gave me that smoldering look I'd learned meant that, at the very least, I shouldn't be expecting ice cream tonight. "Why did you call Corwin?"

"To interview people who were at the press conference. Someone must have seen something. If we could find another suspicious character, it would make my job much easier."

"SODDIT?"

"Do we have an alternative? Corwin was glad to get the work. He's mostly worked for the OSBI these past months, tracking down illegal immigrants. Now that Oklahoma allows law enforcement to seize the property of illegal immigrants, they've gotten very interested in rooting them out. Even if it leaves people with no way to care for their children. Who also can't become citizens under the current laws, even if they were born in Oklahoma."

"Chill, Ben. One cause at a time." She leaned forward and squeezed my hand. "You don't have to run with this case, you know. If you drop out, the court will appoint a lawyer."

"And you know how well that will go for Oz."

"The girls and I will love you no matter what."

"Those girls need to live in a world where people care about one another, where rights don't disappear the moment they become inconvenient."

Christina fell back into her chair. "You're a hopeless dreamer, Ben."

"But . . . you can live with that?"

The corner of her mouth turned up slightly. "Live with it? That's why I married you, you chump."

CHAPTER 21

I spent the next many days dreading the preliminary hearing. We had to go through the motions, but I couldn't remember the last time I heard of a case not being bound over for trial. Magistrates typically handled the hearings, and this was a conservative state, and you don't hang on to your job long if you let accused criminals off the hook. The standard of review was preposterously low. All the prosecutor had to show was probable cause for believing the accused committed the crime—far lower the "beyond a reasonable doubt" standard supposedly required for conviction.

The prosecutor could also proceed to trial by indictment. Let the grand jury do all the hard work—they always indict, and it's done behind closed doors, so the prosecution doesn't have to reveal their case. They don't have to produce exculpatory evidence until "no less than ten days before trial." This is typically done in a huge document production masking the few vital documents in a morass of trivia, leaving the defense scrambling to find the needle in the haystack while the clock ticks down to opening statements.

Preliminary hearings are quicker and simpler but require the prosecution to reveal at least some of what they have. I could only assume that Thrillkill thought this case such a slam dunk he didn't worry about what he revealed—and he wanted to reap the publicity whirl-wind before the election season began.

I managed to get Oz scrubbed up and into a clean suit. Amazing what a difference a good suit can make, something Christina told me for years while I was buying suits at the Goodwill store. He still had the red, tired eyes that almost inevitably follow a stint behind bars. But his spirits seemed up, and he was generally optimistic, even though I told him he had no grounds for optimism about today's outcome.

"Maybe the magistrate will see what a farce this is," he said.

"Let's hope so," I replied, though I thought it much more likely the magistrate would take the easy way out, especially given how much press the case had already received.

"They'll try to hang me because I'm Muslim."

I don't like to argue, but it was best my client had a realistic appraisal of the situation. "That's hardly the only strike against you."

"Doesn't America guarantee freedom of speech and freedom of association?"

"That's the theory." Not so much in practice.

Thrillkill came in looking as if he were Moses preparing to address the Pharaoh. All the cordiality he'd feigned during our last meeting had dissipated. He gave me a curt disapproving nod, then moved on. The reporters in the gallery got the lofty lawman they wanted.

"What's he got up his butt?" Oz whispered.

"A deep desire to be governor," I replied. In any normal circum-stance, someone lower on the totem pole would be handling trial work, but Thrillkill undoubtedly saw this case as an opportunity to score political points.

I noticed someone else sitting beside him at counsel table: a middle-aged middleweight woman I did not know. She was probably from Washington, possibly representing the CIA of the Justice Department.

A few minutes later, Thrillkill deigned to approach my table. "I can make this go away, Kincaid."

"So you're going to drop the charges. Wonderful."

Not even a smile. "You can waive the hearing. Spare your client a lot of misery."

"He'll be automatically bound over for trial."

"That's inevitable. Save the man some pain."

"That would be malpractice. You don't have anything."

Thrillkill shrugged. "Suit yourself. Don't say I didn't warn you."

This was not, of course, a real settlement offer. This was an intimidation tactic, targeting both Oz and me. He knew I'd never take the offer. Even if I thought our cause hopeless, I'd still go through the motions. I wanted a sneak preview of what Thrillkill had up his sleeve.

Magistrate Hamilton took the stand. He'd come from a small practice in Choctaw but was said to be well connected. He had a shock of bangs that covered his forehead, making him appear younger than he was. He struck me as reasonably intelligent and appeared to take his job seriously. But he was also a Republican appointee and had little patience for people he thought were not telling him the truth.

Hamilton banged his gavel. "This tribunal is now in session." He read the case style. "The government wishes to bind the defendant over for trial on the charge of first-degree homicide and treason."

My eyebrows shot up. *Treason?* When did Thrillkill add that? Based on what?

"Both of these charges could carry a death sentence, gentlemen, so I want a clean hearing. No shenanigans. Let's get this done and get out of here."

I wanted a more extensive description of "shenanigans," but I kept my mouth shut. "We can dispense with extensive opening remarks," the magistrate continued. "I have a good idea what's going on here from your pretrial filings. Is there any possibility that counsel could limit their opening comments to one minute?"

Thrillkill nodded obsequiously. "I will do whatever the court requests, Your Honor."

"And Mr. Kincaid?"

"I'm known for being succinct, Your Honor. When I string more than two sentences together, my wife starts yawning."

He did not crack a smile. "You're up first, Mr. Thrillkill."

Thrillkill positioned himself before the judge and spread his arms wide. "Pretty simple, Your Honor. Motive, means, and opportunity are all present, plus the defendant was apprehended at the scene of the crime with the murder weapon in his hand."

I tried not to squirm.

"The motive is obvious. This was a revenge killing, both personally and politically motivated. We know the defendant was previously interrogated by the victim."

Oz and I exchanged a glance.

"We know he bore a great deal of resentment toward the deceased, a CIA agent, and that very day had filed a civil action against Nazir asserting allegations that"—here he glanced at me—"are in all likelihood untrue, unless you believe federal employees are jackbooted hooligans who run around torturing innocents."

He had, of course, chosen the phrase "federal employees" because, technically speaking, the magistrate was also a federal employee.

"The point is the defendant found a lawsuit insufficient to satisfy his raging hatred. He had motive, plus means—the gun found in his possession—and opportunity, because he was apprehended at the scene of the crime."

The magistrate parted his lips as if to speak, but Thrillkill cut him off. "And may I just say with my remaining ten seconds"—apparently, his watch ran slower than mine—"that the evidence will show that the defendant is still associated with known terrorist organizations. He is a person of interest and a dangerous individual." I assume he planted that notion just in case the magistrate later considered the possibility of bail.

"Thank you, Mr. Thrillkill. Mr. Kincaid, would you like to make any remarks at this time?"

As if that were in question. "Yes, sir. Thank you." I rose but I did not leave the table. I wanted to stand near Oz. I wanted the magistrate to be forced to look at him, to see that I was friendly with him, that I trusted him. And that he was totally Caucasian. Thrillkill wanted to make Oz look like the Great Satan, but I wanted the magistrate to see that he was basically a white boy from Nichols Hills, caught up in a whole mess of trouble.

"Let me begin by defining a few terms, Your Honor. My client was not simply questioned. He was tortured. For twenty-one days. By practices denounced by Amnesty International and virtually every civilized first-world nation on earth."

I had to tread carefully here. I wanted to make my client sympathetic, but not to generate grist for the prosecution's revenge motive.

"So I would agree that he had grounds for enmity toward Mr. Nazir, but that is hardly proof that he killed the man. He had filed a civil action and was prepared to deal with his grievance in a legally acceptable manner. The government continued to persecute him, to stalk him and his loved ones, and to engage in all manner of harassment. My own office was ransacked. I don't know if that was to intimidate or if they were searching for information. But I know someone is after my client. And I know that even if he were to resort to murder—which he would never do—he wouldn't be stupid enough to do it in a crowd or to hold on to the gun while he attempted to flee. My client was framed, probably to cover the fact that his initial detention was unlawful, which the civil action would prove."

The magistrate nodded. Thrillkill had a smirking expression on his face, but there was nothing new about that. Prosecutors always acted as if they were certain they'd caught the right guy, even when they weren't, and they always acted as if everything the defense attorney said was a crock.

I did the best I could with what I had. But I'm sure the magistrate noted what I hadn't addressed. Someone did in fact shoot Nazir. If it wasn't Oz—who was it? And why did no one see it happen?

CHAPTER 22

I kept my eyes on Magistrate Hamilton, but he did a keenly professional job of maintaining a disinterested expression. I wondered if he was a poker player.

"Mr. Thrillkill, you must demonstrate sufficient grounds for the defendant to be bound over for trial. Would you like to call your first witness?"

Thrillkill rose. "I would. The United States calls Dennis Benedict."

Benedict was a forensics expert who'd worked in the crime lab since before I was a lawyer. His shock of white hair lent him authority, as did the rimless glasses I'd noticed he only wore when he was on the witness stand. The main thrust of his testimony was that he found Oz's prints on the gun that killed Nazir. None of this was a news flash. The gun was found in Oz's hand, so of course it bore his prints. Benedict was an expert in both ballistics and dactylology, so I wouldn't get anywhere questioning his expertise.

I still took a moment to cross-examine. Not enough to irritate the magistrate. Just enough to show that I paid attention and, perhaps, to raise a few nagging unknowns.

"Did you find any other latents on the gun?"

"Some partials," Benedict replied. "Nothing traceable."

"So someone else might have held the gun before my client did?"

"I can guarantee someone else held it before he did. But that's almost always the case. A gun passes through many hands before it's bought. Manufacturers, distributors, dealers. Those prints fade with time."

"Could someone else have held the gun on the day of the murder?"

"I can't rule out the possibility. But Omar al-Jabbar held the gun last."

The next witness was one of Benedict's associates, Carmen Centrillo. At first, I thought this testimony would be redundant. Then Centrillo laid down the kicker.

"After his arrest, I tested the defendant's hands for gun residue."

Thrillkill nodded. "And what did you find?"

"The defendant had fired a gun. Recently."

That was a problem. One thing to hold a gun—quite another to fire it.

I leaned across to Oz and whispered. "True?"

"I'd been to a firing range the night before. It's a hobby."

Great. I knew just how credible that would sound on the stand. My innocent client coincidentally fired a gun for fun a few hours before the murder. "But you didn't have a gun at the press conference, right?"

"Concealed carry is legal in Oklahoma."

Like I didn't know that. It's what gives you the creepy feeling every time you see a family of rednecks sit down next to you at Chili's.

"Surely by now you realize that people are out to get me," Oz said. "After we filed that lawsuit, it could only get worse. Which it did." He paused. "I expected an assassin. Instead, they used a far subtler means of extinguishing me."

Paranoid rant or God's own truth? I had no idea.

Armed with that completely unhelpful and vaguely credible information, I started the cross-examination. "Can you say with certainty that the defendant fired a gun within an hour of his arrest?" Like any good cross-examiner, I only asked because I knew the answer.

"No. But he fired recently."

"Is it possible he fired a gun the night before?"

Centrillo shrugged. "Anything's possible."

"Is it possible he fired a different weapon?"

"I can't identify the weapon from residue."

"So he might have been practice shooting the night before. Or quail hunting."

"That's not for me to say. But he did fire a gun."

"But you can't say when or what gun or what he shot at."

"True."

That was as good as it was going to get with this government-payroll witness, so I let it rest.

"Next witness," the magistrate grunted.

"The United States calls Officer Marcus Takei."

I knew Takei was one of the officers who searched Oz's apartment after he was arrested. I did not know why Thrillkill wanted to put him on the witness stand. And that bothered me.

Thrillkill took the witness through the obvious preliminaries, establishing that he was an investigating officer with seven years of experience. He was not at the press conference but was called in soon after to search the apartment. He appeared to have followed all the proper procedures before, during, and after entering.

"How would you describe the state of the apartment when you entered?" Thrillkill asked.

"It was a mess."

"Signs of a struggle?"

"No, more like signs of someone leaving in a hurry. And never planning to come back."

"Objection," I said, rising to my feet. "That's conjecture."

"It is," the magistrate replied, "but this is a preliminary hearing, and the evidentiary standards are more permissive than they might be at trial. Overruled."

In other words, sit down and shut up. Objections weren't going to get me anywhere here. Either Thrillkill had the goods to bind this man over for trial or he didn't.

"Describe what you saw on the defendant's desk."

"A lot of paper. Manila folders stacked two feet high. Political pamphlets and brochures and flyers. A lot of propaganda for some Muslim outfit called JUSTICE IRAQ."

It was political, not "Muslim," but I understand the prejudice Thrillkill wanted to create. Takei himself was Asian. Did he mind being part of this racial smear? I was more concerned about why Oz might have JUSTICE IRAQ materials. That was supposedly Mina's outfit, not his.

"Did any of those file folders catch your eye?"

Takei nodded. "The thickest one, on the top of the stack, was labeled NAZIR."

Thrillkill passed a spreadsheet—what arrogant lawyers like to call a "matrix"—to me and then the bailiff, who passed it to the magistrate. "This is an itemization of the documents contained within the file labeled NAZIR. Even at a casual glance, I think the court can grasp the general content."

I could, too. The spreadsheet had three columns. One contained an identifying Bates stamp number, one identified the document by title and date, and the last contained a somewhat argumentative description of the actual contents.

Most of the documents concerned Nazir's interrogation of Oz. A few concerned Mina's and other similar interrogations. There were fourteen Freedom of Information Act requests that produced a collection of heavily redacted documents. Thrillkill made a point of showing that Oz had personal information about Nazir, including where he lived, where he worked, and where he went on the weekends.

He seemed obsessed with his former interrogator.

Thrillkill passed another document to Officer Takei. "Can you identify this?"

"Yes. This is one of many memos I found."

I could see out the corner of my eye that this disturbed Oz more than anything he'd heard thus far.

"Would you please read the portion of the document that I've highlighted in yellow?"

Takei cleared his throat. "'The day of reckoning approaches. We must take action to make the world aware of these injustices. They must be exposed as the murderers and torturers that they are.'"

I didn't bother asking Oz if he wrote that. It sounded very like what I'd heard Mina say in my office.

"Did you search the bathroom?"

"Yes."

"Find anything of interest?"

"Yes. Narcotics."

I snapped to attention.

"What kind of narcotics?"

"Large quantities of OxyContin. Which I'm sure you know is essentially a form of synthetic heroin."

"Tell the court what you mean by large quantities."

"There were three different bottles of the stuff from three different doctors. That suggests he was going to multiple doctors to score more drugs. And one of the bottles held more pills than the prescribed amount on the label. That suggests that he was getting some from the black market."

I rose to my feet, but before I could mutter the first syllable, the magistrate waved me down. "You'll have a chance to cross-examine, Counsel."

Fine. I'd skip the useless objection and wait for a chance to show the speculation for what it was.

I scribbled a note to Oz on my legal pad and slid it across the table: WHAT'S WITH THE PILLS?

He scribbled back in a near-perfect cursive: I'VE BEEN UNDER A LOT OF STRESS.

THREE BOTTLES?

I HAVE A PROBLEM. I'M DEALING WITH IT.

Well, jail would help with that. I had to focus on the witness.

This development had nothing to do with the murder. But it didn't look good. If Thrillkill wanted to be a real horse's ass, he would use it as the basis for another charge, even though that seemed unnecessary when Oz already faced the ultimate sanction. At the very least, Thrillkill could use it for press conference grist.

"One more thing." Thrillkill paused a moment, savoring the moment. "Did you search the storage shed in the back?"

The short hairs on the back of my neck bristled. Storage shed?

"I did," Takei replied.

"Find anything of interest?"

"Yes. Explosives."

My heart skipped a beat. Even though the gallery was mostly filled with reporters, there was an audible buzz when he said the word "explosives." Because in the minds of most people around here, "explosives" means "terrorists."

"What kind of explosives?"

Takei shrugged. "Gunpowder. Fertilizer. Some electronic equipment. Detonation devices."

"Thank you. No more questions."

I leaned toward my client. I knew the magistrate would give me a few moments to consult before crossing, and if I did it quietly, it wouldn't look as if I'd been shell-shocked.

"Explosives?" I whispered.

"Fireworks," he replied.

"Why would you have fireworks?"

"Because I'm an American. I celebrate Independence Day. I take them out to the country. I don't break any laws. The fertilizer isn't even mine. I think the building superintendent stores that there."

"And the electronics?"

"I don't know what he's talking about. I noticed some old beaten-up computers out there. Some people are hoarders. They can't stand to part with anything, no matter how old or useless."

This case just gets better and better, I thought, as I pushed myself to my feet, once again tilting at windmills and unraveling Gordian knots of impenetrable strength.

CHAPTER 23

C ross-examining police officers, and for that matter almost all
government witnesses, requires a delicate balancing act.
Despite the cliché, most lawyers of my generation do not try
to make law enforcement officers look like imbeciles. Most jurors have
generally positive attitudes toward law enforcement, never more so
than since 9/11. Judges don't like it when lawyers are disrespectful to
people who put their lives on the line for the commonwealth, and you
do not want to anger the judge. At least not without good cause. The
courtroom is the judge's playground, and if he or she wants the trial to
go against you, it probably will.

I had to treat Officer Takei with kid gloves. While simultaneously
ripping his throat out.

I decided to leave the Nazir file alone. We couldn't possibly deny
that Oz was obsessed with Nazir. Furthermore, Thrillkill's reminders
that Nazir had tortured Oz for weeks could conceivably work in our
favor. So I went straight to the pills.

"Officer, do you have a medical degree?"

He rolled his eyes. "I wouldn't be here if I did."

"You're not qualified to say whether these prescriptions were necessary, are you?"

"I didn't attempt to say anything like that. But I thought having three prescriptions for the same drug was unusual."

"Do you know why those drugs were prescribed?"

"No."

"So again, you're not in a position to say whether the prescriptions were necessary, are you?"

"No. But I thought it was unusual."

He wasn't budging. "You can't even say it was unusual, can you? Since you don't know what ailment was being treated?"

"I can say that on several occasions I've seen people exhibit violent behavior while under the influence of opioids. And that includes firing a gun in a crowded area."

Score one for the home team. "You also opined that the defendant obtained drugs on the black market. Meaning illegally. From pushers."

"Or perhaps overseas pharmacies."

"But you have no evidence of that, do you?"

"I saw an excessive number of pills in the bottle."

"Have you ever considered the possibility that he transferred pills from one bottle to another? Consolidated? People do that sometimes, don't they?"

"So you're saying there was a fourth bottle of OxyContin somewhere?"

This guy was good. He'd be looking at a nice bonus check this month, I suspected. "What I'm saying is, at this time, you have no actual evidence that the defendant purchased black market narcotics, do you?"

"Not at this time." Takei was smart enough to know when to let it go.

"But we're still investigating," Thrillkill mumbled, just loud enough to be heard.

The magistrate nodded.

"Now let's discuss the so-called explosives. Isn't it true that what you found was in fact fireworks?"

"Fireworks contain gunpowder. They can be and have been used to make dangerous devices."

"Did you find any dangerous devices?"

"I found the raw materials."

"You found fireworks designed to make pretty displays in the sky. But you found no bombs. Right?"

"I also found large quantities of fertilizer. As an Oklahoman, I would think you're aware that fertilizer can be used to make powerful explosive devices."

A reference to the Murrah Building bombing. "Did you find a fertilizer bomb?"

"As I testified, I found the raw materials."

"Do you know who put fertilizer in the storage shed?"

"I know the defendant had access to the storage shed."

"Motion to strike. Officer Takei, please listen to my questions carefully and answer them. Do you know who put fertilizer in the storage shed?"

"No."

"Is it possible the fertilizer was going to be used . . . as fertilizer?"

"I hope so. But given the tenor of those memos—"

"Officer, answer the question."

"I suppose it's possible." Pause. "Though the lawn didn't look like it was getting much love."

I let that pass. It wasn't going to matter. "And finally let's discuss the so-called electronics and detonation devices. What did you actually find?"

"Several computer motherboards. Some smartphones. Which could be used to detonate an explosive device remotely."

"You found a lot of discarded trash, but you found no bomb, right?"

"My testimony was that I found ingredients that could be made into a bomb. I hope we don't have to wait until the bomb explodes before we can do something about it."

"And I hope you never go into my garage," I replied. "Because I suspect you could find the raw ingredients for a bomb in anyone's home. Or garage sale. Or Wal-Mart." I looked up. "No more questions, Your Honor."

I did the best I could with a bad situation. Maybe it was just me and my defense attorney instincts, but I thought the "bomb ingredients" bit was weak, even by preliminary-hearing standards. It might give Thrillkill some play on the evening news. But I thought it sounded a little desperate.

Thrillkill did not redirect. "No more witnesses, Your Honor. We rest."

"Will you be calling any witnesses, Mr. Kincaid?"

He already knew the answer to that question, but he had to ask. "No, Your Honor." The magistrate's decision would be based on the evidence adduced by the prosecution, the party with the burden of proof. All I could do was put Oz on the stand, which would not make the slightest difference to the court's ruling but would lock in his testimony and give the prosecution a sneak peek at what he planned to say at trial. In other words, we had nothing to gain and potentially a great deal to lose. "We move for dismissal of the charges because the prosecution has failed to establish probable cause to bind the defendant over for trial.

"To which we object and oppose," Thrillkill answered. "While we don't claim that our case is perfect at this early juncture, we've met the burden necessary to proceed. And particularly given the extreme nature of the charges and the potential danger to society, I strongly urge the court to deny this motion.

"I believe I understand the situation," Magistrate Hamilton said, "and I believe I'm in a position to rule from the bench. The defendant will be bound over for trial."

Oz looked disappointed, despite the fact that I told him this was inevitable.

"It's true the prosecution's case is far from perfect. I heard a good deal of hearsay in the testimony—double hearsay. At one point I think it may have even been triple hearsay. Heard expert testimony from persons not qualified to give expert testimony. But the evidentiary standards at preliminary hearings are relaxed, and the only inquiry is whether to allow the prosecution to proceed to trial, where a much higher standard will be imposed. I find they have met that burden. The defendant will be bound over."

I patted Oz on the back, trying to be reassuring. This didn't mean anything, my expression said. We would keep fighting.

"To be specific, the defendant will be bound over on the homicide charge. I do not find sufficient evidence on the purported treason charge."

Thrillkill started to speak, but the magistrate cut him off.

"Treason is a constitutional offense designed to prevent threats against the nation. The defendant is charged with attempting to kill a federal officer, but the purported motivation appears to be more revenge than anything else. True, the defendant was politically active, but this is the land of the First Amendment, and political activism is allowed, even in support of causes others may find unsavory. There is no convincing evidence that the defendant was engaged in a plot against the United States of America, and the evidence regarding the alleged manufacture of a bomb was particularly unpersuasive."

Thrillkill took one in the chest. That had to pierce even that blowhard's Kevlar. But he didn't let it show. "Permission to reconsider this matter at the time of trial."

The Magistrate nodded. "You are always free to file additional charges if you uncover evidence that warrants doing so. But at this time, that charge will be dismissed." He pounded his gavel. "This hearing is adjourned. The bailiff will take the defendant back into custody."

"What about bail?" Oz asked me.

"Separate hearing. Later."

"What are our chances?"

"Not good."

"Can you get a message to Mina?"

"I suppose."

"Tell her to continue as before. Stop nothing. I am not important. Only the cause is important."

That sounded just vague enough to give me concern. "Anything else?"

"Yes. Give this message to your sister." He shoved a folded piece of paper into my hand. He must've written it during the cross. "And it's private."

"Anything you tell me is confidential."

"This is between Julia and me."

I took the note, not entirely sure I should.

He hesitated. The bailiff hovered behind him. I didn't know the exact words, but I knew in essence what was coming. "Ben, I didn't kill that man."

"I'll do everything for you I possibly can."

He nodded. "Remember that you said that."

The bailiff took him away, out of sight, where they would put shackles around his ankles and wrists and let him change back into the orange coveralls.

His last statement reverberated in my head for a long time.

It was perfectly natural for a man behind bars to want out.

So why did his words send a shiver up my spine?

CHAPTER 24

Despite the tense atmosphere, the courtroom seemed calm compared to what awaited me back at the office. I expected the firestorm of reporters clustered outside. I did not expect the firestorm inside.

I paid the astronomical monthly rent on this place and thus theoretically had a right to enter, but today I had to fight my way through another throng of journalists. Some of them knew me well enough to realize I wasn't going to entertain questions, but some hurled them at me as I squirmed between bodies and minicams.

I noticed a few from national cable networks and one from the Big Three. This case was attracting major-league attention. Which I knew from experience only made everything a thousand times harder. Especially for the defense attorney. No case was ever aided by 24-7 news coverage, most of which assumed the accused was guilty and slanted every story accordingly.

"Mr. Kincaid, what's your response to the prosecution's press release?"

"Is it true Omar al-Jabbar has confessed?"

"How do you feel about being investigated by the Bar Association?"

That one made me miss a step, but I kept moving.

"Sources indicate your client was building a bomb in his basement. Care to comment?"

I know I should've plowed ahead. How many times am I going to make the same mistake? But that one I couldn't let pass. I'd reached the limits of my tolerance. "Who are these sources?"

The reporter, a female I recognized as a reporter for a prominent local daily, seemed startled that I stopped, much less responded. "I—I'm not at liberty to say."

"Fake news posted to social media?"

"I—I can't divulge—"

"Because you're ashamed to admit how lame it is?"

"No, but—"

"A responsible reporter with a reputable source should have no trouble identifying it."

"Some sources wish to remain anonymous."

"You didn't say it was an anonymous source. Why would it be? My client can't hurt anyone from behind bars."

"Can you confirm or deny the report—"

"You mean the gossip? It's not a report unless it's based on something factual."

She had no reply.

"Or did you just make it up yourself? To see if you could get a quote out of me. And you'll run my response to implicitly suggest the truth of the rumor. You're not a reporter. You're a gossipmonger. And that makes your paper a tabloid. A gossip rag."

"Some sources have suggested—"

"Here's my suggestion. Tell your readers the truth. If you've found a verified fact, report it. And if you don't know something, admit that you don't know it. Don't report gossip as news. It demeans your publication and, quite frankly, demeans you as well."

With that, I pushed my way through the door. This little tirade, of course, would do me no good whatsoever. She'd be gunning for me, the usual media response to anyone who has the audacity to say the emperor has no clothes. Christina would chew me out royally.

Felt good, though.

The office lobby was less crowded but still chaotic in its own way.

Tanya sat in her usual spot behind the counter, and if I didn't know better, I might think nothing had happened the day before.

I offered my best smile. "Any messages?"

"Only a few thousand." She pushed a spindle toward me. "Some famous names on that stack."

"Yo-Yo Ma?"

Her head tilted. "Is that a boy band? No, more like television news personalities."

"That's considerably less exciting."

She ripped a message from the middle of the stack. "Here's one you'll want to give particular attention."

And then my eyes fairly bulged. "I'm being audited?"

"The IRS will arrive Thursday."

"I'm trying a case. I don't have time for this."

"That's more or less the point." Christina stood behind me. "You don't imagine for a moment that this is a coincidence, do you?"

I scanned the message for more details. "It could be."

"Have you gotten to the part about frozen assets yet?"

"What? Which accounts?"

"Virtually all. Personal and business. Frozen indefinitely until the IRS completes its review."

"What's the point of that?"

Christina shrugged. "Officially? To prevent you from absconding with funds the IRS may want to garnish to pay off whatever they find you owe."

"They won't find anything. You know I'm scrupulously honest on my taxes."

"I do know that, but they'll still find something wrong."

"Now you're just being cynical."

"I'm acknowledging that someone sicced the IRS on you, and it wasn't so you could come out smelling like a rose."

"Politicians can't order an IRS audit."

"Nixon did. Repeatedly."

"Thrillkill is not Nixon."

"He wants to be. And you have no idea how much influence or how many friends a well-connected prosecutor might have."

"It's possible this was someone else's idea."

"True. But that doesn't make the situation any better."

"Neither does this story," Tanya said, pointing at her computer screen. "According to social media, you've been laundering money for drug pushers and terrorists."

"What?" I ran around to look. "What happens when you click on the link?"

"You go to a website that tries to steal all your personal information. And has no facts to support the claim."

"That's outrageous."

"Or a great compliment," Christina said. "Fake news shops only target people they think will draw clicks. That's how they drive up their advertising rates. So in a way, this is a compliment."

"Not one I appreciate. Call in Mabel." Mabel Torino was our accountant. "See if she can be here to meet them on Thursday."

"Already done."

"With luck, she can keep the auditors entertained while we do our jobs."

Tanya cut in, though her voice was soft. "Does this mean I won't get paid next week?"

"I don't know." But I quickly corrected myself. "Scratch that. You'll get paid, even if the accounts are frozen."

"How?"

"I don't know. I'll sell my watch."

"That Mickey Mouse watch won't raise twenty bucks."

"I bought it at Disney World!"

Christina rolled her eyes. "And no one else has ever done that."

"I'll find the money." Tanya probably didn't have extensive reserve funds. "You'll get your check."

"Thank you."

"Christina, send a request to the US Treasury. Use the Freedom of Information Act. See if you can find out who initiated this investigation."

"That won't produce anything useful."

"You're already sending a dozen FOIA requests. You can prep one more."

"Aye, aye, Cap'n." Christina picked up the spindle. "Have you been through the rest of these messages?"

"I haven't even set down my briefcase."

She ripped another one out of the middle. "Move this one to the top of the stack."

I scanned it quickly. My lips parted. This is what the reporter was talking about.

I knew there would be backlash. Even the IRS audit didn't surprise me that much. But this did.

"I'm being investigated by the Disciplinary Committee of the Bar Association?"

"Someone filed a complaint," Christina answered.

"Who?"

"They wouldn't tell me. Said they had to protect the identity of the complainant, at least until they decide how to proceed. Some kind of whistle-blower-protection concept."

"Thrillkill."

"Or a pal. No way of knowing for sure. Anyone who's a member of the bar can file a complaint. For that matter, so can clients."

"I'm pretty sure Oz isn't complaining about me. Especially since they're not giving him phone calls. Do you have any idea what I've supposedly done?"

"Only the vaguest. The woman I talked to said there was some suggestion you might have concealed a criminal enterprise."

"Like what?"

"In other words, that Oz told you what he was going to do before he did it."

"That's a complete lie."

"I know. But the best lies have an element of truth. Oz did talk to you before the murder. And he did expose the depth of his hatred for Nazir."

"That's a far cry from revealing a murder plot. So long as he doesn't tell me he's planning to hurt someone, I'm required to keep client statements confidential."

A courier entered with a thin FedEx parcel.

Christina laid her hand on my shoulder. "Ben, this is another distraction. One more thing you'll have to deal with while you're handling a high-profile case for an extremely unpopular client who's getting national attention. It's divide and conquer. Plus, this is bound to get negative press coverage. Bar Association notices are open to the public."

"So they report that the Bar Association is investigating. No big deal."

"You know better than that. The press will report the investigation in such a way as to suggest there's already been a ruling against you. The local paper hates lawyers and Democrats, and you're both. They'll probably run this on the front page. They'll declare your guilt before the case is even heard. Just like the lynch-mob mentality has already decided Oz is guilty."

I crushed the pink slip in my fist. "I wish the Disciplinary Committee spent more time policing people who practice law improperly and less time going after high-profile targets."

"Stay calm, Ben."

"Seriously. We've got the second-floor Mafia extorting money from opposing parties, basically saying pay up or your divorce will take four years and cost a hundred thousand bucks. We've got old-school practitioners who use motions practice and bogus discovery to inflate their fees. But the Bar Association leaves them alone."

"Did you hear the word 'calm'? You do not need to make enemies of the folks who could yank your license at any time."

"Which is why no one ever says anything. Same reason no one calls out the news media when they report unsubstantiated rumors as if they were fact. Everyone's afraid of becoming a target. A hint of gossip and suddenly uninformed trolls are trashing you all over the Internet."

"Welcome to the twenty-first century, Ben."

"I don't like it."

She patted me on the shoulder. "I know you don't. And tonight, you can retreat into a nice Trollope novel and pretend you're living a hundred and fifty years ago. But for now, you have to deal with this case you've thrust yourself into."

"Ben?"

Tanya only spoke a single syllable, but the tremble in her voice made it sound more like a cry for help. "Yes?"

She held up a single sheet of paper, something that had obviously come out of the FedEx envelope. The paper bore no identifying markers.

The message couldn't be more alarming if it had been composed of letters cut out of a newspaper.

DEATH TO TERRORISTS. AND THEIR LAWYERS.

And beneath that, in slightly smaller letters:

WE'RE WATCHING YOU.

When I thought I could speak without being betrayed by my voice, I said, "Who do you think sent this?"

Christina shook her head. "Don't know. Too many possibilities. I'm sure the return address is fake."

"Angry racist? Anti-Arab hard-liner? Survivor of the OKC bombing?"

"The CIA?" Christina suggested, as another disturbing possibility.

Tanya cut back in. Water welled up in her eyes. "Is it true? Is someone . . . watching us? Like now?"

Almost without thinking, I did a 360, looking all around. "No one else is here. No one could sneak past all those reporters undetected." But even as I said it, I knew it wasn't true.

Christina tilted her head. I knew what she was thinking.

"Call Todd Barrow," I said. "Have him perform a sweep. If there are any hidden cameras or listening devices, he'll find them."

"Unless the government has some new tech he doesn't know about."

I ignored that. "In the meantime, let's be circumspect. Sensitive conversations might be best conducted outside. Take a walk to the Myriad Gardens. Enjoy some tropical plants."

Tanya's head fell to her desk. "I've never been so scared in my entire life."

"You need to go home."

"I don't want to leave you without—"

"Chris and I can take it from here. Go home and rest. You'll feel better tomorrow morning." I hoped. Because hiring and training a new receptionist was the last thing I wanted to do at this juncture. "Christina and I have dealt with this sort of thing before. You haven't. Go home and chill for a bit."

She nodded and gathered her belongings.

What I didn't tell her, or Christina for that matter, was that I was just as terrified as she was. This reaction was greater than anything we'd faced in the past, and I knew how ugly people could be when driven to extremes or, worse, when they fought for something they believed in. But right now, they needed—hell, everyone needed—me to be strong.

I faked it.

My gut told me we'd turned over a rock and exposed a rattlesnake. But since we had no idea where it was, we couldn't possibly stop it before it struck.

CHAPTER 25
WITNESS AFFIDAVIT
CASE NO. CJ-49-1886

I knew Kincaid's flunky would find nothing. Our listening devices, the kind I surreptitiously placed in the lawyer's home and office and elsewhere, possessed what techies call a "cloaking device" or a "sonic blanket." They could not be detected by conventional means. Since they contained no metal, a traditional detection sweep would not find them. They were made exclusively of components commonly found in walls, so they would attract no notice. They could not be detected by electronic means so long as they were not recording at the time the sweep was conducted. I deactivated them remotely for a brief time. I doubted that would cost me much. The principals were already taking their sensitive conversations elsewhere. The government's clumsy, lead-boot tactics undermined my much subtler and more effective methods.

I would still probably be able to hear what they said, through their cell phones or by other means. They did not realize yet that they could not escape me. They were flies in a spider's web, only alive so long as the spider wanted them alive.

Our primary concern was beyond my powers of surveillance so long as he remained behind bars, though we had spies on the inside who might recover useful intelligence. Anything he told the lawyer, however, was likely to be repeated to his wife. And I would hear.

The attack on Nazir had turned this city into a powder keg. This heartland town would send its flames virally throughout the nation.

It was time for us to take the next step.

It was time to deploy the weapon.

The lawyer believed he had everything under control. But I observed his reaction to the death threat. He did not know what he was up against. He did not understand the magnitude of the game he had chosen to play.

As always, I relayed my information to my handler.

"Other than that, there have been few developments. The lawyer is headed toward his decadent home."

"Understood. And al-Jabbar?"

"The next step will be the hearing in which the judge determines whether he will be released on bail."

"We do not want that to happen."

"Then it will not."

"Do you have someone who can get to the judge? I hear this egotist considers himself untouchable."

"Everyone can be touched. You only need to know where to touch him."

"Let's offer a generous incentive plan."

"I think an emotional incentive plan might be more effective."

"Whatever works. Just do it."

"I will."

"It would be good to have some ammunition against the lawyer as well."

"It would be simpler to kill him."

A moment of silence. "He would only be replaced by another. Lawyers are the thousand-headed hydra. Control is more effective."

I gazed through my high-powered binoculars, staring through the broad lobby windows. "I have an idea. I will put it into action."

"Not yet. Just . . . be ready. When the need arises."

"As you wish."

"Tell me if something develops. Otherwise, don't contact me again until after midnight."

"Understood." I disconnected the line.

Not everyone has the patience for this work. Most of it is simply watching. Waiting. Maintaining a heightened level of awareness, so if necessary I can spring into action in a split second.

Would that my life was nothing but watching. But it has never been that simple. Not before, across the wide ocean, or now. There are too many factors, too many loyalties, often divided. So many wrongs to be righted.

Watching is only the appetizer. The swift sword of justice delivers the main course.

CHAPTER 26

The next few days passed in a fast-forward blur. I wrapped up the package-delivery case and devoted several sixteen-hour workdays to the legal and media firestorm. The bail hearing was another procedural necessity—some would say antiquity. Given the enormous amount of attention this case had already attracted and the magnitude of the charge, I couldn't imagine this resulting in a favorable outcome. Indeed, Thrillkill's strongest argument might be that Oz should be left behind bars for his own protection.

I wished I could put my family behind bars. At least until this was over.

The Oklahoma City federal courthouse was an undistinguished cinder block, completely devoid of any personality or architectural distinction. It was like federal housing, except it had judges. No one came here unless it was required. Once you passed through the metal detectors and checked the directory to determine your destination, you were filled with a sort of omnipresent unease and, usually, a strong desire to be elsewhere.

Uniformed officers and federal marshals lined the hallways, trying to maintain order despite the bulging assemblage of reporters, rubber-neckers, and, in a few instances, people who were actually supposed to be there. Someone wasn't doing their job, because far more people had been allowed in than should have been, far more than they would ever be able to squeeze into a courtroom. Some thought it was time for the feds to give in and allow cameras, or at least closed-circuit cameras, in the courtroom. I disagreed, but it would eliminate the squabbling over seats.

The environment was calmer in the courtroom. The judge's clerk chatted up the court reporter, obviously killing time till the judge appeared.

Thrillkill tapped me on the shoulder. I didn't even hear him approach. Apparently, he had ninja skills in addition to all the others.

He cut to the chase. "Withdraw your bail request, Kincaid. Save yourself a lot of grief."

"I'm getting a strong feeling of déjà vu."

"You've already lost one hearing. Do you really want to lose another?"

"I can't withdraw my request."

"You're going to lose."

"Maybe. I still can't withdraw."

"If you push for bail, I have to respond. That means a lot of ugliness about your client comes out."

"Something you've kept to yourself?" We both knew that if he had any information he hadn't shared, it should not be admissible at this hearing.

"Nothing you don't already know." He paused. "But I might give it a different spin than you do."

"If you bring up something irrelevant to trash my client, I'll object and file a complaint."

"But the judge will still hear what I said. As will the press."

"So, basically, you're threatening to engage in unethical conduct to win a bail hearing."

"No, I'm threatening to do my job and offering you a chance to protect your client from a lot of embarrassment."

"Still sounds like a threat to me."

Thrillkill headed back to his table. "Suit yourself. Don't say I never tried to help you."

The bailiff announced the arrival of Magistrate Hamilton.

"This hearing is called to order." After determining that all parties were present and the defendant was represented by counsel, he asked the court to read the indictment. Given that this was a homicide case, the clerk would have to read the whole thing.

My eyes rolled back into screen-saver mode. People watched TV shows and thought criminal cases were so exciting. They had no idea.

The clerk read all the special circumstances, then nodded toward the bench.

Hamilton nodded back. "How does the defendant plead?"

We rose. I had advised Oz that he would have to speak for himself. "Not guilty, Your Honor."

The judge was not surprised. "And I believe the United States seeks to deny bail?"

Thrillkill spoke in a booming voice. He wanted to impress the crowd. I presumed he didn't feel the need to impress the judge, because he thought he already had this in the bag. "We do, sir. This is a homicide case, one with political, national, even international ramifications. The defendant has been linked to a terrorist organization. He has committed at least one murder and has been interrogated with respect—"

I guess my reflexes were slowing with age. "Objection, Your Honor. My client has not been convicted of—"

Hamilton waved me into silence. "You are correct, Counsel. Mr. Thrillkill, you know better than this."

"I'm sorry, Your Honor, but this is a capital case, and the defendant was found at the scene of the crime with the murder weapon in his hand. I don't think anyone in their right mind doubts—"

The judge sighed audibly. "Counsel? Last chance. Talk to me, not the reporters."

Thrillkill pursed his lips, as if all these irritating lawyers were getting between him and his quest for justice. "The defendant's acknowledged links to organizations on NSA and CIA watch lists, plus his international connections make him not only a danger but also a serious flight risk."

"My client is willing to surrender his passport," I interjected.

"He probably has a drawer full of them," Thrillkill replied.

"Objection."

The judge removed his glasses, rubbing his eyes. "I did warn you, Mr. Thrillkill. You know the rules. I'm hereby sanctioning you—and I mean you personally, not your office—to the tune of five hundred dollars. Deposit that with the clerk before you appear again in my courtroom."

Thrillkill shook his head and shoulders, an aw-shucks gesture he must've copied from Ronald Reagan. "I meant no disrespect, Your Honor."

"So pay the fine. Did you have anything else to say?"

"No, Your Honor."

Usually, lawyers don't care much for being sanctioned, but I think Thrillkill actually enjoyed it—possibly deliberately invited it. He wasn't worried about the outcome of the case. He thought he had a lock on that. His goal was to cast himself as the underdog, the lone crusader for the rights of the people and the safety of the nation.

He was campaigning in the courtroom.

"Mr. Kincaid?"

"Your Honor, there's no flight risk because, as I said, my client is willing to surrender his passport. He is also willing to wear a GPS bracelet so the government can monitor his whereabouts. Despite his prior detainment, he has never previously been accused, much less convicted, of a crime. He is not a wealthy man, and he does have long-standing ties to this community."

"Is his family in the courtroom today?"

Ouch. Nice catch. "No, Your Honor, given the crowd and the reporters and whatnot—"

"Uh-huh."

"In fact," Thrillkill interjected, "he has not seen any member of his family in years. He has maintained no contact with anyone in this area." He smirked slightly. "Except maybe his lawyer."

"That's not true!"

The voice ringing out from the rear of the gallery was all too familiar. Even before I turned, I knew who spoke.

Julia was in the back row.

The magistrate's surprise was expressed with a mildly raised eyebrow. "And who might you be, ma'am?"

"My name is Julia McKeown. I've known the defendant since high school." Her eyes darted briefly toward the floor. "And I saw him again, the night before the press conference."

That got a reaction out of the crowd—and me. Imagine what they'd think when they learned she was my sister. I stared at her as intently as I could, but she pointedly refused to make eye contact.

Thrillkill turned, stress lines stretching across his forehead. "Wait a minute. Isn't that your sister, Kincaid?" I wondered how he knew that. "Is this some kind of setup? This is the lowest ploy that—"

"You will address your comments to me, Mr. Thrillkill." Hamilton reached across the bench, the gavel poised in his hand. "And no one else."

Thrillkill bowed his head. "Yes, Your Honor."

"I will not tolerate bickering between counsel."

"No, sir."

"This is a serious matter, and you will conduct yourself with the utmost professionalism. Do you understand?"

At this point, Thrillkill was practically groveling. "Yes, Your Honor. Of course. Please accept my apologies."

"I don't accept apologies. I accept professional conduct. And nothing less."

I kept my mouth shut. Yes, the odds were not in my favor today. But at least for once I wasn't the one getting chewed out by the judge.

Hamilton directed his comments to Julia. "I appreciate you coming forth, ma'am. I'm sure that took a great deal of courage. If you believe you have useful testimony, you should see one of the attorneys. But I can't formally acknowledge remarks made by unsworn witnesses from the gallery. Please continue, Mr. Kincaid."

"That's about it, Your Honor. I would add that my client is not going anywhere. He has been wrongfully accused, and he is anxious to clear his name in court."

Hamilton ran his palm across the top of his head. "I'm afraid I must agree with the prosecutor. I think it might be better for all concerned if the defendant remains in custody. I'll set this down for the earliest trial date to which both counsel will agree."

As I suspected. He probably wouldn't let a homicide defendant out in any case, but he certainly wasn't going to do it when there was a good chance he might be harmed before trial. Or devoured by reporters.

"Anything else?" And without waiting for a reply, Hamilton banged his gavel. "The defendant will be remanded into custody. This matter is concluded." Another bang of the gavel and it was over.

Oz took it as best as could be expected.

"I'll be back to visit soon," I assured him.

He nodded. "Thank Julia for me."

"I will."

The bailiff took him away, and I walked to the gallery. I knew the press would converge on Julia as soon as she left the courtroom, and I wanted to prevent it.

I pulled her aside. "Didn't expect to see you here today."

"It's okay. Mom's Day Out has the girls."

"This was still an extremely stupid move."

"I wanted to help. Isn't that what you always do?"

I had no answer. I thought the best idea was for us to get out of there.

"Julia, I think it's time we sat down and had a talk. A real one."

"That sounds grim."

"Doesn't have to be. You still addicted to coffee?"

"Big time."

"Come with me. I know where we can get the best cup in town."

CHAPTER 27

A short drive took us to The Underground. Great coffee and a wide variety of board games made it my favorite. We nestled into a table in the rear. There were no other customers, and the barista did not appear remotely interested, so I thought we might have a real talk. An honest one. Something we should have done a long time ago. Even around Christina, the woman I trust with everything, conversation with Julia was somewhat inhibited. This time it would just be the two of us.

Someone had to break the ice. "When did you start seeing Oz again?"

I could tell she didn't want to answer, but we'd never lied to one another, and thank goodness we weren't going to start now. "About a year ago."

"A year? You've been in town a year, and I didn't know it?"

"It wasn't like that. I wasn't seeing him continuously. Just off and on. I was lonely. You know how that feels. I was going through some problems."

I felt something in my stomach clench. "Drugs again?"

She looked away. "It's just so easy. You're lonely and stressed, and every day is another round of pain. One little pill and you're not feeling it anymore." She ran a hand through her long blonde hair. "Way too easy. Keeps the weight off, too."

"You know, Oz has a drug problem."

"He's working on it."

"I understand that divorce is stressful, but—"

"You don't understand." She lifted her latte and downed half of it in a single swig. "There's been no divorce. I knew it would be hopeless. I just walked away."

And I didn't even know. That was the saddest part yet. Once upon a time, Julia and I had been the best of friends. Our father was an egotistical brute, and our mother was unfathomable, but we two were inseparable. No matter what else might be going on at home, we had one another's backs. Us against the world.

And then things changed. We never fought. We just drifted. She dated Oz in high school, then later married my college roommate. The marriage was a disaster. He was a cop, and she was used to unlimited funds and Porsches and living in that ginormous house in Nichols Hills. She split and married a doctor, had a baby, they broke up, got back together, split up again, etc.

I saw Julia once, during my brief stint with a big law firm, Raven, Tucker & Tubb. She was the one who pushed me to go home, to see our father one last time before he passed. It was probably a mistake. Closure did not occur. The next time I saw her, she left Joey in my care, and the next time was when she collected him. I hadn't seen her since. Not even when our mother died.

Once thick as thieves. Now all but strangers.

"We need to get your family situation straightened out."

"I think you've got enough on your plate right now, Ben."

"As soon as Oz's case is over, you move to the top of the agenda. I don't care what happened in the past. You seem fine now. Taking a child from his mother in unconscionable. Why didn't you consult me before?"

"I wasn't sure I'd be welcome."

I looked up at her. "You will always be welcome."

A faint smile crept into the corner of her lips. "That's good to know."

"So you rekindled your relationship with Oz. I assume this was more than a friendship. A romantic relationship."

"We were sleeping together, if that's what you're asking."

I grimaced. "It is most definitely *not* what I was asking."

She grinned even more. "Same old Ben."

"You know he's with someone named Mina now?"

"Oh, yes."

"But you weren't involved in Oz's politics, right? His . . . organization."

"Have you ever known me to be political?"

"No. Have you met Mina?"

She pressed her fingers against her forehead. "Stuck-up bitch. Can't stand the woman."

"She's been through a lot."

"That's what she says. That's how she stole Oz, playing the poor-pitiful-me card."

"Have you ever met this . . . Abdullah? The mysterious puppet master?"

"Never. Never want to, either."

"Good. I think he's bad news. But to be perfectly blunt, Julia—I kinda think they all are."

"Even your client?"

"Just because he's my client doesn't mean I want him dating my sister."

"Tell me the truth. Do you think Oz is guilty?"

"I have no idea."

"You must have an opinion."

"I think he has dangerous friends and makes dangerous choices."

"I meant an opinion about his guilt or innocence."

"It's my job not to have opinions. I will represent my client with reasonable vigor to the best of my ability. Opinions have nothing to do with it."

"But still .

"Nope. No clue."

"I think Oz is innocent. In fact, I know he is."

"How do you know? Were you at the press conference?"

"No."

"Do you know something about it? Something you haven't told me?"

"Nothing like that. I just know Oz. He wouldn't kill someone, and even if he did, he wouldn't do it like that."

"If you only knew how many wives and girlfriends I've heard say something like that. And be wrong."

"It wasn't Oz. I'm certain."

"I hope you're right."

Our table fell silent. We drank our coffee. We shifted our weight, checked out the view. We were done, basically, except we weren't. Maybe we would never be done.

This time Julia broke the silence. "How can you live in that house?"

I searched for the right words. "It's paid for. Might as well get some benefit out of it."

"I can remember when you couldn't wait to get out of there."

"So can I."

"And now you call it home."

I shrugged. "Nice neighborhood to raise my girls."

"If you want them to be doctor's wives." Her eyes locked on to mine. I could feel them bearing down on me. "I noticed you don't use the bed and bath that used to be mine."

"True."

She gave me a deadeye glare. "You're not over it any more than I am. Maybe we never will be. But living in that house, with all that history—that has to weigh on you."

"I will admit . . . I was hesitant at first. But Christina thought it was a golden opportunity."

"And you would do anything for that woman."

"I would. Yes."

"Even this."

"Even this."

"Lucky Christina." She drained the last of her coffee. "Why couldn't I find someone like you?"

"I can be pretty exasperating. Or so I'm told."

"But she knows you love her. Unconditionally. Doesn't get any better than—" Her voice broke off. "Ben. Look."

My eyes drifted toward the street. I didn't have to ask what caught her eye.

Mina was outside in the parking lot.

Watching us.

"How did she know we were here?" Julia asked.

"Only one way possible. She followed us."

"Why?"

"You know the woman better than I do."

"Probably stalking me because she thinks I want to take away her man."

"You know . . . she was brutalized by Nazir, too."

"So she says."

"You doubt it?"

"I don't know. It would explain her crazy behavior. I can only imagine what that kind of treatment might do to a person. To their mind. Plus, she's Abdullah's sister." She almost smiled. "What relationship could be more screwed up than a brother and sister's?"

I almost smiled back. "Except all of them."

This time she did laugh. "Exactly."

CHAPTER 28

Christina helped me with my necktie. Tying ties has never been my strong suit.

"I should be coming with you," Christina said, as she slid the Windsor knot into place.

"The guy specified only one attorney. If two show up, he'll bolt."

"Do I really seem that intimidating?"

"Not until you speak."

"We can't all get by with the shy-shuffling-bumbler bit." She laid her hand against my cheek. "Maybe I could watch from a distance. With a pair of binoculars. Like a creeper."

"Not necessary. I'm impressed Corwin was able to track him down. Now will you agree that he's a good detective?"

She made a sniffing sound. "He's no Loving."

"He's fine."

"Loving would never let you meet someone like this alone."

"He would if I told him to."

"No. He'd lurk in the bushes and not tell you about it."

Just like you probably will, I thought, but did not say aloud. "Enjoy some quality time with your daughters."

"Or I could go shopping. Once the trial starts, I won't have time.

And I'm practically superfluous at home these days. Julia is doing a great job with the girls."

"She is?"

She gave me a mock slug on the shoulder. "Don't act so amazed. She is related to you, after all, and you're a terrific dad. And she's got prior child-rearing experience, unlike either of us."

"And Emily?"

Her chin lowered. "Julia is terrific with Emily. Especially Emily."

"Does Emily . . . respond to her?"

"No more than anyone else. But Julia is patient. She doesn't mind repeating instructions, if that's what it takes."

"I suppose that comes from working with Joey. She's an expert in—"

"Stop. Stop right now."

"Christina .

"You heard me."

"We have to be realistic."

"Your daughter has never been diagnosed by anyone as autistic."

"Because she hasn't seen anyone."

"And it wouldn't be the end of the world if she were autistic."

I withheld my judgment. "We're going to have to take her to a specialist."

"And on that subject, Julia knows someone."

"She does?"

"Perhaps you're not aware of this, but your little sister is well connected. Particularly in the medical field."

"Maybe she can set up an appointment."

"Already done."

I picked up my briefcase and started toward the door. "Why am I starting to feel like there's a lot going on I know nothing about?"

"Just paranoid." She opened the door and pushed me through it. "Go get 'em, tiger."

❧

Once upon a time, Oklahoma was as dry as it was possible to

be, but thanks to the efforts of legendary lawmaker Robert S. Kerr and others, we legislated our way into becoming a lake state (even if most of them are completely man-made.)

Lake Hefner is a good example. Maybe God didn't want water there, but a lot of well-heeled people did. So they expanded the water supply and created a tourist attraction. The area surrounding the lake is perfect for jogging and playing with the kids, flying kites, and racing the dog. You can catch surfers and sea kiters in the cove, and when the time comes for grub, you have your choice of a wide array of upscale restaurants.

My favorite part is the lighthouse, out on a finger peninsula jutting into the lake. Purely decorative, of course. Not many ships lost on this completely landlocked reservoir. But there is a park bench beneath the lighthouse, and since it is isolated from everything else, and you can see anyone approaching long before they arrive, it's the perfect place to meet a potential witness you don't know anything about.

Corwin had located only one person at the scene of the shooting he thought might be helpful. He was not sure the man would be willing to testify, especially given the outpouring of enmity currently directed toward anyone associated with my client. But getting him to testify was my job. After I determined whether he knew anything useful.

"So you were at the press conference? At the time Nazir was killed?" His name was Emory Walters. White, bearded, on the short side. He managed a downtown Walgreens. Spent most of his time behind the cash register. He wasn't exactly nervous, but I did detect a sense of unease. Maybe he didn't like sitting on a park bench with another guy. Especially one he didn't know.

"I was." He had a slight accent, not the clipped city sound or the Western Oklahoma drawl.

"What brought you there?"

"Curiosity, mostly. I follow the news. I believe we're at a crossroads in American history."

"A crossroads between what and what?"

"Between a powerful nation that becomes more so, and a powerful nation that goes into decline. The Roman Empire in the first century or the Roman Empire in the fourth."

I'd heard enough comparisons between America and the Roman Empire to fill an almanac, but I rarely thought much of them. Seemed like anytime someone needed proof of the unprovable, they retreated to the Roman Empire. Or Nazi Germany. "We may be having some economic issues, but I don't think the Huns are going to overrun us anytime soon."

"But then, neither did the Romans."

"We also don't have a culture based on slavery—"

"Not anymore."

"Or dominated by the military."

"That's a matter of opinion."

"We have a representative democracy."

"Which is entirely controlled by big money and big business."

"The Cold War is over."

"And replaced by hot threats from terrorists, Russia, and North Korea."

This guy was all over the place. I wasn't sure if he was ultraliberal, ultraconservative, or ultra nuts. But I wasn't getting a strong desire to put him on the witness stand. "So I gather it was your interest in politics that brought you to the press conference."

"I'm a huge fan of the work Nazir did for us. He held back the Huns. Which of course is the Middle East."

"Some Middle Eastern nations are friendly to the US."

"Don't be fooled. They'd take everything we have if we gave them the chance. They're on a mission to spread sharia law from one end of the globe to the other."

"Some say that, but there's no proof."

"That kind of thinking led to putting a secret Muslim in the Oval Office."

My Spidey-senses were tingling. "Mind if I ask where you get your information?"

"I'm extremely well read."

I nodded. "FOX News?"

"Actually, I get most of my facts from the Internet."

"Ah. Then they must be true."

"You might be surprised. During the Middle Ages, Europe didn't realize the threat to the Holy Land until much too late."

"You're referring to the Crusades? Europeans who attempted to conquer the Holy Land six times?"

"Seven, actually."

"And you're thinking we should do it again?"

"I believe we should stop reacting and start acting. We know they're coming for us. Much better if we strike first."

"Invade the Middle East. Take over?"

"What would be the downside?"

"Do we take Israel, too?"

"It would save a lot of lives if we did."

Walters was a ticking time bomb, and Thrillkill could make him look like a fool. I couldn't possibly put him on the stand—unless he saw something valuable that I couldn't get from anyone else. "So you were at the conference because you admired Nazir?"

"And his fight against Abdullah. That man is a butcher."

"Do you have any proof of this charge?"

"If you want to get all legal about it, there's no proof Osama bin Laden was behind 9/11. He could never have been convicted in a court of law. So we didn't waste time bringing him to trial. Abdullah is a determined terrorist tool. It's just a matter of time until one of his plots succeeds. When he gets the right weapon in his hands, we'll be toast." He paused. "Unless we allow people like Nazir to do what they need to do to keep us safe."

I did my best to steer the discussion back to the press conference. "Did you hear the gunshot?"

"Of course. Everyone did."

"But no one seems to be sure where it came from. Are you?"

"The sound echoed all around us."

"The shooter had to be somewhere."

"Yeah, but acoustics and ballistics can go seriously wonky. Particularly when there's a lot of concrete around."

"There were hundreds of people watching. How can it be a mystery where the bullet came from? Someone must have seen a gun."

He gave me a long look. "Two words. Grassy knoll."

Point taken. "Did you see my client there?"

"Saw him racing across the plaza like a roadrunner."

"Did you notice if he held anything?"

"No."

"Let me put it more directly. Was he holding a gun?"

"Not that I saw."

Well, that was something.

"Of course, everyone was running every which way at once," Walters continued. "I only noticed your client because he ran right in front of me. Almost knocked me over. And then he got flattened."

My head tilted to one side. "Now what?"

"He got tackled. Knocked down like a linebacker. The first of several."

"Wait. The first of several?"

"Right. One guy knocked him over. Then two others piled on top a second or so later."

"Like they were working together?"

"I don't know about that. It all happened quickly, and the plaza was crowded and everyone was running. Two guys on the asphalt created an obstacle. It's possible the latter two tripped over them. But the end result was a massive pileup. And your guy was on the bottom."

Which could possibly explain him being knocked unconscious. And having memory problems. "How long did this pileup last?"

"Not that long. The latter two got up fairly quickly and raced away. But the other guy—the first to tackle—took longer. Something was going on, but I was too far away to make it out."

"Something like . . . maybe . . . the planting of a gun?"

"Like I said, I couldn't tell."

"Okay." Best not to push. He gave me something valuable. I didn't want to shove him out of his comfort zone. "But that guy, the tackler, did leave eventually."

"Oh yeah. Then your guy tried to run. And the cops got him."

I had to put Walters on the stand. Even if Thrillkill did have a heyday with his outlier politics. "I want to thank you for coming forward," I said. "I appreciate your honesty."

"Every citizen's duty," he replied. "If we don't stand together, we have no chance against the coming threat. It's us against them. The American way versus the sharia way. The true America, and the traitors."

That should have been enough to make me realize he was too dangerous to put on the stand. But of course, I didn't get it. Not till it was too late.

CHAPTER 29

D ays became weeks, and weeks became months. Life passes with an almost surreal fluidity when you're trapped in the clutches of an all-consuming case. One moment I was handling the preliminary hearing, and before I even had a chance to come up for air, I was strapping myself into the same suit and staring at a calendar that had but a single notation: TDB.

I didn't book anything else because there was no way of knowing how long I might be occupied. I didn't pick a suit I liked much, because I knew that by the end of the day I would be a sweaty, dripping, shaking wreck. I didn't bring Christina, though she would've provided much comfort, because I saw no reason why both parents needed to be completely miserable.

TDB stood for "The Day Before." Meaning "The Day Before Trial."

This is why we don't keep antidepressants in the house. Much too tempting.

All defendants handled it differently, usually depending upon their temperament, whether they were incarcerated, and the gravity of the charges against them. In this case, Oz had remained reasonably restrained throughout the pretrial period, so I had every reason to think a meltdown was imminent. His life was literally on the line, and that would unnerve even the calmest soul. Which Oz wasn't.

Some of today's tasks were practical matters that could probably be handled by a competent legal assistant, if I were willing to curse anyone with such work. Making sure Oz had a sufficient clean wardrobe for a trial that would likely go on for many days. They wouldn't let him keep his clothes in his cell, but they would be made available to him at the appropriate time. Proper grooming. Clean shave. Nails. They didn't have to glisten, but we didn't want him coming out looking like Fu Manchu, either. There was no telling what some wacko juror might go off on, and it took only one juror to sway the rest. You could not be too careful.

To give credit where due, Oz looked good when they led him into the small conference room and unshackled him. But I knew it wouldn't last.

"Would you like a guard to remain present?" That came from Frank Gorman. He knew what I would say. He was just going through the motions.

"No thank you."

"You have the right to confidentiality, but I have to advise you that if you are subjected to some sort of injury or affront, the government will not be liable. You are on your own."

"I know." But it gave me a chill hearing someone say it like that, just the same. "Thank you."

Frank left, and Oz took the seat at the opposite end of the table. I gave him my best smile. "How you holding up?"

"No one's killed me yet. Though several have offered. I keep to myself."

"You should've stayed in solitary."

"I'm a social animal. You have no idea how painful that would be."

Less painful than a shiv to the ribs, I thought, but I kept it to myself. "I know you were disappointed that we didn't get bail, but the truth is it was probably for the best."

"I'm having a hard time seeing that."

"Even if the magistrate set bail, it would've been so high you couldn't have made it. Or it would've wiped you out financially if you did."

"I have friends."

"I doubt if you have any with pockets that deep. And if some political organization posted bail, the press would've gone crazy with it."

"I don't care what the press says about me."

"I do," I said, plopping my briefcase onto the small table. "And you should. Because every potential juror out there is probably getting some information about this case, one way or the other, and even if they tell the judge it hasn't impacted their ability to be fair, the truth is everything impacts their ability to be fair. Most of us are not sufficiently conscious of how we reach a decision to say what influences us and what doesn't. Or to put is more succinctly, everything matters."

"You should've gotten some kind of gag order."

"Tricky little thing called the First Amendment usually gets in the way." I pulled some folders out of my briefcase. I probably didn't need them. But I wanted him to see that I'd done the work, I was on top of this, and he was in competent hands. "We have to make a decision about our defense strategy."

"Do you have to announce our defense tomorrow?"

"No. We'll be lucky if we get past jury selection tomorrow. But eventually I will have to give an opening statement."

"Can't you wait till we put on our case?"

"I could, but it would be incredibly stupid, so I won't be doing that. You don't want the prosecutor to have days to fill the jurors' heads with uncontested baloney. You want to tell the jury right up front that we have a different theory of what happened so they can keep that in the back of their brains while he's talking."

I could see his eyes widening slightly, the corner of his lips beginning to twitch. "I'm not going to enjoy this much, am I?"

"Not while the prosecutor is putting on his case, no. I've seen his so-called evidence. He's going to paint you as the world's worst terrorist minion, more than capable of executing a cold-blooded assassination."

"I'm the victim here!"

"And I will bring that out, when I get a chance. Thrillkill will probably allude to your interrogation. He's too smart to leave it to me to mention for the first time. He'll suggest that your prior incarceration is proof of your terroristic leanings. Not to mention a motive for murder."

"And what are we going to say in response?"

Here's where things would get sticky. "We have several choices."

"I hope 'not guilty' is one of them."

"It is. But 'not guilty' has several flavors. Including 'not guilty by reason of insanity.'"

"You want me to claim that I'm crazy?"

I tried to maintain a measured tone. "I want you to consider it as a strategic possibility."

"I'm not crazy."

"Trials are about putting on the best case. Sadly, they are not about truth."

"I thought that was the whole point."

"You were wrong. Trials are a means of dispute resolution. Better than trial by combat, but still deeply imperfect. Trials are won by strategy. Anyone who goes off on a rant or a crusade or thinks they're fighting for truth, justice, and the American Way is probably going to get crushed like a bug."

"I'm not crazy."

I removed a folder from my file. "I've read the psychiatric evaluation. There's enough there. We could make it fly."

"Make what fly? Telling the jury I'm nuts?"

"Telling the jury that being subjected to twenty-one days of incarceration, abuse, and torture unbalanced your mind. You had already been diagnosed with PTSD. Personally, I'd love to get that before a jury."

"What would happen?"

"There's still been no serious legal challenge to the rendition and interrogation passages of the Patriot or Freedom Acts or the torture and torturelike policies implemented after it was passed. I could make you sound extremely sympathetic."

"And extremely crazy."

"I think our theory would be irresistible impulse. It's a form of insanity defense that suggests that, sure, most of the time, you're perfectly sane. But something happened that caused you to snap. You were powerless to prevent your actions."

"And what happens if you make that fly? I get off scot-free?"

"No. But your sentence would be less severe. And you might serve it in a mental institution. Which I can assure you would be less harsh than the prison system."

"How long would I be there?"

"I can't predict. To some extent, it would depend upon your supervisors."

"So you don't know."

"I have many skills, but fortune-telling isn't one of them."

"And you think this is what I should do?"

I considered each word carefully before I spoke. "I think it's your safest shot. The evidence against you is strong. You were found at the scene of the murder of a man you openly despised. You were found with the gun in your possession."

"I didn't do it."

"But this is a solid strategy."

"No. Absolutely not."

"At least think about it."

"I will not lie. I will not pretend I did a horrible thing I did not do."

"Do you want to ask Mina? See what she thinks?"

"I'm . . . not speaking to her right now."

Really? How do you break up with someone when you're in prison? "How about Kir?"

"He's just a kid. He doesn't know anything."

"Julia then?"

"I'm not crazy, and I didn't kill Nazir. I won't pretend otherwise. That's the coward's way out."

God save me from misplaced machismo. "Oz, this is not the time to play John Wayne. This is the time to tuck tail and give yourself some kind of future. You're a defendant and—"

"I'm a freedom fighter."

"Which some people translate as 'terrorist.'"

"This country was founded by freedom fighters. Some of whom committed acts that the British labeled terrorism."

"Ancient history."

"Is it a crime to have strong political beliefs?"

"Depends on what you do about them."

"These are desperate times. We're at war."

"And war never solved anything."

"What kind of dewy-eyed sentimentality is that? We may wish there were better ways of—what was your term?—dispute resolution. But you can't pretend war never accomplishes anything. This country was founded by war. There wouldn't be an America without war. Blacks would still be slaves but for war. Nazi Germany would control Europe but for war."

"We're getting too far afield from the problem at hand. This is a murder case. We'll be better off if we leave the politics out of it."

"Stop being so naive. This case is all about politics. The government was humiliated by 9/11, so it's employing unconstitutional fascistic policies and justifying it with fearmongering."

"This is exactly the kind of rant that would destroy you in court."

"We're up against the enemies of freedom, Ben. They framed me because they want to destroy everyone who opposes them. This is how they get me, and probably all of PACT, out of the way."

"This is a murder trial. Pure and simple."

"There is nothing simple about it!" Oz's shout rocked the room, so loud I saw the guard outside turn his head. I wanted to tell Oz to calm down, but it was pointless. "These people want to destroy me! They want to wipe me off the face of the earth!"

I tried to calm him. "I don't know what the CIA wants. But they will not be the jury box."

"They'll get to the judge. Maybe the jury, too." He trembled like a man in a hurricane.

"No, they won't. I know this judge, and while he's not the perfect choice, he's certainly no CIA tool."

"They'll find a way."

"That defeatist paranoia won't help. We have to pick a defense."

"How can they prove I did something I didn't do?"

"Sadly, wrongful convictions happen all too frequently."

"Doesn't the prosecutor have the burden of proof?"

"In theory. But in practice, many, if not most, jurors think that prosecutors wouldn't bring charges unless they were certain of the defendant's guilt. They assume the prosecutors know more than they can say at the trial. They've seen too many *Law and Order* episodes where judges make irrational rulings that suppress evidence. If we hope to win, we have to do more than just say 'not guilty.' We need a theory of our own. We have to put on the SODDIT."

"Excuse me? What?"

"SODDIT. It's an acronym. Some Other Dude Did It."

"Like who?"

"That's the problem. I don't have a halfway-likely suspect. Who could I make look guiltier than the guy who was caught with the gun in his hand."

"You're smart. You'll think of something."

"I'm not that smart. And I already told you what I think we should do."

"Well, we're not doing that."

"Oz—"

"Please." He squeezed my hand so tightly it left impressions on my skin. "I'm all alone here. Help me."

He broke down completely, weeping and shaking like an infant. I walked around the table and held him in my arms. I knew the guard wouldn't like it, but I didn't think he'd interfere. He'd been around enough to know what people like Oz went through. He wouldn't be a jerk about the contact rules.

"I will do everything I can for you, Oz. That's a promise I made you before, and it still stands."

"I'm going to die, aren't I? They'll give me that injection that tortures people to death while they can't even scream."

He clutched me tight, tight as possible, so tight we were practically one.

I wasn't going to lie to him. "I can't make any promises about the result, Oz. But I can promise this. Christina and I will make sure you get a fair trial. When you go before that jury—you will not be alone."

CHAPTER 30

T he gavel striking the bench never fails to make my heart skip. It's a melodramatic and completely unnecessary gesture, but it works. If anyone doubted the gravity of what was to follow, it would not be for long.

Judge Santino peered through the reading glasses perched precariously on the tip of his nose as he read the case style. "*The United States v. Omar al-Jabbar*, Case Number FJ-49-1886S. The court is now in session. Please note on the record that the parties are present and represented by counsel. I will ask counsel to enter their appearances at this time."

And so began the mindless rigmarole that kicks off the modern-day trial. There is a reason why TV lawyer shows leave all this out. It's tedious. Nerve-racking, when you realize this is the prelude to a determination of whether another human being continues living. But still an endless succession of eminently skippable stuff. Some is required by law, but most is simply habit and routine, lawyers jumping through hoops devised in the Victorian era or earlier, repeated today primarily because no one has the creativity or initiative to do it differently.

Judge Wayne Santino came out of the JAG court and was later appointed to the federal bench. He had a no-nonsense, take-no-prisoners judicial style. He was conservative by nature and appointed by a Republican administration. That wasn't typically the best judge profile for the defense, but the truth was, I liked Santino. He called lawyers on their BS, regardless of which side they were on. He didn't allow anyone to waste his time. And most of his vehemence seemed directed not at defendants, but at lawyers. He had no tolerance for litigation pollution, motions practice, or discovery disputes. A judge after my own heart. The military background was troublesome, but given how much press coverage this case was getting, I knew he'd be on his best behavior.

"Roger Thrillkill for the United States." My opponent then introduced his six assisting attorneys, including the woman who represented the CIA. It appeared the government was sparing no expense on this one.

"Ben Kincaid for Mr. al-Jabbar," I said. Christina introduced herself.

Oz looked good, well scrubbed and well dressed. If you didn't know, you'd never guess that only an hour before he'd been wearing orange coveralls and shackles. Christina spent a fair amount of time selecting his trial wardrobe, mostly blue suits and white shirts. Nothing too exciting, but certainly nothing that would seem criminal or radical or terroristic. The tie he wore was even more boring than the one she'd chosen for me.

Profound human insight was not required to see the strain behind the suit. Which was good, because I've never been a person of great human insight. Other people baffle me. But I couldn't help but notice the dark circles beneath his eyes, the tense posture, the constant crossing and uncrossing of his legs. He was doing his best to contain his anxiety. But there was only so much a human being could do when his life was on the line.

The judge peered up from his paperwork. "Are there any matters that need to be addressed before we select a jury, Counsel?"

Motions were generally made outside the presence of the jury lest they be influenced by something the lawyers said in argument. Thrillkill made some motions that were denied, then I made some motions that were denied. It was all a waste of time, particularly in a high-profile case where the judge wasn't going to do anything controversial that might create reversible error. But lawyers had to cover their tracks. If they missed a hoop, some after-the-fact losing party might say counsel was incompetent. On appeal, the record needed to show that the trial judge was given a full opportunity to rule in your favor on anything of importance. So Christina and I brought up anything that could possibly be of importance.

Thrillkill tried to suppress some evidence, all without success. The judge would never let me appeal based on the suppression of evidence that might help Oz. I made a motion to dismiss based on insufficient evidence. The judge predictably said he would rule on the motion after the prosecution presented its case. I felt stupid making the motion, even though I had to do so. The gun was found on Oz, for crying out loud.

I also made a motion to exclude all discussion of politics and political leanings. "We live in America, Your Honor, and the First Amendment guarantees us the right of assembly and freedom of speech, most especially for political speech. It's completely inappropriate to allow someone to imply wrongdoing based on a party's beliefs. If the court lets the prosecutor do that, we're back in the McCarthy era."

Thrillkill replied in a flat tone. He saved his energy for when it mattered. "Goes to motive, Your Honor."

"Which we all know is not actually an element of this crime," I replied. "Nor part of the prosecutor's burden of proof."

"But it goes a long way toward convincing a jury," Thrillkill answered, "as we all also know."

"That's no excuse for violating someone's constitutional rights."

The judge raised his palm, cutting off the less-than-scintillating debate. "The motion will be denied. If you hear anything inappropriate during the trial, you may object or renew your motion and I'll rule on specific instances. But I will not issue a blanket prohibition. The First Amendment guarantees the freedom to speak, but it does not absolve the speaker from the consequences of his speech. If the defendant's remarks or associations are of probative value, they are unlikely to be excluded."

And so it went. I tried not to take it personally, because I knew this was a lame argument from the get-go. But something about the judge's demeanor bothered me. Did he really curl his lips when he mentioned Oz's "remarks or associations," or was it just my imagination? I recalled what Oz had said before about the CIA "getting to" the judge. I didn't believe it then.

Or, perhaps, I didn't want to believe it.

The judge dispensed with the remaining motions, and we slogged through more nonsense that no one cared about. Finally, it was time to select the jury.

In state court, this could take forever, and in a capital case, it could take forever and a day. Federal courts tend to keep the questioning in check. The judge has the right to do all the questioning himself, and Judge Santino did. Counsel can submit suggested questions in writing. The fact that they are written and submitted in advance usually prevents lawyers from engaging in the tricks and ploys that exacerbate the process, inquiring into personal matters or trying to subtly introduce themes favorable to their case.

Most trial lawyers hate having judges do the questioning. I much prefer it. This relates back to not deluding myself that I possess keen insight into people. The idea that we can predict how these randomly chosen driver's licenses will vote based on a series of questions is preposterous. Sometimes lawyers need to get out of the way and let the process take its course. This was a good example. There is no evidence whatsoever that extensive voir dire produced more favorable jurors. Too often it degenerates into stereotypes, trying to eliminate members of a particular race or gender or socioeconomic class. Better to let the judge handle it, eliminate the few obviously biased, and get on with the show.

The standard questions always include something designed to root out antigovernment or anti–law enforcement biases and looking for anyone with negative past experiences. This time, the questioning was expanded to include negative experiences with foreign nationals, political advocacy groups, and terrorism. None of the first eighteen took the bait, but the questions must have aroused their curiosity. I also managed to get in a question hunting for bias "against people of foreign faiths, including but not limited to the Muslim faith." Two people actually raised their hands on that one. I made a point of removing both from the panel first chance I had.

As the judge would remind us, no one has a right to a perfect jury any more than you have a right to a perfect trial. There is no such thing. You have a right to a reasonably fair jury and a reasonably fair trial. That's as good as it gets.

This preliminary process, streamlined though it was, still took the rest of the morning. After lunch, the judge started on a series of questions that were much more direct. Since the prosecution sought the death penalty, he had to make sure the jurors were "death qualified," meaning they were willing to impose the death penalty if they felt the evidence merited it. No one flat-out admitted they would never impose the death penalty, but five of the panelists were sufficiently squishy on the subject to be replaced by Thrillkill. Which meant new prospective jurors had to be called from the pool of "venirepersons," and then the questioning began again, the new panelists being asked the same questions we'd heard all morning.

By four in the afternoon, I could tell the judge's interest, not to mention his patience, was waning, but we neared the end. I wouldn't take anyone else off without a good reason, and none presented itself. I asked for a brief recess so I could consult with Christina, to see if she'd noticed anything I missed.

"I'm not crazy about the guy on the far-left end of the back row," she whispered.

"The football coach?"

"Right. I didn't like the way he said 'Persians.'"

"Of course, Oz isn't Persian."

"No, but he hangs with them. I think the coach is holding something back."

"Everyone is holding something back."

"He keeps sneaking glances at Oz. With an odd expression."

"He's probably trying to figure out how such a WASP-looking guy has an Arab surname."

"They're all wondering about that. This is something more. He's curious and . . . irritated. Or offended. Or . . . something."

"Like maybe he thinks Oz is some kind of traitor?"

"At any rate, he's going to be particularly susceptible to the garbage Thrillkill will try to shove down their throats."

"Okay, he's gone." Oz didn't object. He was strategically placed between the two of us, so we both had ample opportunity to smile at him, clap him on the shoulders, and offer him Life Savers, standard defense attorney tricks to show the jury that the defendant's lawyers like their client (or, at the least, aren't afraid of him). "Anyone who concerns you, Oz?"

He didn't hesitate. "Lady in the middle of the first row. The checker at Crest."

"You think she doesn't like you?"

He shrugged. "Looks like a hard-ass to me."

She did have a stern demeanor. But in my experience, sometimes the sternest jurors, particularly older women, could be the most insistent that the prosecutors actually meet their burden of proof, rather than voting to convict because the defendant is "probably guilty." "That could be good for us."

"Nah. She's a punisher. I can tell. I've dated younger versions. Insecure and mean. Feel superior if they can point out the faults of others. Did you see how she nodded with approval when the guy sitting beside her talked about his nephew getting two years for possessing a joint?"

In fact, I hadn't, but Christina had. "Law and order freak?" I asked her.

"Or believes the world is losing its standards of decency and we have to be rigorous or civilization will collapse," she replied. "Which is usually another way of justifying meanness."

"Okay. Another juror to remove."

When I did, I could see the judge was not pleased. But I hadn't exhausted my peremptories, so he kept his thoughts to himself and called two more people into the box. Neither presented any problems. By five, it was all over.

The jury was assembled. The trial could now begin. God help us all. And Oz in particular.

CHAPTER 31

Before the trial resumed the next day, I told Oz to brace himself for what he would hear during Thrillkill's opening statement. In truth, I didn't know what the man would say, but I doubted that Oz would enjoy listening to it. In opening statement, the attorney is supposed to preview the evidence that will be produced later. The attorney is not supposed to argue. But lawyers love to argue, so this is like telling a dog not to sniff butts.

The prosecutor always gets the first shot. Thrillkill rose, stood squarely before the jury, calmly and confidently, with no notes, no exhibits, just him and them. I admired his lack of artifice and professionalism. He was an excellent speaker but not overbearing, and in the courtroom, that was best. Jurors tended to dislike lawyers—or witnesses—they felt were putting on a show. They wanted to be observers, flies on the wall, objective witnesses.

"First of all," Thrillkill said, "I want to thank you for your service. I know you have real lives, jobs and families, and errands and other things you could be doing right now. I thank you for fulfilling your civic obligations and playing this vital role in the enforcement of our laws and the maintenance of order in these troubled times."

Thrillkill was already arguing. The first bit wasn't relevant;. That was just sucking up. But the rest of it promoted the idea that this prosecution, and a guilty verdict, were essential to staving off anarchy, fighting back the barbarians at the gate. People are so easily manipulated. The subconscious makes our most important decisions.

"It's a particular pleasure," Thrillkill continued, "to see people willing to stand up here in Oklahoma City. This city has seen great troubles over the years, everything from cattle rustlers to terrorists, but we've always come through it with our chins up and our strength intact. This is a fine city, and our citizens are among the—"

"This isn't relevant," the judge interrupted. "Get to the case."

My eyes widened. That didn't happen often. Your conduct typically had to be egregious to draw an objection during opening. To have the judge voluntarily cut you off meant he found this a monumental waste of time, he was in a seriously bad mood, or he just didn't like the cut of Thrillkill's jib. I hoped for the latter.

Thrillkill cleared his throat and proceeded as if nothing had happened. "This case is important, serious, and will demand your complete attention. But I cannot say that it's complex. In many respects, it's quite simple. The victim, as you may have already guessed from the questioning you received, is Khalid Nazir, a CIA agent who worked to root out terrorist threats before they happened. The evidence will show that the man who killed him was the defendant, Omar al-Jabbar." He gestured in Oz's direction, as if the jury couldn't figure out which one he was for themselves.

"The evidence will show that this man was detained by federal authorities on a previous occasion due to his involvement with a known terrorist group. The evidence will show that he bore a grudge against Agent Nazir and had sworn revenge. The evidence will show that he was at the scene of the crime and was arrested, only moments after the murder occurred, with the murder weapon in his possession. And when a man who has sworn revenge is found at the scene of the crime with the smoking gun, common sense should prevail."

Thrillkill inched a few steps closer, leaning gently against the rail separating him from the jury. "There will be other evidence, conclusive evidence, more than is probably necessary. I want you to reach your verdict without any lingering doubts. You will learn what kind of person the defendant is, his . . . habits and . . . proclivities, his fondness for explosives, and the . . . horrifying ways he spent his time and made his money. Motive, means, and opportunity all prove that he committed this brutal crime as the latest and most lethal cog in an ongoing series of crimes against humanity and the Unites States of America."

Oz and I exchanged a quick glance. Horrifying way he spent his time and made his money? I'd been over everything the prosecution had sent me repeatedly. I hadn't seen anything I'd call horrifying. I hadn't seen much indication that Oz ever made much money, either.

I made a note to ask Oz as soon as I got a chance.

"The defense may attempt to confuse the matter, but you're too smart for that. By the end of the trial, you'll find you have more than enough evidence to find the defendant guilty beyond a reasonable doubt. And then I will ask you to impose the ultimate sanction, the death penalty. This was a hate crime against a federal intelligence officer. This was a politically motivated crime, a terrorist act. And we cannot let that go unpunished. To the contrary, we must strike back with all possible vigor if we hope to keep this nation secure. We want our loved ones to be safe. We must inform everyone who would resort to violence that the United States will find them and punish them as they deserve. Thank you."

A little more jingoistic than I'd expected, but basically a sturdy opening statement. I knew I was nothing like the orator Thrillkill was and hated having to follow his act. I probably should've asked Christina to give the opening, but it was too late now. I had to push myself to my feet and do the best job I could with what I had.

"Ladies and gentlemen of the jury." A little old-fashioned, but I couldn't help myself. My mother taught me to use good manners. I also needed to break the grim mood Thrillkill set, a heaviness that could only incline the jurors to reach a guilty verdict. At the same time, I couldn't be seen as trivializing such a serious crime. Like everything else a defense lawyer has to do in the courtroom, it was a tightrope act.

"Have any of you been to the state fair?" I paused, even though no one was likely to answer aloud. "I'll bet some of you have. The fairgrounds are only about ten miles from here, and every year the same traveling show comes back to town. Some may prefer the rickety rides, or some may prefer the livestock shows. When I was a little boy, I preferred the midway."

I was relieved that the judge didn't cut me off. He probably had a hunch where this was going. This charming anecdote was, of course, totally concocted. Although I'd pleaded, my father never took Julia or me to the fair. He was always working, and he thought the fair was a lower-class waste of time. "Moron heaven," he called it.

I continued my opening. "Perhaps I shouldn't admit it, but I was always intrigued by the carnies and the freak show. A bearded lady? A snake woman? What could these abominations possibly be? The most intriguing to me, because I loved horses, was the World's Smallest Horse. You couldn't see it unless you paid your five-dollar fare and walked up a platform, but judging from the small box up there, that horse must be tiny indeed. Lilliputian. At that time, five dollars was a fortune. With five dollars I could buy thirty-two comic books or twenty paperbacks or the new Partridge Family LP. But one time, curiosity got the best of me. I laid down my hard-earned fiver for a peek."

I paused, ventured a small smile, made eye contact, and proceeded. "You know what? It was a Shetland pony. Small, yes, but hardly freakish. The box had a trick bottom that you couldn't see from the outside. Only the head rose up into that little box. The rest of the horse was underneath. It was all an illusion. Smoke and mirrors."

I glanced down thoughtfully. "At this point, you're probably wondering why I'm telling you this story. It's because I learned two powerful lessons that day. The first? Things are not always what they seem. And the second?" I cast a quick glance back toward Thrillkill. "A good carnival barker can convince gullible people of almost anything."

Oh, I would pay for that one. Thrillkill would be angry for weeks. But I hoped I'd started the jury thinking.

"The prosecutor has given you a preview of some of the facts of this case, but only some, and those were chosen selectively to give you what I consider to be a misleading picture of what happened. He mentioned that my client, Omar—his friends call him Oz—was detained by the CIA. But the evidence will show that Oz was detained for twenty-one days, interrogated extensively and cruelly, subjected to what many would call torture—but he was never charged with any crime. The evidence will show Oz was released because the government did not have and never had any evidence that he'd committed a crime. And here they are back again, with only slightly more evidence than they had the first time around."

Now I had the jury's interest. I had to make sure I didn't lose it. Momentum was everything.

"Yes, Mr. Nazir worked for the CIA, but the evidence will show that he had previously worked for the Iraqi military's Republican Guard as a brutal interrogator who tortured and murdered many American soldiers. After Desert Storm, Nazir switched sides and defected to America. He had a list of enemies as long as Santa Claus's list of naughty children."

I continued in the same vein. "Yes, Oz was at the scene of Mr. Nazir's death, but the evidence will show that more than four hundred other people were there, and if anyone saw who shot Nazir, they have yet to come forward. The evidence will show that Oz was singled out almost immediately, attacked and arrested under keenly suspicious circumstances that suggest that he may in fact have been targeted from the outset."

I stepped closer, giving the jurors my most earnest expression. "I do not ask you to believe anything just because I say it. Don't rely on words you hear from lawyers. Pay attention to the evidence. At the end of the trial, I am confident you will find the prosecution has no proof rising to the level of 'beyond a reasonable doubt.' Furthermore, after we've presented our case, I believe you will be convinced that Oz did not commit this crime"—I paused dramatically, signaling them that something important was coming—"and furthermore, you'll have a pretty good idea who did."

There it was, out on the table. SODDIT. If the jury remembered nothing else, they would remember that promise. I would have to deliver a suspect. Unfortunately, at this juncture, I hadn't a clue who that might be. "Thank you for your attention."

I took my seat. The judge leaned forward, checking his watch. "Very good. Let's begin. "Mr. Thrillkill, you may call your first witness."

CHAPTER 32

S ometimes prosecutors like to lead with a zinger. A powerful or surprising witness to widen the jurors' eyes, convince them of guilt, and make them think the trial is going to be a good deal more exciting than it will probably turn out to be. But not this time. Thrillkill went with the tried-and-true slow-burn approach, leading with a series of witnesses who were arguably necessary but none too exciting.

His first witness was Officer Marlon Parkland, a three-year member of the OKC PD, who was on duty at the capitol building on the fateful day. There was nothing exceptional or remarkable about his background or experience, and Thrillkill ran through both quickly. He was a short man and a little stout, with an expression that suggested he took himself very seriously. Or at any rate, that he did today.

"Did anything unusual occur that day?" Thrillkill asked the officer. He couldn't lead the witness, but his tone was so innocuous it bordered on the absurd.

"A shot rang out during the press conference. From my position in the rear, I saw Agent Nazir's head jerk violently backward. Then he crumpled to the platform."

"What happened next?"

"The crowd reacted. Panic. Screams. Chaos. Everyone ran one way or the other, colliding and crushing. Mass confusion. I did my best to sort things out, but there were too many people for me to make much impact."

"Did anything in particular catch your attention?"

"Yes. I saw some kind of scuffle taking place on the east side of the plaza. Two men engaged in an altercation. I moved toward them with the intent of breaking it up."

So what my witness described as one man tackling another, this witness described as an altercation. And yet I didn't doubt the officer was telling what he thought to be the truth. It was all a matter of perspective.

"What happened?"

"Before I got there, one of the men fell to the ground, the other on top of him. Soon two others had stumbled on top of them. This created an obstacle, and there were so many people moving so quickly that there was significant danger. So I rushed in to intervene."

"Do you know who any of these people you've described were?"

"I never got a good look at the others. But the first man on the ground was the defendant. Omar al-Jabbar."

I saw some of the jurors nodding.

"What did you do when you arrived?"

"First, I established a perimeter, for his own safety. Once I had a chance to focus, I noticed that the defendant held a handgun in his right hand."

"How did you react?"

"I drew my own weapon and ordered the suspect to drop his."

"Did he comply?"

"No. I reached down and took the gun from him."

"And then?"

"By that time, two other officers had arrived. With their help, we hoisted the defendant to his feet and cuffed him."

"Was the defendant cooperative?"

"Not at all."

"Did he say anything?"

"He called us fascists. Said we had no right to arrest him. And he spoke quite a bit in a language I didn't understand. Sounded foreign. Middle Eastern or something."

"Objection," I said quietly. "The witness said he didn't understand it, so he can't identify the language."

The judge nodded. "Sustained."

"Thank you, Officer," Thrillkill said. "No more questions."

This was a classic example of a witness who might be better not to cross at all. Little good could come of it. He was, after all, just doing his job. But I could see Thrillkill elicited the man's testimony the same way he made speeches, selectively choosing what he wanted to emerge and omitting what he didn't. I indulged myself in the notion that I might be able to make a point or two on cross.

I kept my distance from the witness and remained professional. Cops hate defense lawyers, and given how they sometimes get spun around on the stand, I don't really blame them. I tried not to incur his wrath.

"You said you saw the defendant engage in what you described as an altercation. Isn't it true that he was assaulted by the second man? Knocked to the ground by him?"

"I didn't see that." Good response, actually. He chose not to argue. Just stood by what he said the first time. I didn't push it. I'd planted the idea in the jurors' heads. We'd come back to it later.

"You did see the defendant on the ground, though, right?"

The officer nodded. "With the gun in his hand."

"Were his eyes open?"

He thought a moment before answering.

"Yes."

"When you first arrived?"

Another brief hesitation. "I'm not sure."

"So his eyes might have been closed." Good enough. "You said the defendant did not cooperate when arrested. Did he resist arrest?"

Parkland tilted his head. "He wasn't happy about it."

"I don't know anyone who would be. But did he actually resist?"

"He didn't respond when I told him to drop the gun."

"Is it possible he'd been knocked unconscious?"

"He did eventually respond."

"But before that?"

Parkland shrugged. "I don't know. I'm not a doctor."

"You would expect his responses to be sluggish if he'd been knocked out, right?"

"Maybe. He came to life soon enough. Spouting all that foreign stuff."

"You said you saw the gun in the defendant's hand. Do you know how it got there?"

"I assume he pulled it—"

"Excuse me, Officer, but I didn't ask you to assume anything, nor will I ever. Do you know how the gun got there?"

"I didn't see that."

"Is it possible someone else put the gun in his hand? Like the other man in the so-called altercation."

"I didn't see that."

"Is it possible?"

"Anything's possible. But if someone offered me a gun at a crime scene, I wouldn't take it. And if they put it in my hand, I'd drop it. Fast."

"Motion to strike the nonresponsive part of that response."

"Sustained," the judge grunted.

I addressed the officer. "You might drop the gun if you were alert and awake. But you couldn't do that if you were unconscious, could you, Officer?"

"Objection," Thrillkill said. "Calls for speculation."

"Sustained."

I hoped I'd made my point with the jury. "One last thing I want to be clear on, sir. Did you see my client fire that gun?"

"No."

"Thank you. No more questions."

CHAPTER 33

The next two witnesses established the chain of custody for all the physical evidence the prosecution would present. Everything was logged, catalogued, and preserved as it should have been. No surprises there. I didn't cross-examine.

The next witness was a fingerprint expert, a woman, not the same person Thrillkill used at the preliminary hearing. I wondered if that was because there were so many women on the jury. I'd read her report. She would establish that Oz's fingerprints were on the gun and that the paraffin test showed he'd fired a gun recently. None of this was remotely controversial or in question, so the only purpose of my cross-examination would be to explain to the jury what this did and did not prove.

"You said the test showed the defendant fired a firearm." I asked. "Correct?"

Dr. Brenda Adams straightened and smiled. "That's correct."

"But let's be clear—that doesn't prove that he fired the murder weapon, does it?"

It obviously did as far as she was concerned. "Well…"

"You can't prove what gun he fired, can you?"

"His fingerprints were on the murder weapon."

"Which also does not prove he fired that gun, does it?"

"It proves he held it in his hand."

"We already know it was in his hand. But you can't prove that he fired it, can you?"

"I know he fired something."

"Would your findings be the same if he had fired a gun the night before at a firing range?"

"I suppose."

"In fact, the results would be the same if he had fired a gun anytime in the last twenty-four hours, wouldn't they?"

"That's true. But—"

"Did you find any DNA evidence on the gun?"

Too much hesitation. "That's not my department."

"You work in forensics, don't you? I would imagine you know if forensics found any DNA evidence."

"We did not."

"Wouldn't you expect to find something? Flakes of skin. Spittle. Something?"

"In the midst of so much activity—"

"You found no DNA evidence."

"No."

"Thank you, Doctor."

I was playing a game of inches. The prosecutor was building a Lego house, and I was trying to knock it down, one brick at a time. I had a tiny hammer. But Oz's life would depend upon how many bricks still stood when we finished.

⁂

DURING THE BREAK, BEFORE THRILLKILL CALLED HIS NEXT WITNESS, Christina left to make a phone call home. I didn't know how long that might take, but a few minutes later, I was pleased to see her slide into the chair beside me. I probably shouldn't admit it, because I'm a hard-as-nails trial attorney and all, but I always felt a wave of comfort when she sat beside me, in court or anywhere else. Knowing someone had my back was a relatively new sensation for me. Which is why my ongoing attitude was always "anything Christina needs, Christina gets." When it comes to making decisions, she frequently tells me that I'm the boss, but I've never been stupid enough to believe it.

"Everything good at home?" I whispered.

"Seems to be. Julia has the girls under control."

"And you're okay with that?"

"She does have mommy experience."

"Ish."

"She's actually very capable."

"Good."

Thrillkill called Officer Takei to the stand. He was the bombshell witness at the preliminary hearing. His testimony would have a huge impact on the jury, but at least this time I wouldn't be caught by surprise. I had my panoply of excuses and hoped that, even if the jury didn't really buy them, they wouldn't laugh right in my face.

The judge swore Takei in. Thrillkill took him through the preliminaries and established who he was and what he did on the day of the shooting. He did not waste much time getting to Oz's apartment.

"Have you seen these before?" Thrillkill handed him a sheaf of documents that had been premarked as "Prosecution Exhibit 17."

"Yes."

"Where did you see them?"

"In the defendant's apartment."

"Objection." I rose to my feet. "It wasn't only the defendant's apartment. Several people shared the space and had access."

"Nonetheless," Thrillkill said, "it was the defendant's apartment."

"That many other people had access to."

"And now, Counsel," the judge said curtly, "I believe you're arguing, not objecting. Overruled."

But I made my point with the jury, just the same. I wanted them remembering, throughout this testimony, that Oz was not the only person who could've placed suspicious items on the premises. Just in case they took the phrase "reasonable doubt" seriously.

Thrillkill continued. "Did you find these documents in the apartment where the defendant ate and lived and slept?"

"Yes. On the desk."

"Could you describe them for the jury, please?"

"Many appear to relate to an organization called PACT."

"And what is PACT?"

"It's an organization of people sympathetic to Middle Eastern causes and the rights of Middle Eastern people."

"A militant organization?"

"Objection," I said. "Outside the witness's expertise."

The judge shrugged. "He can answer, if he knows."

Takei nodded. "PACT has been associated with several violent crimes in the past."

Thrillkill continued. "What do these PACT documents say?"

"Some are general business documents. Some are written in a kind of code. I can't read it. And some specifically reference Agent Nazir."

"Let's talk about those. What do they say about Nazir?"

"The documents indicate that PACT considered him a threat. One of them specifically says that, and here I'm quoting, 'He must be stopped.'"

Thrillkill paused for a moment, letting that sink into the jurors' heads. "Did you search anywhere other than the desk?"

"Yes, I searched the entire apartment."

"Did you discover anything out of the ordinary?"

"The medicine cabinet was filled with opioids. Mostly OxyContin. A few others. Serious mind- and mood-altering narcotics."

"Objection to the witness's commentary," I said, not bothering to rise.

"Your Honor," Thrillkill rejoined, "I think we all know that opioids alter a person's personality and thinking."

"Then we have no need for this witness's unqualified testimony on the subject," I replied.

"Your Honor," Thrillkill pressed, "when someone is taking large quantities of drugs of this nature, there's no telling what they might do."

"And who's arguing now?" I asked.

The judge almost smiled. "The objection is sustained. The witness will limit his testimony to his personal knowledge."

Takei tucked in his chin. "Yes, Your Honor."

"How much of these narcotics did you discover?"

"Over a hundred pills. And judging by the amounts given on the labels, many had been consumed."

"Thank you. Did you find anything else of note in the apartment?"

Takei hedged. "Not . . . in the apartment."

Thrillkill took the cue. "Did you search the surrounding area?"

"Yes. In particular, a storage shed behind the building."

"Was the shed locked?"

"Yes. I used wire cutters to sever the chain."

"And what did you find inside?"

"Explosives."

The reaction in the jury box was noticeable. Perhaps they hadn't heard the media reports.

"What kind of explosives?"

"Various incendiary devices involving gunpowder. Some electronic devices. And beside the fireworks . . . I found several bags of fertilizer."

Thrillkill knew what he was doing. He chose his clincher with fore-thought and skill.

"Thank you, Officer. No more questions at this time.

CHAPTER 34

My turn. I rose to my feet and walked halfway to the witness stand. "Thank you for coming today, Officer Takei. We all appreciate your devotion to duty."

The officer tipped his head. He wasn't buying it. And well he shouldn't. But I saw nothing wrong with being polite at the outset. In a few minutes, he was going to hate my guts.

"I heard you say you found the documents identified as Exhibit 17 in the defendant's apartment. I didn't hear you say he wrote any of them. Do you know whether he did?"

"Well, I presume—"

"Excuse me, Officer, but I'm not asking you to guess. As the judge indicated, we only want you to testify about what you know. Who wrote the documents?"

"In most cases, the documents are unsigned."

"In most cases. Then in some cases, the documents are signed?"

"Yes."

"By whom?"

"By someone named Mina Ali."

"And that's not the defendant."

"No."

"In fact, when the jury has a chance to examine the documents for themselves, they'll see that the defendant's name does not appear on any of the documents, does it?"

"Not that I recall."

"Did you investigate Ms. Ali?"

Thrillkill stood. "We did, Your Honor, and in fact we may call her to the stand at a later time."

"That doesn't answer my question," I rejoined, "nor does Mr. Thrillkill need to be answering the witness's questions for him."

The judge frowned. "The witness will respond."

"I never questioned that woman," Takei said.

"So you never asked her if she wrote the documents."

"I didn't, no."

"But you told the jury you made a thorough investigation."

"Of the defendant's apartment."

"Except it wasn't just *his* apartment, was it?"

"He had access to it."

"As did many other people, correct?"

"My understanding is that he had roommates."

"The truth is you don't know who wrote those documents or who left them on the desk, do you?"

"I know the defendant was associated with PACT and—"

"Officer, you are not answering my question. Do you know for a fact who wrote those documents?"

"No."

"Do you know who left them on the desk?"

"No."

"These documents contain information about Nazir's use of torture and other 'enhanced interrogation techniques,' but there are no actual plans or threats made again Nazir or anyone else, true?"

"One memo says, 'He must be stopped.'"

"Is it wrong to want torture to end?"

"Another document says, 'The day of reckoning is fast approaching.'"

"So?"

"Sounds like a threat to me."

"You realize that comes from the Bible. Don't you? It's in the Koran, too. Not surprising, since the Koran incorporates a great deal of the Bible. Do you think the Bible threatens the US government?"

"No."

"But a reference to a passage in Isaiah does?"

"You have to consider the context."

"In your case, sir, I think that's all you considered. You found out Oz was Muslim, and you pronounced him guilty on the spot."

"That's not—"

"Here's another document I'd like you to look at. May I approach?" The judge nodded. I handed Takei a brochure. "Would you read the first sentence on the front cover, please?"

He did as instructed, a surly expression on his face. "The day of reckoning is fast approaching."

"Is that another threat to the American way of life?"

"It's an NRA brochure."

At least two of the jurors smiled. "You're an NRA member, aren't you, Officer?" I didn't know, but sometimes you just have to take your best shot.

Pay dirt. "Yes."

"Is the NRA a threat to the US government?"

"Definitely not."

"And yet they use the same dangerous language. In an equally unsigned document. Is it possible this is a common phrase used when urging people to take political action?"

Takei shrugged.

"You do believe in the First Amendment, don't you?"

"Yes."

"That's good to know. Now I'd like you to look at the third document in that exhibit, the one you indicated was written in code." He turned to the page I indicated. "How do you know it's written in code?"

He shrugged. "It's gibberish. Doesn't make any sense."

"To you, maybe. Could it be written in a foreign language?"

He peered at the page. "Looks like American letters to me. Just doesn't make sense."

"Are you a scientist?"

"No."

"Could these be chemical equations?"

"I couldn't tell you."

"This is, in fact, a series of formulae describing a potentially valuable isotope of iridium. This is a draft of an attachment to an article written by an Iraqi scientist named Yasmin al-Tikrit."

"If you say so."

"Now let's talk about the drugs. The truth is those drugs you mentioned were prescription drugs, weren't they?"

"I suppose."

"And all the pill bottles you found bore prescription labels, didn't they?"

"I believe so, yes."

"You mentioned that taking pills could affect someone's behavior. Someone going off their doctor-prescribed meds could alter their behavior, too, couldn't it?"

"That's not my area of expertise."

"Really? A minute ago you knew all about the potential effects of these drugs. Now you don't?"

"Objection," Thrillkill said wearily. "Argumentative."

The judge tilted his head. "Counsel does make a point. But I think the jury has the idea. Let's move on."

Being the hardheaded defense attorney I am, however, I was not quite ready to move along. "You don't have any objection to someone taking medication prescribed by a physician, do you?"

"Of course not."

"Did you make any effort to find out why these drugs were prescribed?"

"I know on the street OxyContin is a popular—"

"Pain reliever," I said, cutting in. "It's a pain reliever, right?"

"Yes."

"Why would a doctor prescribe a pain reliever?"

Takei's silence was even better than an answer. It gave the jury a moment to consider the question.

"You are aware that the defendant served in Iraq, right?"

"Yes."

"You are aware that he suffered severe injuries? That he's been diagnosed with PTSD?"

"Yes."

"Do you suppose that could relate to why a doctor might prescribe pain relievers?"

"I couldn't speculate."

Now I'd made my point, so it was indeed time to move on. "Let's discuss that storage shed. How many people had access?"

"It was locked."

"How many people had the key?"

"I don't know."

"Did Mina Ali?"

"I don't know."

"Because you never bothered to talk to her. What about her brother, Kir? He came to the apartment frequently, didn't he?"

"I don't know."

"Did he have access?"

"I don't know."

"Sounds to me like, after you found the so-called explosives, you stopped investigating."

"That's not true."

"Or to be more accurate, you stopped investigating anyone other than the defendant. Because you'd already made up your mind that he was guilty. Based on unsigned memos and prescription meds."

"That isn't true."

"You mentioned fertilizer. Is it unusual for people in Oklahoma to have fertilizer in the gardening shed?"

"We all know that fertilizer can be used—"

"Motion to strike. Nonresponsive. Let's try this again, Officer. Is it unusual for Oklahomans to have fertilizer in the gardening shed?"

"It wasn't just a gardening shed."

"I bet you have fertilizer in your garage as we speak. True?"

He squirmed. "Possibly."

"Did you discover any bomb components?"

"There were some computers."

"But no bombs. Right?"

"Not yet."

"Isn't it a fact that what you're calling explosives were actually fireworks?"

"What's the difference? Both contain gunpowder and fuses."

"What's the difference? In Oklahoma? In June? Who doesn't have fireworks?"

Takei frowned. "Foreigners."

"Foreigners can't be patriots?"

"People conspiring to bring down the government aren't likely to celebrate Independence Day."

"Except my client isn't a foreigner. He's a US citizen. Born and raised in Oklahoma."

Takei shifted his weight.

"Did you find any evidence indicating that Oz wanted to bring down the government?"

He hedged. "The documents speak for themselves."

"The documents don't say a word about bringing down the government, and you admitted you don't know who wrote them. You're not basing this accusation on evidence. You're basing it on Oz's religion and politics."

"We're trained to keep an eye out for people who pose a threat."

"Such as?"

Takei was becoming agitated, which caused him to speak more freely than he probably should. "Look, we all know who brought down the World Trade Center. We know who supports PACT, which your boy was—"

"You're saying that, because Oz—an American citizen—is also a Muslim interested in political and religious freedom, he's a terrorist."

"I didn't say that. But we have to take care of our people. We'll be the first blamed if we slip up. That's just reality."

"I think the reality is that you targeted Oz because he's Muslim. You decided he was guilty before you got to that apartment, and then you turned garbage into evidence to prove the conclusion you'd already reached."

Takei leaned forward, rising a bit. "We targeted him because he shot Nazir!"

A loud buzz rose out of the gallery. The judge pounded his gavel, trying to bring the courtroom back into order. He was not happy. "Strike that outburst from the record. Anything further, Mr. Kincaid?"

"Yes. Officer Takei, what did you mean just now when you used the word *targeted*." Just to remind the jury that he did.

"I didn't mean that. I was using your words. I meant to say 'investigated.'"

I just let that hang in the air a few moments.

"Anything else?" Judge Santino asked.

"No, Your Honor."

Thrillkill chose not to redirect. I returned to our table. I couldn't read Oz. He probably didn't know what to think of that spectacle. I trusted Christina's instincts.

"Did I do any good?"

She shrugged. "I think you did the best you could with a bad hand."

I nodded. Probably the best I could hope for under the circumstances. But I wasn't at all sure it would be enough to save Oz's neck.

CHAPTER 35

Thrillkill could see the clock just as easily as I could, and I knew he would plan the remainder of the day accordingly. When you schedule your witnesses, there are practical constraints, like the witnesses' availability. But first and foremost, you must never forget that you're putting on a show for the jurors, and jurors like to be entertained (without feeling that they're being entertained). When the trial turns tedious, you can't count on them absorbing anything you or your witnesses say. You have to maintain rhythm and pace.

Thrillkill needed a witness he could squeeze into the remaining time and still feel he ended the day on a high note, leaving the jurors enthralled and itching to convict. It would seem he felt he had just the witness to do the trick.

"The United States calls Traye Conners."

Conners was a middle-aged man, heavyset, a little stubbly, but not unfashionably so. Definitely of white European descent.

Thrillkill quickly established who he was, where he was from, and that he worked in Nazir's CIA office. "What did you do for Agent Nazir?"

"I was his personal assistant."

"Can you describe the duties you performed?"

"About what you would expect." He shifted his weight somewhat awkwardly. He was not the first large man who found it challenging to squeeze into the witness box. "I screened his phone calls. Opened the mail. Typed his correspondence. Kept his calendar. The usual."

"In the course of performing your duties, did you ever have an opportunity to see or read correspondence directed to Agent Nazir?"

"Yes, regularly. I screened his mail just as I did his phone calls."

"Have you ever seen this before?" He approached with the document premarked "Prosecution Exhibit 21."

"Yes, I have."

"Would you tell the jury what it is?"

"This is a letter we received on"—he checked the stamp on the front of the attached envelope—"May fourteenth."

"Could you describe the contents for the jury?"

"It's a death threat."

I saw a woman on the front row of the jury box stiffen slightly. "Objection," I said. "Instead of characterizing the contents, why don't we have the witness read it and let the jury decide for themselves?"

The judge shook his head. "This is not your witness examination, though if you want to do that on cross, you are free to do so."

I'd planted the seed. It was all I could do at this point.

"A threat against whom?"

"Agent Nazir."

"Who's making the threat?"

"The letter is unsigned. But it makes specific reference to"—he glanced down—"the torture and brutal mistreatment of Omar al-Jabbar."

"Did you make any effort to find out who sent the letter?"

"Yes. We launched a full investigation. We take threats seriously."

"What did you do?"

"We organized—"

"Objection," I said. "The witness was asked what he did, but he's about to tell us what his office did. He should only be speaking about activities of which he has personal knowledge."

Thrillkill picked up on that. "Mr. Conners, are you familiar with the investigation your office conducted into the letter?"

"Extremely."

"Were you involved in the investigation?"

"Very much so."

The judge nodded. "You may proceed."

Conners picked up right where he left off. "We used the postmark to trace the letter to a particular post office."

"Which office?"

"The one two blocks from the defendant's apartment."

"Anything else?"

"We ran fingerprint tests."

"What did you find?"

"Nothing one hundred percent conclusive. But some partial prints that would be consistent with handling by the defendant."

"So there's a good chance the defendant held the envelope."

"Objection. Leading."

The judge nodded. "Sustained. Let the witness choose his own words."

Thrillkill rephrased. "Do you have an opinion as to whether the defendant held this envelope?"

"Given the fingerprint evidence, there's a good chance that he did."

"Thank you. Pass the witness."

I'll give Thrillkill credit for moving things along, if nothing else. He was not wasting anyone's time.

I plowed right in, even though I knew I had precious little that was going to make any difference to the jury. "You said the letter contained a death threat, but I noticed you never read the alleged threat. What does the letter actually say?"

"Basically, it warns Nazir—"

"Sir, I did not ask for the Cliffs Notes version. Read us what the letter actually says."

I could see his hands trembled. I didn't normally think of myself as the kind of guy who inspires fear and dread, but being a witness was always nerve-racking. "It says, 'Behold the pale rider will come for you, and his name is death.'"

"And you think that's a death threat?"

"Yeah. What do you think it is?"

"I think it's another verse from the Bible. And what do you know, I just happen to have one on me." I read from the Book of Revelation, the King James Version. "'And I looked and beheld a pale horse: and his name that sat on him was Death, and Hell followed with him.'" I closed the book. "Do you find the Bible threatening?"

"Well, no .

"Then why would you find a Bible verse threatening?"

"It seemed clear given the context—"

"What context? That's all the letter says."

"It has Agent Nazir's name at the top."

"And that makes the Bible verse a threat?"

"That's how I read it."

"Because that's how you wanted to read it. Or, rather, that's how you want the jury to read it."

"Look, we're in the intelligence business. We have to respond to potential threats against our agents. There are many people who would like to take out every CIA agent on earth."

"Would you be willing to admit that, at best, this message is ambiguous?"

"If you say so."

"If someone really wanted to threaten or terrorize a CIA agent, they could probably do a better job of it than this rather vague message."

"Like how?"

"Like saying, 'I'm going to kill you.'"

"Perhaps he's on a religious jihad."

"So you think the defendant is dangerous because he's Muslim."

"I didn't say that."

"Sounded like it."

Thrillkill jumped to his rescue. "Your Honor, this is argumentative. He's deliberately trying to confuse the witness."

The judge drew himself up. "I do get the sense that we are not moving forward. Let's move on, Counselor."

I was done anyway. "Mr. Conners, you said the fingerprints on the envelope could belong to the defendant."

"I did."

"And then again, they might not. Correct?"

"The partial latents we discovered were consistent—"

"Forgive me, but you're not answering the question. Isn't it a fact that they might not belong to the defendant?"

"They are consistent—"

"Which is your convoluted way of saying they might or might not belong to the defendant. Right?"

Conners was pissed. "Whatever."

"Did you take prints from anyone else who had access to the apartment where Oz lived?"

"No."

"You didn't think that might be relevant?"

"Not particularly."

"Because you'd already decided who committed the crime?"

"Because we already had a fingerprint match."

"A possible fingerprint match. And just to be clear, even if this were a one hundred percent certain fingerprint match—which it isn't—that still wouldn't prove Oz wrote the letter or mailed it, right? Only that, at some time or another, he touched the envelope."

"I suppose."

I turned as if finished, but of course I wasn't. I just wanted him to experience that brief moment of relief arising from thinking the persecution was over—and then to tear it away from him. "Oh, one more thing—did you check the letter for fingerprints?"

"What?"

"You checked the envelope. Logically, you must've checked the letter, too."

"Right."

"Now anyone could've touched the envelope at some stage in its travels, but the letter must've been touched by whoever wrote it."

"True."

"But you didn't find anything remotely like Oz's fingerprints on the letter, did you?"

"What we found was a mass of unclear prints that made analysis difficult to—"

"I'm sorry, but you're not answering my question. You didn't find Oz's fingerprints on the letter, did you?"

"No. We found no clear prints. Only smudges."

"So you do not know who wrote or sent that letter. Which only contains a Bible verse. Thank you. No more questions."

I headed back to my table. Christina gave me a little wink. I'd done the best I could to spoil Thrillkill's end-of-day witness.

One Lego brick at a time . . .

CHAPTER 36

Next day, Thrillkill dragged us through several more technical witnesses and laid various bits of his circumstantial patchwork quilt. Exactly the kind of witnesses you want to blow through quickly before the jury is completely awake.

I was surprised that Thrillkill called his PACT witness so early in the trial. When I thought about it a little more, though, I realized how potentially dangerous this witness could be for him. Yes, he wanted to establish Oz's connection with this so-called terrorist organization, and perhaps to elicit some testimony about Oz's bitterness over his arrest and interrogation. But he certainly didn't want PACT going on about the injustice of CIA actions or Oz's torture.

"Do you know the defendant?" Thrillkill asked.

"Yes." The witness, Kaivon Siddig, sat tall in the seat, long, dark somewhat-wavy hair pulled back behind his head. His face bore a seriousness that made you wonder if he'd been born a political activist.

"How did you meet him?"

"He came to the PACT offices, not far from the mall."

"Why?"

"He said he was sympathetic to our goals."

"And what are your goals?"

"We hope to improve the public opinion of and ensure rights for Americans of Middle Eastern descent, especially citizens from Iraq. Most are no different from any other Americans, with kids and mortgages and car payments. Most deplore the idea of random violence perpetrated against innocent people for political causes. Not everyone from the Middle East is a member of al-Qaeda or the Taliban or ISIS. Not everyone supports the Syrian government or, for that matter, the rebels. We want the same peace and safety as everyone else."

"Part of your agenda is to seek redress for past offenses."

"That's the work of JUSTICE IRAQ."

"Your sister organization. Doesn't that by definition make you an antigovernment organization?"

"I disagree. I don't think anyone is naive enough to think the government has never done anything wrong. Sometimes we make mistakes—especially in wartime. That's all the more reason to be diligent about addressing those mistakes later."

"Fair enough. Let's get back to your discussions with the defendant. Did he ever mention any grudges again the US government?"

"Not when I first met him. But later."

"What was his complaint?"

"He felt he had been treated poorly at the hands of the CIA."

"Did he mention the late Agent Nazir?"

"Yes."

"Would you please tell the jury what he said about Agent Nazir?"

Siddig cleared his throat. "According to Oz, Nazir was instrumental in his arrest and . . . interrogation by the CIA." No doubt Thrillkill had instructed him not to use the word "torture."

"Did you ever hear him indicate that he wanted to do something to avenge this allegedly wrongful treatment?"

"I never heard him use the word 'avenge.' But he did say we needed to do something about Nazir. He said if this man were not stopped, there was no telling how many people he might harm."

"And how exactly did he propose to stop Nazir?"

Siddig hesitated—just a fraction too long. "He never specifically said."

"Sir, I know you are possibly sympathetic to the defendant and his political goals, but you are under oath, subject to prosecution for perjury if you withhold the truth. Let me ask you again. Isn't it true that the defendant advocated strong action against Nazir?"

"Yes."

"Isn't it true he advocated violence in support of your cause?"

"At times."

"In fact, he was so extreme you didn't want anything to do with him, true?"

"True. I felt it would be best if we kept him away from JUSTICE IRAQ. We kept him in the less controversial division. Lobbying work."

"You were afraid he'd kill someone."

"I wasn't sure what he might do."

"But you didn't want any part of it."

"Correct. I kept my distance."

"I would've done the same." He glanced at me. "A man is known by the company he keeps. No more questions."

I couldn't decide whether it was worthwhile to cross Siddig. Christina was equally ambivalent. This was a foundational witness. Thrillkill was laying groundwork, but this witness on his own didn't say much. But like the fool I am and I'll always be, I decided to make an attempt.

I stared at Siddig for a good while before speaking. No reason. Just creeping him out. No one likes being cross-examined, even if they aren't lying and want to be as honest as possible. Probably comes from watching too many TV shows where the wily country lawyer extracts some obscure fact he couldn't possibly have known to prove that the witness is a big fat liar.

"Were you aware of Agent Nazir prior to your first meeting with the defendant?"

"Yes."

"How were you aware of him?"

"We had received other complaints about him."

"From people other than Oz?"

"Yes."

"Other people complaining of mistreatment at his hands?"

"Yes."

"Other people who were interrogated?"

"Yes. Or their relatives were. Or loved ones."

"How many such complaints had you heard?"

Siddig shrugged. "I would guess somewhere around ten or fifteen."

"So, in truth, there were a lot of people with grudges against Agent Nazir."

"That's possible."

"A lot of people who might have wanted to see him dead."

"That is possible."

"Thank you. Nothing further."

And then I thought we were done for the day. But I was wrong. Thrillkill rose to his feet.

"Redirect, Mr. Thrillkill?" the judge asked.

He nodded. "Sir, you mentioned that other people complained about Agent Nazir."

"True."

"Did you ever mention these other complaints to the defendant?"

And that's when I knew I had gone horribly wrong. Thrillkill might not have been able to get to this on direct. I would've objected to introducing hearsay testimony from third parties, and the judge would've sustained the objection. So, instead, he baited me into introducing the subject. That opened the door for him to pursue it on redirect.

He set the trap, and I fell for it like a starving mouse after a chunk of cheese.

"Yes, I did," Siddig said. "Not on that first occasion. But at one of our subsequent meetings. I believe it was at his apartment."

"Were you the only one who told him more about Nazir?"

"No. Several of my colleagues did the same. It went on for quite some while."

"What was the defendant's reaction?" Thrillkill asked, as if he didn't already know.

"He was outraged. Infuriated. He does have a temper, as I expect you know. His face turned red and his fists clenched, and he said, 'Someone needs to take that bastard out.'"

"Someone needs to take him out?" He paused, letting that hang in the air for a while. "Meaning someone needs to kill that man?"

"That was certainly how I took it."

"Thank you. Nothing more."

I would've liked to recross, just so the jury had a different takeaway, but I couldn't think of anything that wouldn't reinforce that disastrous testimony. Thrillkill got an even more ominous threat into the courtroom. Which of course in no way proved that Oz killed Nazir. But it didn't sound good. No probative value, but mounds of emotional force.

He played me.

I leaned across the table toward Oz, who looked decidedly disturbed. "Don't worry. We'll fix it tomorrow."

"How?"

I wanted to tell Oz not to blame me because he made some incredibly rash and stupid statements. But I didn't. "I don't know how, but—"

I heard a gasping sound behind my back. After all these years as a trial lawyer, it was a sound I was somewhat accustomed to hearing. Except not from my wife.

She stared at her cell phone, and that was the first sign that something was terribly wrong. She knew juries hated to see litigants staring at their phones. Their reaction was no different from anyone else's when you're at a restaurant or on a date and the people you're with fixate on their phones instead of paying attention to you. It's rude and off-putting. Christina wouldn't do it unless she had a good reason. And there were only a couple of things that would rank high enough on her list. "Is it the girls?"

Christina dropped the phone. "They're at the hospital. Mercy. I'm out of here."

"What happened?"

"Not sure. Julia's with them. Some kind of seizure."

I felt a cold, skeletal hand clutching my heart. "Which . ."

"Emily."

I was already on my feet. "Oz, I'll try to talk to you tonight. No promises."

He nodded, but it didn't matter, because I was already sprinting. Thrillkill held up his hand as if he wanted a confab, but I didn't stop.

Emily.

CHAPTER 37

This was not my first trip to the ER. Not even my first trip to the ER since the girls were born. If Christina is to be believed (and she is, always), I'm a somewhat anxious father, which she found deliciously comical, especially since I came from a medical family. "Usually the health-services crowd is a little calmer," she'd said. Every time the girls sniffled, I wanted to call the pediatrician. Every time they coughed, I wanted to call the CDC.

I never had to deal with anything close to a seizure. Just as well I wasn't there. Though I felt insanely guilty because I wasn't.

Christina and I were in separate cars, but we still hit the hospital about the same time. Someone escorted us into a waiting room. Emily was in a tiny gown and in a crib that had bars rising higher than she could ever climb over. The bars were lowered and a doctor had her stethoscope out. Julia stood to one side, looking like she'd been to hell and back. She held Elizabeth tightly, but she was a mess, sweat streaking the side of her face, deep furrows across her forehead.

"What is it?" I asked. "What's wrong with her? Is it serious? How could you—?"

Christina placed her hand on my shoulder, silencing me. "Let me handle this." She addressed Julia. "What happened?"

Julia shook her head. "I'm not sure. I was holding her in my arms. Elizabeth was playing on the floor. Emily's whole body started shaking, trembling, completely out of control. I've never seen anything like it. Her little head jerked, and her eyes rolled back—" Tears flooded into her eyes. Her voice choked. She covered her mouth as if she might be sick. "I didn't know what to do. She just kept shaking, and I was so scared. I felt her forehead, and she was burning up, so I ran some ice-cold water in the tub and put her in it. Didn't even stop to get her clothes off. Once she cooled a little, I dried her and raced her to the hospital. Didn't even stop for my purse. My car is still parked where the ambulances are supposed to go. To their credit, the second I ran in here with a toddler, everyone on deck gathered to help. They had ER docs looking at her inside of a minute."

I was so confused I could barely process what I heard. "Why would you put her in ice cold water? Did you want her to freeze to death?"

"Actually," a female voice said, "that was probably the smartest thing she could do."

It was the doctor. She'd finished her tests and appeared ready to talk to us.

"What's the story?" I asked. "Is this some neurological disorder? We've had some previous indications—"

The doctor—Sanderson according to her badge—wrapped her stethoscope around her neck. "She has a fever. It probably spiked sharply, and that induced the seizure. Immersing her in cold water brought down the fever." She turned toward Julia. "Do you have medical training?"

"I'm a nurse," Julia answered.

"I thought as much. Good work."

"I wish I could've prevented this."

"I don't know how that would be possible when you didn't even know she was sick."

"What's wrong with Emily?" I said, thrusting myself back in the conversation.

"Hard to say. We took a blood sample so we can rule out extreme causes. But she probably has the flu or some other virus. Possibly an allergic reaction, though I doubt it. Sounds like your sister is careful about what this little girl is exposed to."

"Will this . . . cause brain damage?"

"No, no. This kind of toddler seizure is not all that uncommon. Scary, but nothing to worry about long term."

"Can she go home?"

"I'd like to keep her here overnight, just for observation. I'll give her some baby meds. Watch that fever. Keep her cool. I'd stick with liquids for a few days."

"I—I—" For an alleged trial lawyer, I was having a hell of a hard time articulating words. "We've been concerned that she might be . . . autistic."

Dr. Sanderson's eyebrows moved together. "Seriously? Do you have some reason?"

"Her behavior has been odd."

"At this age?"

Julia spoke. "It's because of me. I have a son on the autistic spectrum."

"There's no evidence that autism is inherited."

"I know. But . . ." She let the sentence trail off, rather than saying, "But I can't get that through my brother's thick head."

Dr. Sanderson ran her hand through her black hair. "If you're truly concerned about this, there's a new program at St. Anthony's—"

Julia nodded. "I've already enrolled her."

My head twitched. I hadn't heard anything about St. Anthony's. I just heard something about an appointment with a specialist. But I noticed Christina didn't seem surprised.

"Good. Then it seems all concerns are being addressed. I'll call your regular pediatrician and give him the scoop. But I think Emily is stable. We'll watch her overnight and send her home in the morning. If you need anything, I'll be on the premises till two. You can have me paged."

"Can we stay with her?" I asked.

Dr. Sanderson smiled. "I think she would be very disappointed if you didn't." She looked at Elizabeth. "Might take that little one home, though. She looks tired."

"I'll do that," Christina said, taking her daughter from Julia. "We could both do with some rest."

"I could take her. I guess," I mumbled.

"Yes, you could, but you'd rather stay here with Emily, and you'll be miserable if you don't. I'll take Elizabeth. We can rendezvous later."

Julia nodded. "I'll keep an eye on the patient."

"Emily is just under observation," I said. "She's not a patient."

Christina smiled. "She wasn't talking about Emily."

CHAPTER 38

A few hours later, with Emily sound asleep in her high-wall crib, Julia and I went downstairs to the all-night cafeteria to find something to eat. I didn't actually get food. Just coffee. Julia cautioned that if I drank coffee, I might not be able to sleep. I knew I didn't have the slightest chance of sleeping, so I might as well drink something I would enjoy. I would've preferred chocolate milk, but bizarrely enough, the cafeteria didn't carry any.

"What's this business about testing at St. Anthony's?"

"They have an early detection and intervention program for autism. They don't normally take children as young as Emily, but I know some people. Starts Tuesday."

"You weren't going to tell me?"

Her eyes averted. "Christina said she'd tell you. Didn't she?"

"Sort of."

"She mentioned that you'd been a little . . . irrational on the subject."

"So I'm crazy now, is that it?"

"Just a concerned daddy." Pause. "A very concerned daddy."

"I'm not even sure I approve of this."

"That's what she thought you'd say."

"Because I'm an unreasonable ogre?"

"Because you'd be afraid of the result."

I felt the knot in my stomach tighten. Of course I was afraid. How could I not be afraid? Wasn't I running as fast as I could to avoid thinking about it? Why wasn't Christina worried? This was our little girl—

Except I knew she did worry. She just didn't let it show.

"How's the case going?" Julia asked. I think we both recognized the need for a change of subject.

"Case? What case?" We smiled. Funny how something that has dominated your thoughts can be eradicated by one distraction—when the distraction is your daughter.

"Do you think you can get Oz off?"

"I won't lie to you. So far it looks bleak. But to be fair, it always looks that way in the early days. The prosecution is determined to make him look as guilty as sin. All I can do is parry and thrust, trying to undercut their case in small ways. The outlook will improve when we put on our case." In theory, anyway. I didn't bother telling her how little I had.

"Sounds like a David and Goliath story."

"The prosecution has an enormous institutional advantage. They have all the money and power of the government behind them. About half the potential jurors come into the courtroom assuming everyone accused is guilty. And Thrillkill is extremely smart and highly motivated."

"But you've won tough cases before. You must have something you can use."

"Traditionally, a defense attorney has three basic strategies: discredit, suppress, and accuse."

"Meaning?"

"You discredit the prosecution witnesses. Hard to do when they're mostly government employees. Jurors might believe they're screwups, but it's hard to believe they're flat-out liars. You can try to suppress evidence on one constitutional ground or another, but this judge is particularly permissive. And that leaves the tried-and-true approach of accusing someone else."

"You think you can make the jury believe someone else did it?"

"The wonderful thing is they don't have to believe it. If you can get them to acknowledge the *possibility* that someone else did it, they can't find the defendant guilty 'beyond a reasonable doubt.' Not in good conscience. Those who take the job seriously and pay attention to the judge's instructions find it hard to convict."

Julia took another spoonful of her low-fat yogurt. "I hear all kinds of people wanted Nazir dead."

My left eyebrow rose. "What do you mean?"

"Just what I said. How many people did that man betray? Or question? Or torture? Pretty infantile, really, to act as if Oz is the only person who wanted him gone."

"Perhaps you could suggest another suspect."

"Oh, I don't know any names."

"Any faces then?"

"Not that I recall."

"You were at his apartment sometimes, weren't you?"

"Sure."

I put down my coffee. "You must've seen some of his disgruntled friends."

"Actually . . . when I was there, he usually made sure we were alone."

This was an area I didn't want to explore. "Tell me what's going on."

"I don't know what you mean."

"I mean you and Oz. Your sudden reappearance. Your involvement with PACT."

"I told you Oz and I got back together. Who said I was involved with PACT?"

"You didn't deny it."

"Well, aren't you the clever one. Am I on the witness stand, Counselor?"

"No. But you can see where I might be curious." And getting curiouser by the minute. "Are you still involved with PACT?"

"Not in an active way. But I'm sympathetic to the cause. If you heard Oz rattle on about it night and day, you might get interested, too. Let's face it—hating people who hail from the Middle East has become the most fashionable hate crime."

"The CIA is watching PACT."

"If the CIA weren't watching them, it would mean they're not doing anything important."

"I know you've been through some tough stuff. I think you've got enough to worry about without inviting trouble."

"You've been through a lot, too. And yet here you are, taking the most impossible, difficult cases. Almost as if you're trying to prove something."

I gave her a long look. "Okay. So we've established that we've both been through a lot." Before I even finished the thought, Julia's hand shot out and grasped mine. She squeezed so hard I felt as if she were clinging to the edge of a cliff.

"Are we going to talk about it?"

I broke her gaze. Those eyes burned much too hot for me.

"I'm a total train wreck," she added. "I need to move on with my life. And you need to get out of that house, Ben. The sooner the better."

"Julia." I held on to that hand. "I couldn't help you before. Let me help you now."

"By helping Oz? You are."

"That's one way. We need to heal. Both of us."

"I . . . don't even know if that's possible." Her voice trailed off. We didn't speak for the next ten minutes.

That silence spoke volumes. It just didn't say anything I wanted to hear.

CHAPTER 39
WITNESS AFFIDAVIT
CASE NO. CJ-49-1886

Much later that night, I was at al-Jabbar's apartment, even though he was not there.

Mina Ali was. I knew my handler would be keenly interested to know why she was there. And what she was doing. The apartment was empty. Al-Jabbar was in jail, and his former roommates had moved to avoid police harassment.

Mina spent at least half an hour going through his desk, his room, his closets. I would be surprised to find anything had been left behind by the government. Certainly, they would leave nothing of great interest.

So why was she there? What was she searching for?

She texted someone. That took me by surprise. I knew she had been trained by her older brother to avoid all cellular communications. Much too simple to intercept, as I had proven on numerous occasions. Did this indicate urgency? Desperation? Because I didn't expect this, I had trouble intercepting at first. I did know her cell number, but by the time I had my network intercept running, I had already missed vital parts of the exchange.

Sent: *MAYBE SATURN HAS IT.*

Received: *IT IS THERE.*

Sent: *IT IS NOT.*

Received: *IT IS THERE.*

Sent: *IM NOT CONVINCED IT WILL HELP.*

Received: *TRY. THE DAY OF RECKONING IS FAST APPROACHING.*

The recipient had a cloaked and encrypted source code. I was certain it was a disposable one-use-only phone, so I didn't bother trying to trace it. These people were professionals. They would not make a rookie mistake.

I was surprised when she went to the storage shed. For a long time, the shed had been covered with crime scene tape, but that had been removed shortly before the trial began. Apparently, the police took the locks with them.

This was the one instance in which my equipment failed me. I could not see inside the shed. Was she still looking for something? Taking something? Planting something?

Mina called her brother, the young one, Kir. I wondered whether I should be concerned. The boy was young and brash and exactly the sort who might decide to tell the police everything he knew in a flash of conscience.

I got this conversation almost from the start. Most was of no import. This is how it ended:

"The pigs are winning."

"It only appears so at this moment." She tried to calm him, with little success.

"They can destroy anyone. Simply by waving their all-powerful hand."

"You're exaggerating."

"Look what they did to you!"

I heard her sigh heavily. *"This is not a productive conversation. And it comes at the worst possible time. I will call you when I am home."*

She disconnected the line. Even then, I could hear the young boy seething.

She spent more time aimlessly working her way through the empty apartment. I thought her purpose, whatever that might be, was concluded. It was almost as if she hesitated to leave. As if she did not want to leave.

But at last she did. So far as I could tell, my duties were complete. I phoned my handler and asked if there were further instructions.

I made sure I had a secure line, using the cell reserved only for these reports. I relayed the highlights and promised photos in the morning.

"Would you like me to send them now?"

"No. I can't look at them now. The morning will be soon enough."

"Is there anything else you would like me to do?"

"No."

"The prosecutor?"

"Pointless."

"The lawyer? His wife?"

"I have that under control."

"Then I will stand down."

"Very good. I will contact you with further instructions tomorrow."

In my mind, I gave a little salute. "I am, as always, yours to command. Good night, Julia."

CHAPTER 40

In my experience, the coroner is rarely the most exciting witness the prosecution has at its disposal, which is why they usually call them early and get rid of them quickly. They must establish that a death occurred, and the cause of death is sometimes of interest. Best to simply get it over with.

In this case, I suspected Thrillkill delayed the testimony primarily because he was afraid of what I might do to the man on cross-examination. Or perhaps I flatter myself. Whatever his faults might be, Thrillkill was thorough, and he had the essential lawyer gift for looking at a situation from all sides.

Clarence Cooper was a respected medical examiner with a national reputation, a pleasant change of pace from some previous forensic "experts," like the former chemist for the OKC police who falsified evidence leading to hundreds of convictions and eleven executions. More recently, Massachusetts had to dismiss over 20,000 criminal cases when it was discovered that a chemist was faking the proof. Cooper knew his stuff, though, and he could be trusted to say nothing that wasn't 100 percent accurate. On the witness stand, he seemed comfortable and calm, always professionally dressed, the picture of authority. I didn't need to worry about devising clever cross-ex questions to trip him up. That was not going to happen. But I could count on him to testify honestly about a few interesting anomalies I'd detected in his report.

Thrillkill established that Dr. Cooper performed the autopsy and outlined his general operating procedure.

"Were you able to establish a cause of death?" Thrillkill asked.

"Yes."

"And that is?"

"Agent Nazir died of a gunshot wound to the head. That caused traumatic injury plus a severing of the blood and oxygen flow. The technical term would be cranial asphyxiation."

"Any mysterious circumstances?"

"No."

"Any other findings relevant to cause of death?"

"The matter is clear-cut. There's no doubt about it."

"Did you match your findings with those of ballistics?"

"Yes. And I found markings on the brain that parallel those detected on the bullet."

"Meaning what exactly?"

Cooper turned slightly to face the jury. "Nazir was killed by a bullet to the brain."

"Thank you. Pass the witness."

I rose to my feet. "Dr. Cooper, I was just wondering—did you perform any toxicology tests as part of your A-scan?"

"I did. It's required by the state. Even when, as here, it's not at all necessary."

"Could you explain to the jury what an A-scan is?"

"An A-scan is the first level of inquiry—trying to determine the cause of death. Here, it was so obvious there was no need to do a more invasive B- or C-scan. And no need for toxicology, in my opinion."

"But you did the tests anyway."

"Yes."

"What were your findings?"

"No sign of poisoning. He died from the gunshot wound."

"But he wasn't exactly clean, was he?"

Out the corner of my eye, I saw a few jurors shift in their seats. Good. Always reassuring to know someone is paying attention.

"He hadn't been poisoned, if that's what you mean."

"That's not what I mean. You found some substances you weren't expecting, right?"

"I never go into any examination with preconceived expectations. Tends to taint one's objectivity."

"Okay, let me be more direct. Did you find any foreign substances in his blood? Like, for instance, intoxicating substances."

Cooper flipped a few pages into his report. "Yes. Here it is on page five. I found traces of both alcohol and cocaethylene."

"Alcohol? How much?"

"Not that much. Around point zero six percent BAC."

"And you performed the autopsy . . . around six hours after his death."

"Yes."

"So at the time of death, the alcohol concentration would've been greater."

"Possibly."

"Or to put it another way—he was drunk in the middle of the day."

"I couldn't testify about his behavior. He did have traces of alcohol in his blood."

"And while we're discussing intoxicating substances, would you please tell the jury what cocaethylene is?"

"That is a by-product produced by the combination of alcohol and cocaine in the blood."

"So he was drunk and high?"

Cooper started to answer, but Thrillkill cut him off. "Objection, Your Honor. I'm shocked that even Mr. Kincaid would sink to this level. Is there any reason to defame the dead?"

Right back at him. "I don't know if this is defamatory, Your Honor, but it's certainly interesting. And relevant."

"It's not relevant to the cause of death," Thrillkill replied.

"I never said it was. But it might give us some insight into the victim. Which in turn might give us some insight into the real reason he was killed. People who take illegal drugs consort with all manner of dangerous people."

There it was. I'd given the jury some small reason to buy the SODDIT.

"The objection is sustained. Mr. Kincaid, your point, though interesting, is outside the scope of direct examination. When you put on your case, you may recall the witness if you like. If you really think that's worth the jury's time."

"Thank you, Your Honor." But why would I do that? I'd already made the only point I would ever make with this witness. I sat down happy.

I wouldn't have been so smug if I'd known I was scant moments away from having the rug pulled out from under me but good.

CHAPTER 41

I'd done everything I could to prevent them from calling Yasmin al-Tikrit to the stand. I was not successful. Her testimony was essentially cumulative, adding to Thrillkill's ongoing effort to demonize PACT. But I feared her science background would give him the basis to unleash all kinds of specters in the jurors' minds.

"You have a degree, do you not?" Thrillkill asked the slender woman who wore tortoiseshell glasses. She was plainly Middle Eastern and strikingly attractive. Her bearing signaled confidence and strength. Even before she spoke, she conveyed a sense of intelligence.

"Yes. In chemistry. A PhD."

"And you work .."

"I am not currently employed."

"But you work, do you not?"

"At PACT, yes."

"Please remind the jury what PACT is."

"PACT is a nonprofit organization dedicated to preserving and protecting the rights of Arab-Americans."

"It's a political organization."

The space between her eyebrows narrowed. It didn't take a psychic to see that she was irritated. "I don't see it that way. PACT fights for the fundamental human rights that all people are entitled to. According to the Declaration of Independence."

"Political rights."

"Among others."

"And PACT has advocated extreme action on occasion, correct?"

"You would have to tell me what you mean by extreme."

"Something other than lobbying congressmen."

"I suppose that's true."

Thrillkill was smart enough to leave it alone. She'd never admit to anything illegal. But he'd planted the possibility in the minds of the jurors. "You knew Agent Nazir, correct?"

"I did."

"And you didn't like him much, did you?"

"No. I didn't."

"Would it be fair to say that you hated him?"

"I had no personal relationship with him and thus no strong feelings. But many of the people I worked with disliked him."

"But your field is chemistry."

"As I have said."

"Isn't it true you're working on a weapon? A chemical or biological weapon that could be used against the United States?"

"No. Privately, in my spare time, at home, I am looking for a renewable energy source. Something to replace the dependency on oil that has done this nation so much harm."

"But your research potentially has military applications."

"The military thinks everything has military applications. I am conducting pure research. I am looking for something to help people, not hurt them.

"You're looking for something that can be used against the USA. The country where you live. You take advantage of our way of life while you secretly try to destroy it."

"Objection," I said. "Argumentative. If I didn't know better, I'd think Mr. Thrillkill was running for office."

The judge shot me a harsh look. He had a low threshold for sarcasm. "Sustained. And both remarks will be stricken from the record. You may continue."

"You have a laboratory at home, correct?"

"As I have said."

"And you receive funding from PACT?"

She hesitated a moment. "I receive a salary."

"Have you created the superweapon they want yet?"

"I never said—"

"I think we can all assume they're not paying you for nothing."

"They're paying me because—"

"Please wait for the question, ma'am. Has this research PACT financed produced any results?"

She stared at him. "I produce results every day."

"Any practical applications, then?"

"Not yet."

"Anything that could be used in combat?"

"Are you talking about my private scientific work?"

"If you say so."

"Then the answer is no."

Thrillkill peered at her, letting an uncomfortable silence play out. Then, in an eerily calm quiet voice: "You know the defendant, don't you?"

"Yes."

"In fact, you're former lovers."

"That's none of your business."

"For all I know, you may still be lovers."

"And it still would be none of your business." She sounded hostile now. The jury did not like it.

"Did you ever hear the defendant mention how much he hated Agent Nazir?"

"Yes."

"And you know Mina Ali?"

"Yes."

"Who also despised Agent Nazir."

"With good reason."

"Sounds to me like PACT is just one big, plotting, bomb-baking hate team anxious to kill Agent Nazir at the earliest opportunity."

"Objection," I said, as loudly as possible. I was grateful for any excuse to interrupt Thrillkill's flow.

"Sustained," the judge said, but Thrillkill was already returning to his chair.

"That's fine, Your Honor. I think we all know what PACT really is. No more questions."

I stumbled through some perfunctory questions, trying to suck the life out of the prior exchange. But I knew I was kidding myself if I thought anything I did would make the jury forget what they'd heard.

"It's okay," I said, clasping Oz's arm. "Thrillkill made a lot of noise, but he didn't actually prove much."

Oz did not look comforted, and the expression on Christina's face was downright sour.

She turned her head to make sure the jury couldn't hear. "He didn't need to. He got the jury to read between the lines. First rule of persuasion. Show, don't tell." She started a second thought, then waved it away.

Didn't matter. I could imagine what she was thinking.

Thrillkill made the jury believe PACT was ISIS, al-Qaeda, the SLA, and every other terrorist organization combined. That would go a long way toward getting them to convict Oz. Hell, they might put him away just to get him off the street.

CHAPTER 42

This might've been the grimmest lunch on record. Christina and I separated from Oz so we could talk openly, perhaps even discuss something other than the case. We splurged on sandwiches from Napoleon's delivered by courier, but it didn't help. This case was heading downhill so fast that it would take a miracle to stop it from crashing at our feet. And neither of us had a miracle on hand.

"I think Thrillkill will finish his case tomorrow," Christina said. "Have you decided who you're going to call first?"

"No. Or who I'm going to call last or in between. I got nothing."

"You've got your client."

"Putting him on the stand would be a disaster. He'll hang himself."

"You may not have a choice."

"There's always a choice, sweetheart." I pursed my lips. "I just haven't figured out what it is yet."

"Maybe you could get someone from the CIA to talk about how they treated Oz."

"The government blocked all my subpoenas. Cited national security concerns. I doubt the judge would allow the testimony anyway."

"Maybe someone from PACT?"

"Haven't we had enough of that? More harm than good, I think." I needed to change the subject before I became suicidal. "How are things back in the office?"

"Oh, about the same. Death threats, harassing phone calls. Tanya is about to go off the deep end. Wants to know if the firm will reimburse her for Valium."

"She'll find her inner strength."

Christina arched an eyebrow. "And you say that because . . . you like her thong?"

I blinked. "She wears thong underwear? I hadn't noticed."

"Uh-huh."

"Anyway, I say that because Tanya has a terrific role model for inner strength. You."

"Well played."

"How are things at home?"

"Same. Julia is a lifesaver. I don't know how we'd get through this crisis without her. She handled that seizure and everything else like a pro. Bad news at Mom's Day Out, though. They've asked for another parent meeting. I think they're going to kick Emily out."

Just as a Tulsa school had done to Joey. My worst fears realized.

"That specialist at St Anthony's has almost finished screening Emily."

"And?"

"Haven't heard anything yet. But soon we'll know if you have anything to worry about. Not that the lack of anything to worry about has stopped you from worrying in the past."

I tried to smile, but I couldn't. "Let me know what happens, okay?"

"I will."

"The straight scoop. Nothing omitted. No paraphrasing or euphemisms. I want to know what's up with my little girl."

"Of course." We both looked away from one another. Because we knew if we didn't, one of us would start to cry. Probably both of us.

My iPhone buzzed. "Rats."

"News?"

"Thrillkill. He's making an offer."

"A good one?"

"Why would he make a good one now?" I scanned the text. "He's hinting that there's worse testimony to come. And if we're smart, we'll cave before it happens."

"Prosecutors always say that. He wouldn't be making an offer if he didn't have doubts."

"Yeah." I pushed out of my chair. "Still, I gotta take it to my client. And this is not going to be pleasant."

⊗

Oz STARED AT ME LIKE I'D JUST SOLD HIS GRANDMOTHER TO THE Republican Guard. "Life?"

"Life."

"That's his best offer?"

"That's the most he's offering at this time. He thinks he's coming from a position of strength."

"How could a verdict possibly be worse than life?"

"Well, it could be the exact opposite of life." I closed the door. "Look, Oz, the decision is yours."

"But you brought the offer to me for a reason."

"And the reason is I have an ethical obligation to present all offers to my client."

"Do you think I should take it?"

I slid into the chair on the other side of the table. I'd had this same conversation at other times with other clients, and it was never pleasant. "You're the only person who can answer that question."

"Because you don't know if I'm guilty or not."

"Frankly, that's not even relevant. The question is how much you're willing to risk on what the prosecutor might do next. I know this— Thrillkill is determined to put you away. He's got the eyes of the world on him, and he's going to make sure this case gives him the political boost he wants. Handled correctly, there's no limit to how far this could take him."

"Thanks. I feel much better now."

"It's not my job to make you feel better," I said, with as much force as I could muster. "It's my job to take care of you."

"So tell me whether to take the offer."

"I can't."

"What would be the reason to reject it?"

I shrugged. "If you accept, you'll have to enter a plea of guilty. Even though it was a plea bargain, most people will only remember that you confessed and were convicted."

"Okay. And what would be the reason to accept it?"

"There's only one. To guarantee you won't be executed."

"How long do you think I'll last in prison?"

As a convicted terrorist who plotted against the US of A? "No telling."

He walked to the window. I could see the pistons pumping behind his eyes. I hoped to God I never had to make a decision of this magnitude. "Tell Thrillkill I say no thanks."

"Are you sure?"

"Was I not emphatic enough? Let me rephrase. Tell him to go—"

"I got the idea. I'll deliver the message."

"I know I'm probably making a hideous mistake. But I didn't kill that man, much as I might've liked to. And I'm not going to let the government steamroller me, not this easily. The world needs to know what the CIA and NSA and people like Nazir are doing. I will have my day in court."

"I never said I'd put you on the witness stand."

"But you will."

"I'll make that decision later."

"I thought the client got to make that decision."

I squirmed uncomfortably. He was right, of course. "We don't have to decide now."

"You're delaying the inevitable, Ben."

"Maybe. We'll see."

He smiled. Just a little, but it was a welcome change of pace. Something I hadn't seen on his face since this mess began.

He slapped his hands against his thighs. "It's about to get worse, isn't it?"

"Yes. But we'll get through it. One way or the other."

CHAPTER 43

"I'm sorry, Your Honor," I said, trying to keep my voice down. "I thought we were having trial by law. Not trial by ambush."

"Stay calm, Mr. Kincaid."

"How can I stay calm? This is inexcusable. Witness lists were finalized a long time ago." I paced from one side of the judge's chambers to the other, which took only about three giant steps. "This is a third-rate shyster trick."

"It's not, Ben." As always, Thrillkill remained cool and unflappable. Of course, he had no reason to be upset. He was the one pulling the trick. "We literally just got word of this witness this morning."

"I'm sure."

Thrillkill's brow creased. "Are you calling me a liar?"

"I'm saying this is damned convenient for you."

"I disagree. It would've been much more convenient if the witness had appeared two weeks ago."

"If he had, I'd have demanded an opportunity to talk to him."

"As far as I'm concerned, you still can. Take a week for all I care."

"I'm going to veto that," the judge said. "No way I'm going to recess the trial for a week so you two can have a chat. Too hard on the jurors."

"If you let this man testify, it will be hard on the defendant."

"Only if he's guilty."

I gave the judge a long look. Unfortunately, it isn't wise to tell the judge when he's being an empty-headed simpleton, or worse, predisposed to convict. But I did my best to imply it with my expression.

"I will give you all the latitude in cross-examination you need."

"Golly, thanks."

"That's the best I can do, I'm afraid. If you really think Mr. Thrillkill is lying, you can file a complaint with the disciplinary committee. But I assume every lawyer is telling me the truth. Even defense attorneys."

Hardy har har.

He rapped the top of his desk. "Okay, then. Trial resumes in ten minutes."

***

A DEATHLIKE PALLOR BLANKETED THE COURTROOM. OR MAYBE THAT was just inside my head. But either way, I felt it.

I'd received all the relevant information back in chambers. Stanley Bell was the classic jailhouse snitch, the sort that turns up all too frequently when the prosecution feels the need to give their case a little extra oomph. Their eagerness to testify is understandable. They want a Get Out of Jail Free card. Or at least a reduction in sentence. They might do it for an extra snack ration or a trip outside the prison gates. Who can say? When your life is lived at that level of monotony, anything is possible.

Sure, as a defense attorney I can bring out the fact that they've made a deal for their testimony, but it never seems to have much impact on the jury. If experts admit they're being paid to testify, as they always are, it can impact their credibility. But the fact that a snitch has made a deal never seems to prevent juries from believing them. Somehow, that gets outweighed by the inclination of the cynical to believe the worst about the accused.

It wasn't hard to see that the next witness had spent some time in jail. Or that it was still his current residence. Prosecutors tend not to dress up snitches much. They want them to look scruffy. It adds to their credibility.

I was expecting the worst. I was not expecting to hear the two most devastating words I could imagine:

"Human trafficking."

"And by that, you mean, sex trafficking."

"Primarily. Labor trafficking, too."

Thrillkill's face was plastered with a keenly unpleasant expression. He wanted the jury to feel his distaste at having to speak to this man, even being in the same room with him. Never mind the fact that Thrillkill was the one who called him to the witness stand. And in all likelihood sent feelers into the grapevine for a snitch willing to testify. "Please describe for the jury the . . . er, activities that caused you to serve your current sentence."

Bell nodded agreeably, striking a note somewhere in the range of entrepreneurial vigor but just short of civic pride. "I had the sweetest operation on South Robinson. In the city."

"Are we talking about . . . prostitutes?" Technically a leading question, but if it got this testimony over more quickly, I was in favor of it.

"Sure, for the white chicks. Um, excuse me, Your Honor. I mean, for the young Caucasian ladies."

The judge made a grunting sound and tilted his head, a grudging acceptance. He bore the same expression of distaste and didn't seem to even want to make eye contact with the man.

"Average age of these young women?"

Bell shrugged. "Maybe fifteen."

"Not . . . eighteen?" The age of legal consent. Not that prostitution was ever legal.

"God, no. Way too old."

"At eighteen, they're over the hill?"

"At eighteen, they're probably mothers. We might keep them around to see if they turn their daughters. Assuming they have daughters."

Thrillkill tucked in his chin. "I gather you were their pimp."

"Hell, no. I mean, sorry, judge. No, sir. I was the CEO."

"Indeed. What does the CEO do?"

"I manage my employees."

"Meaning the pimps."

"Mostly."

"So the pimps take from their prostitutes and give you a cut."

"That's how it worked."

"What do you give them in exchange for your cut?"

"A proper working environment." Eyebrows rose with the sudden elevation in vocabulary.

"You provided a room?"

"They couldn't work my territory without my okay."

"It's your territory?"

"That block was, yeah."

"And how did you earn your territory?"

He made that casual shrugging expression again. "By replacing the guy who was there before me." Amazing how Bell could seem almost impish as he described what was probably a hit, or at the least a serious beating. Imagine what this charisma might have done for him in an honest profession. A little more education, he could've made it in politics. Or on the television news.

Or as a lawyer.

"How long did you command this territory?"

"Almost three years." An eternity in pimp years. "I was the Ruler of Robinson."

Oh God. That clicked. Now I remembered this guy. He'd gotten a lot of publicity at the time of his trial. I read about it daily, even when I lived in Tulsa. The media milked it night and day and, if nothing else, drove home how prevalent human trafficking had become right here in this sweet little red state. Many immigrants, legal and illegal, come through Texas. Even if they're not originally from Mexico, that's the easy way into the United States. About 17,000 people are trafficked into the country each year, mostly through Texas and California. Those immigrants, more often than not, become the labor slaves Bell mentioned, while the American girls—who often start as runaways—more often become sex slaves. Texas has had a desperately bad trafficking situation for more than a decade, and some of those people were trickling north to Oklahoma.

I could object on grounds of relevance, but Thrillkill would ask the judge to give him a little lenience, which the judge would grant. All I would do is slow the wheels and make this take longer than it already did.

"During the time you conducted this . . . business operation . . . did you have occasion to meet the defendant?"

Bell looked at Oz. I felt a chill run down my spine. I'm not simply repeating a cliché. I felt it. I knew this walk on the wild side had to get back to Oz eventually.

"I did."

"How did you know him?"

"He lived near my block. He often walked by, going to the convenience store or Taco Bell or whatever."

I mentally slapped myself. That's right. That sleazy apartment Oz and the others were sharing, the one with the shed in the rear. That was on Classen, not far from South Robinson, the most notorious street in the city.

"Did you talk to him?"

"Eventually. He was more interested in talking to the girls."

So that was it. They wanted to accuse Oz of fraternizing with hookers. It was a smear campaign.

I made a point of not looking at Oz. Even a glance his way would suggest to the jury that I had some question about whether this testimony was true. "Objection, Your Honor."

The judge pursed his lips. "Grounds?"

"Relevance. Even if this were true, which it isn't, it wouldn't relate to the charges on trial today. If Mr. Thrillkill wants to file additional charges, it might become relevant. But I note that he hasn't, which might tell us something about how credible this testimony is."

"Goes to character," Thrillkill said, not waiting to be invited.

The judge frowned. "If that's all it is—"

"And it bears directly on the charges at hand," Thrillkill added.

The judge removed his glasses. "I'm not seeing that connection."

"Give me one more minute, Your Honor. The connection will become apparent."

The judgeexhaled audibly. "If this is just mudslinging, I will consider your representations to me otherwise to be deliberate false-hoods, Mr. Thrillkill. And I will act accordingly."

"I would never do that, Your Honor."

"I hope not. You may proceed. I'll hold Mr. Kincaid's objection in abeyance for the moment."

Thrillkill continued. "What did the defendant discuss with these prostitutes?"

"Objection. Calls for hearsay."

Thrillkill bowed his head. "Allow me to rephrase. Were you present during these conversations?"

"Almost always."

"What was the defendant saying to your young women?"

"He was talking business."

"Was he interested in procuring a prostitute?"

I was already rising to object when Bell answered. "No, he was making sure they had what they were promised. Occasionally asking if they knew anyone else who might like to join them."

Thrillkill squinted. "I'm afraid I'm confused."

Bell was so casual it was almost frightening. "He's the one who brought them over."

"I'm not sure—"

"He got them across the border. He's the trafficker."

The courtroom erupted. The gallery lit up like a pinball machine, chaotic and noisy. In the jury box, lips parted and brows creased.

"Objection, Your Honor. This is exactly what I said it would be. Irrelevant mudslinging from a witness bribed into testifying."

"That's completely wrong," Thrillkill replied, calmly redirecting his attention to the bench. "This goes to motive. It provides one more reason why Nazir, a federal agent, would be investigating the defendant. And it gives the defendant one more reason to want Nazir dead."

I pursed my lips and tried not to sneer. "Motion to strike that talking objection, Your Honor. The fact is Mr. Thrillkill assured the court this would not be mudslinging. And it was exactly that."

The judge craned his neck. "I'm afraid I can't agree with you, Mr. Kincaid. Evidence of additional federal crimes gives the man one more reason to want a federal agent out of the way."

I loved the way the judge acted as if Oz had already been convicted, when in fact he'd only been smeared by a jailhouse snitch. "Your Honor, this is about the lowest, most unreliable form of testimony—"

"And I'm sure you'll go into that chapter and verse during your cross-examination. But as for this evidence, I'm ruling it admissible. Objection overruled."

A few minutes later I stood up for cross, completely torn. I knew nothing I said would make the jurors forget what they'd heard. And the longer I spent with this odious man, the more firmly his words would be etched on the jurors' collective consciousness.

Well, go big or go home. "You've told lies before, haven't you, Mr. Bell?"

"Objection."

"Sustained."

"Let me rephrase. You've been convicted of perjury on a previous occasion, haven't you?"

"Yeah. They nailed me when I denied running my operation on Robinson."

"You lied."

"Well, wouldn't you? I didn't want to go to jail."

"And you'd probably like to get out of jail now, huh?"

"True. But I'm not lying, if that's what you're getting at."

"So you say. But if you didn't have something juicy to offer, Mr. Thrillkill wouldn't have offered you a deal, would he?"

"I guess not. But it's still the truth."

And so it went. After ten minutes of this parrying, I sat down. I was doing Oz no good and probably making matters worse.

I did my best to comfort my client. "Try not to worry. I don't think anyone believed that tall tale," I told him during the break.

"I'm not so sure, Ben. I watched the jurors' faces. They were interested. At best, they're unsure."

"Let them sleep on it. Once the shock wears off, they'll see how unlikely this is."

"I'm going to testify, Ben. We have to show them I'm not a total sleaze."

"Oz, this is not about your reputation. Focus on the endgame."

"What's the point of winning if everyone thinks I'm a sex trafficker?"

"Better than being dead," I replied, but I wished I hadn't. Tried to bite it back, but it was too late.

"One way or another," I assured him, "when we put on our case, I'll rehabilitate your reputation. It can only get better from here."

In retrospect, it would seem I have an endless talent for being completely wrong.

CHAPTER 44

I'd known the sex video was coming since before the trial started, since that fateful day when the genius judge, a paragon of disinterestedness, declared the defendant's sex life to be perfectly relevant. I thought the ruling disastrous at the time.

As it turned out, disastrous was too mild a word. For starters, at the time of the ruling, I didn't know that my little sis was involved with the man, which raised the all-too-icky possibility that I would be listening to a long series of oohs and aahs from my sister. This most recent testimony, however, raised an even worse fear. Now we had to wonder whether we were listening to my client having sex with a chemist or one of the underage women smuggled in and corralled by the alleged trafficking ring.

Thrillkill's plan seemed obvious. I beat myself over the head for not seeing it sooner. Yes, his case was imperfect. His evidence was mostly a long series of suggestions and innuendos, with no hard evidence that did anything more than tie Oz to the scene of the crime with a gun in his hand. But Thrillkill filled the gaps by painting Oz as a disgusting human being, and if he did that well enough, the jury would fight for the chance to put him behind bars—or in a grave.

I asked to meet with Judge Santino in chambers. I also asked that the court reporter be present. I wanted to make sure we had a record for the appeal court.

"Your Honor, once again I must express my strenuous objection to the admission of this clearly prejudicial evidence."

"All my evidence has been prejudicial," Thrillkill said dryly. "To your client's freedom."

"This video is grossly prejudicial and not remotely relevant."

"It goes to motive," Thrillkill replied.

"Even if that's vaguely true, the potential prejudice far outweighs the probative value."

Thrillkill just smiled. I'd like to pretend that was a sign that I had wowed him into silence with the force of my brilliant argumentation, but I suspected the truth was that he knew he'd already won.

"I'm getting a distinct feeling of déjà vu here," the judge said, straightening in his plush, black padded chair. "Which is a nice way of saying you're wasting my time. I've already ruled, Mr. Kincaid. And I've left the door open for you to renew your motion if you hear something you believe to be inappropriate. But we both know this testimony is relevant. This is a woman actually soliciting a murder—"

"She never says murder," I said, making the fatal mistake of interrupting the judge.

He didn't like it, either. He heaved his shoulders and gave me a steely gaze. "Let's let the jury decide what she meant, shall we?"

"We don't even know for certain who's talking."

"Does it matter?" Thrillkill said with a shrug. "One female conspirator in the sack is much the same as another."

"That's exactly the kind of piggish attitude—"

The judge raised his hand, and this time I had the sense to stop. "The prosecutor has edited the video in a manner that I find acceptable. Nothing is included that doesn't have to be there."

"You can tell they're having sex."

"Granted."

"Kinky sex."

The judge arched his eyebrows. "Don't be a prude, Kincaid. Just because it's not missionary doesn't make it kinky."

How old was this guy who just called me a prude? "We still haven't dealt with the whole issue of where the video came from. Who recorded it?"

"My understanding was that the investigating officers found it in his apartment."

"So they say," I replied.

"Do you have some reason to doubt it?"

"We know he was under surveillance by the CIA. Probably the NSA."

"Why would they record someone having sex?" Thrillkill asked.

"Now you're in denial. Sex tapes used to be Hoover's stock in trade."

He waved a dismissive hand. "That was a long time ago."

"I've heard people say the same thing about torture."

Thrillkill made a frowning face but didn't bother replying. "Regardless of the provenance of the recording, there are no doubts about its authenticity."

I kept my mouth shut. I could see the judge becoming irritated, and the fact is there weren't any doubts.

"The edited video will be admitted," the judge said. "You may make your objection or exception or offer of proof or whatever for the record, Mr. Kincaid. And then, could we please get on with this trial?"

⟨✣⟩

"ARE YOU READY FOR THIS?" I ASKED OZ QUIETLY, AS WE WAITED for the trial to resume.

"How could I be ready for this? This is a grotesque invasion of privacy."

"They say you made the video."

"I didn't. Why would I?"

"I don't know. Someone did. Was it Mina?" I assumed she was the woman on the video, though he had never confirmed that.

"Why would she want to do that?"

"I'm just saying that, since you two are in a relationship .

"Actually, I broke that off."

Right. He'd alluded to that before. "Why?"

"She deserves better."

There was something he wasn't saying, something he didn't want to say. But I didn't know what it was. Which left us both in the worst possible situation.

Thrillkill used one of the investigating officers, a new guy, Norman Koljack, to introduce the video. He testified to being part of the initial investigation of Oz's apartment. About the same time Takei discovered the alleged explosives in the backyard shed, he purportedly found this digital recording on a cell phone in Oz's desk.

Like all good mix tapes, this one had a driving rhythm. Unfortunately, the rhythm was provided by an extremely squeaky bed frame. The production values were amateurish, somewhere between Pamela Anderson and Paris Hilton, but good enough to leave no doubt about what was happening. Or that Oz was the man in the video. The woman straddling him was seen only from the back of the head.

Thrillkill cut close to the portion of the video that contained the dialogue he considered relevant. Could anyone be dense enough to believe Thrillkill was putting this video into evidence so they could hear the dialogue? After all, he could've extracted the audio portion. He wanted the jurors to see Oz having sex—and making a recording of it—because even in this more permissive age, that did not make anyone look good. It left them with an awkward, uncomfortable feeling, especially with him sitting right there in the room. Given the earlier evidence presented, the jurors couldn't help but wonder if this was a prostitute, one of the helpless strays he supposedly smuggled over the border so that they could spend the rest of their lives in the sex trade. Luring them into a life of degradation and shame—and tapping them on the side.

This had nearly nothing to do with the case—and it was the most damning evidence Thrillkill had put on yet.

For some bizarre reason, I started thinking about the court reporter and pitying the task that now lay before her. She had to take down every word of this, but at the moment, there were few words. Mostly guttural grunting and passionate moans. Would she attempt to make a record? To capture the essence of the evidence? I glanced her way but mostly detected extreme embarrassment. The same expression I saw on the faces of most of the jurors. But I also noticed they weren't looking away from the screen. We live in the gossip generation, where news has been supplanted by invasions of privacy.

"Oh God. God, yeah. Yeah, baby, yeah. Aww, give it to me, Ozzy. Give it to me hard."

I made a point of not making eye contact with my client.

The woman in the video pulled herself up, arching her back, whipping her jet-black hair behind her. Her fingertips were poised on his hips, lifting herself in rhythm, rocking in coordination with his thrusts.

"Oh, yeah. Just like that. You're so damn big. Just like that, baby!"

Her cries rose in pitch, almost a chirping sound, while her head lolled backward. Oz was either the most fantastic lover in the history of the world—or she really wanted him to think that he was.

And then they exploded, powerfully and simultaneously. If someone was faking, they were doing a damn good job of it.

After the excitement faded, she collapsed on top of him. Her head fell to the right of his, and her hair covered most of her face, again leaving her impossible to identify.

"God, baby, it's so good with you." Her voice was deep and breathless. *"I don't know what I'd do if . . . if this had to end."*

"Then let's not let it end," Oz said, using actual words for the first time in the recording.

"I won't have any choice. I never do. Everyone else calls the shots, and people like me get pushed around."

"No one can push you around unless you let them. Stay here with me."

"I want to stay with you." She wrapped her arms around him and hugged him tight. *"But for how long? Nazir will never leave me alone."*

What seemed like an interminable amount of time passed. Oz opened his eyes and stared straight ahead. *"I'll take care of Nazir,"* he said.

CHAPTER 45

The reaction in the courtroom was subdued—what reaction could you expect in the aftermath of watching two people have sex? But I knew the video had made a powerful impact. Out the corner of my eye, I saw several reporters break for the back door. They had their lead, and they weren't staying around for the color commentary. If anything, the squirming I'd observed in the jury box ended with the video. Now the jurors were left alone with their thoughts while the judge took a ten-minute recess.

If there was any doubt that Oz had a motive to eliminate Nazir before—and there really wasn't—there certainly was no doubt now.

I felt my heart thumping in my chest. This was far from my first rodeo, but I'd never had a client subjected to anything like this level of humiliation before. A sex video, for God's sake. When did courtrooms descend to this?

I felt a hand touch down lightly on mine. "This isn't over yet."

Christina. She didn't have to ask what I was thinking. "I think it might be," I said quietly, careful that Oz didn't hear.

"I'm not pretending this is good. But from an evidentiary standpoint, it's cumulative. What has Thrillkill proved? That Oz had a motive to kill Nazir? We already knew that."

"He trashed Oz. Made him look like a pimp and a pervert."

"You'll fix that when you put on your case."

"Not unless I put Oz on the stand."

She didn't answer. Because she knew the truth as well as I did. That ship had sailed. No one else could defend him against charges of sex trafficking. The defense didn't have the ability to recruit jailhouse snitches like prosecutors did.

"I'm not sure what to do next," I said quietly.

"Take the high road. Repeatedly make the point that you are not indulging in smear tactics, irrelevancies, mudslinging, or rhetoric. You're going to put on hard, relevant evidence."

"I'm not sure people know the difference anymore. Gossip is more entertaining than facts."

"Keep the faith. Most jurors take their job seriously."

"True."

"You see the older woman in the back row, the retired office manager? I'd give you five to one she's going to end up being the jury foreman. She's been paying close attention to everything Thrillkill has done. And she had a pursed-lips expression on her face when he started the sex video. I think she resents him lowering the trial to that level. She'll be receptive when you take a more focused approach."

"Maybe."

"She will." Chris squeezed my hand even tighter. "Remember, at the end of the day, the only real evidence against Oz is that he was found at the scene of the crime with a gun in his hand. Which doesn't prove anything."

Right or wrong, she always knew how to bring me around. Get me out of the doldrums and back where I needed to be.

As the judge reentered the courtroom, I flashed Oz a confident smile. "Don't worry. We're going to fix this."

He nodded. "I trust you, Ben."

I wished to God he hadn't said that.

The judge brought the court back into session. "Does the prosecution rest?"

"Not quite yet," Thrillkill said. "I'd like to recall a previous witness."

I rose to my feet. Something was rotten in the state of Denmark. "I've had no notice of this, Your Honor. Again."

Thrillkill acted as if I was the village idiot. "I don't have to notify opposing counsel of my plans. The witness is on the list I submitted before trial."

The judge nodded. "But traditionally, you can call a witness once. If a new issue is raised during the defense case, you may call rebuttal witnesses, but this is not—"

"Your Honor," Thrillkill clarified, "we need to update some of the prior testimony. Not all the forensic tests had been completed when my witness testified earlier."

The judge rubbed his neck. "This is irregular."

"And you'll recall," Thrillkill continued, "that this case came to trial far more quickly than is standard practice. That was in large part because my esteemed opponent demanded a speedy trial."

I thought the Constitution did that, but whatever.

The judge pondered. "I see no great harm, in any case. I'll allow it."

"Objection," I said, not quickly enough.

"I've already ruled," the judge replied. "Surely you wouldn't want relevant forensic evidence kept from the jury?"

The smirk on his face was perhaps the most prejudicial event in the trial to date, but there wasn't a thing I could do about it.

"The prosecution recalls Clarence Cooper."

Cooper shambled back to the witness stand, still wearing the white coat, still wearing the rimless glasses.

Thrillkill launched right in. "Dr. Cooper, when you were on the stand earlier, you mentioned that your tests were not yet complete."

"That's true," he said, pushing his glasses up his nose.

"Could you please tell us what tests specifically remained incomplete?"

"I had not had a chance to complete my tests on both the gun found in the possession of the accused and the bullet that executed the victim, Agent Nazir."

"Can you explain why?" He glanced my way. "We don't want anyone to think you were dilatory about your duties."

"We had considerable difficulty getting information from the Oklahoma State Bureau of Investigation. To be fair, it's not all their fault. The passage of Senate Bill 1733 in 2012 left a lot of confusion. Basically, almost anyone can buy a gun in this state, and no registration is required, with a few exceptions. This of course makes it difficult for a federal agency to determine who owns a particular gun. Technically, you must pass a federal background check if you purchase from a dealer, but there are so many other ways to obtain guns that this becomes largely irrelevant. Short-barreled shotguns require a federal license, but other weapons do not. Those who can't buy guns legally—felons, the mentally ill, drug addicts, minors, juvenile offenders—simply go to gun shows or pawnshops or buy off the Internet. We had assumed the gun found on the defendant was untraceable." He paused. "And then we got lucky."

"What happened?" Thrillkill asked.

"I put out all possible feelers, which is my standard operating procedure, not expecting to strike pay dirt. Then I got an unexpected hit. Why it took so long, I still don't know."

"Can you explain the nature of this hit?"

"Sure. As you know, Oklahoma is now an open *and* concealed carry state, meaning that you can conceal them, or you can carry handguns up to forty-five caliber in plain view. But open carry does require a permit."

"We appreciate the background information," Thrillkill said, "but can you explain how this relates to the present case?"

"The defendant applied for an open-carry permit. Three days before Mr. Nazir was shot."

Thrillkill's eyebrows rose as if he were surprised by this tidbit. I was relatively sure he wasn't.

"Once you had this new information, did you take any further actions?"

"Yes. This made it all the more important to know where the bullet that killed Mr. Nazir came from. Before, since the defendant claimed that wasn't his gun—"

"Objection," I said, fast and loud. "The defendant has not said one word in this trial yet."

The judge nodded. "Sustained. Please refrain from putting words in the mouths of others."

"But—"

"Or repeating things you may or may not have heard from third parties prior to trial."

"Yes, Your Honor."

"Did this permit application clarify the matter of ownership?" Thrillkill asked.

"Yes. The defendant specifically claimed in writing that this handgun was his own. And requested permission to carry it in public."

"Was the permit granted?"

"It was."

"So he could carry the gun openly in public?"

"Yes."

"Say, at a press conference at the state capitol building?"

"There are a few restrictions to the open-carry law—sporting events, bars, schools, and government institutions. But as long as he didn't go inside the capitol building, he could carry the gun."

"So once you knew the gun belonged to the defendant, and he'd applied for the right to carry it openly, what actions did you take?"

"As I indicated before, given that the gun belonged to the defendant, I wanted to know whether the bullet that killed Mr. Nazir came from that gun. Before, that didn't add much. Now it seemed critical."

I felt the short hairs on the back of my neck rising. There was only one direction this could be going. And it wasn't good.

"What did you do?"

"The standard battery of ballistics tests. Basically, we fired a bullet from the gun he registered, and we compared the markings on it to the markings on the bullet that killed Agent Nazir."

"The result?"

"Let me show you." He pushed a button on his handheld remote, and an image appeared on the overhead screen. "A ninety-four percent perfect match—far more than necessary to establish that the bullet that killed Agent Nazir came from the gun owned and held by the defendant."

Lips parted in the jury box.

"Thank you. No more questions."

The judge nodded. "Cross?"

So many people were ducking out the back of the gallery I wondered who would be around to hear my cross. I wouldn't get anywhere with Cooper, and I couldn't think of a question that could help our situation. I would only give the witness opportunities to repeat his indisputable conclusions.

"No cross."

"The prosecution rests," Thrillkill said, restraining his smile. He'd closed out with a killer one-two punch, first making sure everyone in the jury box detested Oz, and then giving them more than adequate grounds for concluding that he shot Nazir. He hammered the nails into the coffin with finality and overwhelming force.

"I have some motions to make," I said. Despite the futility of asking for a directed verdict, I would. I'd ask the judge to rule that no reasonable jury could convict the defendant based on the evidence presented because as a matter of law it was insufficient to prove guilt, and the judge would try hard to deny the motion without laughing in my face. Thrillkill made his case. He established a strong link between the murder and the defendant.

"I'm sure you do. I'll hear them in chambers." The judge slammed his gavel on bench. "We'll dismiss the jury and resume tomorrow morning with the defense case. Court is adjourned."

Chaos followed. I hunkered down into my shell of three: the lawyer, the comforter, and the man very worried about how many breaths he had left to take.

"We need to talk," I said to Oz. "When you told me what happened, I think you left out a few details."

"I just wanted the permit so I could scare Nazir. He scared me for weeks. Was it wrong to want to do the same to him?"

I started packing. "I don't know if it was wrong. But it may have been fatal."

"I didn't kill Nazir."

"The bullet came from your gun."

"That is not possible. The expert made a mistake."

"That expert does not make mistakes," I shot back. And then I felt Christina's hand on mine.

"Let's get some food," she said. "We'll hash this out later."

We could hash all night long, but it wouldn't change the facts. I could poke and nudge here and there, but I couldn't rewrite reality. Oz had an understandable but nonetheless palpable grudge against Nazir. He brought a gun to the press conference. And a bullet from that gun killed the man.

Oz was getting a lethal injection. Nothing short of a miracle could prevent it.

I've been trying cases for a long time now, and I've had some successes. But I've never once managed a miracle.

PART III
THE PASSION OF HATE

CHAPTER 46

I woke up in a full sweat, gasping for air. The room swirled around me. I couldn't get a lock on where I was. I wanted to scream, but somehow my jaw was locked tight. I was unable to move, unable to make a sound. I inhaled as deeply as I could, but the air burned my throat. It seemed corrosive and failed to make the room stop spinning or my head stop pounding.

I was dying, and I knew I was dying, and there was not a thing I could do about it.

Wake up, you idiot. *Wake up!*

I opened my eyes. There was just enough light to tell me I was in our bedroom. Christina lay beside me, head on the pillow, stirring slightly.

I've suffered from night terrors since I was a kid. People kept telling me I would grow out of it, but so far, no such luck. Perhaps this confirms Christina's assertion that I'm still basically a ten-year-old in an adult body. Sometimes the nightmares seem too real to bear. Even when I know it's a dream, I can't wake up. Not for what seems like an endless, torturous length of time.

Night terrors are considered a psychological ailment, a manifestation of unresolved fear.

If that's true, I've been running scared for a long time.

I pressed my hand against my chest.

"What's wrong, baby?" Christina snuggled beside me. She was still mostly asleep, but her second sense realized her companion was no longer slumbering.

"Nothing. Go back to sleep."

She turned her head just enough to see the orange glow of the alarm clock: 4:30.

"Nah. We'll be getting up soon anyway." She felt her way to the bathroom, ran a little water, and returned. "Here."

She placed a cool washcloth on my forehead. I felt my respiration slow. My heart rate returned to something resembling normal.

Her head rested in the crook of my neck. Maybe I wasn't going to die after all. She ran her fingers through my hair. It was sticky with sweat, but if she was repulsed, she hid it well.

She handed me a glass. "Here. Take some aspirin."

"I don't need that."

"The heck you don't. I'd offer you something stronger, but I think it might impair your ability to function in the courtroom."

"Or improve it." I took the aspirin and gulped them down. A few moments later, I settled back and rested my head on the pillow.

"You know," she said, quietly, "even the best attorneys sometimes lose a case."

"I've lost plenty of cases. And I'm not one of the best attorneys in the world."

"I know some who would differ with that last assertion."

"Like who?"

"Well, me."

I chuckled.

"And I'm sure our girls feel the same way."

"Getting a little desperate now, aren't you?"

"You didn't make this situation, Ben. You had to take the cards you were dealt. You didn't create the facts of the case, and it's not your fault your client neglected to tell you several important details."

"Maybe it is."

Even in the dark, I could see her forehead crinkling. "Have you figured out some new way to experience pointless guilt?"

"I haven't been that sympathetic to Oz. He probably didn't feel he could confide in me."

"Ben Kincaid." I heard the edge creeping into her voice. "You are not responsible for other people's screwups. You are not to blame for—"

"I'm the reason Oz and Julia broke up."

Christina did not reply.

"He was being nice in my office when he said he had some hard times after high school. What he didn't say was—they were mostly my fault."

"What are you talking about?"

"I didn't like him dating Julia. I was still very protective of my little sister. We'd been so close so long."

"But that changed once she had a steady boyfriend?"

"Yes. And I didn't like her choice. He was a jock, popular, typical arrogant rich kid. I didn't think he was smart enough for her. I didn't believe he liked her that much. I thought she was just a means to an end for him. Toward the end of their senior year, there was a big party out at the lake. Senior Ditch Day. You know, lots of booze and sex. Someone started a rumor that Oz made it with one of the cheerleaders."

"Tell me you didn't start that rumor."

"No. I didn't start it." I averted my eyes. Even in the dark, I couldn't look at her. "But I might have . . . helped circulate it."

"To Julia?"

I pursed my lips. "Among others."

I heard my wife sigh. "I'm not saying that was a good thing. But you're still not to blame for his current situation."

"Are you sure? One event leads to another. After high school, his life fell apart. He wasn't the big man on campus. College wasn't for him. And he'd lost Julia. He drifted. Ended up in the military. A directionless kid. A flop at real life. Exactly the type who's easy prey for ISIS and other terrorist outfits."

"You're not responsible for his poor choices."

"We're all responsible for one another. That's the way the world works. At least, that's the way it's supposed to work."

"You can't fix everything."

"Isn't that an attorney's job? To prevent miscarriages of justice?"

"Miscarriages? I hate to be the one who tells you, Ben, but at the moment your client looks seriously guilty."

"Does he deserve to die?"

"I don't think anyone deserves to die. You know that."

"Oklahoma and, on rare occasions, the federal government still practice lethal injection. Even after one embarrassing incident after another. Clayton Lockett, tortured, writhing in agony, strapped to the gurney. Only a few months before, Michael Wilson complained that his body felt like it was on fire. They ignored him. A state court judge said this was so obviously cruel and unusual punishment that he didn't even consider it a close call. The Supreme Court tried to stop the next execution, but the governor ordered it anyway."

"I know all this, Ben. What's your point?"

"Did you see the latest study from the National Academy of Sciences? Based on the growing number of postconviction exonerations, they estimate more than four percent of all death-row inmates are innocent. But we keep on torturing them and killing them just the same."

"You're not responsible for the sins of the world, Ben. You didn't turn the death penalty into a political football."

"This will probably be my last case."

"Ben ."

"Who would trust me after this? I've risked my family's future for what? For a case everyone else in town had the sense to stay away from."

"You haven't even started the defense. You'll pull a rabbit out of your hat. You always do."

"Like what? I've had no luck tracking down the mystery witness who fled from the scene of the crime. I have no defense theory."

"SODDIT."

"Nazir's drug supplier? Which is who? I can only bluff the jury so long. They're going to want a name."

"You'll think of something."

I slunk down into the bed. "And I'm worried about Emily."

Christina pushed herself out of bed. "I think this calls for a grilled cheese sandwich."

"For breakfast?"

"If you like, I'll serve it with a side of Cap'n Crunch."

"Doesn't that sound a little . . . off?"

"I think it sounds disgusting. But it's probably just what you need."

"So I can vomit in the courtroom?"

"Anything to capture the sympathy of the jury." She tossed a warm blanket on top of me and tucked it in at the sides. "Now, you just stay nice and toasty. I'll whip up some comfort food." She caressed my bald spot. "You're going to be fine, baby boy."

I didn't even realize I'd been shivering, but I noticed when the trembling subsided. She kissed me on the forehead and headed toward the kitchen.

"Thank you," I said.

"For what?"

I shrugged. "Pretty much everything. I couldn't do this without you."

She smiled and winked. "Just so you understand that."

CHAPTER 47

Defense attorneys sometimes spend days deliberating over who they should call as their first witness, probably making it far more important than it will ever be to the jury. But after days of hearing the prosecution make its seemingly airtight case, the jury expects some explanation of why this case isn't a foregone conclusion. Capturing the jury's attention is critical. The defense attorney needs to tell the jurors from the get-go that, although law enforcement had to accuse someone, that in no way proves the prosecution caught the guilty party.

On television, people talk a lot about whether someone is innocent or guilty, but no attorney ever has to prove anyone is innocent. Thank goodness—because who among us is ever completely innocent? All the defense has to show is that there is some reason to question the prosecution's claims. They are the Johnny Appleseeds of doubt.

I decided to start with my PACT witness. Sure, he didn't know much about the case, but the prosecution had made everyone at PACT sound like a charter member of ISIS. So I'd rehabilitate the group and, indirectly, rehabilitate Oz.

And then I could work on convincing them he wasn't a sex trafficker, porn freak, drug addict, etc.

I put Fethullah Lkbar on the stand, introduced a bit of his background, and established that he'd been doing clerical work at PACT for about two years.

"Could you describe for the jury what PACT does?"

"We're an information group, primarily. Trying to educate people in all walks of life about the contributions of Arab-Americans, and trying to dispel some of the negative stereotypes out there, particularly since 9/11."

"I imagine that involves a lot of political advocacy."

"Actually, PACT tries to avoid that. We have a separate organization that handles lobbying." Fethullah was well spoken despite his discernible accent. Mina recommended him to me as someone deeply committed to PACT but without a dodgy background that Thrillkill might turn against us. "We see ourselves in much the same role as, say, the NAACP many years ago, when African-Americans were fighting for equal rights and combatting negative stereotypes. They accomplished a lot of good in this country—still do, of course—and we hope someday to make just as positive a contribution."

So far, smooth sailing. Two African-Americans on the jury, so this couldn't hurt. Thrillkill sat quietly and calmly, which either meant he couldn't think of a viable objection or he didn't think this testimony could do him any harm.

"How would you describe your core message?"

"We're trying to teach people not to assume everyone of Middle Eastern descent is a terrorist."

"I suppose there's a lot of prejudice out there."

"There is. But that's completely understandable, isn't it? 9/11 was a devastating, horrific event. Of course, most of the participants in 9/11 originated in Saudi Arabia, technically an American ally, but people don't see that. They just see the color of their skin." Fethullah paused reflectively. "Sadly, we have a long history of that here in the United States."

Nice. I loved the way he used the possessive pronoun "we" rather than "they," inclusive rather than condemnatory, and I loved the way he forced the jury to consider their own possible biases. If I had said it, the jury would've been offended, but coming from a calm, thoughtful witness, it was powerful.

"Would you call PACT a religious organization?"

"Again, no more so than necessary. Part of the prejudice confronting Arab-Americans obviously relates to the fact that we are typically Islamic rather than Christian. We have published brochures pointing out that, at the end of the day, the two religions are not that different. Much of the Christian Bible is found in the Koran. The Koran acknowledges Jesus as an important prophet. Both books are about peace and love and essentially teach us to be nice to one another. Many people only know the parts of the Koran that are misquoted on conservative talk shows—stuff about holy wars and martyrs getting virgins in heaven and such."

Enough with the general background. Thrillkill and the judge were being tolerant, but I knew that wouldn't last forever. Time to get back to the case.

"Do you know the defendant, Omar al-Jabbar?"

"Yes."

"He was involved in PACT's work?"

"Yes, he worked for us when he had time. We liked having him on the Board of Directors."

"Why was that?"

"Most of our supporters are Arab-Americans. But Omar's skin is just as white as anyone else's in this country. He chose Islam. He wasn't born to it. Plus, his status as a war hero gives him special credibility. If a man who fought for his country in Iraq has the courage to say he accepts Arab-Americans as equals, who can question it?"

I nodded. Never a bad idea to remind the court that your client is a veteran. "What kind of work did Omar do for PACT?"

"Greased a few wheels. Attended business meetings. Helped forge strategic alliances. And he made a point of attending social gatherings. Parties, that sort of thing. In fact, he was planning one when . . . you know. All this unpleasantness arose."

"What party was he planning?"

"A Fourth of July celebration. A picnic. What better way to show our allegiance to this nation than by participating in the celebration of its independence."

"What did Omar do to help plan the party?"

"I know he'd obtained a lot of supplies. Food, drink, paper plates. We offered to reimburse him, but he refused." A perfect pause. "And I know he'd obtained some fireworks."

I felt the jury stirring. This was the first instance of what I hoped would be a series of corrections. "He bought fireworks for the PACT picnic?"

"Yes. And agreed to store them at his place till the event. We couldn't have anything with gunpowder in it at our headquarters. I'm sure you can see where that would be a bad idea. We never dreamed anyone would try to make more of it."

"One more thing. We had some testimony earlier about Omar and Mr. Nazir. Basically, the idea was that Omar wanted to "take Nazir out." Did you ever hear anything like that?"

"Oh, yeah."

"You did?" I raised an eyebrow, not that I was surprised.

"Sure. I heard almost everyone in the organization say stuff like that."

"What does it mean?"

"Well, first you need to understand that Mr. Nazir had been quite a thorn in the side of PACT. Omar was not the only person who had been interrogated by him. Nazir treated PACT like a terrorist organization, even though it isn't, and tried to get the IRS to cancel our nonprofit status."

"I can see where that might be frustrating."

"Too many of our members knew that Agent Nazir had been a torturer for the Iraqi Republican Guard before he came to America. He preferred that no one knew about his past."

"Is there more?"

"Yes. You need to understand that the phrase "take someone out" means take them out of the *equation*. That's how people used it at PACT. Everyone hoped Agent Nazir would lose his position of influence and his ability to interfere with PACT activities. But no one wanted him dead. You don't prove you're a peace-loving organization by threatening people and assassinating your enemies."

"In your two years at PACT, did you ever hear anyone advocate any plan involving violence or assassination?"

"Absolutely not."

"And did you ever hear the defendant advocate any plan of violence or assassination?"

"Absolutely not."

"Thank you, Fethullah. No more questions."

Thrillkill was not quick about rising. I could see he gave it serious thought. Fethullah was obviously on Oz's side, so the chances that he would make any points were slender. Still, there was always a chance of backing him into something.

"Sir, you say that PACT had no plans to harm Agent Nazir."

"True."

"And, by extension, that you believe the defendant had no plan to hurt Agent Nazir."

"Also true."

"And yet . . . the defendant did bring his gun to that press conference."

"Objection," I said, bouncing up like a Slinky. "That has not been established."

Thrillkill tilted his head. "The defendant's gun was in his hand moments after the murder."

"None of which proves he brought it there."

Thrillkill paused, the tiniest hint of a smirk on his face. "Very well, then, let me rephrase. Someone who had access to the defendant's gun brought it to the press conference. Would you agree that particular person bore malice against Nazir?"

Fethullah was prepared to answer, but I jumped in anyway. "Objection. Speculative. Argumentative."

"Sustained."

Thrillkill didn't blink. "Did other PACT members have access to the defendant's apartment?"

Clever man. He was putting Fethullah in a trap. If he said yes, he implicated the organization. If he said no, Oz remained the most likely suspect.

And of course, Fethullah answered honestly. "I know some people visited him sometimes. But I don't know that they had access, that is, had their own keys."

"Mina Ali lived there, did she not? Or at least slept over on occasion?"

Something flickered through Fethullah's eyes, like an involuntary synapse firing somewhere in his brain. "True."

Thrillkill saw it, too. "Did their relationship bother you?"

"I don't know what you mean."

Thrillkill stared at him a moment before continuing. "You were interested in Mina yourself, weren't you?" I sensed Thrillkill took a shot in the dark, but he hit pay dirt.

"We had dated. In the past. She left me and started dating him."

"It seems the defendant is quite the playboy."

"Motion to strike," I said. "I don't see how any of this is relevant."

"I would have to agree there," Judge Santino said. "This is about a murder, not who had a date for the prom. Get back to the matter at hand, Counsel."

Thrillkill nodded, nonplussed. "My point is Mina had access to the defendant's gun. Right?"

Now Thrillkill offered an even nastier choice. Incriminate Oz or incriminate Mina. But Fethullah managed to avoid the trap. "Since I don't know where the weapon was kept, I can't say who had access to it."

Thrillkill nodded, resigned. "Thank you. No more questions."

Thrillkill surrendered much too quickly. Which left me certain he had something bigger yet to come.

CHAPTER 48

The next step in my ongoing campaign of client character rehabilitation would be calling Mina's younger brother, Kir. Mina would probably do as well, but her relationship with Oz impacted her credibility, as did her relationship with JUSTICE IRAQ and Abdullah. Kir wasn't a member of PACT, but he knew enough about Oz and some of his activities to speak about them without entering the thorny thicket of hearsay. I planned to use him as a warm-up act, then later to call Yasmin al-Tikrit back to the stand, to destroy Thrillkill's conspiracy theory that she and Oz were conspiring to build a superweapon to use against America.

I wanted to consult with Christina, but she was back at the office, prepping Yasmin. I had to go it alone.

"Would you please state your name?"

"Kir Ali."

"Mina Ali is your older sister?"

"Yes."

I'd let Thrillkill ID Abdullah as his older brother. "Are you a member of PACT?"

"No."

Kir was about as nonthreatening as it was possible to be. He was small and short with a slight slouch. He had an accent but also a bit of a lisp, which did not make him seem like a likely "radical Islamic terrorist." His resemblance to Mina was striking but, if anything, made him seem somewhat androgynous. I could see him joining a boy band, but not a terrorist cell. I had a hard time imagining him getting angry enough to cut in line, much less blowing something up. His Disney Channel demeanor couldn't help but dispel the image Thrillkill wanted, of this entire clan being a closeted terrorist cell. "How did you come to be in the United States?"

Kir then began a longish narrative about his immigration, mostly thanks to his sister. To my surprise, Thrillkill let him tell it without an objection, despite the fact that its relevance was tangential at best.

"What do you do for a living?" I asked.

"I work for an American organization called HOPE."

More alphabet soup. "And what do they do?"

"Basically, we work with the Bureau of Consular Affairs to help Americans with relatives overseas obtain green cards or visas or citizenship status. Whatever it takes to bring their loved ones to safety. We focus on those in greatest potential danger in their homelands. Having been through the process myself, I know how tangled and bureaucratic immigration can be, and of course it has become even more difficult recently. But people's lives often hang in the balance."

"Have you met with much resistance?"

"Sadly, in many people's minds these days, immigration is a dirty word. To some, immigrants are all lazy loafers sneaking across borders so they can get welfare payments. Or they are drug smugglers and thieves and rapists. But that stereotype doesn't match reality. For refugees, or people living in trouble spots, immigration may be the only way to remain alive. We try to help the people who need it most."

"Sounds like worthy work. And not unlike the mission of PACT. How do you know the defendant?"

"He and my sister Mina have worked together. She introduced us. He became just as useful to me in my work as he was with PACT."

"Could you please explain how?"

"In many cases, even after people overcome the seemingly insurmountable challenges of immigration, they are lost and penniless and unsure how to proceed with their lives. Their family may not be able to join them immediately. Having work visas is not the same as having work. It can be a difficult, friendless time."

"I would imagine so."

"Oz has worked hard to help, to ease the often-difficult transition period, frequently using his own money to do it. He's even arranged temporary housing for people."

"Do you know where this temporary housing is located?"

"I know he keeps two apartments to use as temporary housing for new immigrants here in the city."

"Specifically . .

"On South Robinson. Not the best neighborhood, I know. But he's not a millionaire. He's just a good-hearted man willing to put his money where his mouth is. I wish there were more like him. He is a hero to many of us."

I decided to hammer it in, just in case some juror hadn't quite twigged onto the truth. "So he's assisted you with the trafficking . . . of immigrants? Legal immigrants?"

"Yes. Found more than one of them jobs, too. Legit jobs. He's good at learning what their skills are and figuring out where they can be applied."

"Does your sister approve of your work?"

"Very much so. In fact, it was her idea, which I readily accepted. I would not be here but for her. I would do anything for my sister."

"I'm sorry I have to ask you this, Kir, but . . . to your knowledge, did Omar ever place any of these immigrants in the sex trade?"

Kir straightened. "Absolutely not. And there's no chance that could happen without my knowing about it, because I keep careful track of everyone we bring in. Sure, there are lots of prostitutes on Robinson, and everyone knows it, but those aren't our people."

"Thank you." Deal done. Time to move on. "Now earlier, you called Omar a hero. Could you please explain what you meant by that?" And quickly, before we draw an objection .

"He fought for the US in the Iraq War. And was interrogated by this government for his troubles. I don't think I would have survived what he endured. I know he's suffered, but he hasn't let it affect his idealism or his beliefs."

"How exactly has he suffered?"

"Objection. Calls for hearsay," Thrillkill said.

"Not necessarily," I replied. "All depends on the answer, doesn't it?"

The judge made a grunting noise. "I'll caution the witness to limit his answer to his own personal knowledge. But he may answer the question."

I set it up again. "What did you mean when you said that Omar has suffered?"

"I'm talking about his PTSD."

"And you know this because . .

"He told me about it. I drove him to a therapy session one week when his car was out of whack."

"If you know, how often does he attend these therapy sessions?"

"He was going three times a week immediately after he returned, but I believe he's down to once a week."

"Why the decrease in frequency?"

"I guess he didn't need it. I have to say he seems perfectly stable to me, not that I'm a psychologist. But I admire him for taking the matter seriously."

"Do you know if he takes any medication?"

"I do, because we've discussed it, and because I accompanied him to the pharmacy once. He's taking Xanax for anxiety—a very low quantity now. And he takes OxyContin for pain."

"That's a narcotic, right? An opioid?"

"Objection," Thrillkill said. "The witness is not a pharmacist."

"Sustained," the judge replied. Not that I cared. I just wanted the jury to understand why the drugs were in Oz's medicine cabinet.

"Would you say you spent a significant period of time with the defendant?"

"I would."

"How much?"

"Over the course of the past two years? I doubt if a week went by that I didn't see him at least three times."

"At what time of day?"

"On weekdays, usually early in the morning. He'd stop by on his way to work to see if he could help anyone. On the weekends, I usually saw him at night."

"And at any time did you see any indications of addiction?"

"Are you kidding? The man doesn't even drink beer."

"Can you recall any time when he did not seem to be in control of his faculties?"

"No. Never."

Granted, this was Oz's friend, and you would expect him to speak well of a friend. But I hoped this showed the jury there was more than one way to interpret facts. What looks like sex trafficking turns out to be benevolent immigration assistance. What looks like addiction is actually a brave man coping with a serious disorder. What looks like explosives is picnic entertainment. If I got lucky, I might inspire a few of the jurors to wonder if Thrillkill was trying to pull the wool over their eyes.

"Thank you. That's all I have."

Thrillkill found his way to his feet. "Would you consider yourself a friend of the defendant, sir?"

"I would. And I'd like to think he feels the same way about me."

"You wouldn't want to see him go to prison, would you?"

"Of course not."

"But you would agree that the person who killed Agent Nazir should be punished, wouldn't you?"

"Objection. The first two questions went to the credibility of the witness. The last was just rhetorical and argumentative."

"Sustained."

Thrillkill didn't blink. "The previous witness, Fethullah, indicated that it was common practice for people in your acquaintance to talk about 'taking out' Agent Nazir."

"Taking him out of the equation, yes."

"Was it common for your PACT friends to carry guns?"

"No."

"Was it common for them to apply for open-carry permits?"

"Not to my knowledge."

"Do you know of anyone in your group who did that, other than the defendant?"

"I don't know of anyone."

"Did you go to the press conference where Agent Nazir was killed?"

"I did."

"But you didn't take a gun, did you?"

"Of course not."

"Indeed," Thrillkill said, nodding. "Why would you? *You* had no reason to do so. Because you didn't want to hurt anyone."

I was forming the "O" word when Thrillkill cut me off. "That's all. No more questions."

The judge appeared pleased. "Let's break for lunch. We'll start again at one o'clock sharp."

I desperately wanted to consult with Christina. Where was she? She should have been back by now.

I watched the jurors as they rose and trundled off to their prepackaged lunches, probably catered by a local deli. I wanted to see signs of doubt, or curiosity. Anything less than certitude.

As they left the courtroom, not a one looked at Oz or even glanced his way. They didn't want to make eye contact. Not even after I'd explained away all the mud Thrillkill slung at Oz. He still made them uncomfortable.

That was a bad sign.

CHAPTER 49
WITNESS AFFIDAVIT
CASE NO. CJ-49-1886

I detected the target leaving the law office. For such a small person, she moved with great deliberation and speed. Professional women tend to be in a hurry, but this subject showed a particular degree of determination. No matter. I would follow my instructions and complete my mission.

The delicacy of the matter, the immensity of the stakes, and the importance of the cause demanded that I act now.

I followed the target to her residence. Fortunately, my preparations ensured that I would be able to see inside, hear inside, and enter quickly should I be instructed to do so.

This target, though not primary, had been on my watch list since before the onset of the trial. I did not know why. My brief was not to assess threats. My brief was to eliminate them.

From the shelter of a neighboring rooftop, I used my phone to receive visual confirmation. She went immediately to her computer. I could not tell what she was doing, though I would later retrieve that information by accessing the mirror I planted on her hard drive. She appeared rushed, urgent. This was not someone casually checking her email. As her fingers skittered across the keyboard, I realized she was entering a message.

My earpiece pinged.

"Yes?"

"Intercept and disrupt communications."

"Now?"

"And quickly."

"Including Internet?"

"Especially Internet."

"Understood."

This was an escalation I did not anticipate, but that did not mean I was unprepared for it. The step from surveillance to interference is small, but handled clumsily or with inadequate preparation, it can be treacherous.

I returned to my van and activated a scrambling unit. Some might think this overkill. Negating the electricity would be sufficient to disable Internet access, but she undoubtedly had a smartphone in her pocket, and the only way to disable that would be to jam the cell signal.

That would only work so long as she stayed in residence. If she was desperate to get a message out, she would surely attempt to leave.

I had to be prepared to prevent that as well.

Through the hidden cam, I perceived her mounting frustration. She ran to another desk. I switched to a different camera. She sorted through papers, sifting, finding the ones she needed and tossing them into a briefcase.

She was going somewhere. If she left, I could not prevent her from sending a message. A simple trip to the corner Starbucks would give her the Wi-Fi she needed.

"Stop her."

The voice in my ear spoke with unmistakable clarity.

"What measures am I permitted?"

"All of them. As necessary."

"This is a strong-willed woman. I will have to exercise maximum force if I am to prevent her from—"

"I understand. Why do you hesitate?"

"I thought perhaps . . . you might want to reconsider."

"Did you hear my instructions?"

"I did."

"Do I need to send someone else?"

"I will complete my mission." I checked my weapon to ensure that it was loaded and ready. I headed toward the door, on an interception course. "It will be done."

CHAPTER 50

I couldn't get Christina on the phone, and it scared me to death. The judge wanted to reconvene, but I'd asked the bailiff to give me a few minutes to line up my next witness. This was the sort of thing judges always made a show of being grumpy about, but ultimately there was little they could do. If a witness wasn't there, the witness wasn't there. In time the judge would insist that I call someone else or rest my case, but we weren't there yet.

I dialed over and over again, texted, even posted on Facebook. CHRISTINA: WHERE ARE YOU?

I'd known this woman for years, loved her from the start, depended upon her more times than I cared to count. She'd never let me down. Never once.

If she wasn't here, if she wasn't responding—there was a reason.

I tried to think of all the silly, innocuous possible reasons for her disappearance.

I couldn't think of a single one.

Eventually, the bailiff tapped me on the shoulder and asked me to come to chambers. Thrillkill was already there. God knows what he and the judge might've been chatting about.

The judge looked relaxed and uncommonly friendly. Was it my

imagination, or had he treated himself to a little snort of something for lunch? "We need to proceed, Mr. Kincaid. Can't keep the jury waiting forever."

"I'm sorry, Your Honor. I left my witness with my partner. My wife. And now I can't locate her."

The judge frowned. "Christina's flaked? That seems unlike her." As if, sure, we expect that sort of thing from you, Kincaid. But Christina? No. "Nonetheless, we have to proceed."

"I don't see the value of this witness anyway," Thrillkill said, trying to hide his undoubted delight that my case was falling apart. "She's already testified."

"For you. But since my cross was limited to the scope of your direct, I couldn't get into anything that mattered."

"Like what?"

"Like anything helpful to my client."

An amused smile played on Thrillkill's lips. "That should be a short direct."

"You'll have to call one of your other witnesses," the judge said. "You have several names on your list. Get one on the stand."

I wasn't particularly anxious to admit that most of those names were either speculative or bluffs. "I don't have anyone present in the courtroom."

"Then call them up and tell them to get their butts over here pronto!"

The judge was losing his happy buzz.

"What about your mystery witness?" Thrillkill said, still amusing himself. "Didn't you promise the jury that by the end of the trial they'd know who *really* committed the crime? Who is it? The mysterious figure who disappeared from the scene of the crime? Nazir's supposed drug supplier? Why don't you put that witness on next?"

If I hadn't been so keenly aware that murder was a capital offense, Thrillkill would've died right then and there.

"Okay," Thrillkill continued, "if that doesn't work for you, why not call your client to the stand? He's in the courtroom."

"That is not going to happen."

"It will eventually. You have no choice."

"I have a lot of choices."

"It would be malpractice not to call him. He's all you've got. All that matters. You just want to save him for last."

"You don't know jack—" I bit the words back, but it took all the willpower I had. "Your Honor, could we perhaps recess for the day? I'm sure that by tomorrow—"

"No can do, pardner. I need this trial over as soon as possible."

Why? Pressing fishing trip? "I'm not sure—"

"That's the way it's going to be."

Thrillkill steepled his fingers quietly.

The judge continued. "This is just one case out of many on my docket. The most important case in the world to you, I'm sure. But not to the rest of us."

The short hairs stood up on the back of my neck. This case wasn't just important to me. This had made national news. Half the cable news stations were obsessing over it. And he just wanted to get it over with? I was starting to feel uneasy.

"You have to get over this attitude that the world revolves around you," the judge continued. "I gather you were big stuff back in Tulsa, but here you're just another lawyer, one of many I see every day. And if you think I'm going to bend the rules just to—"

"My wife is missing, you pompous blowhard!"

The judge's chambers fell silent.

I don't know what came over me. I've never done anything like that in my entire life. All at once everything I'd kept bottled up inside erupted.

The judge cleared his throat. To my relief, he didn't reply with equal vigor, though he must've been tempted. "I'm sure she'll turn up. In the meantime—"

"How can you be sure? Do you know anything about this?" I couldn't shut it off. "I know Christina, and she'd be here unless it was absolutely impossible. So why isn't she? Why are all my witnesses disappearing? Why is my client going to die for something he didn't do? *Why does my sister hate me?* And—And—"

I found I was crouched over, one hand pressed to my forehead, tears in my eyes.

"And I think my little girl has some kind of brain damage." I fought like hell to keep myself from crying. But I didn't entirely succeed.

"This case has been a tremendous strain on us all," the judge harrumphed, after a long awkward silence. "Maybe an early recess wouldn't be the worst idea in the world—"

He was interrupted by a knock on the door.

I looked up and saw Michael Hickman enter the judge's chambers. I'd seen him come and go throughout the trial, but I hadn't spoken ten words to him since that waste-of-time meeting in Thrillkill's office.

He saw me flushed and barely breathing—obviously had no idea what to make of it—but didn't comment. "I, uh, have some news."

"Does it pertain to this case?" the judge asked.

"Very much so."

"Then let's hear it."

Despite the judge's instruction, he hesitated to proceed. "Mr. Kincaid, I'm afraid this concerns you."

"No," I whispered. "Please, God. No."

"Skip the preliminaries," Thrillkill said. "Just tell us what's happened."

He crouched down close to me. "I'm—I'm so sorry, Mr. Kincaid. I'm . . ." He wiped his hand across his brow. "I'm afraid there's been another murder."

CHAPTER 51

I raced across town, violating every known traffic law. I didn't give a damn. I had to see it for myself. The judge was gracious enough to let me leave, not that he had much choice under the circumstances. Even the most hard-nosed judge on earth had to admit that this was an extraordinary situation.

I raced to the front door. A cop stood outside, protecting the crime scene, while four others circled the perimeter. I recognized the lead guy. Rollins, if I recalled correctly.

I hoped maybe if I kept moving and acted as if I knew what I was doing, he wouldn't stop me. Wrong again.

"I'm sorry, sir," Rollins said, holding up a hand. "This is a restricted area."

"Do you know who I am, Officer?"

"I'm . . . afraid I do."

"Then you know why I want in there?"

"My orders are clear. As of yet I have not received permission to allow anyone in but authorized homicide personnel."

In retrospect, I'm amazed I was able to hold it together at all. I'd already fallen apart in front of a judge. Could a total breakdown be far away? "Are you going to make me beg?"

I could see something was on the kid's mind. He was debating whether to say it.

He finally did. "You're the lawyer who repped Judge Roush, right?"

The gay Supreme Court justice. That was a firestorm, back in the day. Amazing how quickly the world changes. "I am."

He nodded, then gave me a small salute. "I'm sure you know what you're doing. Don't touch anything." He stepped aside.

I didn't wait for him to reconsider. This is an incredible world we live in. Just when you think you've figured everything out, people are full of surprises.

Techs were scurrying around, but I still managed to get a good view of the scene of the crime. And the victim.

Yasmin al-Tikrit. At least, that's who they told me it was. I never could have figured it out on my own. The feisty female chemist hadn't just been killed. She'd been destroyed.

"What happened?" I gasped.

Rollins came in behind me. "Judging from the state of the apartment, she had a disagreement with a person who had an extremely powerful gun. And lost."

"Or that's what someone wants you to think."

The place was a wreck—glass coffee table shattered, chairs upturned, scientific papers strewn everywhere. I spotted a blood-smeared indentation on the wall about eye level. I'm guessing someone's head went into the wall the hard way.

Every research scientist I'd ever met was tidy, orderly. All their ducks in a row. But this apartment looked as if a hurricane had swept through.

"How'd she die?"

"The coroner hasn't spoken." Rollins spoke slowly, obviously not sure he should tell me anything. "But I can see she took a gunshot to the heart and the head, which does tend to cause death."

I looked at her battered remains. "That wouldn't explain . . . all this." She'd obviously been beaten. Blood covered her entire body. Her right arm was twisted back at an unnatural angle. Her right leg was broken.

"Yeah. She's a mess."

"This is more than just a disagreement. This is the work of someone who wanted her to suffer."

"I gather she was some kind of scientist," Rollins said, gesturing toward the paperwork.

"Chemist. Engaged in a research project. Something about renewable energy, if I recall correctly."

I glanced at the periodic table mounted on the wall just above her desk. Some of the elements were smeared with red: aluminum, iodine, potassium, iridium. At first, I thought they'd been marked in blood. I was relieved when, on closer inspection, I realized it was just a marker pen.

I noticed something else on her desk. A visa application. Specifically, an I-130 Petition for Alien Relative. I knew that had to be approved by the USCIS. Usually, the sponsoring relative had to demonstrate adequate income or assets to prove the newcomer wouldn't become a burden on society. And it had to be completed by a lawful permanent resident or a foreign national who had been granted the privilege of working and living permanently in the United States.

Did this have something to do with PACT? Or HOPE? Or Abdullah, the man behind the curtain no one could track down?

I knew there was much more going on than the pathetic little iceberg tip I was presenting in my defense. Ninety percent of this case remained underwater. And because of that, a brilliant woman had died.

And Omar might be next.

I heard a struggle on the steps behind me.

"I'm sorry, ma'am, you can't go up there."

"And how are you going to stop me? I only see four officers. And only two of you have guns."

"Ma'am—"

"If you don't move immediately, I'm filing a police-brutality claim against every one of you. And don't laugh it off, because my husband is the best attorney in the world."

That could only be one person.

I glanced at Rollins. "My wife. She works with me. Do you mind if she comes in?"

I could tell he did but probably thought it better to acquiesce than face the anger of the titan. "She can't touch anything."

"She knows."

I met Christina at the top of the stairs.

"Ben, what in the—"

I wrapped my arms around her so tightly it cut her off in midsentence. Something about a shoulder to the mouth tends to end conversation. I squeezed as hard as I could without cracking her ribs.

"Ben, what is the matter with you?" She tried to push away, but I wasn't letting her go. Yasmin's death was a tragedy, but I'm ashamed to admit that when I realized the victim wasn't Christina, all I felt was inexpressible relief.

I heard Rollins somewhere behind me. "I'd offer to leave you two alone, but that isn't an option. Maybe you should get a room. Somewhere else."

"I was so afraid," I whispered into her hair.

"Well, pull yourself together. I heard you had a meltdown in chambers."

Word travels fast. "When did you see Yasmin last?"

"Not an hour ago. We prepped for her testimony. I think we had it sounding pretty good, not that it matters now. She was going to dismantle the lopsided, slanted, deceptive portrait Thrillkill painted of Oz. Then she checked a text, and suddenly there was nothing I could do to keep her in the office. She raced out the door, promising she'd be back at the courthouse in time."

"That's a promise she's not going to keep."

"No joke. I blew an hour looking for her. Sorry I didn't see your texts. I turned my ringer off. What happened here?"

I filled her in on what little I knew about the murder. "It probably relates to the Nazir case."

"But it's possible it doesn't."

"In addition to being tragic, it's devastating to our defense. One more blow to an increasingly impossible case."

"Oh, I don't know." Christina crouched down, peering at the battered remains of Yasmin's face. "Tragic, but surely you can see the upside to this."

"An upside? To murder?"

"Put your feelings in a box, Ben. Think about that case you're trying. What's been your biggest defense problem?"

I mulled that over. "No SODDIT."

"That just changed."

"Because .

"Oz is in custody, so he couldn't possibly have committed this crime. Someone else is out there. And assuming you can get the judge to permit you to introduce evidence of this new murder—"

"Which is a big if."

She granted that with a nod. "But if you can, or if the jurors hear it on the evening news, then they'll realize there's someone capable of committing murder. Someone who isn't Oz. Any unanswered questions work in Oz's favor. They create doubt."

I tried to run the angles through my head. "It's still not much."

"It's more than you had this morning."

True enough. I felt like a complete vulture, trying to spin this hideous murder to my advantage. But Christina was a pragmatist. And I had a man's life in my hands. I didn't have the luxury of being above it all.

This recess wouldn't last forever. The judge had been generous, sort of, but tomorrow morning he would expect the trial to resume. We would undoubtedly have a flurry of motions that would kill at last an hour. I'd try to admit evidence of the new murder; Thrillkill would try to suppress it. I couldn't know the outcome for certain, but the judge had ruled with Thrillkill on every matter of import so far. Why should this be any different?

Christina still stared at that horribly mangled corpse. "I don't know if you ever seriously doubted this, but you want to put Oz on the witness stand. Next."

"Why?"

She laid her hand on my shoulder. "Because everything just changed."

CHAPTER 52

W e had to wait for an uncommonly long time for the judge to return to chambers. He'd decorated it with the usual suspects: photos of grandchildren and OU football memorabilia, a few throw rugs, and some framed prints illustrating "DETERMINATION" and "INTEGRITY," which I suspected were carryovers from the previous occupant. Nothing that would distract anyone for long.

Santino had a private bathroom, which he eventually emerged from. Apparently, breakfast was not agreeing with him. He all but lumbered to his large oaken desk, rested his hands on the ink blotter, and gave me a steely eye. "Convince me you're not wasting my time."

I cleared my throat. Seemed we were going to cut straight to the heart of the matter. "We're not, Your Honor. I will respectfully suggest that, given the violent death of one of the prosecution's own witnesses, the playing field has changed."

"I will have to disagree with that statement," Thrillkill said. He reclined in the most comfortable chair, making a point of appearing unruffled.

"There's another murderer out there," I said. "Not my client. Someone is killing off people in this Iraqi immigrant community."

"Mr. Kincaid," the judge replied, "the fact that another murder has occurred does not prove your client wasn't guilty of the first."

"And if I may add something," Thrillkill said, "Agent Nazir was not a member of this community. There's a huge difference between monitoring PACT activities and being a member."

"There's a difference," I agreed. "But huge? Not so much. They all knew each other."

"We're not going to dismiss," Thrillkill said, "if that's what you're after. Your man was found at the scene holding the murder weapon, his prints on the gun and powder on his palm. He's guilty, and we all know it."

"I don't know it," I shot back. "I just know someone really wants us to believe it. Which is not the same thing."

The judge looked frustrated—never a good sign. "What is it you seek, Mr. Kincaid?"

"I want the jury to know about Yasmin's murder."

"No. That's not relevant. It will only confuse matters."

"Your Honor, I was planning to put her back on the stand, to correct the misapprehensions Mr. Thrillkill created with his selective direct. Now I can't do that."

The judge pursed his lips. "I'll inform the jury that you wanted to call her back to the stand but . . . she was unavailable."

"I'm sorry, Your Honor, but that's not good enough. The jury will never have a fair understanding when one lawyer gets to use a key witness and the other doesn't. I wanted to bring up additional matters when she was on the stand the first time, but you told me to wait till I put on my case. I'm putting on my case now, and guess what? I can't call her."

"I have many powers, Mr. Kincaid, but raising the dead is not one of them. I'm not calling a mistrial, either. This case has dragged on much too long. No mulligans."

"I suppose," Thrillkill said, still markedly unworried, "we could consider retracting the prior testimony of the deceased."

"The jury has already heard it," I pointed out.

"I could instruct the jury to disregard her prior testimony," the judge said. "Exclude it from their deliberations."

"And we all know how much good that will do. You can't unring a bell. They've been prejudiced by the slanted questions put to her on direct."

Thrillkill chuckled. "You mean by her truthful answers?"

It was all I could do to keep from wrapping my fingers around the man's unctuous little throat. "You don't see anything you don't want to see. Because you're more interested in your political career, and you don't care if an innocent man dies if it helps you get elected."

Thrillkill sat up. "Excuse me, Kincaid, but don't take your petty—"

"Gentlemen!" The judge actually pounded on his desk. "Let me remind you that even though we are in chambers, this trial is still in session, and we are on the record, and any comments you make will be directed to the court, not to each other. Do you understand me?"

We both nodded, chins tucked. I felt like I'd been taken out to the woodshed—because I had. And I deserved it. This case was turning me into a crazy person.

"I'm sorry, Your Honor," I said. "But I don't think this problem can be fixed by telling the jury to ignore something they've already heard."

"Then tell me what you want. Short of a mistrial. What would make you happy?"

I saw my opening. Even though I thought it was hopeless, I took my shot. "I want the jury to know that I'm not calling Yasmin back to the stand because she's dead. I want my client to be allowed to testify about what went down between him and Nazir. The interrogation. Including the torture. Twenty-one days of incarceration without being charged. I want them to understand how this country treated a war hero, basically because he had the audacity to convert to the Muslim faith and to show sympathy to people in need. I want them to understand what this case is really about, not just selective bits and pieces, so they can reach an educated conclusion about what happened. I know you could probably argue that it's not probative, but it's the only way the jury will ever really understand this case."

Judge Santino nodded. "All right then. Granted."

I was stunned. My throat locked up. I was so surprised I couldn't find words to reply. Thrillkill seemed equally caught off guard.

"But here are my restrictions, Kincaid, and I expect you to follow them to the letter."

"Yes, Your Honor. I will." Perhaps it would've been smarter to hear what they were first, but I was still shell-shocked from having a tiny bit of success.

"One." The judge raised fingers as he ticked off his conditions. "Your client may discuss his war record and his treatment at the hands of the CIA. Two, you may introduce evidence that Yasmin has died, thus preventing her from being recalled. You will not mention that she was murdered or in any way suggest that her murderer was also the murderer of Nazir." His lip curled slightly. "Take your SODDIT somewhere else."

"I can live with that." I didn't love it. But this was not the time to argue. I didn't need to bring up theories about her murderer in court. It had been all over the news and the front page of the newspaper. Jurors are always instructed to avoid all contact with the news media, but I didn't believe for a minute that they did. It was fundamental human nature, from the Garden of Eden on, for people to seek out knowledge. Everyone wants to feel like they understand what's going on around them. Why would jurors be any different?

"Three," the judge continued, but instead of extending a third finger, he clenched them all into a fist. "You will stay on target, discussing these prescribed subjects and nothing else. This courtroom will not become a referendum on the relative wisdom of US intervention into Middle Eastern affairs, immigration, racism, religious prejudice, or anything else. We're going to talk about the murder of Agent Nazir."

"Understood, Your Honor. Thank you, Your Honor."

"Any problems with this, Mr. Thrillkill?"

The man was obnoxious to the core, but he did know when it was time to be quiet. "If that's the court's ruling, we'll live with it."

"Thank you." He gave me the evil eye. "Can I assume your next and probably final witness will be the defendant?"

"Yes, sir."

"I will be watching every word he says like a hawk. Make sure he doesn't cross the line."

"I will, sir, but—"

"No buts. None."

"He feels very strongly about the US invasion—"

"That's another word I don't want to hear."

"I'm not sure it's possible to tell his story without some reference to recent events. It's like explaining Noah's Ark without mentioning rain."

"You'll find a way."

"And I know the court doesn't want to rob the defense of its best ammunition."

"You think politics is your best ammunition?" Santino removed his glasses, then leaned back into his chair. "I thought you were smarter than that, Kincaid. Maybe your rep isn't all it's cracked up to be."

Swell. Just when I was starting to feel minutely good about the case. "I'm not following."

"Kincaid, your best shot isn't talking about politics. Or the CIA. Or who had a motive against whom. I've been on this bench a long time. I've watched juries. I understand how they think. They know the lawyers will cross swords. They know there will be conflicting stories and everyone will suggest the other side is evil and blah blah blah. It's like squabbling parties after a divorce. It's always the other person's fault. Bottom line, juries don't pay much attention to all that. What they do pay attention to is evidence. Like the fact that your client's gun, the one he held in his hand at the scene of the crime, fired the bullet that killed Agent Nazir. That's what the jury will remember. And bloviating about Iraq will not cause them to forget it."

CHAPTER 53

O z composed himself on the witness stand with more grace than most people in this stressful situation. He seemed to have made a real journey over the course of this case. When he first came back into my life, he was angry, bitter, filled with rage. After the murder, he was scared, panicked, certain the bastards had found another way to take him down.

But today he seemed strangely tranquil. And although I wanted to think that was because he had supreme faith in my lawyering abilities, I knew better. Had he come to terms with his situation? Accepted his fate? Found an inner resilience? Or simply stopped caring? I didn't know. But I needed him to remain calm on the witness stand, so this was a good development.

Even when I told him about the judge's ruling, which meant we spent the entire night redesigning his testimony, he seemed to take it in stride.

"This helps us, right?" he asked.

"I think so."

"I know so," Christina added.

"At least now the jury will understand what really happened."

"Agreed."

The jurors appeared pleased when I called him to the stand. They all knew the defendant didn't have to testify, but in my experience, they're disappointed if the defendant doesn't. It's like seeing a play that skips the final act. They don't feel like they've been presented with the whole story.

I didn't spend a lot of time on Oz's war record. That spoke for itself. I've always thought attorneys erred when they had their clients make overt plays for sympathy, like when personal injury lawyers let people whine on about their pain and suffering. Here in Oklahoma, anyway, most folks are uncomfortable with public displays of emotion. We tend to respect people who bear their crosses with equanimity. I didn't think Oz needed to rattle on and on about the horrors of war. Everyone already knew.

"Were you ever injured?"

"Yes. Shrapnel in the leg. A concussive bomb near my head deadened my hearing for a while." He shrugged. "I saw friends get much worse."

"Any other symptoms?"

"I was diagnosed with PTSD. Got some treatment. And as you heard, some medication, which I'm still taking, though in smaller doses." He glanced at Thrillkill. "Which is one reason all those free samples from the VA hospital last so long."

"When did you return home?"

"About two years ago. I considered a third tour. But I felt that if I didn't get some kind of career started at home, I never would. And to be truthful, I was beginning to question our involvement in the Middle East. The longer I was there, the harder it was to figure out why. It seemed more about oil and less about weapons of mass destruction and—"

"So you returned to Oklahoma." I could see the judge frowning. I cut Oz off before it got too political. "What did you do when you returned?"

"My plan was to get a degree at UCO and get into construction management. But I was introduced to an organization called PACT."

Not mentioning the man who introduced him, Abdullah. Good. "Why?"

"I mentioned that I questioned our military intervention. I also questioned my faith. Perhaps I was influenced by all the people I saw willing to give their lives for their religion. Most of the Christians I knew didn't seem nearly so committed. Go to church on Sunday, then do whatever you want the rest of the week, that sort of hypocritical thing. I won't bore you with the details. But over the next six months, I began attending a mosque in Choctaw. Eventually committed to Islam. Changed my name to acknowledge the conversion experience."

"How does that relate to PACT?"

"They were hoping for a more public, more aggressive education campaign. And I was exactly what they wanted. I can see that now even more clearly than I did at the time."

"What do you mean?"

"Well, for starters, I'm white, and I'm a war veteran, but I'm committed to the Islamic faith, and I think our repeated interference in the Middle East has been a titanic blunder. I've seen other members of my faith subjected to prejudice based on the color of their skin or the spelling of their last names. I've seen bigotry in many forms, and I know how destructive it can be. PACT wanted to do something about all that, and I was ready to help. We were preparing for a major campaign when I was . . . taken."

"Would you please explain what you mean by taken?"

"I was arrested by federal agents."

"What was the charge?"

"No charge. They said they wanted to talk to me."

"And did they?"

"Yes. For twenty-one days."

"Please tell the jury what happened."

"I was arrested and held at a federal detention center. I was kept in a tiny cell, often cold, sometimes with blaring loud noise or music. I was frequently stripped and left naked. I was at times restrained or chained to the wall. I was subjected to sleep deprivation, extreme temperatures, what in the military they call 'stress positions.' Bright lights in the face. Manhandled to keep my eyelids open. They would put a towel over my head and dunk me in a tank of water. Never long enough that I would die. But long enough that it would feel as if I were dying. Over and over again."

I let the room go silent for a while. I thought it was okay to let him understate everything. Better than playing the drama queen. But I wanted to make sure it sank in, just the same.

"And this went on for . .

"Twenty-one days."

"Who was doing this?"

"At first, I didn't know. Eventually, I learned it was the CIA. Acting domestically, though some say that violates their charter."

"What was the purpose of the interrogation?"

"They sought information about a man named Abdullah Ali."

"Do you know Abdullah?"

"Yes. He's one of the founders of PACT."

"Why would the CIA care about PACT?"

"The attitude of my interrogator seemed to be that PACT was more than a nonprofit political-advocacy group. They claimed PACT was a cover for a terrorist cell. They thought Abdullah was a terrorist ringleader. They said he was developing some kind of weapon that would be used against the United States."

"Was PACT a terrorist cell?"

"No. The most dangerous thing I ever did was try to get a bulk-mail license."

"Is Abdullah a terrorist?"

"I had no reason to think he was a terrorist. But at any rate, if he had secret activities, it had nothing to do with me."

"And you told them this?"

"Not all at once. At first, I stood on my constitutional right to avoid self-incrimination. The Fifth Amendment, remember that? But extensive torture and abuse . . . well, there comes a point when everyone gives in." His head lowered.

"Did you tell them what you knew?"

"Yes. Which was of no use to them. I knew nothing about terrorists or weapons."

"And they didn't release you?"

"Not for twenty-one days." He shook his head. "I'm a war veteran.

I've seen bad stuff. I've been injured. But I've never experienced anything as brutal and cruel as what I got at the hands of my own government."

I checked the jury, but their expressions weren't giving me much. All I could tell for certain was that they were paying attention.

"Were there any other possible reasons the CIA might be suspicious of you? Other than your involvement with PACT?"

Oz drew in his breath, then slowly released it. "They might have known about my . . . brief flirtation with ISIS."

Several of the jurors leaned in closer. I knew we needed to bring this up before Thrillkill did. But I had to handle it just right if I didn't want it to convince the jury of his guilt. "You're talking about the jihadist terrorist organization, right?"

"Right. The Islamic State of Iraq and Syria."

"Can you tell us what you mean by a brief flirtation?"

"ISIS tries to recruit lonely, disaffected Americans, often targeting the rich or the bored or the voiceless. Young people who haven't found their place in the world yet. And that of course would be the perfect description of me just after I returned from service. Disillusioned and lost."

"ISIS reached out to you?"

He nodded. "I didn't know that's who it was at first. I just started getting online messages from people who wanted to teach me what it meant to be a Muslim. They never said anything bad about Christianity. They said Islam was a correction of Christianity. Like a software update. Christianity 2.0. Each day I got a new lesson, starting with the fundamentals of praying, which included the *wudu*, the ritual washing of face and feet, hands and arms, before each of the five daily prayers. They told me Muslims placed their heads on the ground when praying, and gave me a Bible verse that showed Jesus doing the same thing."

"They were trying to recruit you."

"They were. They are masters of social media. They have many people trolling the Internet, luring in isolated, lonely people. Packages started to show up at my apartment. Hijabs, prayer rugs, books. 'There is no God but Allah, and Muhammad is his messenger.' Unquestioned acceptance of polygamy. Eventually, that became talk about the Islamic

State and how it wanted to build a homeland in Syria and Iraq where the holy could live according to sharia law. We Skyped a few times. They spent thousands of hours on me. Sent me little gifts, chocolates. Gift certificates for Barnes & Noble. Offered me money."

"Did you ever meet these people?"

"Yes. They encouraged that. Told me it was sinful to only associate with unbelievers. Eventually they suggested face-to-face get-togethers at a local mosque. I attended two meetings, then got out. They were way too radical for me. Kept pushing me to travel to a Muslim land. Even if I agreed with what they were saying, which I didn't, I would never have agreed with any plan to use force or violence to achieve political change."

"But the CIA found out about this."

"Yes. They raided an ISIS computer server and tracked the email to me. Accused me of plotting with ISIS, which was absurd. If they'd read the email, they'd know it was absurd. Which is why I always thought that was an excuse, not an explanation. There was some other reason they were interrogating me. They wanted information about PACT and Abdullah. And I had nothing to give them."

Oz told his story well. He was not holding back, but he wasn't self-pitying or melodramatic or anything else that might turn the jury off. And he hadn't given Thrillkill a reason to jump to his feet.

"What did you do when you were finally released?"

"Tried to put my life back together again. I'd disappeared for almost a month, and no one knew where I was. I lost my job. Made PACT suspicious of me. Lost my girlfriend."

"Did the CIA offer you any assistance?"

His chuckle was more than a little bitter. "No."

"Did you enter counseling?"

"I was already there. The GI Bill covered some PTSD therapy. I was angry. I'll admit it. I think being held for weeks without being charged is unconstitutional. I don't care what the law says, it's wrong. I felt I'd given a lot to this country, and it owed me better. And don't let anyone fool you with this crap about 'enhanced interrogation techniques.' We're talking about torture. The US tortured people for information. And no one ever walks away from being tortured without permanent scars. That—" His voice jumped, quavered, but he cut it off. "That—" He tried again. "That messes you up for the rest of your life."

"The prosecutor has introduced evidence indicating that you had a grudge against the deceased. Agent Nazir."

"He was my chief interrogator," Oz said quietly. "He orchestrated the torture."

I nodded. "Any other cause for enmity?"

"PACT felt he was engaging in improper surveillance of a legitimate political lobbying organization. Which, sadly, the US has a long history of doing. The government tried to suppress labor unions way back when. The FBI bugged Dr. King and Eleanor Roosevelt. Agent Nazir had an ugly history, and he bore hostility toward anyone who might expose it publicly. PACT wanted to take Agent Nazir out of the equation."

"Did that mean you wanted to kill him?"

"Of course not. I've seen enough killing. I hope to never see it again. It offends my religion, and it offends me as a human being."

"But you owned a gun."

"Yes. And I wanted the right to carry it, too. If you'd been subjected to the kind of treatment I had, you'd feel the same way, I guarantee."

"You took it to the press conference where Nazir was shot."

"I took it everywhere."

I nodded. We'd done about as much as we could do. If I'd forgotten anything, I didn't know what it was. Time to wrap it up.

"Omar, did you want Agent Nazir dead?"

"No."

"Did you shoot Agent Nazir?"

"No."

"Do you know who did?"

He looked straight at the jurors. "I do not."

"Thank you. I'll pass the witness."

CHAPTER 54

T his was one witness Thrillkill couldn't skip, even if he thought cross would accomplish little. To allow the defendant to testify without questioning anything he said would be tantamount to accepting his word as gospel truth. A prosecutor could never allow that.

As it turned out, Thrillkill had way more up his sleeve than I realized.

Thrillkill rose, but he did not immediately speak. He glanced at his notes, then set them aside. He settled into a position at the edge of the defendant's table, paused, strode a little closer to the witness. Not close enough to seem overbearing, but hardly invisible. Imposing might be the correct word. Unavoidable.

"I will ask you to admit that at the time of the murder, you bore significant ill will against the United States government."

Oz thought for several beats before answering. Good for him. "I fought for my country on the battlefield."

"Not at the time of the murder. At that time, you supported anti-American interests."

"I completely disagree." Stay calm, Oz. Stay calm.

"You opposed US involvement in the Middle East."

"After I returned from service, I exercised my First Amendment rights to speak out against something I opposed. That's not anti-American. That's what defines America. Freedom of speech."

"Our former vice president said those who don't support American policies are helping the terrorists."

"He needs to reread the Constitution."

A little too much sting for a defendant, but I don't think the jury minded much. Thrillkill was obviously needling him.

"But the fact is—you were helping the terrorists, weren't you?"

"Absolutely not. Never."

"You worked with ISIS."

"Never at any time did I so much as lift a finger to advance ISIS's political agenda, which I completely oppose."

"You helped Abdullah Ali."

"I helped PACT."

"And you're aware that Abdullah is on the CIA's watch list."

"The CIA watches literally tens of thousands of people. Most of them are of Middle Eastern descent."

"Because they are suspected terrorists."

"I'm not in a position to explain CIA motivations. I don't think you are, either."

The more defensive Oz acted, the more suspicious he became. As "un-American" as it might seem, the witness stand is one place where we do not admire those who stand up for themselves. It tends to lead, to quote Shakespeare, to a feeling that the witness "doth protest too much."

"You will acknowledge that Abdullah was suspected of terrorist activity?"

"I never saw any evidence of any terrorist activity."

"I will direct the witness to answer the question," Thrillkill said, putting a little force into his voice. "You were aware that Abdullah was suspected of terrorism?"

"Yes." Oz paused. "But then, so was I."

"Another point the jury should bear in mind," Thrillkill added, with more than a little snark. "And what a coincidence that the two of you should be working together."

"Objection," I said. "They weren't working together on terrorism, and the prosecution has never put on the slightest evidence suggesting that they did."

"I apologize," Thrillkill said. "I meant nothing inappropriate. I'm sure these two suspected terrorists were working on something completely innocuous."

My jaw clenched. "Are we going to try this case on evidence or snotty innuendo?"

The judge looked even angrier than I did. "Counsel are both directed to be quiet. Immediately." He gave us a fierce look. "I will have no more talking objections. State your objection and be quiet. I can rule without coaching." He paused to gather his thoughts. "This objection is sustained."

Thrillkill continued unruffled. "Sir, would you admit that the fact that the CIA detained you for twenty-one days suggests that they had serious reason to suspect you of terrorist activities?"

"No. Desperate people do desperate things in desperate times."

"And in your view the CIA is desperate."

"Objection," I said. "Relevance. Also, lack of personal knowledge."

"Sustained."

Thrillkill feigned frustration. "They must've had some reason to keep you so long."

"As I've said, they were hoping I had information about Abdullah. Which I didn't."

"They didn't detain him."

"They can't find him."

"But they held you—"

"The US kept six men at Guantánamo Bay for more than twelve years without charging them. Then shipped them off to Uruguay. Does that prove those men knew anything? No. It proves the US used them, then wanted them out of the way."

"Why would Agent Nazir want you out of the way if you weren't—"

"Because I was dating someone he had a prior connection to. Someone he had tortured and humiliated. Mina Ali."

"You were in a . . . romantic relationship with her."

"That was Mina in the video you showed. How can we pretend

Americans have any privacy when people like you are allowed to put our private affairs on display?"

Thrillkill cut him off. "That was Mina Ali?"

"Yes."

"How long had this relationship been going on?"

"Not that long. Nazir probably thought that if two people he had mistreated became allies, the truth about his past might become public knowledge. Nazir tried to embarrass Mina to break us up." He took a deep breath. "I didn't make that sex video. Nazir did. The master spy. He recorded us, then tried to use it to humiliate her. Showed it around the family, the mosque. Her family demanded that I marry her. When I declined, Mina had to leave her mosque, was shunned and shrouded by her family." His teeth clenched tightly together. "In other words, once again, Nazir had destroyed someone's life. Without mercy or remorse."

CHAPTER 55

This is why lawyers hate surprises. People think trial attorneys are masters at thinking on their feet, being spontaneous. Wrong. The secret of good trial practice is advance preparation, slowly and carefully considering every possible contingency. But all that planning falls apart when there are important facts no one bothered to tell you.

Had Oz just made himself more sympathetic to the jury? Or had he given them another reason to believe he killed Nazir? This was the most complicated trial I had ever managed, and it was proving much too complex for this bear of little brain.

Evidently Thrillkill was having the same trouble assimilating all this, because he changed the subject. "You refused to release your psychiatric records, true?"

"I was never consulted."

"I'm sorry. Your therapist refused to release your records."

"Objection." I knew I was playing into Thrillkill's hands, but it had to be done. "Medical records are privileged by law. It's completely inappropriate for counsel to bring this up on cross."

"Sustained."

The ruling was obvious. But Thrillkill wanted to remind the jury that Oz was seeing a therapist—which suggested to the old guard that he had some kind of mental problem. He also wanted to plant the suggestion that Oz was hiding something.

"You acknowledge that you've seen a therapist, correct?"

"I already discussed that."

"There must have been a reason."

"The military encourages soldiers to seek counseling when they return stateside. Especially if they've been wounded."

"And the reason they promote this therapy—"

"Objection." I sensed where this was going, and I wanted to stop it dead in its tracks. "The witness does not establish military policy and has no way of knowing why policies were put into place."

"Sustained."

Thrillkill tried again. "I assume the reason therapy is recommended is that in the past people suffering from PTSD have engaged in violent or dangerous activities."

"Objection!" I said, too loudly. "This is outrageous. Now he's trying to convict the defendant based on the fact that he served his country."

Thrillkill looked appalled. "I was not—"

"The objection is sustained," the judge said curtly. I was not surprised to see that a former JAG court judge didn't care much for this line of questioning. "Mr. Thrillkill, I think it's time for you to move on."

Nothing warmed my heart more than seeing the judge get rough with someone else.

"You serve Abdullah's organization."

"I've worked for PACT. I've aided the cause of equal rights for Arab-Americans."

"And you've worked to bring more Muslims into the United States."

"True."

"Why would you do that when you have so many disagreements with the US government?"

"Now you're being disingenuous. If you'd lived a day, or for that matter ten minutes, in what's left of Iraq or Afghanistan or Syria, you wouldn't ask such a foolish question."

I could see Thrillkill weighing whether he wanted to take that baton. He didn't.

"Did you discuss these complaints against the United States with your friends in ISIS?"

"I have no friends in ISIS."

"Sounds like you engaged in extensive discussions with them."

"They tried to recruit me. They were unsuccessful. I've never done anything that would hurt my country."

"You accepted gifts from ISIS agents. You smuggled prostitutes across the border."

"I did no such thing. I helped people build better lives. In many cases, prostitution is exactly what the people I helped were escaping."

"So you insist that you were not involved in the sex trafficking that is so prevalent in the area where you live."

"Correct. I know nothing about it."

"Nothing. Hmm." He shuffled a few papers. "Were you responsible for bringing over a woman named Karma Khan?"

He nodded. "I remember Karma. Her aunt works as a maid at the La Quinta in Midwest City."

"Were you aware that she's currently working as a prostitute?"

"No," Oz said. "I'm sorry to hear that. If it's true."

"Since you're challenging the veracity of my statement, let me present you with her arrest report." No point in objecting. Oz's remark opened the door. "May I approach the witness?" He passed the report to Oz, then retreated to his usual position. "As you'll see, she's been picked up for soliciting. Twice."

Oz laid down the paper, the sadness evident on his face. "I'm sorry to hear that."

"So your testimony is that you didn't know?"

"I didn't." His voice choked slightly.

"Spare me the crocodile tears, sir. You brought her over for the express purpose of turning her into a prostitute."

"That's a disgusting lie."

"Would you please read to the jury the location where your protégé was arrested?"

He read the addresses off the arrest sheet. They were both on

South Robinson, the area Thrillkill had mentioned before. Near where Oz lived.

"But you didn't know she was a prostitute."

"I still don't know that."

"So you're claiming both arrests were mistakes?"

"The police have made mistakes before. And I see no indication of any convictions."

"How many times do you expect the jury to believe that story? If law enforcement made as many mistakes as you suggest, this country would be in anarchy."

"Objection," I said. "Argumentative."

"Sustained. Mr. Thrillkill, your job is to ask questions. Nothing more."

"Yes, Your Honor. I'm sorry. I'm just having trouble getting straight answers."

I jumped up. "Your Honor—"

Thrillkill held up his hands. "I'm sorry. Withdraw the remark." As if that would make it go away.

"So to recap," Thrillkill continued, "you didn't know Karma Khan was a prostitute. Working in your neighborhood. Did you ever see her on your drive to work? Perhaps on a street corner?"

"No." Oz contained himself, but I could see rage boiling behind his eyes, and I'm sure everyone else could, too.

"Did you ever make any attempt to check in on the young women you brought into this country?"

"In the first place," Oz said, "it wasn't just women. In the second place, it's not really possible for me to follow up on them after a point. Unlike the CIA, I do not stalk private citizens. My role was to help them obtain a visa and find work. Once that's completed, they tend to move on."

I tried to send Oz psychic commands. Stay calm. No matter what happens.

"Once you'd obtained a green card for these women, did you turn them over to someone else?"

"Employers, if that's what you mean."

"And by employers you mean pimps?"

I jumped to my feet. "Objection!"

Thrillkill shrugged. "It's a fair question. If the answer is no, he can say no."

The judge's lips curled. "I'll allow it."

"I did not turn anyone over to a pimp," Oz said, teeth clenched. "I don't know any pimps. "Most of the people we brought over are now productive members of society."

"Are you sure? I thought you said you didn't keep tabs on them."

I could see Oz's hands gripping the front rail. "I am not a pimp. I am not a sex trafficker. I have never been and would never be involved in such a thing."

"But you've killed people. Haven't you?"

Thrillkill came back with that so quickly I could see it was all planned. He wanted Oz to lose his temper. He wanted Oz to look dangerous.

If he could accomplish that, the evidence, or lack thereof, wouldn't matter so much.

"Only on a field of combat," Oz replied.

"I imagine taking your first victim is the hardest. After you've killed your first human being, the others probably come much more easily."

"Objection," I said calmly, trying not to escalate the anger factor in the room.

"Sustained," the judge said. "Let's get back to the murder at hand."

"Were you aware that Agent Nazir was investigating links between sex trafficking and terrorism?"

"No," Oz replied. His voice had traveled from having a hint of an edge to being almost all edge. "Agent Nazir did not confide in me about his work."

"He had a theory that terrorists were using the underground railroads employed by sex traffickers to bring terrorists into the country. In other words, that the two activities were closely connected."

"Is there a question here?" I asked. "Or is the prosecutor just giving us gratuitous hearsay testimony from the dead?"

Thrillkill didn't wait for a ruling. "My question is whether you were aware of any such link, sir?"

"No," Oz replied. "How could I be? Since I knew little about terrorists and absolutely nothing about sex traffickers."

"You seem terribly oblivious to the world around you. Very closely around you. You're in constant contact with terrorists and sex traffickers, yet you want us to believe you know nothing about them." Thrillkill shuffled a few more papers. "Are you also denying that you owned a gun?"

"No."

"So you weren't involved in terrorism, and you weren't involved in sex trafficking, but you did make sure you had a weapon on hand."

Oz hesitated. "I live in a dangerous neighborhood."

"I know. It's full of terrorists and prostitutes. Everyone there, probably, except you." He shuffled a few more notes. "And you don't deny applying for an open-carry license."

"No."

"What would be your reason for wanting to carry your weapon openly?"

"I already discussed that. Safety."

"You can't protect yourself with a concealed weapon?"

"It sends a message."

"So you were trying to scare people."

"I was trying to prevent people from messing with me. Soldiers carry their weapons openly, too, and for a reason. It discourages attacks."

"You know what?" Thrillkill said. "I've lived in Oklahoma City my entire life. Even spent some time down on South Robinson. But I've never felt the need for a weapon. Much less one dangling from a holster around my waist."

"You haven't been chained to a wall like an animal for twenty-one days."

Thrillkill pounced. "So you carried the gun because you were hoping to get even with the men who did that with you."

"No."

"Particularly the chief interrogator."

"No."

"You hated Nazir and you wanted him dead."

"Well, what if I did?" Oz sprang out of his chair, leaning against the rail. "That bastard deserved to die!"

A shroud fell over the courtroom as his words reverberated in the dead space. It was like a moment trapped in amber. I'm sure Oz wanted to take it back as soon as he'd said it. But it wasn't going away.

I didn't know whether an objection would help or hurt. Thrillkill had needled him, baited him, and ultimately gotten the reaction he wanted. He wasn't so much asking Oz questions as gently gliding a noose around his neck.

Oz fell back into his seat, tiny tears seeping from the corners of his eyes. "You don't know what it's like. Being humiliated like that. I served my country, and my reward was shame."

"And you blamed Nazir."

"He destroyed my life more than the military or the Iraqis or anyone else. He left me with nothing."

Thrillkill spoke quietly. "Sir, you did in fact carry a gun to the press conference at which Agent Nazir was killed, didn't you?"

"Yes." His voice was little more than a croak.

"And that was your gun. The one you bought, you owned. The one for which you got the permit."

"Yes."

"And that gun was in your hand when you were arrested, wasn't it?"

It was as if he'd lost the will to resist. "Yes."

"And you heard the testimony of the ballistics expert. Stating that your gun was the murder weapon?"

"I did."

Thrillkill nodded. "No more questions."

CHAPTER 56

I made no stops on my way home from work. Christina tried to console me, saying even the best attorney can't rewrite history, but it didn't help. I thought the case was winnable, and I'd let victory slip through my fingers. I still didn't believe Oz shot that man. But I knew the jury did. I couldn't figure out how anyone else could've done it. And I couldn't come up with another plausible suspect.

Oz put his trust in me. And I failed him.

And Julia.

I didn't even want to go home. Julia would be there. Probably Christina already told her the grim news, but that wasn't nearly as bad as having to face her, having to tell her that this man she cared about was headed to a lethal injection, and it was all my fault. She'd been doing great with the girls. Christina was talking about asking her to stay permanently. But now? I'd be lucky if she could stand to be in the same room with me.

Sadly, there was nowhere else to go. And I was desperate to see my girls.

Christina met me at the door. With a grilled cheese sandwich.

"Is that for me?"

"Well, I've heard other wives greet their husbands with a martini, but since you detest the taste of alcohol, this will have to do."

"Thanks," I said, hanging up my coat. "But I'm not hungry."

"What does hunger have to do with grilled cheese sandwiches? It's not like you eat them for their nutrients."

"I'm not in the mood."

"Suit yourself." She set the sandwich down on a plate.

"Girls in bed?"

"Of course. They're fine. There's someone else I'd like you to see before you look in on them."

Someone she wanted me to see? "You haven't gone out and bought me a puppy or something, have you?"

She shook her head. "Something much better." She opened the den door.

"Skipper!" And a second later, a huge, barrel-chested man of my acquaintance strode out the door in a white T-shirt and tattered jeans. "How the hell ya been?"

Loving. My investigator of many years. Complete salt of the earth. A more devoted man never lived. He wrapped his arms around me and squeezed so hard I thought he'd cripple me. But to tell the truth, I didn't mind too much.

I was anxious to catch up and see what had been happening in his life lately. Seems he'd been to Australia, done a walkabout, taken up meditation, and found his center, whatever that means. But it wasn't long before the discussion turned to the trial in progress. "Hear you're up against the wall on this one."

"It's a tough case."

"Against a prosecutor who's trying to screw you over."

I shrugged. "He wants to run for governor."

"So he needs a conviction. Regardless of whether he nails the right man. Some things never change, huh?"

"True enough."

"You know he's in with the CIA. And they're still tryin' to cover up Roswell. They got all the evidence stashed at Area 51."

I decided to give that digression a pass. "You're looking healthy, Loving. I think you've dropped a few pounds."

"It was overdue. I had to get myself together. But I got my head back on straight. And I feel like a million bucks. I run my own private investigation agency now. And I don't take any cases I don't want or don't believe in. It's made me a new man."

"I'm glad to hear it. What brings you here?"

"What do you think?" He gave Chris a smile. "Your little honey said you needed help."

"I do not need help."

"She predicted you'd say that. So I dropped everything and got my butt over here."

"You didn't have to—"

"Of course I didn't have to, Skipper." He slapped me on the shoulder hard enough to leave a welt. "But you stuck your neck out for me more than once. 'Bout time I did the same."

I gave Christina a stern look. "It would appear you've been a busy bee."

I heard Julia's voice. "Oh, you don't know the half of it."

A second later, she emerged from the kitchen—followed by my former office manager.

"Jones!"

"Hey." He wiped his hands on his apron. "Julia and I were whipping up a little dessert."

"Baked Alaska?"

"For you? No. Rice Krispie treats." He grinned. "Hear you're still fighting the good fight, boss."

"I'm not your boss anymore. Not that I ever really was."

"Old habits die hard."

"What have you and Paula been doing?"

"Just keeping our heads above water. I think you know she became assistant director of the whole Tulsa City-County Library system. Unfortunately, no one under fifty seems to want print books anymore. The libraries are all about e-books and computers. She resigned and started her own small publishing business. She writes and edits. I handle the business end. We're getting by."

"That's terrific. I'm sorry Christina dragged you down here. I'm sure you have many—"

"Nothing more important than you, boss." He didn't have to touch me. I felt the hug in his eyes. "Nothing at all."

I glanced at the table. That sandwich was starting to sound good, but it would be rude to eat in front of my guests. "I think we've wasted your time. The trial will likely end tomorrow. I don't have any more witnesses. I wanted to call the guy who was spotted running from the scene of the crime, but I couldn't find him."

Loving put a thumb to his chest. "I did."

"What? Overnight?"

"Nah. Chris called me days ago."

I glared at my spouse. "You didn't mention it to me."

Christina shrugged. "Seemed pointless—unless he found something. Which he did."

"How? The police couldn't find the guy."

"I have a habit of going places the police don't," Loving reminded him. "And Jones was a big help. For once."

Jones ignored the jab. "Online data searches. Credit card companies don't use packet protection nearly as well as they should. Got some interesting leads from the CIA, too."

"You hacked the CIA?"

"You think Snowden is the only person who knows how to crack a firewall? If anything, he just showed how easy it is. And how much the government spies on our personal lives. Which, when you think about it, is a bad combination."

"So who is this guy?" I asked. "Does he know anything useful?"

"I'm not saying he'll win your case single-handedly. But he definitely throws a few added wrinkles into it." Another grin spread across Loving's face, ear to ear. "And that's not all I got."

"Another witness?"

"Sort of. Who's the other important player in this case you haven't been able to get your hands on?"

I thought for a moment. "You found Abdullah Ali?"

"And I got him where he can't get away."

My eyes narrowed. "Tell me you haven't broken laws."

"Which laws?"

Best not to know.

Jones did a dead-on Marlon Brando impression. "Loving made him an offer he couldn't refuse."

"When can I talk to them?" I asked. "Where are they?"

"See," Jones said, "that's the most interesting thing about this. There is no 'they.'"

"I'm not following you."

Jones and Loving exchanged a knowing glance. "Abdullah *is* the guy who disappeared from the scene of the crime."

CHAPTER 57

Trying to get the judge to accept an eleventh-hour witness is never a pleasure. And in a capital murder case, where the stakes are so impossibly high, every irregularity is a struggle. Add the fact that the eyes of the nation were upon us, and the prosecutor was counting on this case to augment his political plans, and you had an even tenser situation.

I did have one factor to my advantage, however. Thrillkill had added a new witness during his case. I think my fleeing witness had more credibility than his jailhouse snitch. And no judge wants to give a defendant anything he could potentially use on appeal.

Judge Santino peered at me through those thick, black glasses. "You're saying you had no inkling you were going to call this man to the witness stand prior to last night?"

"Your Honor," I replied, "I didn't even know this man existed prior to last night. I mean, I knew there was a man named Abdullah Ali. But I had never met him and had no reason to believe I could find him."

"And yet," Thrillkill said, in his usual suggestive louche voice, "you did."

"My investigator brought him to my attention last night."

"Your investigator? Corwin? Or that big guy, the one who went on the walkabout?"

How did Thrillkill know about that? I didn't know about that myself till Loving told me the previous night. "I don't see what difference it makes. The point is we found him, and he has relevant knowledge."

"And you were able to convince him to testify. Against his own best interests."

I tilted my head. "My investigator can be extremely persuasive."

The judge turned his attention to Thrillkill. "You have any objections? Other than the obvious?"

"Other than the fundamental unfairness of calling a witness I've had no chance to investigate?"

"I'm not required to give you a witness list or to tell you anything about my case in advance," I noted.

"You indicated the defendant was your final witness."

"I thought he was."

"And then," Thrillkill said, spreading his hands wide, "a miracle occurred."

I ignored the sarcasm. "Every trial attorney should be entitled to at least one miracle."

The judge overruled the objection, and I called Abdullah Ali to the witness stand. He was dressed in traditional Muslim garb, a crochet taqiyah and kurta. I will confess I tried to get him into a Western suit and tie, maybe something from Dillard's, but he refused. I didn't feel good about encouraging him to hide his heritage, but at the end of the day, my job was to prevent Oz from being executed, so the less "other" this key witness looked, the better.

Abdullah's beard was mostly gray, and his voice had a lot of gravel in it. He appeared about sixty, but I wondered if he was older. He seemed calm and well mannered. As he spoke, I began to understand why. In his life, he'd faced situations far more intimidating than a jury.

He explained that he was raised in Iowa, but at some point, his father got a job at the US consulate in Saudi Arabia. As a result, he had frequent contact with US military personnel. At the age of nineteen, he started college, two years in a Saudi Arabian school followed by two years at Oxford. After he finished his studies, he traveled to Afghanistan. "In the eighties," he explained, "I became a freedom fighter."

"Please tell the jury what that means."

"It means, as the name suggests, that I fought for a nation trying to preserve its freedom from invaders."

I decided to beat the jury to the punch. "So you're saying you were a terrorist."

"Far from it. We never used any terror techniques." His weight, facial hair, and friendly demeanor suggested Santa Claus, not a terrorist. "We didn't even have explosives. But we were effective. The area you call Afghanistan has been subjected to more invasion and attempted conquest in the last hundred and fifty years than any other place on earth. Its peoples are accustomed to fighting for their homeland."

"Did you work with the Taliban?"

"The Taliban did not yet exist, not in its current form. Neither did al-Qaeda or ISIS."

"Did you know Osama bin Laden?"

"I knew of him. He was prominent in the fight against the oppressor." He paused. "The fight against the Russian invaders. Because he and I both fought with the United States."

"You helped the US?"

"We all did. Of course, the US was not officially involved, but in reality the US was actively attempting to prevent Russian expansion. And we were successful. After much bloodshed and misery, the Russians went home. But the toll on Afghanistan was unimaginable. Once the Russians lost interest, so did the US. They withdrew all support. That war-ravaged nation was left with no infrastructure, no army, no schools, virtually no government. Starvation became rampant. Petty warlords replaced legitimate governments. Chaos reigned."

"And you blamed the United States."

"I did not. But many did. Osama bin Laden did. It was the abandonment of Afghanistan that fueled his hatred of the US—and we all know where that led."

"This is a fascinating history lesson," Thrillkill said, rising. "But what has it got to do with this case?"

"If the court will just give me a moment," I said, "I think that will become clear."

"I'll give you some leeway," the judge grunted. "But not forever."

I returned my attention to the witness. "You explained why some people who fought in Afghanistan in the eighties bore resentment toward the US. Did that include you?"

"No. I took a different view."

"Which was what?"

"I felt that the only long-term solution to this repeating pattern of aggression was to eliminate the incentives. In the nineteenth century, when Great Britain invaded our lands, it was to expand their empire. When it became evident that a diverse empire of unwilling subjects was unsustainable, they retreated. Similarly, during the Cold War, the US sought to prevent the expansion of the so-called Communist threat. Since that time, the primary reason for US interest in our region has been oil."

"I'm sure you're aware many would dispute that."

"And they are free to do so." His hands spread open, his beard curling in a genial smile. "But you have asked me to provide my view. The first US invasion of Iraq used the pretense of saving Kuwait, a nation about which the US cared nothing. A nation of barbarism, decadence, and greed. Please. The US went in to protect its oil supply. The next time, the US used nonexistent weapons of mass destruction to justify the invasion. But the true mission was keeping the Strait of Hormuz open. To maintain the free flow of oil. If not to control it."

"Some would say the US went to Iraq because of 9/11."

"Well, bin Laden was in Pakistan, as US operatives had known for some time. So why invade Iraq and Afghanistan?"

I left that question alone. The jury had enough background to understand where this testimony was going. Time to move on.

"After the fighting in Afghanistan in the eighties ended, did you remain politically active?"

"In a manner of speaking. I lived in Iraq and, using my science background, worked in a laboratory there."

"Did you work with anyone we might know?"

"Yes. Yasmin al-Tikrit. My dear, late Yasmin."

"The jury heard from her earlier. She was your colleague?"

"And friend. She and my sister, Mina, were close. There was nothing they would not do for one another. Mina had been able to help her in a time of need, and she remained faithful to Mina and our family ever after."

Out the corner of my eye, I spotted Mina in the rear of the courtroom. Their brother, Kir, was with her. Neither looked particularly pleased.

I continued. "We've heard talk about a so-called superweapon. Did you work on that?"

"No. We were trying to devise an efficient, renewable energy source. Something other than oil. To end the political interest in our region. We did so with the support of the Hussein government. The so-called energy crisis of the nineteen seventies produced fear and desperation in Washington. Of course, the US had enough oil to supply its domestic needs, especially if it implemented some minor conservation measures. But your President Carter lowered the speed limit and suggested that people turn down the thermostat—and the nation all but impeached him for it. It became clear the US did not want to conserve, and that meant it needed foreign oil. We felt the only way to keep the US out of our lands was to find another energy source."

"Was that realistic?"

"Speaking as a scientist, I believe it is not only realistic but inevitable and necessary. Current estimates show our known oil reserves will be completely depleted around 2050. What do we do then? Alternative, sustainable energy sources would have already been developed but for the efforts of American Big Oil."

"That sounds a little paranoid."

"It is no different from the way RCA suppressed television until Philo Farnsworth's patents expired. It is no different from how Big Oil used its influence to delay the development of the electric car. They reap enormous profits. Why would they want that to end?"

"So, despite living in an oil-rich nation, you were developing a new energy source."

"Correct."

"Yasmin said her work could have military applications."

"She said the government could adapt her work into a weapon. What else is new?"

"There's a big difference between a power source and a weapon."

"Is there? Please, take the example of nuclear fission. That could be a source of limitless energy, if we learned to use it safely. But that is not why it was developed. It was developed—and deployed—as the most devastating weapon ever seen. Solar energy similarly has the potential to be a source of endless energy, or a horrible weapon."

"So you disfavored military applications of your project."

"I did. Which is why I ultimately resigned from the project. Eventually, I was granted admission to the United States. I worked in Oklahoma City at Chesapeake for years. Then I heard that my old colleague Yasmin had come to the US and lived not far away. You can imagine my interest. Eventually, my concerns about the status of Arab-Americans led me to form PACT. My work had produced a sizable savings, and I had little need for it, so I donated it to the cause."

"You were familiar with Yasmin's work?"

"Yes, but we did not fund her work. That was the US government. That is why she was allowed to emigrate. I believe the CIA kept a careful watch over her."

Thrillkill rose. "Is it my imagination, Your Honor, or did Mr. Kincaid indicate that at some point this would have something to do with the homicide case?"

The judge nodded. "He does have a point, Counsel."

"I understand. I'll get right there. Thank you for your patience." I was happy to put in as much background as I could. But now it was time to move on. "Sir, did you know the victim? Agent Nazir?"

"I did not know him personally. But I had heard others speak of him."

"Others such as whom?"

"Omar, for one. And of course my sister, Mina."

"What was the general tenor of these remarks?"

"They were aware that his agents watched them, and PACT, which would make anyone uneasy." He reached into his pocket and withdrew a string of beads. "But for two people who had been extensively interrogated and abused . . . the feeling would be much more powerful. They were fearful. In an all-consuming way. So much so that it almost made it impossible to function. I tried to help, but there was so little I could do."

"How did you try to help?"

"Talking to them. Encouraging Omar to explore his legal options."

And now, at last, our first meeting made sense. "Like filing a civil lawsuit."

"Exactly. Something proper. We'd had too much violence in our lives. This is supposedly a nation governed by laws."

"Omar testified that when he was interrogated, Agent Nazir wanted information about you."

"So I have heard. I do not think Nazir actually believed that I was a terrorist. I think it is possible he opposed the political ambitions of PACT. I think he disliked anyone who knew the details of his past, especially those like my sister who had been subjected to his brutality firsthand."

"But he singled you out."

"The CIA attempted to persuade me to continue my scientific work for them after I came to the US. Unlike Yasmin, I refused. That may have made certain people in the government suspicious. Or simply angry."

"Did you know about the press conference given by Agent Nazir?"

"Indeed. We were all most interested in what he would say."

"Did you attend?"

"I did."

"Did you see anyone there you knew?"

"Yes. I saw Omar—just before the shot rang out."

"Did he have a gun?"

"Yes."

"Did he fire the gun?"

Abdullah looked straight at the jury. "He did not."

"How can you be certain?"

"Because I was watching him when I heard the shot. I was approaching to greet him. He did not withdraw his gun until after we heard the gunshot. He probably thought he needed to defend himself, but only a few seconds after he withdrew the gun, someone tackled him. Knocked him to the ground. Then more people piled on top, wrestling Omar to the pavement. They shouted for the police, yelling that they had the killer."

"Did they?"

"They most certainly did not. As I said, Omar did not even have his gun in his hand until after the shot was fired."

"You're certain of that."

"Completely."

"What did you do next?"

"I am afraid I left the scene quickly. I feared this was not a safe place for someone of my ethnic background. Too often police officers needing a suspect will grab anyone readily available."

"Do you know who killed Nazir?"

"I do not. But it seemed to me that the shot came from the other side of the gathering. In the area of the oil derrick at the end of the south plaza."

The salient point here is that it was a good long way from where the cops found Omar.

And now we got to the rough patch. But better it came voluntarily than was dragged out by Thrillkill. "Did you tell the police what you saw and heard?"

His head bowed. "No." His fingers kneaded the beads. "I am ashamed to say that I did not."

"Why?"

He pointed to himself. "You see how I look. You see how I dress. I saw several police officers, and bystanders, eyeing me suspiciously simply because I am of Arabic descent. I did not wish to get involved. I—" He stuttered, then fell silent. "I was afraid."

"If you were innocent, the police shouldn't be a threat."

His head rose. "Because in the US, the innocent are never wrongfully convicted?"

I didn't bother replying.

He continued. "Because in the US, race never plays a role in convictions? You know as well as I do that non-Caucasians are convicted at a grossly higher rate than white people. What if they decided I was the killer? What if the CIA decided I was a person of interest?"

"Did they have any reason to suspect you?"

"I was in the area. I have an Arabic name. I am Muslim. Omar was arrested on little else. I am stopped every time I board an airplane. People move away from me, refuse to sit with me. The CIA was already interested in me. This could easily be the excuse they needed to detain me for twenty-one days."

I played the devil's advocate. "Surely, if you're innocent, there's no reason to be afraid of questioning."

"Your CIA tortured hundreds of people during the Bush administration and lied about it to Congress. They later admitted many people of my faith were held by mistake, but those people were still subjected to interrogation and torture for weeks. Your government lied about NSA surveillance of private communications, the so-called PRISM program. Once the lies become too frequent, who will trust you? All it would take is for someone to suggest a national security risk, and I could be held indefinitely for years. And subjected to your 'enhanced interrogation techniques.' At my age . . . I would not survive it. As so many others have not survived it."

"So you remained quiet."

"To my shame, yes. I did. I disappeared to a cabin near Grand Lake, where I thought I could not be located. Until your investigator found me."

"Why are you speaking now?"

He averted his eyes. "Your colleague convinced me that I had a duty to Omar. And to Allah. He is a spiritual man, your investigator. He opened my eyes."

I think Loving also threated to bust CIA heads if they came after him, but I was content to leave that part out. "Thank you, sir. No more questions."

CHAPTER 58

Judge Santino gave us a ten-minute break before the cross-examination began. I read through Christina's notes and read my own, trying to anticipate Thrillkill's line of attack. I was deep in the trial lawyer's zone when I felt a soft touch on my shoulder.

"Mr. Kincaid."

I recognized the voice. Mina Ali, Abdullah's sister. And standing just a step behind, their brother, Kir.

She understood I didn't have much time and didn't waste any. "You know what that man will try to do to Abdullah."

"He will try to discredit my witness. That's more or less the point of cross-examination."

"He will try to insinuate that Abdullah is a terrorist."

I nodded sadly. "You're probably right."

Her lips tightened, reminding me of when she told her story in my office, back when this case first began. "What do you intend to do about it?"

"I can object to anything inappropriate, but I can't stop Thrillkill from talking."

"He will damn my brother with false lies and half-truths."

"You're likely correct, but I can't prevent it."

My words only made her angrier. "Do you see the man sitting in the rear of the courtroom? The ginger man with the ill-fitting suit?"

I took a quick look.

"I have seen him before," she continued. "He works for the CIA."

I shrugged. "I suppose he has as much right to be here—"

"Are you blind? They have set my brother up. Thrillkill will force lies from Abdullah's throat, and then that jackal will seize him before he leaves the courtroom."

"Unless your brother confesses to a criminal act—"

"They do not need a confession!" Her voice was loud enough to attract attention. "The merest suspicion is enough to detain someone for weeks."

"She's right about that," I heard Oz murmur.

"I understand your concern," I said, hoping to calm her. "But there's not a thing I can do about it."

Mina threw up her hands. Kir stepped forward. "You call this a justice system," the young man said. "And yet there is no justice anywhere to be found."

"I think that's extreme."

"All the power is in the hands of Nazir and people like him. Until the power is evenly distributed, justice will not return. No one will be safe."

Another time, this might have led to a fascinating discussion, but I simply didn't have the time, and I was worried Santino might reappear and hear some of this anti-American diatribe. Christina cut in an asked them to speak to her outside. I knew she wouldn't let them back into the courtroom till they got a grip on their emotions.

Thrillkill knew as well as I did the importance of the evidence the jury had just heard. He'd put on a good case, but he had no eyewitnesses. Now I did. And juries generally think eyewitness testimony is the most reliable, though it is actually among the least reliable, because people's eyes and memories play tricks on them. Given his political sympathies, Abdullah's testimony could be called into question. But even a questionable eyewitness was better than none.

"First of all," Thrillkill said calmly, "I'd like to clear up a few matters regarding your background. At one time, you worked for the Iraqi army. True?"

"Yes. Military service was required."

"So you worked for the army."

"As a scientist."

"Working on a weapon."

"No. A sustainable energy project."

"With potential military applications."

"All research has potential military applications. That has been true since the wheel was turned into a chariot."

"Did you work on any other weapons projects?"

He hesitated just a fraction. "Yes."

"Such as."

"I was occasionally asked to assist with conventional weaponry. Duplicating it. Making it more effective."

"You made bombs."

Abdullah looked downward. "I am sorry to say that I did."

"You want to trash the CIA for doing its job, but the truth is you were out there helping Iraq kill people."

"I did as I was instructed by my superiors. Until I was able to extricate myself from the situation." He fidgeted, shifting his weight from one side to the other.

"How long did you work for the Iraqi army, you and Yasmin?"

"About two years."

"And in that time, approximately how many bombs did you construct?"

Abdullah kneaded his hands. "I have no way of knowing that."

"How many American boys died as a result of the bombs you made?"

"Objection," I said, though I knew perfectly well Thrillkill had already made his point.

"Sustained," the judge intoned.

"I'll rephrase." Thrillkill smiled. "Would you be willing to admit that your work resulted in the deaths of some American soldiers?"

"As I recall, the American conquest of Iraq only took about a month."

"But fighting continued."

"Yes, even after the so-called mission was accomplished, there were skirmishes. But the Iraqi army was disbanded. A move that had devastating consequences to the infrastructure of our country."

"Could some of your weapons have made their way to Afghanistan? Or the Taliban? Or ISIS?"

"I have no way of knowing this."

"I think you have blood on your hands, sir. Your work proves exactly why everything the CIA did was necessary, and why they were right to take an interest in you and your activities."

"Objection," I said. "Is this a cross-examination or a Republican after-dinner speech?"

The judge almost smiled. "The objection is sustained."

Thrillkill was not deterred. "You were pals with Osama bin Laden, weren't you?"

"I would not say we were pals."

"You worked on the same side."

"He never worked for the Iraqi army."

"You both fought against the United States."

"No, sir," Abdullah said, his voice rising. "I only fought to stay alive. As did most of my kinsmen."

"But you will admit that you knew the man."

"A long time before. In Afghanistan."

"You had friends in common."

"Not that I'm aware."

"But it's possible."

"Objection," I said. "Mr. Thrillkill has made his point, such as it is. He was always anxious when he thought I strayed from the case. But he hasn't even mentioned the murder yet."

The judge nodded. "Let's have testimony that relates to the homicide."

Thrillkill nodded politely. "Did you approve of the death of Agent Nazir?"

"Omar did not kill Agent Nazir."

"You're not answering my question."

"I will never approve of murder. I believe it is a crime against Allah."

"Really?" Thrillkill pulled a face. "I thought you folks all believed that if you murdered for a good reason you went to heaven and got serviced by those sexy virgins."

"Objection!"

The judge tilted his head. "This one is not entirely irrelevant. I'll allow it. Please answer the question."

Abdullah's irritation was plain. "The particular passage of the Koran which you are grossly misquoting applies to a holy war. Not an assassination."

"So flying planes into the World Trade Center—was that a holy war or an assassination?"

"Objection!"

"Overruled. The witness will answer."

Abdullah complied, though it was clear he had no desire to do so. "In my opinion, it was neither. It was simply an act of terrorism. And I have never heard of any deity that rewards terrorism."

"But isn't that what the men who flew the planes believed?"

"I don't know. I never met any of them."

"Isn't it true that in your faith—"

"Objection," I said, as forcefully as possible. "Are we having a debate on comparative religions now? I thought we were going to talk about the murder."

"That objection is sustained." The judge gave Thrillkill a stern look. "Do you understand what I'm saying?"

"I do, Your Honor. I thank you for granting me this leniency." In other words, he'd already done his best to discredit the witness by playing on prejudice, implying that Abdullah was a terrorist based on little more than his nation of birth and his religion. "Let me ask you a different question. Since Omar is your friend, and you approve of his work—you don't want to see him die, do you?"

"Of course not. I don't want to see anyone die."

"And, in fact, you might be willing to do whatever was necessary to help him out of a tight spot, wouldn't you?"

"If you are implying that I am lying, I must tell you that I am not."

"You lied to the homicide investigators, didn't you?"

"I do not know what you are talking about."

"They asked for eyewitnesses to come forward. You did not come forward."

"That is hardly the same as lying."

"Some would say it's exactly the same. You kept quiet for a lengthy period of time, then suddenly appeared at trial at the last possible moment to bail out your friend. Can you see where that might look more than just a little suspicious?"

"Objection," I said. "That's not really even a question. More like the prosecutor is practicing his closing argument."

"Sustained."

"Let me rephrase. You testified that you didn't come forward earlier because you feared retaliation."

"Yes."

"From the CIA."

"Or any other American law enforcement or intelligence agency."

"But you're talking now. To help your friend."

"To prevent a gross miscarriage of justice."

"And you expect us to believe that the man caught with a gun in his hand didn't kill Agent Nazir."

"I know that he did not. The gun was not in his hand when the killing shot rang out. From somewhere else."

"You're the only one who heard that mystery handgun fire."

"Actually, to me, it sounded more like a shotgun."

"That no one else heard. We've had a lot of different reports from different witnesses. But no one mentioned the oil rig. Nor did we find any other potential suspects."

"Did you look? My impression is that you grabbed the obvious suspect and never investigated further."

"You think you know more about that gunshot than anyone else there?"

Abdullah struggled to remain calm. "I have perhaps more experience with gunfire and combat situations that most Oklahomans."

Thrillkill let out a thin smile. "No one else heard a sniper in the oil derrick."

"Did you ask?"

"Motion to strike the nonresponsive reply."

"Granted."

Thrillkill hesitated. He had probably done everything he could do with this witness. But I suspected he wanted to go out with more of a bang. If he was going to bury the eyewitness and eradicate all doubt, he needed more oomph.

"You say you have experience with battle situations and the sound of gunfire."

"Sadly, that is true."

"Are you familiar with ballistics?"

Abdullah bowed his head. "It is not my main field of inquiry, but ballistics is a science. And I am a scientist."

"Are you aware that the ballistics evidence shows conclusively that the bullet came from the defendant's gun? The gun you yourself admit he had on his person at the time of the murder?"

"I have heard of this. I have not seen the report. Or the bullet."

"Do you have any reason to question the report?"

"Objection," I said. "He's not here to testify about ballistics."

Thrillkill shrugged. "He's a scientist, as he keeps insisting."

I tried a different tack. "This is outside the scope of direct."

The judge pondered a moment. "The witness did mention the gun and the gunfire in his testimony. I'll allow it."

"So what about it?" Thrillkill continued. "Do you have any reason to question the hard-and-fast scientific evidence that the murder bullet came from your friend's gun?"

"I have every reason to question it. I believe this state has some considerable history of falsifying evidence for criminal trials. And the federal government lied about this war before it even began."

"You're accusing us of framing the defendant?"

"I only say it is not impossible." Abdullah seemed tenser with each sentence. Beads of sweat trickled down the side of his face. I could see he'd been pushed too far. "Historically, when America wants a conviction, it does what it needs to get one. Anytime you want some of our people where you can torture or humiliate them, you *lie and lie and lie again!*"

Thrillkill just let it hang. Kept his mouth shut while the ensuing silence pierced the air like a knife to Abdullah's heart.

Finally, he said, "I think I see what this witness is all about now. No more questions, Your Honor."

CHAPTER 59

W e took a short break after Abdullah stepped down. I asked the bailiff to take him out through a back exit. Even if the CIA were stalking him, he wouldn't be arrested here. Then I grabbed Christina and started running through every idea I had. If we closed our case on that last note, I would not hold out much hope. I could see Omar felt much the same.

Fortunately, thanks to last night's confab, we had one more trick.

Christina slid into the seat beside me.

"Is he in the building?" I asked.

She nodded. "Tracked him down to courtroom 214. Judge Farris."

"Good man. He'll loan his expert out, I'll wager."

She nodded. "Already asked."

Judge Santino returned to the bench and banged the gavel. "Mr. Kincaid, does this conclude the defense?"

"No, Your Honor. One more witness."

He was surprised. "I didn't know—"

Thrillkill rose. "Neither did I."

"Well, I'm sure you won't mind." I gave him my best smile. "I'm just recalling one of your own witnesses." I turned back to the judge. "The defense calls Clarence Cooper."

Thrillkill's forehead knotted. "I don't see the point of that. He's already testified twice."

"For you. Not for me."

"And I don't know where he is. I wasn't prepared—"

"He's in courtroom 214, waiting to testify in another case. And Judge Farris has said he will allow him to leave to testify here. It won't take long."

For perhaps the first time in the entire trial, I saw a tiny touch of concern creep across Thrillkill's face.

"Any objection, Mr. Prosecutor?"

"I suppose not," Thrillkill replied. Probably meaning he couldn't think of one.

The bailiff collected the witness, and ten minutes later I began. Cooper still wore his white coat. I was beginning to wonder if he slept in it. "Dr. Cooper, you've already testified, so I won't waste time reestablishing your credentials in the field of ballistics, among others. You've testified that the bullet that killed Agent Nazir came from the gun owned by the defendant, correct?"

"That is correct." I could see Cooper didn't know why he was here, either. And that would worry anyone.

"Your conclusion was based on markings found on the bullet that killed Agent Nazir, correct?"

"Yes."

"How did you determine what markings were made by the weapon in question?"

"After the gun was seized by the police, we fired a test bullet, then compared it to the bullet that killed Agent Nazir."

I nodded. "Fascinating. How can you fire a bullet without damaging it?"

"There are many different techniques. In my office, we fire the bullet into a block of gelatin. The gelatin slows the bullet without marking it."

"Could someone else do the same thing?"

He blinked. "I'm . . . now . . . do what?"

"Fire a bullet and stop it. So it isn't damaged."

"I . . . suppose. I don't know why anyone would want to."

"So then the bullet could be reused. Inserted into another weapon. And fired again."

"Yes, but the second weapon would also leave characteristic marks—"

"What if it didn't?"

Cooper stopped short. "You lost me."

"Don't feel bad. I didn't understand this till my investigator filled me in last night. He's been firing guns since his daddy took him quail hunting back—well, never mind. Point is, he knows guns. And he tells me that if someone fired the bullet from Omar's gun, recaptured the bullet, and put it into another gun, it would look as if the murder bullet was fired from Omar's gun, even though it wasn't. Or, at least, wasn't most recently."

Cooper shook his head furiously. "But the second weapon would leave marks, too."

"What if the second weapon had an extremely smooth barrel? Like, say, a shotgun. A brand new, extremely well-cleaned shotgun. Which, come to think of it, is what the last witness, the *only* eyewitness, thought he heard."

"Even then, the shotgun would leave some mark—"

"But not much, right? So an examiner would predominantly see the markings of the first weapon."

"It wouldn't be exactly the same—"

"But it's never *exactly* the same, is it? No two bullets are ever exactly alike, even when they came from the same gun, right?"

He shrugged. "True."

"When you say there's a match, you're saying the two bullets are mostly the same, not exactly the same. And the procedure I described could conceivably produce two bullets that looked mostly, if not exactly, the same, even though one was shot a second time from a different weapon. Correct?"

I could see the jurors stirring. This definitely had their attention.

Cooper worked through the possibilities. "The killer would need access to the defendant's gun."

"True."

"He'd have to fire a bullet in advance, recover it, then put it into his shotgun."

"True."

"Most people don't have blocks of gelatin lying around."

"What if he fired into a swimming pool? Would that work?"

"Well .

"If he fired into the deep end, the water would stop the bullet without damaging it, and the bullet could be recovered later."

"I suppose. But there's no evidence—"

"Sir, I have not asked you if there's any evidence, or what you think happened. But I will ask you this question. Is the procedure I just described possible?"

He twisted his neck. "I suppose in theory."

"So, in theory, it is possible that the bullet was fired from Omar's gun, then fired again from a different weapon on the day Agent Nazir was murdered. Correct?"

Thrillkill sat up straight and was no doubt threatening his witness with daggers from his eyes. I moved between them.

Cooper hesitated before answering. But in the end, his scientific objectivity won out. "I think it all sounds terribly contrived," he said. "I've never heard of anything like this being done before. But I suppose it is possible."

"Thank you, sir." I had what I wanted and knew when to get out. "No more questions."

Thrillkill rose awkwardly. "Do you think it's likely—"

"Objection." I'd won a little doubt here. I wasn't going to let him take it away without a fight. "The witness already said he'd never heard of anything like this before. So how could he possibly assess its likelihood?"

The judge tilted his head. "I will have to award that point to Mr. Kincaid. Sustained."

Thrillkill tried again. "Did you, during your investigation, see any indication that anything like this contrived twice-fired bullet business was done?"

"No."

"Thank you. No more questions."

I sprang back up without being invited. "But, sir, the whole point of this procedure would be to *prevent* someone from realizing it had been done, right?"

"I suppose so."

"So you wouldn't be likely to detect any indication that the bullet had been fired twice."

"Also true, I guess."

"And you did say that it was theoretically possible, correct?"

"I did say that."

"Thank you. Nothing more."

I sat down. Thrillkill waved his hand in the air, his nonverbal way of saying he'd had enough.

"The defense rests."

"Very good." The judge shuffled some papers. "Let's take ten, then counsel can proceed with closing arguments."

The court adjourned. The gallery was talking, and the jurors bore somewhat perplexed expressions. I'd given them all something to think about, which was the most I could do. Take what looked like certain guilt and make it a tiny bit less certain.

Christina squeezed my hand. "You did good, Ben."

"I agree," Oz said.

He actually smiled, and I hadn't seen that in a while. "That doesn't mean I changed the jury's mind."

"You don't have to change their minds," Christina said. "You just have to plant seeds of doubt."

"Did I?"

She glanced at Omar, then at me. "You did the absolute best you could with the case you had."

"Will that be good enough?"

"That's up to the jury. Now let's see you argue that stupid politician into the mud."

CHAPTER 60

Whether I liked it or not, the prosecutor got first whack at closing argument. Lawyers spent many an hour, usually in a bar over a glass of scotch, arguing about the relative merits of recency and primacy—or to put it the way normal people talk, whether it's better to go first or last. Some jurisdictions allowed the prosecutor to do both by giving them a rebuttal. More often than not, though, the rebuttal was used not to refute but to give soul-stirring, teary-eyed jeremiads about the "thin blue line" and other routines designed to make the jury forget about the evidence and convict to protect society from evil. I knew this judge disfavored rebuttals and wouldn't give Thrillkill one unless I said something of heart attack–inducing surprise. That wasn't going to happen.

Thrillkill was an excellent orator, something I knew I would never be. He showed no sense of nervousness, even though he had a lot riding on this speech. He strolled slowly from his table, watching the jurors, looking some of them in the eye, smiling confidently. At last, he settled in a central location. Then he took a few more moments of silence. I was expecting a dramatic flourish or gesture.

Instead, he shrugged.

"You'd think convicting a guy found at the scene of the crime with the murder gun in his hand wouldn't be that complicated."

And he let that sit with the jury for at least two or three ticks of the clock.

"I don't fault defense counsel for doing his best to muddy the water. That's his job, and he's done it admirably. Even at the point where some lesser men might've given up, he's still in there swinging, trying to make everything look so much less obvious than it is."

I tried not to bristle or to take the slam personally.

"What have we established in this case?" Thrillkill asked, pacing slowly before the jury box. "Let's review. Motive. The defendant bore a strong grudge against the victim, Agent Nazir. He admitted that. For that matter, he had a bad-on against the entire CIA. His gang of friends encouraged him to 'take out' Nazir, including one extremely attractive foreign activist with whom he had sexual relations."

Thrillkill was entitled to his interpretation of the evidence, however skewed it might be. I knew objections would not be welcome unless Thrillkill did something egregious.

"Opportunity. The defendant was, in fact, at the scene of the crime, and he was in possession of a gun. He has admitted both. In fact, he recently applied for an open-carry permit so he could wear the gun in public. Spectators at the scene of the crime were so certain he was the shooter they tackled him and prevented his escape."

Thrillkill paused. "And then there is the matter of evidence. Cold, hard scientific evidence. The stuff that no defense attorney can argue his way around. All the courtroom shenanigans and trickery will not change facts. And what are those facts? The bullet came from the defendant's gun. That gun had been fired recently. Paraffin tests showed that the defendant himself had fired a gun recently."

He spread his hands wide. "What more do you need?"

He pivoted. "Yes, I heard the defense attorney try to sell you some convoluted science-fiction explanation about bullets being used twice or coming from an alternate dimension or something. All I can say is— come on. Which seems more likely to you? That there was an elaborate frame that only a PhD in ballistics could understand, or that the man who repeatedly told people he hated Nazir and wanted to take him out actually did? The top ballistics expert in the state told you that bullet came out of the defendant's gun. End of story."

He paused reflectively. "And, yes, we had one alleged eyewitness say he watched the defendant at the time of the murder and that he did not fire the gun. This was, of course, a friend, a coworker, and a sympathizer with their political cause. Should we put any faith in that testimony? Think about it. Why would he be watching the defendant at the time the gun was fired? Why would anyone be looking that way while Agent Nazir delivered an important address? One he'd presumably gone to the state capitol for the purpose of hearing? Does this make any sense? I'm not even going to touch the nonsense about the mysterious shotgun at the oil rig. There were several hundred people at that press conference. But only one guy heard a shotgun fire from the oil rig?" He allowed himself a small grin. "This is a state where most people know what a shotgun sounds like."

He pivoted slightly, paused, then turned back to the jury.

Christina scratched a note on my legal pad: HE'S PUTTING HIS MEAN FACE ON.

"There is one other . . . strain of testimony we've heard, ladies and gentlemen. And much as I'd rather ignore it, I'm forced to address it square on. As I said, I don't fault the defense attorney for doing his job, trying to confuse you and gum up the wheels of justice."

Not exactly how I'd describe my role .

"But I *will* fault . . . *anyone* . . . who attacks this great nation we live in. The United States of America."

Here we go. I knew it was coming. How could a politician resist? Behind her hand, Christina made a "barfing" face.

"Granted, we have freedom of speech, but that doesn't mean I have to like everything people say. And I do not like it, not one bit, when people abuse that freedom to attack this nation. We may not be perfect, but we are the finest nation in this world, the finest nation there has ever been in this world, and we should not be subjected to criticism from . . . well, darn it, from those who are jealous or bitter or for whatever misguided religious or terroristic reasons want to tear this great nation down."

Chris and I exchanged a look. He treaded close to the mark here. I thought even this judge might not look too harshly on an objection to this rhetoric. But I kept my mouth shut.

"We all know that America has enemies. We have to do whatever it takes to protect the American way of life. Sometimes we may even have to do things we'd rather not. The only people who never get their hands dirty are the people who never accomplish anything. But the idea that all these people are actively working to bring down this nation, targeting the CIA, targeting its agents, and then trying to turn their evil into an excuse—that's just disgusting. There is no excuse for murder. They don't get a free lunch because their politics is different from ours."

He centered himself and leaned against the guardrail, getting as close to the jury as it was permissible to get. "And let me make one more thing clear. This case is not about war crimes. It's not a referendum on foreign wars or US foreign policy. It's about murder. One murder. One murdered CIA agent. And that's all it's about. No matter what your politics may be, no matter what you believe about the United States or Iraq or anything else, you will agree that murder is wrong. And here we had a cold, cold-blooded murder committed by that man." He whirled around and pointed dramatically at Oz.

"Do we want this to happen again? Do we want this scene repeated every time someone has an ax to grind? Or do we want to draw a line in the sand, right here and right now, and say no, sir. Here in the United States of America, we do not condone murder. Here in the United States of America, murderers will be punished."

He pushed himself back from the rail. "Ladies and gentlemen. This man was arrested at the scene of the crime with the gun in his hand and gunpowder on his palm. Let common sense prevail. Do what you know is right. For all of us. For the nation. For the safety of your children."

He made eye contact with each juror, then resumed his seat at the prosecution table. Hickman gave him a firm smile and a slap on the back.

The judge cleared his throat. "Mr. Kincaid?"

Christina passed me another note. GIVE 'EM HELL, SLUGGER. Well, I'd do my best.

CHAPTER 61

"Y ou probably think I'm going to stand up here and disagree with everything the prosecutor said. But I'm not."

I know my limitations as a speaker. I'm never going to master the suspenseful pause or the dramatic gesture. I didn't have Thrillkill's flourish. But over the years, I've learned how to get someone's attention.

"Truth is I agree with much of what he had to say. It doesn't look good, does it? Arrested at the scene of the crime with a gun. Bullet came from the gun, gunpowder on the palms. And I'm not even going to suggest that my client didn't dislike Agent Nazir. He did. Big time. Why else would he file that civil suit? He thought Nazir wronged him, and he wanted the man punished."

Pause. "But that does not mean he wanted the man killed." Another pause. "And there's no proof that he did kill him."

I proceeded. "Mr. Thrillkill wants you to think your job is to establish guilt. He keeps saying, 'Hey, use your common sense.' 'What's more likely,' he said at another point. But make no mistake about this —your job is not to establish what is more likely or what makes more sense. Your job is not even to determine whether you think he's probably guilty. To return a guilty verdict, you must find him guilty beyond a reasonable doubt. As the judge will explain when he reads your instructions, this is an extremely high standard. You might privately suspect he's guilty, but still not think the prosecution has proved it beyond a reasonable doubt. We have this high standard because we don't want anyone convicted wrongfully. It does happen, sadly, when jurors forget what a high standard this is and start using common sense or deciding what they think is most likely. If people truly applied this standard for what it is, wrongful convictions would never happen."

I paused, shuffled around a little. I'd given them a lot to think about, and I wanted to give it a few moments to sink in before I moved on.

"What Mr. Thrillkill calls confusing and gumming up the wheels of justice is anything but. To the contrary, it's making sure the wheels of justice run smoothly, without embarrassing mistakes that destroy people's lives. If there is any doubt—and let's face it, there's a lot of doubt here—it is my ethical duty to bring it to your attention so that you can do your job right, too."

I took a few steps back, which inevitably drew the jurors' eyes to Oz. I thought this was a good time to remind them that this wasn't just a bunch of abstract ideas we were tossing around in civics class. This was a debate about a human being's future.

"So is there any doubt? True, my client was arrested at the scene of the crime. But several hundred people were there, and many of them disliked Nazir just as much. Like Yasmin al-Tikrit. Like Abdullah Ali. Yes, my client flunked the paraffin test, but he admitted that he'd been at a gun range the day before. Why should that surprise us? He owned a gun and he practiced regularly so he could bear it responsibly. Yes, he had an open-carry permit for it—but doesn't that make it even less likely that he would use it to murder someone? If nothing else became clear when Omar took the witness stand, I hope you understood that he is not a stupid man. He would not do a stupid thing. And murdering someone in broad daylight with the gun you got a permit for shortly before is just plain stupid."

I continued in the same vein. I could tell I had their attention. Which of course did not mean they were buying any of this, but it was better than thinking they were bored.

"There is the troubling ballistics evidence. I will be the first to admit that. But is it conclusive? Does it eliminate all reasonable doubt? Remember—even the prosecution's expert admitted that it was possible the bullet was fired first from Omar's gun, then recovered and put in a smooth-barreled shotgun and refired. I could've called an expert witness to say the same, but then you'd have to wonder if that was just someone saying what I wanted them to say and collecting a paycheck. So instead, you heard it from the man Mr. Thrillkill called the leading ballistics expert in the state." I smiled a tad. "If the top expert in the state admits that it is possible, who are we to disagree? And more to the point, how can we say there is no reasonable doubt when the top expert in the state says that there is."

I stopped for a moment to collect my thoughts. I was about to enter treacherous waters, and I knew how important it was that I get it right.

"We've had a lot of discussion of the politics surrounding this case, the ethical debates about the Patriot Act and the Freedom Act and enhanced interrogation techniques and intervention in the Middle East. I'm not going to talk about that. Except to say this. Omar is an American citizen. He was born and raised right here in Oklahoma. The fact that he has converted to Islam or changed his name does not make him any less American or any less entitled to constitutional rights. The fact that he was interrogated by the CIA might explain some of the animosity between the parties, but it does not prove innocence or guilt. Nor does the fact that Oz worked for an Arab-rights organization. Or that he was approached by ISIS. Or that he had consensual sex with an adult. If you ask me, the admission of that completely tasteless and irrelevant evidence tells me the prosecution is much more desperate than they want you to realize. If Mr. Thrillkill had as much confidence in the evidence as he suggests, that disgusting exercise in character assassination would never have seen the light of day."

Okay, I'd said what I had to say. It would be nice to go out with a bang, but that had never been my style. I just laid it on the line and trusted the jurors to do their jobs. Which was basically what I told them.

"When you entered that jury box, you swore an oath. You said you would perform your duties to the best of your ability. Your duties, simply stated, are to follow the judge's instructions and to reach a verdict. The judge will give you many instructions, but the one that matters is the one that says you cannot convict unless you find the prosecution has proven beyond a reasonable doubt that Omar al-Jabbar killed Agent Nazir. And the problem with that is there's doubt all over the place. Lots and lots of doubt. And all it takes is one to preclude a guilty verdict. I respectfully submit that you have no choice but to find my client not guilty."

CHAPTER 62

Some people think cross-examination is the hardest part of trying a case. Some people think the closing summation is the hardest part. They're both wrong.

The hardest part is the waiting.

"Have you talked to your sister much lately?" Oz asked as we sat together in the almost-empty courthouse coffee shop, waiting.

"I've been busy."

"She's watching the kids?"

"And surprisingly good at it."

"Doesn't surprise me." He looked down with a little grin. "She's a wonderful woman. Confused, off to a slow start. But still wonderful in her own way."

Since they'd been sweethearts, at least twice, I trod gently. "She can be somewhat . . . frustrating. Inconsistent."

"Imagine what it's been like for her. Bad enough growing up in that house, with that father of yours."

I looked up. "How much did she tell you about him?"

"Not as much as I'd have liked. But I got the distinct impression he could be a tyrant."

"True that."

"And she had to deal with having a genius overachiever for a big brother."

"Wha-a-a-at?"

"Don't be modest. I was in high school with the both of you, remember?"

"I was the least popular guy in the school."

"You had your friends. You were shy, sure. But everyone knew you were headed for great things. And everyone treated her like the ditzy little sister."

"I don't remember any such—"

"Julia's a smart woman."

"I know she is, but—"

"Sometimes it's hard to find your own way in the world."

"She married when she was only—"

"She'd have done anything to get out of that house. And away from that man."

I fell silent. That part, at least, I knew was true.

"She needs you, Ben."

I didn't know what to say.

"I needed you, too. And you've been here for me. You're always here for your clients. And your wife. I can see how devoted you two are to each other and your daughters. But your sister needs you, too."

"I—I—have tried to look after her, but . . ." My sentence trailed off.

"Well, think about it." He polished off his Styrofoam cup of java. "I might not be around in the future to remind you."

⚝

THE JURY RETURNED ITS VERDICT JUST A LITTLE OVER FOUR HOURS later, which as capital-crime juries go is practically lightning speed. Usually takes twenty minutes or so to choose a foreman, then at least an hour to read through all the instructions. Trial attorneys go back and forth on the meaning of a speedy verdict. Some say it means guilty; some say it means not guilty. I think the only thing it means is that the first vote comes in unanimous, or darn close. If the vote is split, one side will try to convince the other, and that can take forever. I've known judges who've kept the jury late and didn't bring in food, obviously hoping hunger and fatigue would persuade a few to relent and give way to the majority. But that wasn't necessary this time. Which told me that at least most of them were already on the same page before they even started to talk.

I just hoped they were on the right page.

Word got out to the media quickly, because by the time I returned to the courtroom, it was more packed than it had been since the first day of trial. The reporters asked for predictions, but I ignored them. Predicting was a fool's game. And I might come out of this looking foolish enough as it was.

Julia came for the verdict reading. She'd managed to drop the girls off at the church. For whatever reason, she wanted to be there.

I pulled her aside. "You understand . . . I have no idea how this will go."

"What do you mean?"

"I mean there's a good chance—"

"Either way, I want to be here."

I nodded. "If you're sure."

"Either way this turns out, I want Oz to know that some people in the world still love him."

I couldn't argue with that.

Christina and I resumed our seats at the defense table. Thrillkill went to his corner. The jury slowly filed back in. None of them made eye contact with Oz.

My stomach was an aching, gnawing centrifuge of anxiety and pain. I tried to remind myself that I was the lawyer and my life was not on the line here. It didn't make anything better. To the contrary, I think it made it worse. I tried to write Christina a note, but my hands shook so badly I couldn't even write.

I watched in silence as the foreman gripped the document that would determine the future for at least three people in this room: my client, the woman in the gallery, and me.

The foreman spoke. I knew nothing would ever be the same again. Not for any of us.

"Foreman?" the judge said.

The man Christina had predicted would become the foreman rose. "Yes?"

"Do you have a verdict?"

"We do."

The bailiff walked to him, took a piece of paper, then carried it to the judge. I did my best to read it from the back, but there wasn't enough light. The judge looked it over, made sure everything was correct. If they'd made any technical mistakes, he'd send it back and have them fix it rather than risk having it challenged on appeal. But today there was no problem. He passed it back to the bailiff, who returned it to the foreman.

"As to the first count." Christina took my hand and held it. "On the count of murder in the first degree, we find the defendant Omar al-Jabbar .

I closed my eyes and prayed.

"Not guilty."

Oz threw his head back in relief, a joyous smile on his face.

"As to the second count, murder in the first degree with special circumstances, we find the defendant not guilty. As to the third count, manslaughter, we find the defendant not guilty."

And the courtroom erupted. Reporters dialed their cell phones as they raced toward the door. Judge Santino pounded his gavel. I knew he would poll the jury, just to make sure that was the agreed verdict of one and all. But I'd heard enough. Somehow, we'd come out of this alive.

More specifically, Oz had come out of this alive.

I felt a wave of relief rush over me so intense I thought for a moment I might pass out. I don't think I realized how worried about this I was till that moment. I felt as if I'd physically shoved the executioner out of the way and stolen his ax.

As I scanned the courtroom, I saw one unexpected person making his way out of the courtroom—Fethullah Lkbar, the witness who had rehabilitated both PACT and Oz. I hadn't even noticed him in the courtroom, but now he headed out just as quickly as the bottleneck in the aisle would allow.

"Mr. al-Jabbar," Judge Santino said, "you have the court's thanks for your cooperation. You are free to go."

The judge continued talking, but no one was listening much. I don't think that surprised him. He thanked the jurors for their service and announced an adjournment. We'd reassemble tomorrow morning at nine to handle all the postverdict rigmarole.

Christina threw herself in my arms. "I love you," she whispered.

"Not as much as I love you."

"Not as much as I love you both!" Oz added, and he threw his arms around the both of us.

Julia offered her congratulations, exchanged a long look with Oz, then headed out to pick up the girls.

"Let's go straight home," Christina said. "We'll get ice cream and celebrate properly."

It sounded like such a wonderful idea that for a moment I almost allowed myself to believe it might happen. My phone told me that news of the verdict was already breaking all over the media. It took maybe half an hour to finish the required paperwork, including Oz's release papers. Then we made our way out of the courthouse and found my car. Just as I was about to start the engine, I felt my phone buzz.

I'd received a text message.

I HAVE JULIA.

I guess it showed in my face. "What's happened?" Christina asked. "Is something wrong with the girls?"

I shook my head. I couldn't even speak.

She knew something was wrong. "Then what?"

The next text message was a photograph. Julia, bound and gagged. She looked scared. I saw blood trickling down the side of her face.

"Ben, tell me what's going on."

I couldn't force the words out of my mouth. Another text came in.

DO AS I SAY OR SHE DIES.

"Ben, what is it?"

I turned my phone around so she could see. "It's Julia. She's been kidnapped."

CHAPTER 63

I didn't know what to do. Common sense told me to call the police, but I was warned that if I did, Julia would die. Could this person have eyes on or inside the police station? I couldn't discount the possibility. The police were never good at keeping secrets. Especially to protect a loathed defense attorney.

"Ben, do you have any idea who this is?"

I looked at her grimly. "Yes. But that doesn't tell me how to help Julia."

Christina left to pick up the girls. Oz offered to come with me, but I sent him home. I knew he was concerned about Julia, but, frankly, his presence just made everything more complicated. I told him to go home and, if he couldn't rest, get over to our house and help Christina.

I tried to figure out the smartest course of action, but I couldn't, so I just followed the instructions that came in by text. I had failed Julia so many times. I couldn't stand the thought of failing her again. I'd had enough experience with the criminal world to know that if she wasn't found in the first twelve hours or so, she probably never would be. At least not alive. I had to convince this person that I was cooperating so he would allow me to make contact. If I knew where she was, there might be a slight chance I could save her.

And then I received a reminder that my wife was psychic, or, at the very least, brilliant beyond all measure.

She sent me a text: CALL MIKE.

Of course. That wasn't exactly the same as calling the cops, right? And Mike knew who he could trust, who he couldn't, how to keep something on the down low. I could call him without going anywhere near the police station.

Five seconds later, I was talking with my old college chum, the man who was now the head of the Tulsa homicide department. I hadn't seen as much of him as I'd like since he married Kate and got promoted, but we were still close enough that I could call in a favor. Especially under these circumstances. Especially when it involved his ex-wife.

This wasn't his jurisdiction, but he made some calls, called in a few favors, and generally assured everyone I wasn't the total and complete asshole the cops thought I was.

After that, it went a little better.

Mike dispatched a private operative named Childs to our home. He wore plainclothes and did nothing suspicious. I had errands to run, so he got to my home before I did.

"Do you know where Julia was taken?" Childs asked.

"She never picked up our girls," I explained. "So it must've been after she left the courthouse but before she got to the church."

"Have you had any signs of trouble?"

"Only related to the case. None relating to my sister." Should I tell him about the connection between Julia and Oz? I didn't know.

"What kind of trouble?"

"Crowds outside my office, verbal brickbats, death threats."

"You get death threats a lot?"

"It comes with the territory. This is a deeply conservative state. Defense attorneys aren't always loved as they should be."

"I was told your sister has a history of . . . erratic behavior."

"What are you suggesting? Do you think she just went out for a walk? Posed for a fake photo?"

"No. But I do get the impression that this was not something cooked up at the last minute."

"Why would you think it was? I can tell you this with certainly. My sister would never have abandoned those two girls."

"I believe you," Childs said. "But you got to admit it's a hell of a coincidence."

"What's a coincidence?"

"This kidnapping. Just after the verdict was delivered."

"Why would anyone think it's a coincidence?" I replied. I didn't. That was something I learned from Mike. What looks like a coincidence to others often turns out to be the key to solving a case. You just have to deduce the unknown or unspoken reason for the two corresponding events everyone else writes off as coincidence.

"So you think the kidnapping is some kinda revenge for you getting the killer off?" Childs asked, more than a touch of irony in his voice.

Where to begin? "First, my client didn't kill anyone. That's why the jury acquitted him. Second, it seems obvious that someone has been watching Julia, and probably my house, for some time. And for some reason, the instant the trial was over, that someone decided to snatch my sister."

Childs pulled a face. "You seem to know a hell of a lot about this crime."

"I have a brain, and I can use it to discern the obvious." I restrained from saying more. I needed to chill.

"I guess you think getting your client off makes you some kinda criminal expert?"

Again, I withheld my true thoughts and contented myself with "This isn't my first rodeo."

Childs grunted and left. As he passed through the front door, someone else came in. "You hangin' in there, Skipper?"

Loving. Never been so glad to see the big man in my entire life. "I'm fine," I lied. "Worried about my little sister."

"I knew you would be. That's why I came."

"How'd you find out about the kidnapping?"

"Chris texted me."

"Did she tell you Julia was seeing Oz?"

"I guessed. You think that has somethin' to do with the kidnapping?"

"Maybe. You got anything yet?"

"Nothin' much. Been mostly listenin' to see what I could pick up." He glanced over his shoulder, as if eavesdroppers might be anywhere, then looked back at me. "I did manage to, um, liberate some files from the cops."

"About this kidnapping? How—"

"No, the murder."

"I've seen everything they've got on Nazir's death."

"No, this is about the other one. The woman. The brainiac." He withdrew a file from under his overcoat.

The file concerned Yasmin al-Tikrit. I didn't see how that could be connected, but I sat down and thumbed through it just the same.

The case remained unsolved, and it looked to me as if the police had no significant leads. Since no one was found at the scene with gun in hand, they didn't know where to start.

I rifled through the crime-scene photos, but they just brought back ugly reminders. I didn't need to relive it all. Her battered body. The bloodstained desk. Her scientific papers.

Wait.

I took another look. I'd noticed something unusual when I was there before. I just hadn't known what to do with it.

Maybe desperation is the mother of all invention. This time the cogs snapped into place.

"Oh my God. Oh God."

Loving hovered over my shoulder. "What is it?"

"It—It's all starting to make a crazy sort of sense."

"What?"

"This crime scene. What Abdullah said on the witness stand. What Oz told me the very first day in my office. But I was too stupid to understand."

"You know who killed this woman?"

"I think so. And Nazir."

"Does that mean you know where Julia is?"

"No. But I know who took her. There's only one person who would do it—only one person who would have any reason." I threw the file down on a coffee table. "I am such a fool. I've been operating in the dark. All along."

Loving knew me well enough to understand where I was headed. "Skipper, I hope you're not thinking about doing something crazy dangerous."

"Let's get out of here. While we still can." I headed quietly toward the door.

"I'm comin' with you," Loving said.

"You don't even know where we're going."

"And I don't care. But wherever it is, I got your back."

"Thank you, but no. Much too dangerous. I—" My phone buzzed.

I had a text.

And a location.

CHAPTER 64

Downtown Oklahoma City was the weirdest cross section of good and bad on the face of the earth. The renovation of Bricktown into a pedestrian pleasure park had been a titanic success. The river cruise, restaurants, Thunder games, and shopping had wrought a fantastic change to what had previously been a dismal area no one visited unless they had no choice. Some of the area housing had been renovated and yuppified. But if you traveled more than five blocks in any direction, you could see some of the most depressing, poverty-ridden hovels imaginable.

Which of course was where I was headed now.

I couldn't help but notice I was also only a short drive from Oz's apartment and the stretch of South Robinson that received so much attention during the trial. Oklahoma City was moving in the right direction, but it still had lots of work to do.

Loving and I parked a block away and walked cautiously toward the two-story house. When we were almost directly in front, Loving laid a hand on my shoulder. "We should call Mike. Give him a heads-up."

"He'll have uniforms out here in five minutes."

"Yeah." Loving shoved his big hands into his pockets. I could tell something else was in there. Loving never carried guns—didn't believe they made anything better. That didn't mean he was completely unarmed. "Might be better if they did."

"This is a change of heart. You usually prefer to work alone."

"Well . . ." His eyes scanned the house. "There's a lot at stake here."

I knew what he meant. He was accustomed to having to take care of me. He'd done it often enough in the past. But having Julia in the mix added too many variables. I'd suspected before that Loving maybe had a sweet spot for Julia, perpetual screwup slacker that she was. He didn't want her death on his conscience.

"There is a lot at stake," I said. "More than I've had time to explain to you."

"What does the kidnapper want?"

"Out of the country."

"Makes sense. Now that Omar is off the hook—"

"The police might reopen the investigation and get it right this time. Except they won't. They'll make public statements about how justice was denied and go on acting as if they tried the killer. Too embarrassing to admit they make a mistake. Especially on a capital crime. But this kidnapper doesn't know that." I paused. "Why would anyone think I could get a killer out of the country?"

"Anyone who's seen your house . ."

"Right. Would think I'm loaded. What a joke. I couldn't get myself out of the country for a two-week vacation." I checked my watch. "Time to go in."

Loving nodded grimly. "I'll take the rear. Don't go in till you get my signal."

"Let me text first."

"Is that smart?"

"You haven't read the texts. Our kidnapper is not thinking logically. Panicking. I don't think surprise is the right approach."

"You're the skipper."

I pulled out my cell phone. The night was abysmally dark, not a shred of moonlight. I could barely see well enough to tap the right buttons.

I resisted the temptation to text using voice recognition. IM HERE.

Must've had the phone in hand, waiting, because the reply shot back within seconds. COME IN AND I'LL KILL HER.

Another chill raced up my back. I CANT HELP YOU IF I CANT SEE YOU.

A second later: JUST GET ME OUT OF THIS FILTHY COUNTRY.

I knew the four stages of hostage negotiation, as well as the stupidity of lying to someone holding a gun. But the truth was we didn't have time for all those stages. The situation was desperate and deadly. So a lie seemed expeditious.

IM MAKING THE ARRANGEMENTS. I HAVE YOUR PLANE TICKETS. PASSPORT. YOU HAVE NOTHING TO WORRY ABOUT.

For the first time, I had to wait for a response. Thought I was going to throw up while I waited.

SLIDE THEM UNDER THE DOOR.

Here's where I had to get tough.

NO. WANT TO SEE JULIA'S ALIVE AND UNHURT.

Another painfully long pause.

SHE'S ALIVE.

The bottom dropped out of my throat. Keep it together, I told myself. She needs you thinking clearly. Now more than ever.

I tried the forceful approach. IM COMING IN.

I almost felt sympathy. I understood now where it all came from, how the whole mess began. But it made little difference. I had to get this done.

I could see through the windows that another family with small children lived downstairs. Another reason this situation had to be contained.

Another reason this could end badly if it went down wrong.

Eventually my answer came.

ARE YOU ALONE?

I lied again. YES.

NO COPS?

NONE.

Had to wait a little while for the next one.

NO WEAPONS. STAND JUST INSIDE THE DOOR.

And a moment later: IF YOU TRY ANYTHING, ILL KILL HER. THEN YOU.

I started forward.

A set of rickety, white wooden steps on the side of the house provided access to the upstairs apartment. Separate entrance for a separate tenant. Unfortunately, there was no other entrance. I spotted Loving in the rear, keeping watch.

I reached the top of the stairs. My hand shook as I reached for the doorknob. Keep it together, I told myself. You can handle this. You can do it. Just a little while longer.

I pushed the door open and stepped inside.

Julia was duct-taped to a kitchen chair. She could barely squirm. Some kind of gag stretched across her face, contorting her expression, making her look wide-eyed and desperate. And scared. Which she undoubtedly was.

Kir Ali stood behind her. He held a shotgun pointed at her head.

The murder weapon?

Her blouse was caked with blood.

His hand shook worse than mine. "You've seen her. She's alive. Put the stuff on the floor and get out."

I shook my head. "You have to let Julia go."

"I can't do that." His voice trembled, and his eyes were wild. I judged him to be over the edge and on the brink of doing something violent. He never would've resorted to this if he weren't desperate. "If I do, you won't help me."

"I'm not helping you till she goes free."

I could see his fingers tightening around the trigger. "Don't screw with me."

"I'm not."

"I'll kill her. I will. You think I won't, but I will." Sweat flew off the sides of his head. "I've killed before."

"I know. Agent Nazir. Right? You pulled off the miracle shot from the oil derrick?"

"You think I'm a killer?"

"I don't think you want to be. I think you're a victim of horrible circumstances, like almost everyone in this mess. I'm sure you felt you were out of options. You have sharpshooter experience, don't you?"

"In Iraq, boys are trained to be snipers when they are five."

"My theory is you used a long-range acoustic baffle to disguise the source of the shot. The derrick gave you the cover I needed."

Kir started at him, stunned.

"In the chaos afterward, you hid the gun beneath the derrick and calmly walked away. Probably recovered it later."

"Do you know what that bastard did?"

"Yes. I understand why you killed Yasmin, too." I paused. "But you made a terrible mistake."

"You don't understand anything."

"Your people wanted her research. The ones you work for. And she wouldn't give it to you."

"I had no choice! Now put the stuff on the floor."

The flaw with that being, first, I had no stuff, and, second, I was certain he'd refuse to release Julia. Might kill her. Anything was possible, given his current state. He thought terrorists were out to get him, and they probably were. He thought the police wanted him, and they would, if they didn't already.

I locked eyes with Julia. She seemed less desperate, almost resigned.

I'd seen that look in her eyes before.

She thought she was going to die. And she thought there was nothing she could do to help herself.

This time I was going to save her. I *had* to save her. This time.

"Kir, you know this isn't going to work. Put down the gun and let me take Julia somewhere safe."

"You don't know what will happen to me!"

"I think I do. You've been working for ISIS, right? Or some similar group. That's why you killed Nazir and framed Omar. That's why you killed Yasmin and why you've been trailing me and my friends. Omar wouldn't play ball, Yasmin wouldn't give you her research, and your freedom depended upon Omar being wrongfully convicted of murder. At this point, your terrorist masters probably think you're a liability. So you decided to kidnap"—my eyes met Julia's—"your handler."

"You . . . you know."

"I should've seen it sooner. Even when Oz went into chapter and verse about how ISIS recruits the lonely and lost and isolated, it didn't occur to me that there was a much more vulnerable target out there, one connected to money and assets and with a history of poor judgment. A history of jumping from one outstretched arm to another, anyone offering a moment of comfort." I paused. "My sister."

"And you know about Yasmin?"

I lowered my eyes. "More than you, unfortunately."

"What do you mean?"

This was about to get treacherous. Dangerous for Julia and me. But it had to be done. "I figured it out. When I saw the periodic table on the wall at Yasmin's workplace, I noticed that four of the elements were marked in red. Didn't mean anything to me at the time. Scientists do bizarre things. Maybe it had something to do with her research. And then a short while ago, I looked at a photo, and it finally clicked. Yasmin marked potassium, iridium, aluminum, and iodine. The chemical symbols, moving across the table from left to right, are K, IR, AL, and I. They spell out your name. That smart woman identified the man threatening to kill her. The man who ultimately did kill her."

"I had no choice. She did it, you know. She made the breakthrough. The first step toward the superweapon."

"And you didn't want the US to get it."

"Are you insane? The US must have it, you fool."

"Then why did you take—"

"Don't you see? The US owned Yasmin. It was inevitable that she would share her research with them, given time. I cannot put the genie back in the bottle. But I can make sure both sides have access to it. This is World War Two and the atom bomb all over again. The world could never be safe so long as only one side had the bomb. That's what alienated the USSR. That's what started the Cold War. We would have no defense against American imperialism if they had a weapon that could kill huge numbers without damaging buildings or spreading radiation. The entire world would be pawns in American hands."

"So you're going to give it to terrorists?"

"I'm going to give it to everyone. Terrorism is in the eye of the beholder. The history of American aggression shows that all they ever do is destabilize a region. If there is no balance of power, America will police the world."

"That could never happen."

"Anything could happen. The US talks about human rights while torturing prisoners. The US talks about privacy rights while eavesdropping on its own citizens' conversations. The US talks about sovereignty while invading other countries to support its ravenous need for oil."

This sounded much too much like a rant I'd heard before. And finally the light dawned. "You work with Abdullah."

"I did."

I bit my lower lip. "He really is an ISIS scout. When the online attempt to recruit Oz didn't work, Abdullah decided to throw him to the dogs. Probably upset about him breaking up with your sister, too."

"He turned her into a whore!"

I nodded. "I thought that was a factor. So you took out Nazir and framed Oz." I pressed my fingers to my forehead. "Nazir was right about Abdullah."

"Nazir was a bastard."

"No wonder he wanted to interrogate Oz." I thought a moment longer. "And of course, inevitably, Abdullah converted you. He's just as dangerous as Nazir said he was."

"Nazir deserved to die! He tortured my sister!"

I felt a painful aching in my stomach. I so much did not want to advance this conversation. But it had to be done. He had to know. "Kir . . . Mina is not your sister."

"You lie."

"Your mother was unmarried. Raped. If the pregnancy had become public, she would have been shamed and disgraced. Her career over. She had no family, no protection. So Mina agreed to basically adopt you. Pretend you were her little brother. Abdullah covered the tracks and made it all look right."

"You liar!" The shotgun wavered. I could see the muscles in his arm tighten. "Are you saying Nazir was my father? You filthy lying American!"

The expression on Julia's face urged me to stop talking. But I had to finish. "I don't know who your father is. I don't think anyone does, and it's probably better that way. Mina's mother had recently died so they pretended you were her child."

"Filthy American. You will say anything to save yourself!"

This was the hardest conversation I'd ever had in my life. And my sister's life dangled in the balance. "I'm not lying to you. I wish I could've told you sooner, but I hadn't figured it all out yet. Once I did, my friend Jones did some online research. He has access to CIA databases and about anything else that can be found online, which is basically everything these days, if your hacking skills are strong enough. He confirmed what I suspected. Even Abdullah couldn't eliminate all the traces."

"What are you talking about? You filthy liar."

"I'm telling the truth. Hard as it is. I think it's time you knew where you came from. So people will stop taking advantage of you."

He pressed the shotgun hard against Julia's face, screaming. "Who is my mother?"

"I think you already know. You heard Abdullah in the courtroom, talking about how close she and Mina were. How they would do anything for one another. And the truth is—they did."

"No. Please. No." He crumbled to his knees, but the shotgun remained aimed. "No."

"The first time I met you, Mina mentioned how smart you were in school. Especially in science." I tried to steady my voice. "You get that from your mother. Yasmin al-Tikrit." My voice completely caved. "The woman you murdered."

CHAPTER 65

"Y ou lie!" Kir screamed, so loud it sent a trembling sensation across my skin. The shotgun flailed from one side of the room to the other. *"You are lying!"*

"No. The lawyer speaks the truth."

I whirled. Abdullah stood behind me. I didn't know enough about guns to identify what he was packing, but it was big and looked as if it could fire off a thousand rounds a second from now till doomsday.

"I will thank you not to move," he said evenly.

I had hoped that telling Kir the truth might stun him or at least distract him enough that he would lower the shotgun. Abdullah's sudden appearance threw a deadly wrench in my plans.

"I have tried to help you, Kir," Abdullah said. "But you betrayed me."

"So it's true," I said. The gun was pointed my way, but right that second I didn't care. "You're everything the CIA thinks you are. I'm amazed you agreed to testify."

"Your investigator knew too much about me. He threated to go to the authorities. I chose the lesser of two evils."

"You were behind this all along. Except you manipulated Kir, this impressionable young innocent, into doing your disgusting work for you. You're the real murderer. Of Nazir and Yasmin."

"I needed Yasmin's research. Acts of violence have become too commonplace. They no longer instill terror as they once did. We needed something new. But despite her debt to my family, she would not turn it over. So I sent this young puppet to get it for me."

Kir whipped the shotgun around toward Abdullah. Standoff. Abdullah had the faster and more powerful weapon, but Kir could still do plenty of damage. "I've done so much for you. I killed Nazir. I framed Omar. I followed this lawyer and his friends."

"As you should." Abdullah smiled. "I have been training you since you were a toddler. Playing the strong older brother. Making you an asset."

"You beat me. Degraded me."

"I did what was necessary."

"You used me."

"Not well enough, it would seem. I told you to obtain Yasmin's research."

"I did."

"I told you to bring it to me."

"And I will. At the same time I give it to the US."

"That is not acceptable."

"I will give it to both of you or none of you."

"You will give it to me or you will die."

Kir's face turned a bright crimson. "If you kill me, you will never find it."

"I will torture you before you die. You will talk."

"Do your worst. You will get nothing."

Kir tried to speak bravely, but I could see he was terrified. For all that he shook, Abdullah remained calm, which gave him a huge advantage. "It is possible you might withstand torture," Abdullah said. "Though unlikely, I think. But would you remain silent while I tortured your handler? This American woman? I have always suspected you had feelings for her. What about her brother, the lawyer?" I felt his gun pressing against me. "Will you keep your information hidden while I pull him apart limb by limb?"

A cold shiver ran down my back. I didn't doubt this manipulative killer would do it.

"I will not give you the weapon," Kir said defiantly. "Not unless both sides have it."

"Then perhaps I will have to torture Mina."

"Your own sister?"

Abdullah pushed his shoulders back. "The Koran says someone who betrays his people has no family."

"You will not hurt her."

"I will. Unless you give me what I want." I stared into the black coals that man had for eyes. And I did not doubt he would torture his sister. Or anyone else who got between him and what he wanted.

Abdullah spotted me looking at him. "If you are waiting for your man to rescue you, I am afraid it will be a long wait. I saw him outside and disposed of him."

My heart rose into my throat. I'd put Loving in danger one more time and . . . and . . . "What does that mean?"

His only reply was a smile. He grabbed me by the neck and pushed me to my knees. "Give me what I want, Kir. Tell me where it is, or I will kill everyone around you, everyone you know or care about."

I watched a thousand emotions race across Kir's face. He didn't know what to do. "I have made so many mistakes."

"Don't give in to him, Kir," I said. I felt Abdullah's grip tighten around my neck.

"But—he will kill you."

Like I didn't know that.

"And Julia."

I made eye contact with my sister. "Don't give in. Either of you."

"I am so tired. Of all these lies. Of everything." His eyes turned wet and cloudy. "And I have killed . . . my own mother." His face contorted with pain. "I must be punished." Kir reached out as if to hand Abdullah his shotgun. Then, all at once, he whipped the barrel around and pointed it at his own head. "Goodbye, false brother. You may reshape the world. But you will do it without my help."

"No!" I twisted out of Abdullah's grip, leaped forward, and tackled

Kir. Too late. My scream was drowned out by the report of the gun. Blood splattered into my face.

Abdullah rushed toward us, but he was too late to stop anything.

"Stupid boy," he muttered. "Stupid, foolish boy. Just as weak as your mother. She trusted the Americans. She was seduced by comfort."

I resisted the temptation to kill him with my bare hands and focused on the boy. Thanks to my tackle, the shotgun blast had drifted to the side of his head. He would end up mangled, but he might not end up dead. "We need to call an ambulance."

"There will be no ambulance. He is better off dead."

"No one is better off dead." Kir was unconscious, and his pulse was faint, but he was still breathing. He could be saved.

"You'll never get the weapon now, Abdullah," I said. "You might as well leave and let me call for help. Go disappear again."

"Would that it were so simple. But I fear now you know far too much." He pointed his gun at me. "Your final mystery will be the one surrounding your own death. Yours and your sister's."

Behind him, on the stairs, I saw Loving's head appear. The right side of his face was caked in blood. But he was alive. He moved slowly. Understandably. If Abdullah heard him coming, he could gun Loving down before he took another step.

I played for time. "Fine. Kill me. But not my sister. She's the only sister I have."

"She betrayed you. And your country."

I stared at Julia, not him. "She made a mistake. Who hasn't? There was another time when I betrayed her."

Julia's head shook violently from one side to the other.

"But I'm going to try to make up for it." Behind Abdullah, Loving had reached the top step.

And then, all at once, the scene exploded into chaos. The whole mess probably took ten seconds, but it seemed like an eternity. Loving tackled Abdullah, but the strong man did not fall.

He swung around firing the gun.

Bullets drew long lines in the wall.

Loving dropped to the floor. Was he shot? I couldn't tell.

Screams erupted from downstairs.

I don't even remember thinking about it. I just rushed forward. I kicked Abdullah between the legs, then pounded the hand that held the gun. It fired again. The bullet went into a countertop, narrowly missing Julia.

I managed to get on top of him, one arm pressed under his chin, the other pinning down the arm with the gun. But he was stronger than me. Mike had tried to give me some self-defense lessons once. Right then, I wished I'd been a more attentive student.

I knocked the gun out of his hand. It skittered across the floor.

Loving picked it up.

Thank God.

"This is over," Loving growled. "Skipper, get out of there. Take Julia with you. This asshole moves, I'll kill him."

Loving did have a knack for making people believe his threats. Abdullah stayed on the floor.

I was already at Julia's side, tearing away the tape. "What now?" she said. "The people below heard the shots. Cops will be here in no time."

"You have to get out of here."

"But . . . Abdullah will tell them—"

"I know. That's why you have to go."

"He'll tell them that I helped them."

"The feds will be far more interested in him than you. For the present. But you do need to disappear."

Loving rolled Abdullah over and pinned his arms back. He wrapped flex-cuffs around the man's wrists.

"There's no time to discuss this." I tore off the last bit of tape, then wrapped my arms around her. "I love you so much, Julia. And I am so sorry . . . for everything."

"No, Ben, I—"

I cut her off. "There's no time. Get the hell out of here."

Loving handed her his car keys. "Take my car. Leave it somewhere I can find it."

She took the keys. "Ben . . . it can't end like this."

"It won't. But you need to go. I'll tell the cops you ran off and I don't know what happened to you. It'll be true. They won't look that hard. Your terrorist associates might hunt for a bit, too, but they'll have more pressing matters to pursue in the long run. Just keep your head down, and you should be fine."

She threw herself around me, her face pressed against mine. "You never betrayed me."

"I never will again. Go."

She pressed her lips to my ear. "Emily is just fine. She's not Joey."

"I know. Go."

She took the keys and disappeared into the night, just as I heard police sirens wailing in the distance.

CHAPTER 66

Four months later, I saw Julia for the last time.

The truck stop on I-40 just before you get on the turnpike was best known, to the extent that it was known at all, for wicked, greasy fried chicken and the world's greatest array of porn magazines, discreetly tucked away in high shelves and plastic bags. For my purposes, this location had only two advantages. I wasn't likely to bump into anyone I knew. And if someone needed to depart in a hurry, they could fade away in about a dozen different directions.

Perfect for a reasonably well-known attorney and his little sister on the lam from the law.

I had to wait about forty minutes, which gave me far more time than I wanted to sample the truck stop's coffee, if that's the right word for that sludge. Even had a side order of Slim Jims and one of those hideous stuffed burrito things. I felt guilty about it, but they were short on yogurt and wheat germ.

Julia had dyed her hair, cut it short, and wore a torn hoodie, hood up. Glasses, too. I wondered if they corrected anything, other than an onlooker's immediate recognition of the former cheerleader from Heritage Hall Prep.

She slid into the booth opposite me. We were tucked away in the corner, close to the exit, but still so secluded I didn't think anyone could possibly spot her.

"I like the specs," I said. "Armani?"

"Ha ha." She leaned in close, wiggling her eyebrows. "It's a disguise."

"Thanks for calling. I was worried."

She nodded. "Bought one of those phones at a convenience store. Used it once and tossed it. Had to wait until I was sure the feds weren't monitoring your phone calls."

"Even if they were, I think you were sufficiently cryptic. That reference to Flondie wouldn't mean anything to anyone else."

A big smile brightened her face. "Oh my God. That hideous doll you used to carry around all the time. Where did that come from? It didn't even have clothes. And it wasn't blonde." She pointed a finger. "You were seriously messed up."

"Mother bought it for you. I liked it better."

"I never was the dolly sort."

The table fell silent. I reached across, not quite touching her. "Are you okay? Do you have everything you need?"

"I'm okay. How's Omar?"

I shrugged. "Left the state. Was in the process of changing his name."

"Again?"

"Again."

"But he was acquitted. Is he afraid ISIS will go after him?"

"No. He's afraid the average Oklahoma redneck will go after him."

"What's happening to Abdullah?"

"He's been charged by the feds with espionage and conspiracy and terrorism. They've put the case on the slow track so they can gather more evidence. They were grateful to Loving for catching him, but the truth was neither of us had much evidence against him."

"And Kir is still alive?"

"Just. He's making a slow recovery. And, sadly, as soon as he gets out of the hospital, he'll be arrested."

She lowered her eyes. "I wish he hadn't done what he did."

"Me, too. But I get it."

"Are the cops looking for me?"

"I'm not sure they understand your role in what went down. Loving certainly didn't tell anyone. Abdullah can't really incriminate you without admitting his involvement. I think he's hoping that if he doesn't speak out against you, then I won't speak out against him. And he's right. So just keep your head down. I doubt anyone is actively looking for you. Few years and this will all blow over."

"Maybe."

I nodded. "Maybe."

"But in any case—no fatwa."

"No." At least, I hoped to God not. "How did you ever get mixed up with those people?"

She twined a strand of dyed hair between her fingers. "I told you how dislocated I was. Divorced. Lost custody of Joey. Didn't know what to do next. Had my life completely pulled out from under me."

"It happens."

"Yeah. To me. Let's face it, Ben, I've been a total screwup since the day I stepped out of high school. Maybe before."

"You're being too hard on yourself."

"I'm being honest. So here I was, lost and alone, completely without direction. And then these people came calling. Offered me a chance to do something with my life. Something that mattered."

"Terrorism?"

"They called themselves advocates for political change."

"No doubt."

Her fingers curled into tiny fists. "I just wanted to do something that mattered. Like my big brother does."

"What? Wait a minute—"

"You know I've always looked up to you. Here you were, crusading for your clients, helping out the little guy. And there I was, messing up my life over and over again."

"You should've called me."

"Yeah. I should've. But I didn't." She smiled again, just a little. "Glad I got to see my nieces, though. They're adorable. And Emily is not remotely autistic. I knew it all along. But now it's been confirmed by experts. She's just off to a slow start. She'll catch up soon enough."

"Thank you for taking her to those specialists. While I was busy with the case. It took a big load off Christina's mind, too. Although now . . ." I let it trail off. The rest was obvious. Christina wouldn't have allowed Julia through the front door if she'd known Julia was involved with terrorists. Bottom line, she endangered the whole family just by showing up.

"I know," Julia said. "But I did enjoy it, while it lasted. Even though it meant returning to . . . that house."

With that, the mood darkened. Some burly, bearded trucker came in and started flirting with the ample woman behind the counter. The popcorn popper started its staccato song.

And Julia and I stared at one another.

"Our father was a real bastard, wasn't he?" she said at last.

I pursed my lips. "I prefer to say he was wrapped up in his own world."

"A complete egotist. And so judgmental. And competitive. And completely lacking in human empathy. If you weren't just like him, you weren't anything. I keep telling myself it's time to outgrow blaming everything on Daddy, but . . . what he did ."

We stared at one another across the counter.

"Okay," she said, "I'll be the one who puts it on the table. He hurt us. Badly. Repeatedly. I remember seeing your glasses fly across the room, he hit you so hard. Bashed your head into the side of a car. Made your mouth bleed. Knocked you unconscious."

I closed my eyes. "I will never forget that time in the bathroom."

"You and me both."

"I heard him walk in on you. I don't know what you were doing—"

"I was showering in the tub. I don't remember what he was mad about. He was such a control freak. Spent the day completely ignoring his family, then came home and complained because everything wasn't exactly the way he wanted it to be."

"I heard you crying out. And I did nothing." I swallowed. "Then I heard your head pound against the tile."

"He hit me, while I was naked and vulnerable, so hard it knocked me back against the wall. Then I slipped and fell, which was even worse."

"And I did nothing."

"When he saw the blood, he started to cool. Stomped out. Lucky he didn't go after you next. The following day he sent me to a doctor. Told everyone I fell in the tub. Left out the details."

"And I sat in my room and did nothing. And, of course, we never said anything about it."

"We were little kids."

"I betrayed you."

"There was nothing you could've done, not that time or a hundred others. Except gotten your head bashed in, too. He did that often enough as it was. I know this is why you've always been willing to go to such extremes for me, Ben, but you don't owe me anything. Face it, it was child abuse, and we were both victims. You were too young and too small to help."

At last I managed to open my eyes. "I still remember it. That time. And every other time. I can still hear you screaming. That's why we don't use that bed or bath."

"You never forget being hurt like that. Ever. You can block it out of your conscious mind. But you never forget. It colors everything for the rest of your life."

"I think . . ." I tried to choose my words carefully. "I think a lot of your issues can be traced back to that man."

"And yours, Ben."

"What? I—"

"I'm not the only one who sees it. Christina does, too. Why are you so quiet? Reserved. I know, because I was there. You learned it was safer to keep your thoughts to yourself. Anytime you spoke up, it was an opportunity for that bastard to put you down, either with his tongue or his fist."

"I don't know .

"Look at you! Why does such a high achiever remain so insecure, feel so unaccomplished? Because your father never approved of anything you did, went to his grave complaining that you'd disappointed him."

"He did that to everyone."

"That's exactly right. He never approved of anyone unless they did exactly what he thought they should do, which usually meant becoming a clone of him, or his nineteen thirties idea of what a man or a woman should be."

"But he's gone. It's been years. It's time—"

"Why are you so worried about your girls? You, Ben Kincaid, the best father I've ever seen."

"I remembered Joey .

"No." She removed the fake glasses and peered deeply into my eyes. "It's because you're afraid you'll turn into the kind of father you had."

I wanted to say something, but I knew if I tried, I'd choke. So I kept my mouth closed.

"Our father would've never spent enough time with Joey to notice anything was wrong. You figured it out the first week you spent with him. If our father did notice, he would've blamed someone and given it no further thought. You tried to find a solution. You are nothing like our father, Ben. Thank God. You're making sure you are everything to your girls that he never was to you."

I didn't speak until I was sure I could keep my voice steady. "There are similarities sometimes. I can see it. Between him and me."

"No."

"Yes. And why was our father the way he was? Remember how he used to complain about his own father? Never had a nice word to say about the man. The cycle of violence and abuse is passed down from one generation to the next."

"Until someone has the courage and strength to end it. And that person, Ben, is you." Her voice cracked. "I'm amazed you can live in that house."

"It . . . hasn't been easy," I whispered. "And I'm tired of pretending I like it there. I have some thoughts."

"Like what?"

"Kir needs help. He's a stupid kid who made some horrible mistakes. He's not evil, and I don't think he ever wanted to hurt anyone. He needs therapy. He's basically got PTSD, just like Oz. He was manipulated, pressured, forced. I'm not sure he should get a free ride, but I don't think his life should be completely destroyed. I doubt anyone could ever punish him as badly as he'll punish himself. He was abused from the day he was born."

"Like us."

I couldn't let myself go there. "He might be able to work a deal with the prosecutor if he agrees to testify against Abdullah. But they won't volunteer anything. If he doesn't get an experienced, aggressive lawyer, he's going to be completely railroaded. I can't represent him. Christina forbade it. Our family was too involved with these people already, and she's drawing the line."

"Understandable. But a good lawyer costs money."

"Exactly."

"And you don't have the money to pay for it."

I paused. "We could."

The light came to her eyes. "If we sold the house."

"I don't want to live there. You don't want to live there. It's three times the house I need and not my kind of neighborhood."

"It's in your name."

"It's half-yours. I'm not doing anything without your approval. I figure we'll give the lion's share to Kir's defense. Try to help the next victim. Stop another cycle of abuse from repeating. And then we give the rest to you. Just to make sure you're comfortable while you keep your head down. That's going to require some cash."

"You don't have to do this, Ben."

"I want to do this." I grabbed her hand. "Please, let me do this. Just this once. Let me do this for you."

She looked at me a long time. "If you're sure." She swallowed. "Not like I have a lot of options."

I slid an index card across the table. "Here's instructions on the drop-off. Loving will handle everything so I stay out of it. As soon as I can sell or borrow against the sale, I'll slide you some cash. And you can disappear for as long as necessary."

I looked up and saw tears flooding her eyes.

"Julia . . . stop. This is a good thing."

"I know," she said, her voice cracking.

"Then why the tears?"

"I'm just—" She raised her hand to her face. "I'm just remembering why I love my big brother so much."

She took the card, and we embraced. A few moments later, she was gone.

After waiting a decent interval, I stopped by the men's room to wipe my eyes and blow my nose, then headed home to give Christina the news. We had a lot of work to do in the days ahead. We were going to be busy. But I knew she'd understand. She always did.

I hope now it's clear why this was my most important case, important enough that I assembled all these memories and affidavits and tried to create a record that made sense. I saved Oz from a death sentence. But the person I really saved was myself.

I couldn't help Julia, not back then. But this time I did. A little.

ABOUT THE AUTHOR

William Bernhardt is the bestselling author of more than forty books, including the blockbuster Ben Kincaid series, the historical novel *Nemesis: The Final Case of Eliot Ness*, two books of poetry (*The White Bird*, *The Ocean's Edge*), and the Red Sneaker series on fiction writing. In addition, he is one of the most popular writing instructors in the nation, hosting an annual writing conference and small-group writing retreats throughout the year. His monthly Red Sneaker Writers newsletter reaches more than twenty thousand people, and the Red Sneakers phone app reaches many more. He is the only writer to have received the Southern Writers Guild's Gold Medal Award, the Royden B. Davis Distinguished Author Award (University of Pennsylvania) and the H. Louise Cobb Distinguished Author Award (Oklahoma State University), which is given "in recognition of an outstanding body of work that has profoundly influenced the way in which we understand ourselves and American society at large." In addition to his books, he has written plays, a musical (book and music), humor, children stories, biography, and puzzles, and has contributed to the WWII computer game *Burden of Command*. OSU named him "Oklahoma's Renaissance Man," noting that in addition to writing novels, he can "write a sonnet, play a sonata, plant a garden, try a lawsuit, teach a class, cook a gourmet meal, prepare homemade ice cream, beat you at Scrabble, and work the *New York Times* crossword in under five minutes." You can contact him by email at willbern@gmail.com or through his web page, www.williambernhardt.com.

AUTHOR'S NOTE

I want to thank my wife, Lara, and my family for their constant love and support while I forged this return to the Ben Kincaid universe. I also must thank all the readers who insisted that Ben should return, even after I foolishly insisted that I was finished with him. I begin to suspect I will never be finished with him.

I also want to thank all my patrons whose generous support means so much to me: Jason Willis, Glenn Vermillion, Georgia Lee, Kathy McCullough, Belinda Bruner, Gary Conrad, Jennifer Ludwig, Glenda Thompson, Debi Harris, Jim Wolf, Mike Baker, Charles Robison, Sylvia Bauer, Brenda Partington, Mary Jo Hughes, Sue McMurphy, S. C. McCole, Doreen Anne Knight, Sarah Talton, Anthony DeWitt, Miori Dunseith, Donna Vieth, T. C. Miller, Selma Mann, Karen O'Brien, Bob Mandala, Kevin Caliendo, RJ Johnson, Richard Knight, Winona Cross, Ann Elizabeth Compton, Justin Robbins, Robert Silberstein, Charles Templeton, Nikki Hanna, Dwayne Morris, Barbara Power, Loree Johns, Jana Porter, Sylvia Schneider, Roxie Kirk, Bailey James, Kimball Peterson, Lee Ann Cole, Theresa Key, Jennifer Reeves, Debbie Rhoades, Marni Graff, Nancy Meacham, Rebecca Weaver, Richard Lacey, Luke Hughes, Elise Roenigk, Dave Johnson, Shane Wilson, Madeline Flannery, Doris Degner-Foster, Dan Friedman, Kim

Bailey, Leigh Singleton, Ginny Gardner, David Pfeiffer, Cherie Waggie, Otto Penzler, Adam Goldworm, Gini Campbell, Diana Corrigan, Sean Silver, Fran Thomas, Bren Keenan, Jon Weimer, and Dan Millman.

You can obtain more information about my patronage program and its benefits at: https://www.patreon.com/willbern.

OTHER BOOKS BY WILLIAM BERNHARDT

The Ben Kincaid Novels:

Primary Justice

Blind Justice

Deadly Justice

Perfect Justice

Cruel Justice

Naked Justice

Extreme Justice

Dark Justice

Silent Justice

Murder One

Criminal Intent

Death Row

Hate Crime

Capitol Murder

Capitol Threat

Capitol Conspiracy

Capitol Offense

Capitol Betrayal

Other Novels:

Nemesis: The Final Case of Eliot Ness

Dark Eye

Strip Search

Double Jeopardy

The Code of Buddyhood

Final Round

The Game Master

Challengers of the Dust

Midnight Before Christmas

The Red Sneaker Series:

Story Structure

Creating Character

Perfecting Plot

Dynamic Dialogue

Promising Premise

Sizzling Style

Excellent Editing

Poetry:

The White Bird

The Ocean's Edge

For Young Readers:

Shine

The Black Sentry

Princess Alice and the Dreadful Dragon

Equal Justice: The Courage of Ada Sipuel

Made in the USA
Columbia, SC
01 November 2017